Down the River

by

David Wilma

For Kellen

Sixth great-grandson and the next generation

May 29, 2007

Eloise Howard Buchanan, Director
Manuscripts Division
The Free Library of Philadelphia
1901 Vine Street
Philadelphia, PA 19103

Dear Ms. Buchanan:

Thank you for taking the time with me on the telephone this morning. What follows is the known provenance of the enclosed manuscript. As I mentioned, I represent the estate of Henry Ward Beecher Lewis, Esq. who practiced law here in Philadelphia in the early 20th Century. He was a grandson of Abolitionist Phyllis Wallace Lewis (1794?-1867) and was himself a leading figure in the African American community in Philadelphia. He died in 1940 leaving no heirs and his will left all his assets to local charities. He entrusted his professional papers to the firm of Baily and Dore, an antecedent of this firm. The papers were forgotten until 2005 when they were discovered in an office move. Among the records of Lewis's legal practice was a sealed envelope with an instruction that it not be opened until twenty years after his death.

The envelope contained the enclosed manuscript, apparently in the hand of Phyllis Lewis. The task of determining the document's value and its disposition fell to me with the able assistance of your archives staff. Mrs. Lewis's 1867 obituary in *The Christian Recorder* states that she was born a slave and after receiving her freedom in Kentucky in 1813 migrated north to Ohio. In the 1820s she moved to Philadelphia where she married the Reverend Emmanuel Lewis of Philadelphia in 1830. Along the way she acquired an education and became quite literate. With Reverend Lewis she wrote anti-slavery pamphlets and newspaper articles, gave speeches, and provided aid to escaped slaves. The Lewises had three children who survived to adulthood. One son died in the Civil War.

Some of the disclosures in the manuscript are not entirely complimentary to the heroic image of Mrs. Lewis presented in her obituary. This is probably the reason that Henry Lewis had the envelope sealed.

I have been unsuccessful in locating any heirs to Mr. Lewis. Since Mr. Lewis bequeathed all his papers to this firm, we are free to dispose of them as we see fit.

This firm wishes to donate the enclosed manuscript to The Free Library of Philadelphia. This is being done with the stipulation that the manuscript be preserved and that it be made accessible to all patrons of the library. Our firm makes no warranty as to the authenticity of the manuscript.

Enclosed is a document of transfer which should be signed by the authorized representative of The Free Library of Philadelphia and notarized.

Thank you for your assistance in this matter.

John L. Martin
Attorney-at-Law

Philadelphia, Penna.
August 23, 1867

My Children:

The doctor admits to me now that I will soon join your dear father in the arms of Our Lord. Or so I need to believe. In addition to my meager worldly goods, I commend to you this document that I have compiled over several years. I no longer fear retribution on this earth for my acts, and I will leave it to God to judge my life. All I seek from you is understanding and a promise to preserve my memory.

You have often heard my story of a journey over fifty years from chains to this comfortable parlor, from property to a voice for the liberation of Our People. The chronicle of my salvation, my education by kindly Christians, and our long travail to abolish slavery is well known. That story is not without embellishment, but this record does not correct every inaccuracy or dispel every myth. The popular version of the life of Phyllis Wallace Lewis has served Our Cause well enough and I will leave that person where she has been placed.

From your earliest years, you have heard others describe me as brave and selfless and determined. You have seen me stand in front of crowds and congregations as a model for all women of our race who fight injustice, and you have heard me preach. Twice, my enemies attempted to kill me, but that only made me work harder. Phyllis Lewis is a name often mentioned alongside that of Frederick Douglass and Sojourner Truth, and I am honored to be invited into their holy company. But you will see that there is someone else here, someone I tried to leave behind me when I crossed the Ohio River.

You and the rest of the world have probably assumed that my life as a slave on the frontier was simply too horrid to remember, let alone speak of, and that my silence on the matter of my bondage was sufficient to express my suffering that my drive as an abolitionist said enough about what bondage had done to me. I was whipped and I was starved. My family was torn from me. This much you already know.

You have accepted from my evasions that my past was a perdition I cared not to visit, which is true. But visit them I did, in secret, every day as I worked and studied and struggled and fought. Every night the pain of memory gave way to sleep. The things I saw have been with me every moment for more than fifty years, and it is time I surrendered them to posterity. There is always more to history or perhaps, as you will see, there is less.

Each of us has some moment in life which we see for the rest of our days, something wonderful such as the birth of a child or the sadness of a death. We can describe every word and every sound of those events where other details of the day are forgotten. Like a newspaper item cut from the page, that story endures, but the rest of the day's events are discarded, lost.

I have listened to testimonies from men and women who have accepted the Word of God, been born again, and who are saved. In our church, the faithful speak of how they met Our Savior and how He came into their hearts. A few of the accounts were truly dramatic, such as the man reprieved on the scaffold just after the hangman dropped the hood over his face. Since the War the stories are of the terrible suffering in the struggle to preserve our Union and to free the slaves, of young men's bodies ripped apart by minié balls and cannon shot, and of so many friends and loved ones gone forever. I have heard the accounts of sin and dissolution, followed by some travail which the sinner survived by the grace of God and by faith to then be resurrected.

Every testimony begins with something small like a breath of wind in a sail or a bugle in a sleeping camp. The bugle signals the opening of a great and horrible battle. A mother recalled placing a bowl of soup in front of her small daughter, described meticulously the meal she had prepared, the warm biscuits, the fresh butter, and every one of the words her little girl said to her. Then the cyclone struck them with unimaginable fury, and her home, her family, all that she knew in the world, vanished. The epiphanies that each of these people experienced all started with something simple: an ordinary act that is then frozen in memory by the worst of God's creation.

I can recite every detail from the afternoon that the Morgans died. I can tell you the color of their horses, the smell of the trees, and the taste of the dust. I can describe every word spoken as clearly as if I heard it at breakfast this morning. I remember it all, not because of the screams and the blood, but because beginning that day, God chose me and tested me. Those dead men cost me my children and they almost cost me my life. But their blood paid for my freedom just as the blood of our Savior paid for our salvation. My freedom grew and blossomed into freedom for millions, but never for those whom I loved.

For me the breath of wind, the bowl of soup, or the bugle's note is a yellow dog waking from his nap in the shade. The farm is a sad affair. The house is built of cut lumber rather than of logs suggesting some affluence on the part of the owner when construction commenced. But the boards never knew paint, and the mossy roof shows crude patches. Any plans the builder had for a substantial home atrophied many seasons back. A porch extends across the front where the tools of homemaking – a tub, a stool, a churn, a saw – lie where last used instead of being stored in an orderly fashion. Smoke from the embers of the breakfast fire seeps from wide cracks in the chimney.

I am seated on a log in the shade crushing boiled corn with a heavy wooden mallet. The wide trough is worn deep from years of labor. The remnants of yesterday's dried product becomes part of today's meal. I lift the tool and let it drop, using long and tiring experience to pulp the corn with little wasted effort. I do not even have to look. I take the work slowly, knowing that my masters expect no speedy conclusion to my task and that only other work awaits me at the end.

A few feet away two dogs slumber. The spotted one snores away. He is the simpler of the two, only a little less aware napping than when awake. The yellow one is closer to me, seemingly asleep as well, but he never really rests. He is always thinking, listening, calculating.

I add more corn to the trough and raise the mallet. I glance at the yellow dog just as his eyes open and one ear moves slightly. The mallet falls into the corn. Thump. He is still a moment. I raise it again, and he raises his head. He is instantly alert, searching the tall cane in the creek bottom. Someone approaches, but all I hear are the flies buzzing in the heat. Despite my sadness and the repetition of my work I consider what might have awakened him.

His eyes narrow. His throat tightens to loose a cry. My world changes forever.

Virginia

I was born the property of David Morgan in Virginia in about the year 1794. I do not know the date precisely because Morgan did not record the births of his slaves, but by counting back from other events, I settled on the year 1794. Slave sales and reports of runaways were carefully documented, because these transactions represented value gained, traded, or lost. A slave who died was money lost, but a slave birth warranted no documentation for Morgan since a baby could do no work. Our master did not count his property until it had value and brought him profit. My worth came when I was about six years of age and was tall enough to swing a stick and herd stock.

My mother's name was Ella, and we slept in a windowless log cabin in which she could barely stand and which provided us little more than room to sleep. Our bed was made of boughs on the ground and a few blankets. A tiny, mud fireplace provided some heat. We ate with others in their cabins or outside, where group meals were the custom. I saw nothing of my mother during the day because she worked the fields. I saw women tend tobacco with babies strapped to their backs and I can only assume that is how I spent my first year. Once weaned, I joined the other babies.

An old woman herded us about like so many geese or ducks. Perhaps the age of five or six was not so much the point of being productive as when the inactivity became troublesome. Climbing a fence indicated a certain skill that might evolve to some bad purpose, but could be directed to a benefit for the master. While the women cooked or carded flax or made baskets or washed the master's clothes, the children played in the dust among the flies, if the weather allowed, or we wandered the farm in search of food and diversion. In winter we clustered around a fire in a cabin. Of those first years I remember very little, and of my mother, even less, except for her warmth at my back and a soft voice in the night. Never knowing my mother or a father left more than just a void within me. A hard place grew that no one ever saw, a hard place that served me well in the years to come. That spiritual could have been written for me:

Got one mind for white folks to see.
'Nother for what I know is me.
He don't know.
He don't know.

Billy, the boy with the club foot, first took me to the fold to instruct me how to drop the fence rails that snaked between the fields. "Push girl!" he shouted, "push!" I struggled under the rough split wood, but I was much too small to budge the massive chestnut beam. I fell to the ground in tears. Disgusted, he hobbled over and knocked the fence down himself, and I jumped out of the way to avoid a damaged toe. In a year I could do it by myself. Billy showed me how to use a stick to goad cows out to the pasture. Between his halting gait and my short legs, we managed to keep up with the ponderous beasts.

"You watch yourself," he warned. "You get under one of them cows, and you end up like old Hamper and his half a face." Hamper was born with a monstrous countenance and the ability only to mumble. But he had a strong back and the master had ample need of that. "And don't let one of those hogs get a finger. You lose a finger, you get the lockjaw. You get the lockjaw, they cut off your hand. You lose a hand, Master get rid of you."

Although I did not grasp it completely at the time, I understood enough to know that being "got rid of" was a bad thing. I heard adults whisper these words and "sold away" with great apprehension. What they feared, I feared. I presumed at the time that it involved one of the demons who snatched lazy or disrespectful children in the night. Hamper's hideous face and the stump of an arm concerned me more than the demons, however.

2

In spite of the risk of pain and disfigurement though (a child does not understand death), I was immediately struck by the fact that I, a mere child upon whom the world showers its needs and wants, who had no importance and no power, could actually cause one of these great brown beasts to go in a direction that I chose! Me! You can only imagine the thrill I felt being able to whip a cow, many times heavier and taller than little me, and have her move. To be sure, they were all accustomed to the daily routine of pen to pasture, so it wasn't as if I taught them anything. But for the first time in my life I could make something happen, and I could not have been more excited if I had a new toy made of corn husk.

Naturally, it was the overseer and the drivers who decided where the cattle would go each day, but I was the one who made them do it. Once I got the stock to the appointed pasturage, I watched that they did not blunder into a neighbor's lot or begin to graze in the corn or beans or wander into the woods to disappear. Allowing stock into food crops intended for people and market earned a whipping. If a cow ate food the loss came not off the master's table, but out of the slave pot. It only took one swipe with my own stick in the grip of an annoyed field hand to teach me that.

One sunny day, all I had to do was make certain that none of the cattle crossed the stream. Tobacco had exhausted the field and only manure and time would help bring it back to some use. Since there were no tasty corn stalks nearby to entice the animals away, I handled this easily from a rock on the bank as my charges grazed on the weeds. The water wandered alongside the pasture lazily across a muddy bottom pocked with thousands of animal tracks. Bugs danced across the surface in some race against invisible fish. I soaked my leathery feet in the clear water and drew random designs in the mud with my stick. The clink of tack prefaced a blocking of the sun. I looked up to see the master's massive horse twisting his head against the bit. High up on the its back sat the master, he who flogged and fed and sold away, the most powerful being in my universe.

Even through the eyes of a child and across all these years, that image of David Morgan remains one of a man much too small for his horse. During the war, I saw General Phil Sheridan ride by, his powerful steed and imperious bearing calculated to mask his small size. My first thought then was not of the Hero of the Shenandoah, but of Master David Morgan of Patrick County, Virginia. David Morgan never led a deadly army of thousands, with cannon and horses and wagons, but he exerted no less power over me and the other slaves on our plantation. From his horse, Morgan towered over anyone on foot, an important object for anyone in need of dominating his surroundings. When I received the Word of God before I was baptized a Christian, my image of a higher power was not of Jesus on the cross or some old man with a long white beard, but of David Morgan on a horse wearing a wide hat that almost covered his face.

Slaves tried to slip out of the master's way when he approached, the alternative being to remain hard at work. Not that Morgan was naturally cruel and whipped people out of hand, but the easiest way to avoid trouble was to avoid the master, indeed any white man. I had always been told to stay away from white people and was admonished at every turn never to speak to a white man unless he spoke to me. And I was never, ever, to look a white man in the eye. I had seen the master at a distance and heard the whispered warnings, so it was with great anxiety that I found myself not only close to this mighty dangerous apparition, but fully under his gaze.

From my rock down in the creek, I could not see the master's face, but I knew who was there, and I could tell he was looking at me, only me. I froze, trying to keep my eyes down. I looked at his tall boot and ugly spur in the bright metal stirrup. From his wrist hung a short leather whip. He was still for a moment, meeting the moves of the horse with the slightest workings of his hand. Then he took hold of the whip.

I had seen the white overseer do the same. He would flick the handle of his whip into his palm as a signal that pain would quickly follow. The slave had an instant to contemplate the impending pain. The overseer then lifted his heels and elbows, swung the whip up, and brought it down with the full force of his body. Not only did the leather slash into head and back, but for many the blow was enough to knock them to the ground. It was my turn for a thrashing. Morgan lifted his arm slightly and I knew I had never been beaten as I was about to be. Morgan snapped it down sharply against his tall boot with a loud crack that pierced my body.

I cried out and wet myself. I jumped up and splashed through the stream into the pasture and up to the nearest cow, engaged in nothing more offensive than chewing her cud. I smashed at her with my stick, driving her across the field, fully expecting lashes across my back. I glanced back toward the creek, but the master had already turned the mare away in a slow walk, his body gently rocking with the horse's step. I stood there, smelling no better now than the cow, grateful to him for not beating me.

Kentucky

I tended stock for two summers when Morgan moved west. That was the year 1800. Morgan planted his middling plantation in Virginia to tobacco, but leaf ravages the soil, and slaves stayed busy clearing new land when not tending the delicate plants, worming, weeding, picking, and curing. A field is good for only a few years in tobacco before it is left fit only for poor pasture. A planter constantly searches for more land, like a bear or a panther always tracking the next meal. Morgan ran out of land and the country over the mountains held promise for him as it has for so many others.

The first to disappear were Billy and Hamper. They followed another planter down the road as if they were simply being hired out. Billy struggled on his bad foot to keep up with the mounted man. Hamper smiled as best he could. I never saw my mother leave. I heard how it happened years later.

The overseer ordered her away from carding flax and sent her to see the master. She found Morgan astride his horse with another white man, a slave, and a cart. The white man's brown frock coat and a black felt hat marked him as another planter.

"Ella, go with Mister Fairburne here. You're with him now," Morgan announced.

My mother brought her hands to her face and emitted a long sad cry of "eeeeeeeeeeeee!" before turning to run.

"Enoch," Fairburne stated casually as if reminding the slave to empty a chamber pot.

The slave took a few easy strides and seized my mother with both arms. He lifted her from the ground, and she thrashed with her legs. "My baby! My baby! Phyllis!" she cried as Enoch carried her to the cart. Without being bid, the slave bound my mother' arms with rope set in the cart for that purpose. My mother's fear and anguish prevented her from fighting well and Enoch's superior strength and practiced skill easily overcame her efforts. He worked her elbows behind her and quickly had her pinioned. Her feet presented less of a problem as she succumbed to the inevitable. In less than the time it takes to saddle a horse, my mother became a sobbing, distraught bundle of paid-for property hauled away with potatoes and squash.

The new owner turned his horse to follow the cart with "Best of luck to you, Morgan."

"And to you too, Fairburne."

To prevent trouble, Morgan snatched my mother away quickly like an annoying thorn stuck in flesh best removed in one sharp motion rather than worried out slowly to greater pain. Thus I became an orphan of the slave trade.

Esther found me at my cabin. I suspected something troubled her, but she quickly distracted me.

"Your mama not home yet. Why not come and stay with us tonight?" A night in a cabin with other children made me forget all about my mother. Thomas and Albert and I had played together until I went to the fields, and I found them cheerful company before the fire. Esther made more than enough supper for us, placing the surplus fritters into a basket. The hot, tasty fritters filled us up and fits of laughter soon left us sleepy. The dying fire watched me doze off.

My slumber was broken by Esther's soft voice. "Time to go." We stumbled into pandemonium. A bonfire illuminated all the farm's carts, yoked to oxen. The Morgans, father and son, both sat their horses walking back and forth snapping orders to men and women who loaded bundles and boxes and baskets into the carts. The master's wife, clutching a shawl against the cold, directed the loading of his belongings. I found the scene exciting and fascinating, and the boys and I warmed ourselves at the fire as the commotion continued. When the tumult began to abate, Esther took us from the fire to a cart where she piled the two boys on top of sacks.

"Phyllis," she told me, "you stay behind this cart. You'll be with the stock, but not till it gets light." More shouts and the cart with the boys bumped forward. They quickly dropped off to sleep as I walked behind looking forward to the wonderments that lie ahead. A man led each pair of oxen. Often his wife trudged along beside him as if they might lose each other in the dark. The whole exercise of keeping up with the great wheels, whose hubs I could just reach, and staying out from under the ponderous oxen prevented me from considering that I was leaving something behind.

Dawn pushed back the chilly night and clouds greeted our day. I walked behind the cart down a road I had never seen. We passed small farms and a few planters' homes where cook fires reheated suppers for a morning meal. The chimneys leaked smoke indifferently into yards and pastures. In twilight, slaves and some white people tended stock, cut wood, and carried loads. Every one of them looked hard at our caravan as it headed west, but no one betrayed a thought or a feeling. Were they envious? Fearful for us? Fearful for themselves? Or just curious?

Thomas and Albert and I were the only children on the journey. Morgan could not be troubled with anyone not up to the trip or life in the new land and the other children disappeared. But Peter was the driver and letting the slave who drove the other slaves keep his children bought his and Esther's continuing allegiance. Such was the dark reasoning of slavery.

The excited, high-pitched chatter of an outing soon dissipated to a silent slog as each saved his energy for the journey ahead. In all, our party was about twenty slaves, a multitude to me. The only white people were Morgan, his wife, Anna, their son, William, his wife and baby girl. And there was the overseer. The white men rode horses and the Morgan women rode in the front carts. Occasionally the white women walked, but the overseer and the slaves always walked. Once the sun came up, I trailed alongside the stock, whipping back into line any animals which stopped to eat

9

or drink. I saw Morgan frequently, sitting his mare off the edge of the track, the drooping brim of his wide hat obscuring his scowling face.

With the nudge of a knee, Morgan cantered up along the line his ugly whip hanging carelessly from his wrist. But his strength and the fear he evoked also represented a center around which my world revolved. Here was a predictable force, a safety of sorts, like a river that at once gave life in the form of fish and water and travel, but also took life with a swift current and floods. My very existence moved with the master, and I easily succumbed to the idea that as long as I served him, all would be well. I had to be careful not to be caught staring at him; still I could not help but be drawn in by his power.

Two ruts took us through the rolling Piedmont past other plantations then small farms that got rougher as we traveled. I noticed differences in the trees and in the soil. The rocks grew larger and I saw mountains for the first time. Trees crowded the trail until it became a dark, leafy tunnel. Permanent, mortised fences gave way to crudely stacked saplings, then no fences at all. The people changed too. Whites grew poorer and wilder and spoke to each other in strange tongues. Few Negroes appeared. Other travelers camped just off the trail, families with a cart and a mule, or just a mule or two, but nothing the size of our party. We stopped once about midday to cook and to rest. At dusk we camped, allowing the hobbled animals to graze. The women cooked up mush, fry bread, and perhaps some freshly killed meat. William Morgan possessed a keen skill with his rifle and he provided our party with venison. It was autumn when we moved. I remember because I wore moccasins. At night, I huddled with Thomas and Albert under rough blankets. While we twitched and giggled, people talked around the fire.

"Be walking like this ten, twenty days."

"Master say the new land rich."

"I hear he got a whole valley in Kentucky."

"I hear he got a whole county."

"How much is a county?"

"More'n you can walk across in a week."

"A month."

"A year."

"Shawnee in Kentucky."

"No. Shawnee been whipped. All run off west."

"Some left, though."

"Maybe. Best to stay close."

"Shawnee don't steal niggers."

"Shawnee steal anybody. Kill anybody. Cut your nose off. Eat that tongue of yours. Might not bother to kill you to eat that tongue."

"Nawwwww."

"Best to stay close."

The cold was enough to keep me close to the fire or under a cart, but worrying about Shawnees helped.

The caravan entered the mountains that crowded in close to the trail. As my gaze went up to the wondrous heights of mountains, I tripped on roots and rocks. I had never seen nor imagined the land turned on its side and reaching for the sky like that. These mountains were to be my world for the next fifteen years and for the remainder of my days, the rest of the world stood next to those mountains. I compared the buildings of New York and Philadelphia to the Alleghenies. Pennsylvania had mountains too, but not like these. Before the trail tipped down into Kentucky, we stopped seeing settlements or plantations or farms of any sort. The last day, we drove the cattle single file along a game trail barely wide enough for the carts. The track followed up a clear stream to a place where the valley broadened out to bottom land, thick with cane and immense poplars, oaks, maples, and beeches. We turned the cattle and hogs out onto the leafy forest floor to fatten on mast. The great carts surrendered their burdens one last time and our camp transformed over the next few weeks to crude lean-tos and hearths of stacked stone.

To clear the new land in Kentucky, slaves girdled the great trees carving wide deep scars in the bark so that the trees would die. The leaves quickly fell adding their manure to the rich, black loam. Men marked off the green meadows into fields and pastures and attacked the forest with broadaxes and saws, first for fence rails, then for logs. The oxen dragged the largest felled trees to the river bank where men bucked the logs then rolled them over the pits built into the bank to saw lumber. After we built the master a large cabin (I helped some) and the overseer a small one, we put up stables and more fences. Only then did the slaves build homes for themselves, smaller but tighter and easier to heat than the ones for the white people. The master had a stone hearth and chimney with mud mortar. Our chimneys were of sticks and mud, but these did not last long, and eventually we got stone chimneys too. Being a mere child my efforts remained the simplest and lightest of tasks like filling chinks in log walls or tending animals. My excitement at the trip over the mountains gave way to work and the life of a slave where fatigue framed every day and the only joy came from food and rest and a little laughter. But since I knew nothing else, I had no sense of anything different, anything better.

I marveled at the new land, which was greener and rockier and taller than Virginia. The chestnut and oak and poplar amazed me with their size, and the forest offered us an unlimited bounty. In all my travels over the years, I cannot recall seeing a country so full of life and promise. We had plenty of meat that first year. Deer and bison came out of the dense cane to feast on the young corn only to become meals themselves. William Morgan and men with guns waited in the night for the thieves to slip up on the crop. Our men got quite good at timing several shots together to bring down two trespassers at once. The gunshots that woke us promised fresh meat. What we did not eat went to a smokehouse or was traded. We worked hard, but we ate well that first year.

This is really where my story begins, along the Louisa Fork of the Big Sandy River, which tumbled out of the mountains before meandering north to the Ohio. I left childhood on this rough plantation in a fertile valley hemmed in by hills, a place of bondage and labor, but also one of security and order and happiness. Anything that ever represented comfort to me, such as my bed or my home, recalled a vision of that clear stream shouldered by rocky hills and cushioned by tall trees. Since we came down out of the mountains, the direction of the future and of progress always felt downstream. The past and loss were back behind us, back over the mountains. Ahead was progress and plenty.

It was at Morgan's that the events that shaped my life unfolded, all in the shadow of a small white man on a large horse.

The Orphan

S ome of us crowded into that first smoky hut with the fire in the middle. Our crude shelters gave way to cabins and I settled in with different married couples. As babies came, I ended up with Mariah and Ike for whom children were not part of God's plan. I can't call them my stepparents because all the Morgan slaves were my parents, and we were one big family.

I cannot remember missing my mother or experiencing any sadness at her loss probably because I saw so little of her. Children are marvelously malleable, and tragedy washes over them like a spring rain, briefly unpleasant, but soon past. Did her absence form me or did I inherit some trait that left me immune to any lasting pain from having my mother sold away? I grew up on the Morgan place as everyone's child, but as no one's child. Thomas and Albert died the second winter so that left me in the middle as far as age; too old to need a mother and too young to warrant a husband. The babies became little children who developed friendships with each other which I never knew. The adults were not inclined to include someone so young in any of their matters. I took on chores that did not require much help and if I ended up working with others, I was given less to do. I picked worms off the tobacco plants and hoed beans and hunted ginseng, but I also helped with washing and cooking, carding, and weaving. I participated in conversations only as an observer, never a principal. My questions received short answers with little opportunity for a continuing discourse. My opinions elicited no responses at all. This is not to say that I was ever treated badly or shunned, such as white people do to each other; it is just that I am aware now that something kept me apart from them. From this, I assumed early in life a habit of solitude and autonomy, never expecting anything from anyone else. Later I came to understand that the origin of my blue eyes set me apart.

I don't remember just when I came to live in Mariah's cabin. I slept under a blanket on straw and leaves to one side of Mariah's hearth, and she and Ike shared their straw pallet to the other side. My first bedmates were the bugs that took up residence in my meager mattress, until I learned that they found cedar shavings distasteful. In winter, after Ike's urgent grunting yielded to slow, even breathing, I could join them for the warmth. But Mariah always positioned herself against her snoring husband, leaving me her back, the most intimacy I ever knew from her. She taught me to cook and to weave, but she never sang a song for me nor ever told me a story. When I went down with a cough or a fever, Daisy rather than Mariah brought me tea brewed from red alder bark. Never cruel nor even discourteous, Mariah still never gave me a smile. Ike was a big, strong field hand, best left in the charge of others. He regarded me as some slave assigned to sleep in his cabin, which I was, and spoke to me only if I asked him a direct question. Until I married, I learned to be my own best friend.

I first learned of my eyes in Mrs. Morgan's hand mirror. I was bringing washing up from the creek, and she had left her looking glass on a bench next the front door. I had seen her and William's wife Susannah using it to fix their hair. Mariah warned me never, ever to touch it or any of the mistresses' other possessions. Such treasures were irreplaceable on the frontier, and any slave who broke a mirror suffered greatly from the master not to mention the enduring curse. I did not touch it, but I looked. The small glass was encased in a polished wood case with a handle. As I peered into it, the image moved. Closer examination revealed a stranger, a girl I had never seen before, with fair skin and blue eyes. Only then did I realize that the stranger was me and the eyes were mine. Blue eyes. I stood hypnotized.

16

"There it is," I heard the master's wife remark shaking me out of my fixation. "I suppose you've never seen a mirror before, have you, Phyllis?"

I mumbled some obsequity and started to leave.

"Go ahead and look," she said. "You won't break it."

I glanced at her in one of our earliest direct interactions. She was short, like Morgan, and blonde and she had blue eyes too. Instead of the tight expression I had ascribed to white people, mostly because of what I had heard, I discerned a certain composure, a comfort with her world. That she would invite me to look in her mirror suggested that I was no threat and neither was she. I looked again in the mirror. The stranger looked back at me. I turned my head one way and she turned her head. I marveled at this wonder.

"I need it now," Mrs. Morgan interrupted patiently. "You get back to your work now." She picked up the hand mirror and disappeared into the house.

A Hard Lesson

Late one night, after the fire had died out of sight, urgent whispers spread through the slave cabins and jolted me awake.

"Ruth been caught stealin' sugar!" Sarah loved to carry tales, this time about Morgan's cook. "That no account Draper find her out on the road," she hissed. "Brought her in 'cause she didn't have a pass."

A slave away from his owner was at the mercy of any white man, unless he carried a pass or was known to be on the master's business. As hard as life on a plantation was, the risks abroad argued against flight.

"Draper!" Mariah shot back. "He wouldn't know a pass if it bit him on the leg. He can't read. I hear Missus say so." Mariah stood at our crude door, and I could see Sarah against the moonlit night. I knew of Draper too. Morgan tried him as overseer for a time, but he was too quick with his blacksnake and lazy to boot. He now wandered the mountains and valleys, trapping and trading skins for whiskey, willing neither to move on nor to do real work.

"He don't have to read what she don't have," Sarah said. "Mas' goin' to give him a dollar for her."

"Was she out to see her blacksmith?" Mariah asked.

"What, do you think she out for, a cup of tea? She sayin' she forgot the sugar was in her pocket. But it was for that blacksmith."

"Where she now?"

"O'Hara got her tied in the barn."

"I thought slave catchers got five dollars."

"You think Mas' is goin' to pay five dollars to someone like Draper? He not a real slave catcher."

"You think Ruth'd try to pay him off herself," Mariah said.

"You mean with the sugar?"

"No, not with the sugar. Knowin' that Draper, and knowin' that Ruth, he *did* trade with her, but Draper brought her in anyway."

Sarah rushed to the next cabin to deliver her news, fattened with Mariah's contributions. Sarah could be counted upon to embellish any tale and you could never tell how much of what Sarah said was true. Still, I could see that Ruth faced serious trouble.

"I hope Mas' lays 'em on her," Ike muttered as he reached over to stir the fire from his bed. Small flames struggled out of the coals and reflected off his broad face, but finding little fuel, expired to the memory of heat.

"Hush," Mariah said as she rejoined her man. "You could be one of them who has to hold her down. How you goin' to like that, up close while he whip her? You probably dream about bein' that close to her."

"Fine with me. Her and her yellow skin and her white woman's dress. Always lordin' over us. Wonder if she sleep in the kitchen now?"

"You just better hope he don't ask if you know about it. If he think we know she was sneakin' out on him and stealin', we're all in for somethin'. If he ask you, you don't know nothin'."

Theft was a crime, and even at fourteen I could not dispute the justice for stealing something as precious as sugar. The only sweetener I ever tasted was sorghum or honey, so a slave stealing real sugar not only represented the loss of something expensive, but the crossing of that line between black and white, a far greater transgression. Stealing sugar represented a threat to the order of the world.

In the morning, word came down: the master wants everybody at the big tree. An immense oak, one survivor of dozens we had felled in the valley, marked the boundary between the slave cabins below and the master's family who lived further up the slope. No slave traveled above the tree without a specific purpose, and he stayed there no longer than was required. By the same token, Morgan rarely frequented the slave cabins downhill, leaving that task to the overseer or his son, William. If we saw Morgan at the cabins, it was on his horse and with his short whip.

Reluctantly the Morgan slaves, in the brown and gray dusty homespun reflective of our lives and spirits, shambled in twos and threes up to the tree where the master waited. Each one of us wanted to be last. Morgan stood facing us with his arms folded, his weight on one leg as if his carriage were late. He wore a fresh white shirt, tan breeches, and those tall brown riding boots. That cool summer morning, he left behind his hat, showing us his close-cropped grey hair and hard hazel eyes. We stopped at the tree and clustered around the trunk like shipwreck victims clinging to scrap of timber in an angry sea. Two women carried infants and several wide-eyed urchins clung to their mothers' dresses. I tried to keep out of his sight behind the trunk along with Mariah until we heard that voice.

"Get out from behind there!" Morgan ordered. "I want to see all of you!"

I took a place at one side of the group, my eyes down, already skilled at watching the master without looking at him. About twenty feet separated me from Morgan. Despite his short stature, the slope gave him the advantage over me. I stared at an oak gall on the ground. Morgan did not whip his slaves much; he did not have to. But when he did, he knew how to whip. He whipped for the best effect, not just for the poor wretch on the ground, but for the rest of us. A loose cow, a cabin burned by an untended fire, sleeping instead of working – all invited stripes. Of the worst offenses, particularly running away, Morgan had little fear. He thoughtfully crafted whippings so that not just the miscreant received his leather education, but the onlookers learned from the ordeal as well. In a manner of speaking, when the Morgans whipped, everyone felt whipped.

The elder Morgan had a certain flair for ceremony, an almost theatrical talent in that way. If some act of negligence or even rarer act of malice came to his attention, he made certain he delivered an extreme display of temper, not widely viewed, but in front of one or two. These wagging tongues carried his explosion back to the slave quarters in magnified iteration. The retelling improved on his anger to the extent that the master walked up walls, performed somersaults, and shrieked like a madman. Even the unlettered slave knows the difference between someone who is simply intent on doing harm and one who is crazed.

Morgan customarily administered whippings, not in the morning when the punishment might be lost in the day's labors, but in the evening when we all shared a few waking hours of community. We could slumber with screams and blood in our minds.

"Victor!" Morgan would announce, ordering the hapless victim to shuffle forward, embarrassment as strong an emotion as fear. Improbably, almost every slave was taller than David Morgan, making the quaking prisoner look even more incongruous next to his judge. "I have a lame horse because of you," or "The dogs got into the smoke house and ate my meat," enumerated the precise nature of the offense. In a civilized culture this would be called indictment, trial, and conviction. But slavery was not a civilized world. On a plantation all is the whim of the master. Jewell talked back to the overseer once and Morgan heard it. She thrashed about on the ground against the men on her arms and legs while O'Hara lifted her shift to lay into her backside. I am certain that the ignominy of her nakedness hurt as much as the stripes themselves. Making the other slaves participate in the punishment confirmed Morgan's power over us. Being so close to the squirming, bawling victim gave everyone a taste of the whip. We heard about backs flogged bloody and mutilations on other plantations, so we believed we had a good, fair master.

O'Hara the overseer and Draper dragged Ruth up from the barn, one to an arm. When she saw the gathering at the tree and Morgan calmly waiting, she began to bellow like a terrified sheep. The white men brought her in front of Morgan and let her go. She collapsed onto the ground and crawled across the dirt towards him. The blue house dress that she had received from Mrs. Morgan was dirty and covered with bits of straw. More straw and feathers stuck to her wild black hair. She barely resembled the haughty woman who slept in the white people's kitchen and who was so quick to notice my muddy feet or my dirty shift.

Ruth reached out toward Morgan's feet, crying, "Please, Mas', I– I–"

"Shut up, you thieving pig!" he screamed as he dropped his hands into balled fists. I had known the master all my life, but I had never heard that voice before. It seemed to come from deep within him, and it hit me like a blow to the stomach. All the faces reflected awe and fear, and I heard a muffled sob. Draper grinned, showing teeth on only one side of his mouth. O'Hara laughed. Mrs. Morgan watched from the porch of the house.

"You find this amusing Mr. O'Hara?" Morgan snapped.

"No sar," O'Hara answered, recoiling, his usual reaction in Morgan's presence. Morgan barely tolerated the Irishman, as much for his obsequiousness as for his race. Morgan held the same contempt for Hibernians as he did for Africans.

"Well, you are correct. This is not amusing. Not at all. No. This is actually very sad," Morgan answered. The mock desolation changed quickly to viciousness. "Ruth thinks she can steal from me. She thinks she can steal from my grandchildren. She thinks she is smarter than me. She has taken food from my table, and she has betrayed the trust that I have placed in her."

Ruth whimpered up from the dust, "Naw, suh, please..."

"Quiet! I don't want to hear you. Don't say another word!" He then looked at all of us. "Ruth here has stolen from her master. I have given her food and a warm place to sleep and clothing. I have given her easy work in the house. She answers my charity and my goodness with theft, with ... betrayal. She has insulted me, and she has tried to make me the fool! This slave has stolen from me, David Morgan. She must be punished!"

If there was such a thing as a good master, Morgan might have been one. But I will never believe that a man who would exercise ownership over another human being, however benignly, could be construed as fair or good. I certainly cannot call Morgan, bad though. (I must remind myself that such judgments are to be left to The Lord, and it is for me to forgive.) If it is necessary to compare people, they perhaps should not be held up against the whole of society, but against others like them. I could not compare David Morgan to Abraham Lincoln, who did not own slaves, but I could compare him to Edward Osborn who did. In that setting, Morgan was not a bad owner. He did not take advantage of slave women, and he did not approve of those white men who did. If he found an overseer molesting a slave, he sent the scum packing. That did not stop Morgan from accepting ownership of the mulatto children born in his slave cabins. Yellow children brought a fine price. Morgan did not mistreat his slaves needlessly, any more than he mistreated his horses. But David Morgan could be quite dangerous.

"A master has great responsibilities," Morgan said to O'Hara, but the runty Irishman was not his intended audience. "I must feed them all and clothe them all, and I must make certain that there is order here. What would happen if slaves were allowed to steal?" O'Hara could never possibly answer such a profound question. "God help us if every slave decided to steal and run off."

Ruth started to get to her knees and pleaded, "Please, Mas' Morgan, I didn't run–"

"Shut up!" screamed Morgan again, and his heavy brown boot shoved her back to the ground.

"And William, you know the worst of this?" Morgan turned to his son, taller and fairer than his father, although always smaller in his presence. The son took after his mother in countenance, but without her loyalty or her sense of hard work.

"No, Pa," William answered, unimpressed by the whipping of a simpering slave. William preferred victims who resisted their fate.

"Every nigger in the county will hear about this. Every nigger will know what Ruth has done. Now, every nigger will know what I did about it. She thinks she can steal and that I will not notice. If I do not do something about this right now, right this minute, these niggers will think I am soft. They might even think that Ruth is smarter than I am. We can't have that, can we?" No reply. "William?"

"No, Pa."

I rarely heard Morgan call us niggers. We might be Coloreds or Negroes or Africans or hands, but almost never niggers. Ruth made weak sounds on the ground that may have been words. That day Ruth, the privileged house servant, was one of us, just another piece of property.

"O'Hara, your rope," Morgan ordered calmly. No one made a sound, but I was certain that Morgan heard my heart beating. O'Hara stepped forward with a rope used on horses. Morgan pointed into the tree. O'Hara clumsily swung the line up into the tree without success. A second try failed too. On the third attempt it snaked over a limb, dropping to the other side. I saw that Morgan was going to give her a real flogging, but Ruth looked up and seemed puzzled. Her tears had turned the dust on her face into streaks of mud on her amber skin. Morgan took the end of the rope, and he began to tie a substantial slipknot. I had worried that I would finally be one of the slaves ordered to hold Ruth, yet I was strangely fascinated at this novel way to whip someone, hands hoisted over the head. Victor had told of such a whipping in Virginia. The strung-up victim twisted away from the lash only to take stripes across the front of his body.

"Get her up here," Morgan ordered. O'Hara and Draper took Ruth by the arms and hair and lifted her to her feet. She just hung between them, unable to stand on her own. While Draper held her up, O'Hara grabbed her hands and held them out toward Morgan and the rope. Morgan stood in front of her, his hazel eyes fixed and cold. I had seen that look in him when he traded horses and when he made speeches at elections. He concentrated on his task and he intended to win. Whatever Morgan did, he needed to win. Morgan held the open rope in front of Ruth's face. I was behind her and could not see her eyes, but I heard her bawl.

"Ruth, you are no good to me anymore," Morgan stated calmly, decisively. But Ruth was beyond understanding him. O'Hara thrust Ruth's wrists toward Morgan as if he were forcing her to pray to him, the heathen African begging the white man for salvation. Draper held her by the shoulders, grinning with anticipation.

"I cannot trust you now. I cannot let you in my house or near my grandchildren. I cannot even sell you. What good is a cow that

25

won't give milk anymore? She's just meat on a rope." His eyes did not move from Ruth, and he repeated a bit more softly, "Meat on a rope." A woman behind me gasped, earning her an elbow.

In a twitch, Morgan dropped the noose over Ruth's head and cinched it quickly around her neck.

"Haul on that line!" he ordered.

Draper fell on the rope over the limb and began pulling. O'Hara quickly joined him. Both men seemed as surprised as any of us, but they were completely under Morgan's sway. Ruth grabbed at the rope on her throat as the white men lifted her to her toes. She gagged "A-k-k-k-k-k" and spun around so that we could see her face, eyes and mouth wide open. Now that they had her weight, Draper and O'Hara pulled inexpertly until she was off her toes a few inches and swinging free. She kicked and twisted as she fought the hemp closing off her throat. Her eyeballs bulged and her tongue filled her mouth. The choking soon stopped and her struggles slowed until, first one hand, then the other, dropped to her side. She just swung there, mouth half open, eyes vacant. The only sound was the creaking of hemp against the oak limb.

Slaves spoke of bad Negroes being hanged and they even joked about it, but the idea that Morgan would hang a woman for stealing sugar was outside the realm of possibility, beyond imagination. Killing a slave was the destruction of valuable property worth hundreds of dollars, like shooting a horse or burning down a barn. I was at the same time stunned and sick and transfixed. As hard and sometimes as painful as life on a farm was, there was little real cruelty. I butchered cows and hogs and game, but we knocked them in the head and cut their throats so that they died quickly. The animals fought some, but it was over in a few seconds. They surrendered their meat to us, untainted by their agony.

This thing with Ruth, however, was raw brutality, and I could not comprehend it, particularly in that safe and familiar valley. I think we all knew that our master was capable of violence, but beyond his flashes of anger and the odd whipping, we had never really seen it. Ruth swung slowly her hands and feet twitching ever so slightly.

"Let go!" ordered Morgan, and the white men released the rope, Draper a little less readily than O'Hara. Ruth dropped to the ground like a sack of grain, and her head slammed onto the hard ground. Her long, dirty, curly hair covered her face. Morgan stepped over and loosened the noose. Ruth gasped for air and choked and coughed. Her hands went to her throat to pull at the noose, and she took in a deep breath.

"Haul her up!" Morgan told the white men and Draper pulled on the rope which he still held in his hand. Reluctantly this time, O'Hara lent his weight to the task.

"Nooooo!" rasped Ruth as she struggled to her feet to fight the noose, but in an instant she was swinging again, kicking. Her fight stopped more quickly this time and her arms again went limp. Her eyes stared blankly past us as her body rotated, no longer a human being, just... meat on a rope. Two women cried softly. William seemed unimpressed. Mrs. Morgan flushed and her lips pursed in anger.

I stole a glance at Morgan. He wasn't watching his cook strangle slowly under the limb. He was watching us. He was watching me. Those around me stared at a spot on the ground beneath where Ruth was dying. They couldn't watch her choke and they couldn't look at Morgan and they couldn't look away.

"Drop it," Morgan commanded as casually as he would summon a cup. The body crumpled once again, and Draper seemed to enjoy letting go as much as hauling up. Morgan and reached down again to loosen the halter. But this time he shook the loop open and wrested it from her neck, letting her head flop into the dust. She gasped again and coughed and gagged.

Morgan held out the noose right towards me and spoke calmly, slowly. "Any of you ever think about stealing from me, ask Ruth what it is like to be hung. Ask her what it's like when the darkness falls over you and you start to cross over into the great beyond. Any of you steal from me, you will *beg* me to whip you. You will *beg* me to shoot you. You will *beg* me to cut your throat." He showed no emotion. He could have been directing the division of a hog or the saddling of a horse, instead of the murder of a human being. "O'Hara, Ruth works the fields now, and I expect a full day out of her today. Mariah! You cook me my breakfast." He then pointed at me. "Bring her with you."

With that, Morgan turned and walked into his house. O'Hara told two of the women to see to Ruth. The rest of our people drifted quickly but silently down to chores, just happy to be free of this. O'Hara snarled some commands to Peter about the day's work. I looked at Mariah, whose eyes were wide with surprise. She turned without a word, hurried up to the side of the master's house and the kitchen. I followed, full of shock and terror and sadness, but also with no little excitement at this change in my own fortune. Both Mariah and I had been promoted from field work to the house. Working at the master's house allowed access to better food, better clothing, albeit discarded by the master and his family, and generally easier duties. Our status among our people rose too. We could hear what the master said and would be first to carry any news of the little plantation. People would gather around us in the small chance that we had some morsel of gossip they could carry or keep.

It was undoubtedly Draper who started the story around. He had his dollar from Morgan, a taste for whiskey, and a need to sound important. By the time we visited town a week later, everyone, white and Negro, heard that Morgan hanged Ruth for eating a spoonful of sugar. A white boy told me Morgan hauled Ruth up with just one hand and that it took an hour for her to die. The boy knew because he had seen it with his own eyes. People said Morgan would hang a woman for burning his breakfast and Morgan's slaves were so frightened of him that none of us would never tell what really happened that day, so don't believe anything any of us said.

Morgan never spoke of the incident again. That fall, he was elected commissioner and head of the militia. It was his county.

The Master Returns

The summer after Morgan hanged Ruth, I don't know what was hotter that day, the fire burning in front of me or the sun. Esther and Daisy and I worked near the cabins, butchering a pig which had gotten into the corn. Mariah mastered Ruth's kitchen work quickly and she took care to leave me with chores that kept me away from the rest of the Morgan family. I traveled back and forth between the main house and the slave cabins all day. I chopped wood, emptied night jars, and pounded laundry. My house chores completed, Mariah sent me then to find Esther. At the time, I assumed Mariah just regarded me with the same unimportance as before, but I suspect now that her behavior was motivated by a desire to ensure that I was not tempted as Ruth was. Mariah did not care to share the benefits of good food and better clothing that Ruth had squandered. Had anything gone missing, Mariah justifiably feared that she might wear stripes or a rope burn. Mariah needed me close enough to take the most thankless tasks yet far enough away to not to pose a threat to her and her position.

We usually killed hogs only after the weather turned cold in November. This summer, a marauder expressed a particular skill at getting through the fences and into the corn so Morgan allowed the men a gun to kill it. William Morgan, ever the great hunter, found less joy in waiting for a corn thief than in tracking him down. After one night of fruitless vigil he passed along the honor of the kill to Peter and the men. It took several more nights of sentinel duty before the hog finally fell to a bullet. Mariah roused me out of my bed long before dawn to go to work. Only by acting quickly could we prevent the meat from spoiling in the heat that abated only slightly after sundown.

By full light, the carcass hung by its hamstrings, and we went to work with knives. Esther showed me where to find the vein at the neck. The innards spilled into the pot and off came the head to be quartered and soaked in brine. We still lost the lights and the liver to the heat. Those organs usually went to the slaves. By afternoon, the best meat had been salted down and hung in the smokehouse or was roasting for the master's dinner. The slaves had some fresh pork as well, a rare treat. I skimmed fat out of another iron pot set over a smoky fire. From the dark color of the fat, the hog had been feeding on chestnuts, promising sweet-tasting meat.

Though not as tasty as bear fat, hog fat was what we used the most. Daisy had ways to mix it with yarrow and ginseng to treat sickness. Esther and Daisy cut fat into small pieces and threw the bits into the near-boiling water. The hottest work fell to me, the youngest. I had to crouch near the fire and steaming kettle and carefully remove the top layer of hot grease with a gourd. Only my dress, really a long sack with arm and head holes, protected me from the flames and grease. I had dropped my rope belt to let the fabric hang away from my body and allow a little air inside. The pot we were using had made the trip with us from Virginia, and if it wasn't cooking up mush or a stew, it was tanning leather or dying cloth. My job at the fire at least meant that I wasn't tormented by the flies that swarmed over the bones and meat and bloody hands. The small black creatures covered the sides of the little crocks that I filled and I had to watch that they not get trapped in the lard and turn up later in the master's breakfast.

My coarse shift hung on me dark with sweat and only frequent visits to a water bucket nearby kept me from drying up entirely. Fifty years later, it is hard for me to imagine the work that I did in that heat. Even though time can temper the experiences of youth, I never saw a hotter day. Cows and pigs clustered in the shade next to buildings and under trees. An ear flicking at a fly was the only indication that the heat had not killed everything. Otherwise the farm looked dead. Any of the petty differences and contests between the animals were traded for bits of shade together and some refuge from the summer oven. Crickets screeched from the trees, angry at the summer and the sun. Three vultures sulked in a distant scrag, unwilling or unable to struggle aloft in the soggy air. It was like the photographs you now see of the War, where bodies are scattered along fences and ditches, still and lifeless. No wind made its way into our valley, so the air simmered back in on itself like the cauldron in front of me. The thick air muted the green of the trees and crops with a mist, and left the once sharp ridge tops indistinct.

O'Hara, the overseer, sweated too. He was supposed to keep us at our tasks and that meant he had to be out in the sun as well. He was not pulling at a hoe or hauling on a saw, but he had to be out with us just the same. There was a small joy at making him work at making us work. O'Hara came to Morgan's one day sniffing out the rumor of a small position. The hairy Irishman's deep chest sat atop ridiculously short legs. The first time I saw an ape in a circus in Philadelphia, I was reminded of the hunched O'Hara, arms hanging loose in front. His dark brown hair and beard never knew a comb, and he wore what Morgan threw away or slave homespun.

I have found it ironic that slave owners managed to recruit so many drivers from among the Irish, so recently slaves themselves. Years later, I saw them flee famine, living skeletons with runtish children, stupid from hunger, so I can easily imagine what O'Hara left behind him. Tyrants recognize that it is useful to lift one slave up over another and let him wield the whip instead. A man unable to strike back is willing to flog another in a bargain for food or freedom or power. If one cannot escape, the next best thing is to be less a slave. O'Hara was no slave, but until he had the means and the motive to move on, he was just another piece of Morgan's stock.

That particular day, O'Hara started no one with his strap. He suffered just like any other pig in the shade. If O'Hara had one reliable attribute, it was his unreliability. He interested himself in getting through the heat and into the evening and a swallow of whiskey, not in seeing that the master's property turned a profit.

31

Twenty slaves, scattered over three hundred acres of fields, pens and woodlots, were too many for a one man, even on a good day. To watch everyone, the overseer had to keep moving, looking down each row of plants or checking in on each chore. But that August, even breathing was laborious, so he found his own place to hide.

Infrequently, he stirred and, after finding a drink of water (or something else) he stumbled after his old spotted horse. He tugged the worn-out saddle to see if the cinch had come loose – or had been loosened – and then he started his comical act of mounting. Too short to just step into the stirrup of even that small horse, he had to lead the animal to a fence or a rock and climb up on that before finding the stirrup. He held the animal still with one hand while he worked his foot into the iron with the other. Sometimes the horse stepped away just as O'Hara yanked at the top of the saddle, forcing him to kick helplessly as he hung there before dropping off to try again.

Finally in the saddle, O'Hara kicked the animal forward, never faster than a walk. He barely knew how to ride, having come from a country where farmers did not even have horses for their plows. A sow lifted her head from the dust to see what could be so important to move in the sun. On learning that it was just O'Hara, she returned to her slumber.

O'Hara rode on to find someone to torment. "Put your back into it you sorry cow. You call that a pile of wood? I saw you sleeping there you blaggard." No one knew what a blaggard was. Any of us could bend onto a hoe or pull at a bundle just as his horse staggered into view. O'Hara was too lazy and too hot that day to expend any effort beyond an insult. He snarled and we cowered and the charade stumbled through the day, more comic than cruel, more inept than oppressive. It was reflective of his intelligence that he bothered at all when Morgan was away.

Despite the heat, three thin dogs stayed wide awake at the butcher block. The mongrel issue of hounds that had migrated with us through the mountains, all wore an indeterminate brown color. Two had spots and one sported white feet. Unknown and unowned, these vagrants could be counted upon only to be near the trash pit or the butchering. They might make some noise if a cat or a bear or a wolf hunted too close, but they left it to braver breeds to confront anything remotely aggressive.

The thieves circled the butcher block and the pile of bloody meat, heads low, tongues hanging out, hoping for a handout or an opening to steal. Esther took a bone, stripped of flesh, and waved it about. "Here you go dog," she teased. "How'd you like to chew on this?" She feigned a toss to one side and two dashed out for it, but she threw it the other way to the feet of the third, the small one with white feet. Eyes wide with surprise and terror, he snatched it up and fled, pursued by the teeth and snarls of the other two. A chase, the swirl of a fight, and the strongest won the meal, meager as it was. The losers contested the decision a short while before returning to the possibility of a whole bite of meat instead of just a bloody bone. We were losing much of the hog to the heat, so Esther was not really wasting food.

One at a time, the dogs crept close, eyeing Esther and looking for a moment of inattention. Esther bent over the meat pretending to cut more, which tempted a robber to come in and pick out his own snack, but such a venture carried a price. As swift as each of them was, none was as swift as Esther, or rather, as swift as her whip. She owned a braided leather for herding, cracking it near the stock, but never striking. "Ho cow," snap! "Ho pig," snap! "Ho boy," snap! I found her whip unattended once and tried to snap it like she did, only to earn myself the mark below my eye that you can still see today.

One spotted dog worked in close, thinking Esther did not see him, and just as he darted in for the meat, she snatched up the handle and snap! The thief yowled off, one pained front leg tucked up, as much in shame as in pain. We laughed together at her skill and the dog's defeat, knowing that she had inflicted no lasting injury.

Esther was past mid-life, which for a slave was about thirty years of age. Work, children, and disease gave any slave woman only about forty or fifty years on this earth. Esther resolved to enjoy some of it. Already broad in the face, her brown eyes flashed with awareness and calculation. She smiled and joked with everyone and everything. She could even joke with the master occasionally, though very carefully. Only when she buried her children did I ever see her cry.

"You just try it, dog," she teased. "You come on in and get you a piece of hog. Nice juicy chunk of fat. Bet you can taste it now. Mmm. Come see how it feels. I bet I could crack you clear back to that fence. You try it. Maybe you think you're pretty fast?" Their eyes locked and a hungry animal measured the risk, then skulked away to consider another approach. The heat rendered this sport leaden at best.

Esther took care to see that each of the six or seven women at Morgan's had some role she could call her own. Sarah became the weaver. Mariah cooked. Daisy healed. We all helped with big chores like butchering, and at harvest. Slavery being built on strict layers of power, it was too easy for the slaves themselves to make others slaves. Morgan expected Esther to maintain order among the slave women, which she could have done like the animals, each one dominating another until the least is treated as the runt. Esther possessed wisdom enough to see that we were better than the animals and no one should be a runt.

I stoked the fire to keep the water hot enough to render down the fat, but not so hot as to roll a boil that would mix water into the grease. Water in the lard made it pop and spatter in the pan. Grease burns are slow to heal and leave ugly scars. The short handle of my gourd brought my hand close to the fire and the fat. I dipped carefully into the top layer, removing it before I got burned. I learned to make small dips quickly, filling the gourd only part way. A dog might sniff at a crock and taste the smelly liquid, but by the time the fat was cool enough for a tongue, we had covered it with cloth for sealing later with beeswax.

Another dog far down the valley broke my tedium. I heard it only because the thieves around us turned their attention briefly in that direction. After some consideration, our pests abandoned the bloody offal and headed down the road. They trotted away yipping and barking as if this new item of interest truly held more importance than fresh pork. Esther spoke what I suspected.

"Mas' comin'."

Several minutes later, David Morgan rode into view, slumped atop his mare under his wide, dark hat. He had ridden to town two days before, and his return always drew notice.

Esther started the discussion around the smoky fire. "Look who comin' for a visit."

"Why that Saul, Mr. Harmon's boy," Daisy volunteered. "Mas' Morgan hire him out."

"But old Harmon die last month," Esther replied, always first and best at reading the signs. "I say Mas' buy the boy." I was only half listening because my full attention fixed on the beautiful African striding cheerfully down the road with a bundle over his shoulder. Esther must have noticed my distraction. "Jump it, girl! You never see a horse before?" and she took a good-natured swing at me with her whip. I was jolted back to the pot and the fire, but I managed to keep one eye on this new development.

I had just that year begun to notice young men. Of Morgan's twenty or so slaves, only six or seven were men. And there were just two near my age. Patrick already had a wife and Jack was simple. The other men had wives too. I got to go to town every few weeks and each visit witnessed new feelings in my belly as I saw and even spoke to men of my own color and age. I had become a woman that spring, and the slave women began joking about marrying me off. They knew I abhorred Jack, so they speculated often about whether our children would have my fair skin and his persistent drool. They tormented me when young men from other farms manipulated a reason to travel over to Morgan's carrying some message or lending a hand. They always drifted to where I was working, supplying Esther and Mariah the sport of running them off.

Morgan stopped up by his house and swung down from his saddle. He handed the man the reins, and the slave bobbed his head. As Morgan disappeared, the man loosened the cinch and broke the saddle's wet grip on the blanket and the mare's back. He stroked her head, and I saw him lean toward her ear, which twitched in his direction. Then he turned down toward where we were working and the mare followed. As he walked ahead of her, the reins hung loose between them. Most people, white and black, would have tugged on the hard bit to force the animal to the barn, but this man thought to introduce himself to her and to make her comfortable. She followed him, not because of the iron in her mouth, but because he had asked her to. To watch them, you would think they had been together for years.

Like most of us, Saul wore a homemade straw hat woven of split hickory. Instead of homespun, though, he wore good clothes. His blue linen shirt, soaked through with sweat, had a collar and buttons, and he held his brown trousers up with galluses. And he wore real shoes. He was by no means prosperous, but compared to the rest of us, he exuded affluence. As he drew closer, I could see his kind face and a bright, confident look. I was torn between staring at this vision and spooning the fat from my kettle. If I spilled any hot grease on me, I would have a painful wound for months. If I dripped it into the fire, the whole pot could ignite and Esther would take her whip to me. Our visitor attracted more than just my notice. Esther watched him too.

Morgan or the overseer often gave Esther orders to have the women prepare certain foods or ready carts or the wagon for town, because they knew she would get it done. Her husband, Peter, served as driver for all of the Morgan slaves, but Peter paid a substantial deference to his wife, whose intelligence and good will struck even the white people. It fell to Esther to distribute food and clothing and she went to town with the family almost every trip. She showed her approval of others by choosing who went along, but she spread the chores evenly. That day, she took charge of greeting the visitor, one hand on a hip, the other holding a bloody butcher knife.

"Where'd you get them nice clothes, boy?"

"My old master die and Missus give 'em to me," he responded in a clear voice that made me want to melt.

"Your old master? Who's your new master?" Esther asked as if she didn't know.

"Mas' Morgan. Mas' David Morgan," the beautiful man said proudly. "He buy me from Mrs. Harmon yesterday. He got a paper."

"The Widow Harmon? Well, how she going to work that place of hers?"

"She sell it. Movin' back East. Mas' Morgan say I should take care of Brownie here and then go find Mister O'Hara."

"Where you gonna live?" Esther pressed her examination of the new man.

His eyebrows cocked a bit as he joined the game. "Maybe I throw in with you? I'm sure you got room in your corner."

"Pretty clothes and a pretty boy, but a sassy mouth! That mouth get you whipped yet if my Peter don't shut it for you first."

"I say there room for two of us to keep a good woman like you happy," he shot back brilliantly. Had Esther found her equal? "Let me talk to this Peter. He might like the help." Daisy blurted out a shrill laugh.

Esther frowned and warned Saul, "You best take care of that horse there or you won't need that smart mouth to get your whuppin'." Esther turned to me and I could see that she approved of the new addition to our community. "Phyllis, take this boy..." She turned back to the man. "What's your name, boy?"

"Saul."

"Saul. Girl, take this Saul down and show him where we keep Brownie and where Mas' Morgan keep the tack."

My mouth went dry and my feet felt stuck in the dirt.

"Jump it, girl!" Esther ordered, and she grabbed her whip.

All I could do was point to the barn and start stumbling in that direction. I think my mouth hung open like Jack's did. I certainly felt just as clumsy and just as appealing. As I walked to the barn, Esther called after me, "And that all I want you to show him, girl! I see the way you walkin'. Don't you pay no mind to that mouth of his. You be back up here in a blink or I be the one show's you." My face burned, not from the heat of the rendering fire, but in mortification.

"C'mon, Brownie," I heard Saul say, "let's follow this pretty lady." He ran his immense hands over her soggy coat. If I had not been in love with him before, I certainly fell in love with him beginning at that very moment. He followed me to the low barn of cut lumber that served as the Morgan stable. We called it the barn, but it had started as just a hayrick with an overhang. We added to it every year, and by then three sides had walls. It was large enough to keep the weather off of fifteen or twenty head of stock. I pointed out Brownie's stall and the racks where we hung saddles and harnesses.

As Saul tended to the mare, I couldn't take my eyes off him. His old master must have been smaller than he was, because the manufactured clothes were tight against his powerful muscles. He was the most beautiful thing I had ever seen. He never spoke to me or looked at me, though. He directed all his comments to the horse.

"Yes'm, Brownie, you a pretty girl. Long, strong legs you got. Nice haunch too. Firm. Good to feel." He pulled off the hot saddle and soggy blanket, throwing them over a fence rail. Thick fingers tenderly traced the marks left by cinch and saddle as if to acknowledge the loyal service she had just given her rider. "Your master got lots of pretty things around here, Brownie. Lots of pretty things." He found the curry comb and a rag. As he drew the comb over her wet flanks, her skin shivered to his touch.

"Phyllis!" Esther called. "You get up here and get to your work!" Her angry voice had no trouble penetrating the barn. "Get back here right now or that backside of yours don't look so good to Saul no more!" I rushed out of the barn, back up to the rendering pot. I knew the big grins from the women were not from Saul's obvious ability with animals.

At the pot, I resumed my careful dipping, even though I remained captivated by Saul's voice and enthralled by his lovely eyes. I managed to keep the dogs at a distance and still avoided setting myself on fire. Every spare second, I glanced down at the stable to catch some glimpse of Saul. I happened to look up toward the house. Morgan stood hatless in his shirt sleeves under the oak tree where he strangled Ruth. He lifted a tin cup to his lips and watched me.

The New Man

In our deep valley, dusk lingered for hours before yielding to a black sky crowded with stars. The heat that baked us all day relented as if God had opened the oven door and allowed in a hint of breeze from downstream. One more day of hard work ended, and Morgan's slaves gathered to dine on roast pork.

I have to smile at myself now as I describe our meal as "dining," since not only did we lack white linen, fine china, and bright cutlery, we had no table. Indeed, we had no chairs, just some logs sawn short and turned on end to make stools, and some longer pieces that served as benches. Our table service came from shaped clay and carved wood. For silver we used our fingers. But I can assure you that no formal gathering in a Philadelphia parlor saw happier or more grateful guests than Morgan's people sharing a fresh-killed hog.

Daisy had charge of roasting the meat, while simple Jack turned the spit, the glowing coals and crackling fat holding him completely in thrall. Firelight reflected off sweaty faces, bright with the small pleasure of decent food. Meat was a special treat, since we got so little of it, and the half dozen children laughed and squirmed about. Hands slapped and waved without thought at flies and mosquitoes that intruded upon the scene. One temporary relief from insects came when the smoke from the cook fire changed direction to exchange insect bites for coughs and burning eyes.

Saul's addition to our little community added some excitement too. Prisoners in dungeons describe how they welcome the slightest change in their dreary existence, even if it is some sort of calamity. Slaves are no different than prisoners in that sense, craving the slightest variation in their dreary lives. Saul joined the group from the men's cabin, having exchanged his old dead master's clothes for the usual work brown. He found a place in the circle on the log next to me, but the curiosity of the others prevented me from maintaining his attentions. Hungry people crowded around Daisy and the fire for their supper. Esther, usually the first to eat, passed up her turn to start the interrogation

"What'd old Harmon die of, boy?"

"Don't know," Saul answered. "He just die. Got sick one week, die the next."

"What about the other people?"

"Just Mama. She go to Virginia with Missus."

Daisy had her own questions. "What about the men?" she asked as she cut chunks of sizzling meat away from the carcass. "Tim?"

"Harmon sell off Tim and Joe last winter. To a man over in Paris."

"Not what I hear," Peter mumbled through a mouthful of food. He tossed a bone back over his shoulder which produced barks and snarls from the dogs circling in the darkness. We all enjoyed throwing our scraps in random directions out of the firelight and laughing at the variety of sounds produced.

"What you hear?" Daisy challenged.

"I hear they sold to a trader, down river."

Heads turned from food to Peter.

"Who tell you that?" Daisy pressed.

"Hear it from one of Mayo's boys. Jacob, I think." A pause. "No, Phillip."

"Phillip," Daisy spat. "He just tryin' to make trouble. Mayo catch him spreadin' tales like that, he get some licks. He find *himself* on a chain."

"Maybe they get over to Paris, and then they sold down the river," suggested a voice in the circle, but no one had an answer.

I noticed that Esther just stared into the fire from her accustomed seat, a large poplar stump hewn into a chair, her throne. She spoke up to be heard over the clatter of licking and chewing. "How'd you work that place by yourself, boy?"

"Hard," Saul said, wiping his chin. "Me'n Harmon and Mama and Missus do it all. He weren't afraid to switch us, but he was there in the field as long as we was. That probably what killed him."

"Work never killed nobody," Peter said, ever the authority on nothing.

"Well, he worked hard as me. But he was a old man."

"Why'd he sell those boys off?" Esther continued, but I think she knew the answer. I think Esther always knew the answers to the questions she asked.

"Couldn't feed us, he said. Try cotton, but he can't plant enough. Try tobacco. But tobacco kill the land. Only need all of us at plantin' and harvest. He hire us out, but last year, the white men send us back home. I hear him say, 'darkies no good in this country'.

"There was five," he continued. "Ma, Tim, Joe, Daniel, and me. Mas' Harmon bring us from Virginia. Prince William County. Daniel got sold over to Mayos. Then Tim and Joe go. A sad day. Old Harmon don't say nothin', he just take 'em to town. I think they know. Kept me, 'cause I young, I guess, and I know stock. And 'cause of my mama."

"Your missus sell you to Mas' Morgan. She sell her land too?"

"Yup, to Mr. Osborn, Mr. Edward Osborn. He want to buy me too, but she sell me to Mr. Morgan. I hear Mas' Morgan mean, got a temper."

"He can be mean, all right," Peter said. "You find out how mean he is, you don't do your work. Or you run off."

"Don't see no reason to run off," Saul told him. "No sir, see lots of reason to stay at this place."

"And what's that?" Daisy teased.

Saul didn't reply at once, and his silence caused me to glance up. Every face in the circle grinned at the two of us. My face burned in embarrassment until Saul answered. "Good food, for one," he said, holding up a clean bone. "How about young Mas' Morgan?"

41

"Mas' William?" Peter answered. "He rather go to town."

"Or hunt" from a voice across the fire as a bone crashed into the coals and sent up sparks.

"His missus dead, I hear."

"She die when little David come. Got the two girls too."

"Unless you count in town." Again from across the fire.

"He got children in town?"

"And a wife," Daisy said. "If you want to call her that."

"If you call her a wife," Peter added, "then he got wifes all over." This brought laughter all round. Some were back on their feet, holding out a plate for Daisy to saw on the haunch.

"Do I got to stay out of his way?" Saul still wanted to know.

"He prob'ly won't even know your name. You just do your work, and you don't have to watch nobody."

"What about Missus?"

"O'Hara!" somebody hissed. The circle fell silent and eyes dropped as the overseer wandered unsteadily into the firelight. He shoved a wooden plate at Daisy, who took it and went to the meat over the fire. She cut away some pieces, and even in the dim firelight, I could tell she caught gristle and lots of fat.

"Give me some meat, damn you," the Irishman slurred.

"Stringy hog, Mas'," she told him as she handed back the plate.

O'Hara wrinkled his nose over the food, holding it to catch some fire light. Either satisfied or unwilling to press the issue, he doddered off. No one spoke, until we were certain he had returned to his small cabin.

"He don't trust you much, do he?" Saul asked Daisy. "Where he come from?"

"Where any of 'em come from?" Peter said. "Up the road. Over the hill. Some day he go back down the road."

"There be another one," a voice assured us.

"I got to watch him?"

"Stay out his way. He do everything he can to stay out your way."

"If he the overseer, I don't see how I can stay out his way."

"Just do your work and stay 'way from his liquor."

"I already see he like his liquor."

Esther interrupted the pointless exchange. "Osborn got more land than he can work. Why he want Harmon's?"

"Can't say as Mr. Osborn mention it last time he had me up to supper," Saul said easily. Hoots and moans acknowledged his joke.

"You a smart boy," Esther told him. She addressed her next question to no one in particular. "Why he want land he can't work?"

"Maybe he just want to own it," Saul suggested. "White folks want to own things. 'Specially niggers."

"You hear white folks talk about it?" Esther asked.

"No, but my mama did." Saul let that sit.

"Well, tell me boy. You keep bein' so smart, maybe I tell O'Hara you got a secret jug someplace. He think you don't like him, you don't give him some."

"Don't be so sure I ain't got no jug. He be my friend, maybe we change 'round who stay in what cabin."

"That's it," from across the fire.

"Tell her."

"Uh huh."

I couldn't remember anyone ever teasing Esther like that, and I added Saul's wit and pluck to the list of things I already loved about him.

Esther was not to be diverted. "What your mama say?"

"Well, Mr. Osborn, he come over soon as he hear Mas' Harmon die. He all dress up and ridin' that nice gelding. Mama say he got to be the prettiest white man in Kentucky. He real sweet to Missus, tell her how sad he is Mas' Harmon die. How whole county goin' to miss him. He worry about Missus and say his missus worry about her too. He tell her that unless some man come to marry her, she never goin' to be able to run her people and get her place to work. He say he give her a good price for the place and the hands, and she can go back to her people with cash money.

"Then Morgan come on up. 'Nother day. He want the place, too, and the stock. My mama say Missus tell him she promise the land to Osborn. Morgan say he buy us, but Missus want to keep Mama. So he just buy me. Here I am, waitin' to move in with you." Saul pressed against me to make it my joke too. That was the first time he ever touched me.

Esther ignored Saul's aside. "Osborn say what he goin' to do with that place?"

"He say he want to work it. Get niggers or tenants or somebody."

"Or sell it," Peter offered.

"Why he do that?" Saul wanted to know. "He just buy it."

"Make money," Peter answered. "That's what white folks do. Osborn, he probably just want to get one over on Morgan."

"Why he do that?"

"Bad blood."

"How come?"

"Everybody know 'bout Osborn and Morgan," Sarah said, undertaking her self-appointed role has herald and tabby.

"I don't."

"Harmon keep you up there tied to a tree?" she baited. "You don't talk to nobody?"

"I guess I don't. Maybe tonight, you can talk to me?"

"Walter," she said to her husband, "you goin' to let him do me like that?"

"Till I'm done with my dinner," Walter mumbled, "he can do what he want."

"What about after dinner?" Daisy said "You take care of him then?"

"Hush," Esther snapped, ending that discussion. Punished by the whole universe, slaves have no one to punish, so we often took our anger out on each other. Esther and Peter not only enforced work, but they enforced peace too, he with his size, and she with her cleverness.

"Or you can tell me now," Saul said, toning down his waggery.

"Or maybe I won't." I never heard Sarah elect to keep her mouth shut.

"Morgan know Osborn's daddy back in Virginia," Daisy started, doubtlessly pleased to use Sarah's own vanity to rob her of an opportunity to carry a tale. "They fight in the Rev'lution. Osborn come to Kentucky and start a place, but they don't do so good. Morgan do him a favor and get him a job o' work to mark out roads and land. He rather look fine and talk big about how he goin' to be rich. Only Morgan get him off that job. I hear he ruin the job."

"He just don't do it," Sarah corrected, not about to let Daisy take all the credit.

"Morgan shame Osborn," Daisy continued. "Osborn try to go agin' him for election. He jaw on Morgan all the time. He hate Morgan. Morgan hate him."

"Election?" Saul asked. I found myself learning too. I heard some of these things before but paid no attention. Words like election and politics and revolution were concepts as remote as China and India. But now Saul wanted to know, so I wanted to know.

"Boy, you got a lot to learn," Daisy laughed. "The white men get together and decide who goin' to be judge and sheriff. Who goin' to run the county, who go to Frankfort."

"And they give out whiskey," Peter added. "One comin' up this fall."

"Whiskey for darkies?" Saul asked.

"Not supposed to," Peter said, "but we get some."

"What Frankfort?"

"That where they run Kentucky," Daisy explained. "Morgan, he want to go, I hear."

Seeing Saul consider this new information made me want to understand too, if only to join him in something. My mind drifted away from the hard body next to me, to my own secret feelings, and to the world outside of Morgan's valley. I remembered Virginia and the journey to Kentucky and I knew Prestonsburg, but these were things I had seen personally. I never thought about something I had never seen. I was drawn to ponder the idea of land and sky beyond my own experience. Questions crowded into my head, demanding answers like hungry little pigs pushing for teats on a sow. Anxious to be included in something that Saul was doing, I formed a question of my own.

"Mas' leavin'?" I blurted out, surprising the group. If I had dropped out of the sky into the circle just then, they could not have appeared more startled.

"Not for good," Daisy told me after a moment. "They just go for a few weeks. Make laws. Then come home." Her tone was patient but signaled condescension.

"How far he go?"

"Frankfort. Down river." This was a lot for me to grasp and these ideas overwhelmed my sense of speech. I remembered the beautiful man next to me and worried that my attempts at conversation made me seem stupid.

"Where Osborn get his money for Harmon's place?" Esther asked, pulling the discussion back to her interest.

"Don't know nothin' about money," Saul answered.

"Osborn not rich," she commented. "Spend his money on those clothes, that horse."

"He got slaves?" Saul asked.

"Did. Three. Sold 'em away"

"Down river?"

"No, over to Appleton."

"How he work his place?"

"He got boys."

"Maybe Mas' hire us out to work Harmon's," Peter suggested. Like everyone everywhere, slaves enjoyed endless conjecture at some meager change in lives of monotonous toil. The general discourse drifted through various circumstances and all the imaginable consequences. Being hired out meant hard work and perhaps some danger, but it also meant the opportunity to see and do something new, depending on the weather and the master. A few weeks in different fields or at new tasks broke the tedium that shackled us as much as our bondage did.

When the last bones of that hog flew off into the darkness or into the fire and all the permutations of white people's greed had been exhausted, people left the circle for their cabins and the solace of sleep, however brief. Saul and I sat alone staring into embers that glowed like the smoldering warmth within me. I did not understand what was happening to me, but it felt good and it felt right.

That day, Saul stepped along the road ahead of every other person in my life. His easy smile and his warm brown eyes filled an emptiness I never knew had existed. Once he was there, it was as if he had always been there, and I could not imagine my life without him. Calling me by name in his soft voice, left me drunk with confusing new sensations. The one time I tried alcohol made me dizzy and sick, but Morgan's liquor did not cripple me as much as the first brush of Saul's fingers against my neck. What I once might have regarded as the sour stench of an unwashed field hand became on Saul a reminder of his strength and the bond between us.

"Where your people?" he asked me as we watched the fire die.

The question took me completely unawares. I was used to enquiries such as "where's that bowl?" or "how you expect me to finish this with you just standin' there?" but never any curiosity about me. Everyone at the Morgan place knew my history, and I knew nothing of any interest to them. I had to stop and think and form words that I had never spoken before.

"Virginia," I managed.

"Where your mama?"

"Gone away."

"And your daddy?"

"Don't have a daddy."

"Everybody have a daddy," Saul said. "Maybe he give you those eyes?"

I did not know what to say. I thought my eyes were just something like the birthmark on Sarah's neck or a harelip. I certainly had a grasp of breeding, having witnessed the conception and birth of several generations of stock, but I never connected my eyes to a parent. Mariah had told me about my mother and if I asked her about my father, she told me to fetch more water or to cut some wood. When I mentioned my eyes, she did not even respond.

All I could say to Saul was "I don't know."

"Well, they pretty eyes," he said and I felt another ripple of desire wash through my belly.

We sat in silence, close but not touching, and I could feel his sadness. All that he had known in life, his mother, his friends, the farm where he grew up, even the white people he had no choice but to trust, was gone now. It was as if every person and every thing had been washed away by some great flood, and he was left stranded on the shore with the clothes on his back. He had been too busy all day, traveling, meeting new people, and learning new things to consider what he had lost until those quiet moments alone with me. Some coals collapsed, sending a small cascade of sparks onto the ground, and he looked up.

"Ever wonder how come the sun be up in the sky? What you think?"

I had no idea how the sun came to be up in the sky, but Saul knew and he cared if I knew. He told me the story he heard from Daniel who came on a slave ship.

"The sun and the ocean was good friends. They talk and they laugh and good things come from the sun and the ocean together. Lots of things. Fish and rain and the cool wind. And the sun, he live on a mountain top and he go and visit the ocean, but he never ask the ocean to visit him. You see, the sun, he worry that the ocean be too big for his home, 'cause the ocean the biggest thing there is. And he feel bad because he could go see the ocean and the ocean always nice to him and show good manners. The sun want to show good manners too, so he finally ask the ocean to visit him. Well, the ocean, he come to the mountain top where the sun live, and sure 'nuff, the ocean was too big and he wash up the sides of the mountain. But the sun, he too proud to say that his house too small, and he jump to the sky to save himself. The sun, he stay there and he never go back to the mountain top. Now, the sun in the sky, and the ocean down where it is."

And Saul told me how there came to be night and day and the other stories from Africa. Saul made me think. He started me on a mental journey that I have followed to this day. Saul was the smartest man in the world. His words came from around numberless fires on numberless nights stretching back centuries and far across the sea. Where the Greeks had written down their myths, which were then copied and recopied and translated and published into the books I later learned to read, the African only had the fire, the stars, and evening after evening of repetition and memory. In addition to those first sparks of womanly hunger that coursed through my loins and legs, Saul kindled something that a slave had no right to hope for – an imagination, a mind, and the dream of escape.

Out in the dark on another night, I gave myself over to Saul's patience and caring, and I learned God's purpose behind the flames that glowed within me. Or perhaps Saul surrendered to my lust? No matter. Together, he and I forged love out of that furnace of passion. The grins and lewd comments the next morning from Esther and Daisy and even Mariah made me feel, for the first time, like one of them. I now knew the substance of the earnest noises in the darkened cabins and the unspoken tie between those whose bodies unite. As an unlettered slave girl on the frontier, I experienced none of the shame or regret about love that I later heard from high-born white women or even pretentious colored women who whispered obliquely about their husbands. Love and its concurrent pleasures were as natural and as beautiful to me then and now as a sunrise that bid a flower to open to the sky.

I know that all this must come as a surprise to you, since I was married to your father for twenty-eight years and by whom I bore five children, three who survived. I had, I still have, a great love for the Reverend Emmanuel Lewis, and I know that he felt the same for me. But ours was a union of intellect and of spirit, fired by a commitment to our cause and to our faith. I learned much from him, and I am honored to think that he learned something from me. We respected each other, and over the years, we rejoiced in each other's accomplishments. He was a good husband, a good father and a good friend. Would that more men such as the Reverend Lewis find their places at the head of families and in front of their communities. I feel his loss deeply yet.

My feelings for Saul, however, probed other depths in my fifteen-year-old body. If my emotions could be given voice, what I knew with the Reverend Lewis was the hearty shout of "freedom" and "justice," a moving speech, a rousing hymn in the cadence of marching battalions. What I experienced with Saul screamed like a panther in the summer night, starting deep inside my belly and rising through me in a great, breaking wave and lifting to the sky. Just as the two separate lives that I have lived stretch between slavery and freedom, so do my two great loves extend from the raw and feral to the civilized and genteel.

Every little thing that Saul said seemed to open a new door for me. Father. Mother. The past. The future. Each of these ideas flew through my head like the great rivers of pigeons that coursed overhead, fluttering, turning, rolling. Some thoughts disappeared in the turmoil. Others landed close by to be taken as a meal. Just as with the pigeons, I had to learn to take only what I could comfortably eat or put away. The ideas, like the birds, were inexhaustible.

Saul liked to play with me. I might say something, and he would answer with a childish "why?" I would innocently answer and his response was another "why?" It was not long before I was out of answers to his whys, but his simple game kept me thinking. When the answer began to go beyond earthly solutions, I reflected on the creation of the universe, but without any final resolution. I can say with confidence that it was Saul's coltish whys that prepared me for the Word of God when I finally received it. Saul developed my mind as if it were a new field being cleared of the trees that blocked the light to the young corn. When I first heard the message of Our Savior, it was the seed tucked into black loam, patted down, and watered to sprout under the sun of knowledge.

Saul was a careful man and just as he would cautiously examine the different sides to an unbroken pony, he watched his new surroundings and waited. He examined more than just the young girl who caught his eye. He studied everyone, slave and free. Beginning a new life for himself under circumstances outside his control, he needed to assess the landscape. He may have spent his life on a farm in a lonely hollow, but he was a keen observer and he applied his knowledge of animals to people. He listened for what annoyed Peter and for what pleased him. He took care to saddle O'Hara's horse and helped the stubby overseer to mount. He never mentioned liquor to him lest the Irishman think for a moment that Saul could be an ally or an obstacle in the pursuit of drink. If another slave commented about his work or the way he handled stock, Saul always nodded and agreed that was a good idea.

Saul was careful with the women too. After his comments about moving in with Esther or meeting Sarah, he never joked like that again. He did that not only out of respect for me but also to ensure that he was no threat to them or to their husbands. When he heard Sarah spread a tale, he waited for others to reply, and he listened for verification from elsewhere. He even took the time to greet simple Jack and to praise the work of his oxen. Had Saul been born in different skin, he would have been elected to office. No one can ever please everyone, though.

The heat wave that oppressed us the day that Saul arrived relented, and a gentle wind blessed the valley. That farm hacked out of the forest became a harbor of delight, where birds made glorious music and every tree and bush bespoke wonder. I was in love. I would never be in love like that again.

My work at the house and around the farm crawled by slowly as I anticipated each day's end and Saul. Whenever I passed a window of Morgan's house or walked outside, I craned my neck for a glimpse of him at his chores. If I saw him, I would stop and stare until he passed out of view or until Mariah cuffed me to get me back to work. If I didn't see him, I trudged on to my next task.

The Price of Folly

O ne of the few pleasures in the sad life of a slave was the opportunity to create or to fashion anything useful. To do something better than anyone else, especially better than any white man, remains one of the secret joys of our race. The slave might be property, subject to sale or abuse or worse, but no one can sell or beat from him the satisfaction of looking upon the well-crafted result of his own skill. Mariah secretly enjoyed hearing the sounds of satisfaction from the owner's family at dinner or supper, even though they rarely thought to express it to her. Esther knew that she ran a peaceful and efficient community but would never hear that from her owner. And Walter's abilities as a builder were evident on the best farms in the county and in town, although his work was always credited to the white man who held him in bondage.

The Morgans had Walter and the men put up all manner of farm structures, and with each new project the walls rose straighter and smoother and the designs grew more elaborate. Morgan's house had gone up according to his own plan, but it was Walter who supervised the sawing of logs, the planing of boards, and the erection of beams. The mortises were all cleverly crafted to accept matching tenons so that just their weight held them fast together. Walter had no training, other than what he picked up from other journeymen and masters. His was the sort of talent seen in any true craftsman or artist, as natural and as a part of him as his massive hands. Morgan hired him out to work on the courthouse in town and to superintend the construction of other planters' homes.

Morgan's home was unlike the popular vision that you may have of the Southern plantation. We lived on the frontier and in country that never really prospered like the cotton and cane and rice counties elsewhere. Those crops, tended by armies of slaves, left the masters with cash to build their palatial mansions with Greek columns and windows and galleries on all sides. Not so in the Big Sandy country. First, we had to mill all the lumber ourselves, so no cut boards went to features unnecessary for survival and shelter. Second, all the nails and metal and glass had to travel over the mountains from Virginia or up from the Ohio, so even though a rich man could afford these symbols of wealth, he did not use them frivolously.

Morgan's house was one of the grandest in our county, but it was still a simple affair, unpainted, just two stories tall and six rooms, three downstairs and three upstairs. A narrow staircase provided access up to the childrens' room and to William Morgan's room. The master and the mistress slept downstairs in one room and the family gathered for meals around the hearth. Mariah cooked in the summer kitchen outside or on the hearth when it turned cold. The master's bed came from Virginia, but the rest of the beds and most of the furniture were home made. My home today is larger and grander than the Morgan mansion, but he was a pioneer and interested in more than ostentation.

Morgan used Walter to acquire wealth in the new county. Walter spent more time working for other white men than at the Morgan farm. Since Morgan had more slaves than anyone else in the county, he enjoyed the ability to offer labor to white men who could not or would not own their own slaves. Simple Jack and his ox team skidded heavy logs and Patrick could build barrels. All could bring in a harvest. Morgan earned money and influence and the slaves returned with important intelligence, gleaned by Esther and passed along to the master.

When work at the Morgan farm waned, Morgan took idle hands to town on market day where he offered their services for a few days or a few weeks. Morgan let the planters know that should a hand return with scars or tales of mistreatment, he would reconsider the arrangement in the future. Morgan was not above insisting on new clothing for the hand from the planter as one condition of service. Morgan also cleverly dispatched husbands separate from their wives to ensure that each would return on a regular basis during their service to be questioned by Esther in a timely manner.

I do not know who wanted the cabin, whether Saul went to Walter, or Walter went to Saul, or Esther suggested it. I only knew at the time that my newly awakened desire for Saul was thwarted by more work. Walter took Saul into the woods, and I hated the carpenter for taking my man away. I heard their chopping and the crashing of trees. Jack skidded first the locust logs out of the forest with his ox and Walter marked off the walls, setting stobs in the ground. This all took place in the evening after our regular work. This was summer when the crops were in, so there was time while it was still light.

They had no yardwands, no plumb lines, and no diagrams, just Walter's eye and a serious aspect under his beard. Axe heads flashed overhead and wood chips flew as the men cut logs into lengths and notched the ends. The cabin sills took locust and the walls took poplar. Once or twice with a grin Saul attempted an unspoken contest to see who could cut through the tree the fastest. The contests did not last long. Effort is precious to a slave, and Walter did not waste his sweat. Even though Saul had youth and speed, none of Walter's swings failed to hit the mark or to remove the maximum amount of wood. Without changing gait or exerting any more effort, Walter easily bested Saul, who flailed amateurishly at his cut. But Saul was an easy study, and he soon approached – but never met – Walter's skill.

The men rolled the nocked logs up into place with rope and handspikes. As the cabin took form they lay down rails and winched the logs up onto the growing walls. A gap indicated plans for a door. When the walls reached the appointed height, a roof stretched overhead to take on rafters and crude shingles. A wattle chimney climbed the end on top of a stone hearth.

Although I watched Saul and his wondrous muscles, mesmerized, the project evolved apart from me, as if it were someone else's business. I understood that Saul was building the cabin for himself and at night he excitedly described to me the things he had learned from Walter. He talked about "the" cabin and "it." Preoccupied by my newly discovered carnality and anxious to slip away again into the darkness, I gave little thought to practical considerations such as tomorrow or next week. All I knew was now and tonight. My realization that the cabin was to be my home did not come for some days, or rather some nights.

As I lay in his arms on the cool grass under the stars, toying with the stubble on his face, he whispered, "When we live in the cabin, I still want to come here with you. Like this. I want to hold you while I look up at them stars." Such was the proposal of marriage. My acceptance was to bury my face in his chest and make him submit to me again.

One feature of the simple structure escaped my notice at first. When I knew what I saw, I still did not understand its importance and I certainly could not have predicted the consequences. Just as the most evil is often done by those believing they are doing good, so too do so many things deemed to be a benefit turn out to have the opposing effect.

All the other slave cabins had one door and a chimney. Morgan's slaves had thrown them up quickly against that first winter with little attention to refinements that came later. Although each rude shelter was a little larger and a little tighter than its predecessor, they all had the same basic design. The men's cabin was the largest and, next to mine, the newest. Their chimney had caught fire because the bachelors were less careful with their fires than the women. The whole building went up in a fury of heat and light and not a little excitement. Walter superintended a larger replacement, but still very simple, one door, one chimney. None of the slave cabins sported a window. Windows required more work and would have just admitted more cold.

But Saul wanted a window for his bride, and Walter was only too happy to include one in his plans. Like so many great engineers, Walter saw only the good in his work, never imagining any damage as a result. Saul's log cabin would have a window with a single shutter. Morgan's house had windows with glass shipped up from Catlettsburg or over the mountains, and a stone chimney. The houses in town had glass windows and the planters' houses did too. There was no glass for slave quarters.

After the chimney was mudded up and the door hung with leather straps, Saul and I met there instead of our usual spot among the trees. We were man and wife after that. There was no ceremony, no singing, and no feasting. The slaveocracy did not approve of slaves marrying in the civil or ecclesiastical sense. Marital unions were always subject to dissolution as one or the other is sold away, so why introduce an institution into a slave cabin that might prove troublesome?

I slept that night with my husband on a tick of fresh cedar chips. Our new home still smelled of the forest and had yet to take on the taste of soot, unwashed bodies, and last night's supper. The hearth had yet to see a fire, and we had no idea even if the chimney would draw. Meadow grass still made up the floor. I could look up from our bed out the open window across the tops of trees at a few lovely stars. The joy I felt in the darkness in the arms of my own man in my own house cannot be measured or expressed. Life could not be better.

Before dawn, the slave quarters stirred for another day of work. Each cabin woke slowly, in its own way. I listened to familiar sounds from a new vantage. First the coughs of rousing sleepers, then the same questions and greetings and complaints. Time to get up. Shut your mouth. Let me sleep. Smoke curled out of doors and chimneys and mothers spoke softly, then firmly to drowsy children. Fry bread from the day before or boiled oats usually served as a slave's breakfast, but I did not have any wood in the new cabin with which to build a fire, let alone any mush to serve my man. We would grab what we could from the pot in the men's cabin.

"Boy!" Peter called to Saul. "Pull up your britches and get Brownie saddled! Mas' got business!" Saul struggled to his feet thumbing braces over shoulders. He hurried out the door, which then banged shut on leather hinges.

I got up and watched him through my window as he disappeared into the darkness. I leaned out and took a lung full of that glorious morning. The opening was little more than a square hole hewn out of the wall and I could just fit my head and shoulders through if I bent over.

"Good day," I said to Sarah as she returned from a visit to the trees. Sarah seemed stunned when she saw me. Shocked is probably the correct term. She said nothing and I noticed, but without appreciating the reason.

Then Mariah came looking for me. "I see you got you a nice new house," she remarked, "with a nice window to watch the world go by. My, my. Fancy Lady. That's what we call you now. Fancy Lady." I was accustomed to Mariah's sharp tongue and did not sense any change in her demeanor. "Come on, Fancy Lady, you got work to do." I hurried after her in the gloom, past smoky little cabins and hungry livestock pressed against rail fences. I had to build the Morgans' breakfast fire and empty their night jars.

That evening presented a problem. I had been in Mariah and Ike's cabin and customarily ate with them or with Saul and the men. We ate many of our meals from one pot over a common fire, but often families with children cooked their own corn and beans out of the slave ration. The five single men ate and cooked together, and since Saul's arrival, that is where I had my supper. But now that Saul and I were a family, I wanted to gather the rudiments of keeping a home, the central piece being a pot or pan of some kind. Daisy was the best cook we had and she had collected, through some crafty trading, two small iron cauldrons and one iron pan with a long wooden handle. I never saw all of them in use at once, and I assumed that she could spare one. I found her turning a small stone mill reducing corn to meal.

"Daisy, can I have one of them pots?"

"What for?"

"To cook," I replied. "Me and Saul want to cook." I think that was the first time I spoke aloud a reference to my new husband and my new home, and it still felt strange, like some kind of an act or even a lie.

"You don't need no pot," she snapped. "Eat with the men." Daisy returned to her grinding. I was puzzled. Mine was a reasonable request. Just a few days before, Daisy laughed at my attention to Saul. She was always cordial to me, if not friendly, but was

never that gruff. All of us respected one another's meager possessions, clothing, tools, crude bits of furniture, but we also enjoyed
a strong sense of sharing within our tiny community. To give what
you did not need was normal if not expected. To be sure, a pot was
a valuable item, but Daisy had several and I was without. It made
no sense for her not to share with me.

Saul and I ate with the men while Daisy fed her husband and
children from a single vessel. I told Saul of my desire to cook for
him, even if it was just to warm some mush. We could collect other
items as time went on, a few blankets, some stools, and crocks to
store food. Something to cook with seemed to me like a necessity
though. Saul told me not to worry. We soon forgot the pot.

Morgan sent Esther on some errand, which was not unusual.
Peter may have been the driver and in charge of the slaves, but
Esther was in charge of Peter. He had good enough sense how to
get work out of us and to keep Morgan and O'Hara happy, but
it was Esther's hand in matters requiring imagination that made
Peter valuable to Morgan. Esther saw that the best use of simple
Jack was at a single task, and she got Peter to pair up him with the
oxen. She saw that Ruth was never going to fit in with the rest of
the slaves, and she gave Peter the idea to mention that Morgan
could trade her to Willoughby for a field hand. Willoughby had a
number of mixed bloods, and he undoubtedly would have an eye
for Ruth's fair skin.

So that evening Esther was not around when Peter got to thinking, as best he could. I cannot testify to this, but I believe that
someone got to Peter and made him believe that unless he had a
window, he could not be a proper driver. Peter walked up to where
Saul and me sat on our log. I had my hand under Saul's solid arm
and I held him close, my base instincts yielding to the higher joy of
simple companionship and proximity. The men lounged around
with their pipes and talked about nothing. Esther never would
have allowed what happened next.

"Boy!" Peter announced as he approached. "Esther and me
goin' to take the new cabin. You take my place."

Esther always prevented Peter from using his office for personal profit. He and Esther handled all the slave rations and their

two children always ate well, but never at the expense of the rest of us. As the driver he rated better quarters. Saul was the inferior to Peter in age and position and size, so by any measure, the matter was decided. There are volumes written about worse abuses than the higher ranking man taking the best cabin, and from the safe distance of a half century, it is difficult not to grant to Peter this prerogative. Saul's intelligence and character helped him get along in this new society. Unfortunately, Saul's experiences left him unprepared for a situation where he was being robbed of something he could rightfully claim as his. He was also unschooled in how to deal with a child wife who was too stupid to keep her mouth shut.

What happened next changed the course of history, certainly the course of my history. I was fifteen years old and oblivious to greed and power. My swim in the sea of passion and ecstasy stripped me of any reason, and I responded to Peter, as they say, with my heart instead of my head.

"That my cabin!" I protested. "Saul build it for *me*." Saul's hand clutched my arm, but I ignored his signal.

Peter tossed my remark off with, "Well girl, it my cabin now. I the driver, and I get the new cabin. I get the window."

"Saul build that cabin for *me*. You build your own cabin." And then I fired the shot heard round the world. "Saul fight you for it."

Nobody talked back to Peter. The other hands took Peter's orders out of long habit and with the knowledge that to do otherwise risked his wrath. Peter enforced his will readily with his size and strength, though Esther tempered Peter's rashness.

The next few seconds recede into a fog not improved with the intervening decades. Peter stepped over to me and swung his massive hand down. He could have struck me with his fist, but he chose to slap me full on the side of my face, suggesting some reason on his part and not anger. He knew how to keep order for Morgan, and I am certain now that the action felt as natural to him as slapping a horse.

The pain from being kicked by a mule or slapped by a giant does not begin immediately. The body takes an instant to understand the assault. In that instant the world just rolled away from me, and I heard myself hit the ground. Then I tasted blood in my nose. Through the ringing in my head I began to ache. These sensations prevented me from seeing what followed. Sarah related the whole incident with great relish, not because of my mortification or the other consequences, but because it was an event she saw herself. Sarah's tales usually involved others' observations improved with her own interpretation.

"That Phyllis," she recounted, "she come off that log like she was dropped or throwed, which she almost was. It weren't that far, just here to here. Smack. Weeeoooo. Thump. Well, that boy Saul, right when that girl hit the ground, he got him a fist, and he plant it square, flat dab on Peter's chin. Right there. Right on the tip. Bam. Peter, he just finish knockin' that girl, and he not ready for that boy. 'Sides, who ever hit the driver? But that boy, he hit Peter right on the end the chin. Right there. Bam.

"So Peter, his head, it snap back and he fall down. Down he go, and he fall into the fire. Well, if you ever see somebody fall into a fire you know what it like. It like a 'splosion, crash, and the fire go everywhere. People go everywhere, 'cause of the fire. It like to burn me alive. Peter lie there in the fire for maybe a twitch, maybe not that long, and he up and he screamin'. He hurt and he on fire and he mad. Oh, he mad! And he on fire. Well Ike, he start beatin' the fire out on Peter's back and Peter, he sock Ike. Somehow they get the fire on Peter's back with some water in a bucket, but the bucket hit Peter in the head and he really mad now and he down on that boy like some hawk on a mouse. Nobody hit the driver, nobody."

When I rejoined the realm of the conscious, Saul and Peter were rolling on the ground thrashing at one another like two small boys. O'Hara heard the commotion and came running with his whip. He started beating the two men mercilessly.

"Ya stupid naggars!" he shouted. "I'll whip ya to next month. Stop it! Stop it!"

Finally, they rolled away, arms over their heads. I don't know what hurt Peter more, Saul's fists, the ignominy of being struck, his burns, or O'Hara's blows, but the driver had sufficient grounds for moaning like the injured bull he was.

As for Saul, he just lay there, his hands to his head. I crawled over to him to hold him and to bawl and to bleed, devastated by the violence done to us and to the peace that I had always taken for granted.

The next day, Morgan had Saul properly whipped. The men held him on the ground while O'Hara laid twenty on his bare back with a horse whip. Saul did not cry out until eight. By the end, he begged for O'Hara to stop and for the master's forgiveness. Daisy and Mariah pinioned me to keep from earning stripes of my own. I bit off my screams into the rag they had stuffed in my mouth.

Peter and his sons took the new cabin, and Walter and Daisy got Peter's. After some shifting around Saul and I ended up in one of the first cabins we built back in 1800. It was adequate shelter, warm in winter, and cool in summer, but I could just stand and Saul had to stoop under the low roof. The chimney drew well enough. The previous occupants had added small amenities, such as little shelves and pegs. Saul's back healed, but he bore marks for the rest of his life. This annoyed Morgan, since any potential buyer would think Saul surly and hard to handle. Peter's back recovered, but he could not work for a week, further raising the master's ire.

A grim silence descended upon the slave quarters. People ate in their cabins and the men spoke little amongst themselves. Laughter vanished. The women went about chores sullenly and communicated only when necessary. Even Mariah's curt orders to me fell to nearly nothing until she waved me away from the house to leave her alone.

If Peter could take a cabin, he could take anything. If he could hit a fifteen-year-old mouthy girl who might protest the loss of her home, he could hit anyone for anything. All of us understood again that at the bottom, bondage represented the complete absence of justice, void of hope. It is one thing to work hard and be subject to another man's orders and greed, because most people, white and colored, are under someone's thumb in some way. But to finally see that you had no rights – except the right to suffer – confirms the impossibility for anything better. It is bad enough to be trapped and to have no future. It is worse to know it.

Esther returned from Morgan's errand to a community sound-less in pain and despair. All her even-handed management of food and work and relations shattered under a brute's slap against a young girl with more tongue than brain. She scolded Peter, she scolded me, she scolded everyone. She got Walter to offer to cut a window for O'Hara and for any slave who wanted one. One of Daisy's pots appeared at my door.

But the bell could not be unrung.

Esther

Saul worked the animals, mostly Morgan's horses. This kept him away from Peter, who superintended the field hands and heavy labor. Saul quickly demonstrated his ability with colts and word got around the county. Owners brought their green animals to Morgan and with Saul's soft touch and patient voice, they were transformed into useful and even valuable saddle horses. I continued to spread my time between the house and tasks in the cabins, such as pulling flax, carding, and spinning. I did my turn in the fields too.

Saul and I kept to ourselves. Our intercourse with the others held only to those transactions necessary for work and for living. I did not respond to comments about the weather or the crops and I lowered my eyes in any conversation. Saul dismissed idle questions about the stock no matter how well intended. He spoke to horses more than he spoke to anyone else, even me. We stopped gathering with the other slaves in the evening. If we had any waking moments of our own, which was not often, we repaired to our cabin or slipped into the forest, anything to avoid the others and anything to be together. This self-ostracism became our escape, not just escape from the unpleasantness of the conflict with the others, but escape from our bondage. For a few moments in the new darkness and into the night, we were not property, but human beings with thoughts and dreams. Until Saul came into my life, I might have been satisfied, or at least accommodated, to my condition of solitude. He taught me what I could have and could not have.

Our favorite spot in warm weather was down the creek where some boulders and trees screened us from the quarters. It was close enough to answer a summons from Peter and still gave us the seclusion we sought. We even ventured time there when clouds or wind insisted otherwise. Certainly the best times were that first autumn before the warm days succumbed to the cool nights and then the first rains..

"You never want to go down the river," Saul mentioned one evening as he stared at the languid current. The sun had long left our narrow slice of sky, and the dusk crept slowly into the valley. Wood smoke from the dinners of slaves and of slave owners hung overhead like a soft curtain that had lost its window. Bits of voices, some sharp, some gay, echoed indistinctly in between the slow steady blows of an axe.

"Down this here Beaver Creek there the river. The Louisa. Then down there, way down, more river. Ohio. Further down is Mis'sippi. Hard in Mis'sippi, they say. Work 'til you die. But I'm thinkin' that there somethin' else down there."

"How you know?" I asked. I had gotten used to pressing him for more information. He often taunted me on my statements and my ideas, and I grew to enjoy returning the challenge. (I learned later that the Greeks originated this method of teaching. I say the Greeks stole it from Africans.)

"This old Shawnee trade with us. He show up with meat he trap. We give him tobacco, flour."

I grasped for what little I knew of history. "I thought the Shawnee run out. Gone west. Gone south."

"Not all. Some stay. This one, he call himself 'Pata-lani' or somethin'. Never could say it. Means rabbit. We call him Rabbit. He move like a rabbit. We be workin' or sittin' and look up and there he be, watchin' us. Then 'ffftt,' he gone."

"What he look like?"

"Oh, he light, like you, but he don't look African. Or white. Sorta...Injun."

"What he wear?"

"Just clothes, like us. He wear a rag on his head. No hat. He live off by himself, trappin', tradin'."

"How he talk?"

"He don't talk much. We use signs. He know some words. Tobacco. Meat. White. Joe do the talkin'. Joe always do the talkin'."

"What your mas' say?"

"Oh, he don't mind. But the boys tell me to never say nothin' to him or to any white folks about Rabbit. They hunt him down. Somebody like Draper take his scalp. But I think Rabbit take Draper's scalp first. Still, don't say nothin'."

"Why he stay? Why he don't go with his people?"

"The boys think he kill somebody. Shawnee. He can't be with Shawnee and he can't be with white. Or colored. Colored was about all he could talk to. He lost between ever'body, I guess."

An image of the outcast emerged, crouching behind a tree, listening, watching, gauging his next move. I immediately felt a kinship with this mysterious figure, as if a third person had stepped out of the forest and joined us by the water. If Saul and I could be pushed out of our community, so could someone else. What had happened to us had apparently happened to this Indian. What caused his expulsion from his people? Murder like Philip said? An argument over a house? A woman? Power? Maybe he was falsely accused?

I grappled with the idea of the outcast and how an individual was part of the collective only as long as it suited both. Little did I know then that this question had confronted those far more studied than I will ever be, for centuries. But that lazy evening by the creek, my primary conclusion was that the casting out could happen to anyone, even to white people. I considered the short list of whites in my world, and the only ones I could equate with such estrangement were Draper and O'Hara. I certainly experienced none of the affinity to those miscreants such as that I felt with the Indian I had never seen, but I knew of being separate.

"I kind of lost too now," Saul allowed. "Don't belong at Harmon's. Don't seem to belong here."

"You never be lost with me," I told him. "We never be lost if we together." I pulled Saul closer to me and he touched my face with his coarse hand that smelled of old leather and horse sweat.

A single leaf floats past, resting lightly on the surface of the stream. The leaf curls inward as if to protect some delicate treasure. Bouncing softly against a stone, it stops for an instant, turns slightly, and drifts free. Another stone, a pause, a lift, a shift, and the journey continues until the leaf is out of sight. Across the creek, a log angles down into the water. Other leaves have collected against it, pressed in on one another by the current. At first the leaves hold their form. Then they slowly lose their individuality until they constitute a single, soggy, mass. The log holds fast, snagging more leaves, although a few manage to glide past. I know that the water will eventually win out. The log's strength will rot and ultimately yield to the soft but relentless current until the corrupted remains too wash away. By that time, however, the trapped leaves will have settled to the bottom as so much mud. In the mean time, the single leaf detaches from the mass and spins back out to the current, making its way out of sight, to what fate, I knew not. I cannot tell you the number of times the memory of those leaves returned to me. As I contemplate crossing over to the Other Side I see where that stream is life. And death.

Summer slipped into autumn and its profusion of color that ringed fields shorn of their corn stalks. Piles of ears awaited shucking, and animals stole everything they could from Morgan. Squirrels and crows gorged themselves in broad daylight. I was carrying ashes from the house when Esther called me down to the stable.

"You goin' to town today," she announced. "Help me with these." I loaded some baskets of corn and apples into the two-wheeled cart already hitched to a horse. We had planted apples for Morgan from cuttings we carried from Virginia and the fruit proved popular in the county. Esther sat on a basket, took the reins, and started down the track. I followed on foot. Soon, Master Morgan and William rode up and took position ahead of Esther. They wore almost identical black hats, wide brims with flat crowns, and baggy, once-white shirts. Their coats draped from the ties on the cantles out of deference to the still warm weather..

William balanced a long rifle across his pommel. He seldom went abroad unarmed. The Shawnee had left the Big Sandy country more than ten years before, but William always found something to shoot at. At any distance, it was easy to distinguish the taller son from his father. William's skill and ambition as a hunter served us well those first years. All he had to do was hunt, which suited him perfectly. Hardly a day went by that he and one of the men did not return with a deer or bear or the quarters of a bison. What we did not feast upon within a day was smoked and jerked or traded. Mr. deRossett in Prestonsburg bought the skins for soldiers' hats.

Even with room in the cart, I did not climb aboard out of my habit of isolation. I had to step out to keep up with the horses, but the trip to town was a welcome respite from the physical and societal desert of Morgan's valley. Today, I marvel at the distances I once covered on foot. I followed the small procession for about a mile before I noticed Morgan and William confer. William turned to Esther and jerked his thumb. The riders touched spurs to flanks and broke into a canter, disappearing into a fine dust.

Esther turned back to me. "Get up here girl, Mas' want to make some time."

I rushed ahead and hopped on, allowing my bare feet to dangle off the back.

"No, up here," she ordered. "You throwin' off the horse." A cart must be loaded more carefully than a wagon. If the load sits too far back, the traces pull up on the animal, robbing him of his ability to do what he does best, pull. Put the weight too far forward, and he carries more than he needs to.

I climbed over the load while the cart rocked and jolted. I found a position at the balance next to Esther and quickly settled into the motion of the ride. We bounced along the track, which followed the meander of the stream in a compromise between grade and distance. Indians originally cut the narrow path tunnel through the forest. The roof of branches blazed with crimson maples, golden birches, and flaxen poplars. Woodland smells replaced the manure and rot of the farm. Pollens and seeds drifted through the shafts of sunlight that pierced the forest. Tree limbs crowded over us in a dense canopy broken only by an occasional ford or a tiny farm. Absent were the taunts of the countless crows that clustered around the farm, replaced by softer, slower calls of mountain birds. The blue of the jays and the red of the cardinals treated my eye.

Small farms broke the mountains' monopoly on the country. Pioneers no better dressed and little better housed than I coaxed corn, tobacco, oats, rye, and hemp out of the soil. But the fields seemed better tended than Morgan's, with fewer weeds and burrs. When I traveled north for the first time, I marveled at the neatness of farms, built and tended entirely with free labor.

Esther had not been involved in the matter of the cabin or the pots or whatever it was. The relations between us were untainted by those events, and I felt less of a separation from her. Nonetheless, I hesitated to start a conversation as we bumped along in silence. Finally, Esther spoke.

"Mas' got business in town. Might have somethin' for you to do. If you stay close and watch."

The master's affairs held more mystery for me even than the stories of the stars and the myths of Africans. I knew that Morgan conversed with other white men until they shook hands and exchanged papers and objects and shared tobacco and whiskey. Our Master always seemed to stand in the middle of any group and other white men came to see him, another lead dog.

I had been to town a few times on market day, but my notice then focused on the noise and the sights and the activity. To be involved in the master's business worried me. I knew not to be drawn into something I did not understand. No slave who expects to survive goes happily into a new situation or takes many risks. Safety is always with the familiar, even if it is bondage for life. Despite all Morgan night soil and dirty laundry I had carried, anything to do with white people remained foreign to me.

Then the spirit of adventure began to take over. Not only was I about to see and do something new, I was to receive knowledge not shared by the other slaves. I don't know whether to blame that weakness on Saul's tutoring or whether I bore the propensity in my blood, but the unknown began to lure me as the smell of whiskey beckons the drunk.

"When we get to town," Esther continued, "you stay with me. You keep your mouth shut this time. But I think you know that now. You just stay close. You watch and you listen."

"What's this business?" I wanted to know.

"First," Esther answered, "you remember you don't say nothin' 'bout what you see or do in town. Nothin'. You say anythin' to anybody, even that man of yours, I see you dance with O'Hara's snake. You don't say nothin'."

I pictured being held on the ground, naked to all as O'Hara laid into my back.

"You hear me girl?"

"I hear."

"Good. Now listen close. Mas' got a election coming. He not so sure 'bout his friends. That Edward Osborn, he talkin' up against Mas'."

"The man that buy the land from Saul's old master?"

"That him."

"And Mas' hate him?"

"Mas' don't hate nobody. Don't love nobody neither, I think. But Osborn, he hate Mas. Mas' don't like Osborn, but he don't hate him. I hear him tell Mas' William not to hate. Make you crazy. But I don't think William he listen."

"Mas' William hate Osborn?"

"No, but he get a temper. And he let himself be over ladies. And when he drinks."

We rode on through the fine dust and diagonal sunlight and questions began to form in my head.

"This election," I asked, "all the white men come to town and drink whiskey?"

"They s'posed to do more than that, but that all some do. They all come and choose who they want sheriff and judge and such. They vote. If they say Morgan, then Mas' be elected. Osborn want to be sheriff."

"If he get enough white men to vote for him, Osborn be sheriff. He make the laws. He have one over on Mas'."

She pulled up away from the stream so as not to allow the horse to drink and dropped off the cart. I watched her approach the dam of sticks and mud where cool water spilled through gaps in a pleasing sound. Esther stepped up the bank and regarded the beaver's lodge from several angles. She returned to the cart and we started off again.

"I been watchin' that pond. Beaver's pulling more logs into his house. Cold winter comin'. I wonder how long that beaver hold out. Somebody make him into a hat."

But I was more interested in the idea of business. "Osborn make the laws," I asked, "he make a law against Mas'?"

"No, sheriff don't make the laws. They make the laws up to Frankfort. Sheriff have the law though. He use the law like a long knife. You catch on, girl. He use the law again' Mas'. Might not be so good for us. Mas' rich because he the boss. He the boss, he take care us. He not the boss, no tellin' what happen."

I rocked with the motion of the cart and reflected upon this new situation. Here came more information than I had ever expected to possess about the man who owned me and about the society that owned everyone. I grasped that I was participating in some great secret. This burden filled my chest the same way desire for Saul burned in me. White people were dangerous and to be avoided. Betrayal of their secrets carried a great price. Indeed just the mistaken belief of breathing a secret risked stripes or disappearance. I can trace my skill with secrets during the years of our struggle for freedom to the lessons I received from Esther.

We got to town after two hours. Ten years after its founding, Prestonsburg remained a dirty scatter of inept structures at a bend in the river. A simple grid of rutted streets ordered the houses and low clumsy buildings, which looked as if they sprouted from dissimilar seeds scattered in the wind from the brick court house in the middle. Buildings varied from a two-story tavern and a few clapboard homes to log cabins. Fences, vegetable plots, small barns, and open ground filled in the scene.

Esther reined up the cart in front of a pile of sticks outside town. "Moses!" she called. "Moses, you in there?"

A patch of grey fur emerged from the confusion of wood. The hut made my windowless cabin look like a real house. The fur grew out of the oldest Negro I had ever seen. The tangle of ancient hair completely surrounded the wrinkled skin of his face. His grin revealed no more than four yellow teeth, and he wore rags in such disrepair that I could not tell the nature of the original garment.

"Ah," the man croaked, "my fine lady. Come for more of old Moses? Old Moses still got his fire. Come over h'yar. Oh, and somebody new? You been tellin' on me Esther? You been sayin' what a man I is?" He struggled to his complete height and still stood shorter than I.

"Everybody know what a man you is, Moses," Esther assured him. "I can't help but talk about you."

"For that, no Moses for you lady. Nope, can't be storyin' like that. Man have his pride."

"Well, maybe if I give you somethin' you take me back?"

"Maybe. What you got?"

"I got some 'sang." Esther retrieved from the cart a small parcel wrapped in cloth that I had not noticed before. "How that?"

Moses hobbled over to us. "Well, give it over h'yar and I think on it." He took the bag, opened it, and sniffed at the ginseng root that grew wild and began to fetch a good price. "I think on it."

"What's the news in town, Moses? That old boy make you marry his daughter yet? Or is it his wife?"

"Don't know nothin' 'bout that. Ev'body talk about your master."

"What they say?"

"Osborn snatch that Harmon place from under your master's nose. Just slip in there and grab it. Osborn brag about it. White men think it funny. Morgan get one boy, but Osborn get the land."

"Who he brag to?"

"Brag to ev'body. He say your master not boss no more. Things goin' to change here bouts. You got anythin' to eat for old Moses?"

"Got fritters. Made just this mornin'." Esther produced another small parcel of cloth and opened it, handing down the brown corn cakes. Moses returned a craggy grin.

"That be nice. That be real nice." He sniffed the food and then bit off a piece chewing slowly. "Mmmmm."

"Who think it funny?"

"White men."

"Which white men?"

"Oh, that Auxier fella. Paul Paxton think it funny. Slap Osborn on the back. Some man I don' know from Catlettsburg. Not from here."

"How 'bout Lackey? He think it funny?" I knew Lackey to be married to Morgan's daughter, William's sister. A rift with the son-in-law could be critical.

"Mmmm. Don' recall he 'round."

"Graham?"

"No, not the judge. You got any liquor for Moses?"

"No liquor, Moses. You wait for election day."

"Plenty liquor then, plenty." Moses closed his eyes as he savored the fritter.

"What man from Catlettsburg?" Esther pressed.

"Up on a boat. Askin' about niggers for sale. No one sellin'. Your master got the most niggers." Esther prodded him for details of when he heard Osborn brag and where, but he could not elaborate. He asked Esther for a blanket and for more food. She promised him some on her next trip. She clucked at the horse and the cart lurched forward.

"Moses here long as anybody remember," she told me. "He come when they fight Injuns, fifteen, twenty years ago."

"Who own him?"

"Nobody own him anymore. His master die. But he so old by then, Moses, nobody take him. Nobody own him. He live off what white folks and coloreds give him and what he can find. He sell that 'sang for cash money. White folks figure he know where to dig." We passed the first of the houses of Prestonsburg. "Now, you stay close to me. We go to the landin'. Like I say, you watch and you listen."

Prestonsburg

The river landing at Prestonsburg was a churned width of mud on a gradual bank between town and water. A small keel boat with its house in the middle nosed at an angle onto the soggy shore. Several canoes carved out of tree trunks rested on their sides as if discarded by some giant. The only activity came from three white men and two white boys carrying sacks from a pile on top of the bank down a precarious path onto a raft of logs lashed together with a deck of crude lumber that cleared the water by less than a foot. The cargo grew in a more or less orderly fashion in the middle. Esther estimated that these were small farmers and had probably built the raft themselves. They would float down to Cincinnati or perhaps St. Louis and sell everything, even the raft for its lumber, for cash. Two Negroes lounged nearby under some trees.

"Why don't those men work?" I asked.

"Them boat men don't own no slaves. The boat men can't use coloreds 'less they pay the owners. They do the work themselves. Keep their money. If they have money. These folks, they squat on land, get out a crop, and move on to someplace else. Maybe they buy the land." I was beginning to understand the ownership of property, a concept I later came to understand it only too well.

Each man hefted a bag before stepping and balancing carefully down the slope onto the springy plank. The two boys managed careful cooperation to move each bag aboard. No one stood by with a switch or a rope end to keep them moving. The men and the boys took on their work with the same resignation as any slave, but as each of them hurried back to the shore for another load, they regarded their surroundings directly without the downcast stare or the side glance that I practiced myself. The men noted the two slave women and the cart with the tired horse but did not interrupt their task. I had never seen white men work that hard before, my first vision of free labor.

"Stay with me and listen," Esther muttered. She walked toward one man, bearded and dressed in rough clothing stained across the front with dirt, tobacco juice, and the other colors of a hard life, not too different than any slave. He wore a pair of homemade leather shoes and an ancient top hat from which his wild blond hair sought escape.

Esther stopped within ten feet of the stack of bags he and his mates were moving and called, "Oh, mister." As soon as he turned to her, she focused at about the level of his knees. "You be buyin' for down river?"

"We got plenty, girl."

"Got some good corn here, apples too," she told him. "Nice apples. Morgan apples. More'n we need."

"Got no cash, girl."

"Can't eat no cash, Mister." Her voice was higher pitched and much less authoritative than usual. "Maybe we trade?"

The mention of the master's name made the man stop. "You Morgan's girl?"

"Yessah. He say I can trade. Maybe you got oats?"

"Where's your pass?"

"Don't got no pass, mister. Mas' Morgan say I his girl an' I don' need no pass."

"Colored got to have a pass, you off your place."

"Yessah. But Mas' Morgan, he commissioner. He say I don' need no pass."

"I call the sheriff, he put you in jail. You get a whippin'."

"Yessah, you right." Esther dropped her head and crossed her hands in front of her in submission. "But the sheriff, he already see me. He used to seein' me in town. I go get him, if you like, sah."

Although looking down myself, I caught the look of disgust on his face. "We got some oats. Potatoes too."

"Mas', he like taters. This his house girl. She fry 'em up for him."

Careful to look at the ground, I felt the man examine me. Then he walked past us to the cart. He pulled at a basket of apples and pushed his face inside. The horse shifted weight, causing the cart to move. The man shoved a hand down and pulled out some fruit from the middle. He took one, turned it over, and bit into it. After a few chews, he tugged at another basket, then another, each time digging deep to insure that the middle was as good as the top, all the time holding onto the first apple. The slaves in the shade continued to look in another direction, but I could tell they followed the proceedings very closely.

"You got, what, ten here?" he asked.

"Twelve I think, mister," Esther said, "I coulda swore it was twelve."

"Twelve then. Give you six bags potatoes."

"Mas' he have my hide I come back with six taters, Mister. Make a saddle outa me. Ride me all over the county. He 'spect me to come home with leas' twelve. More. Maybe I look at them taters?" She started toward the load on the ground.

"Keep your nigger hands off my property," the man growled and Esther froze. He went to his bags and opened one, holding it for her. His partners stopped their work to watch from the base of the plank.

Esther cautiously walked over and peered inside. "That what they like down deep?" The man glared at her and moved around the top layer exposing no more than a few of the dirty brown balls. "How 'bout that one?" she asked, pointing to a bag in the middle. The man looked at the sack and then back at Esther his lips grim. He grunted and moved bags half-heartedly to gain access to the one she indicated. He opened it then shook it a bit in a pretense of display.

"Them mighty fine taters, Mister. But my Mas', he whip us both near to death we come back with less'n twelve. And they smaller bags. He prob'ly whip us anyway. You be down in Cincinnati havin' a fine old time, and we be beggin' him to stop. You got plenty taters. Havin' your oats and them apples help you get a good price for it all." She hung her head. "I got a bear skin you can sell for two dollars. Cured it myself. I throw it in." She stepped back to the cart and pulled out a dark brown hide. The boat man joined her just a little too quickly. He reached across and grabbed a handful of fur, rubbing it between thumb and forefinger.

"Twelve with the hide," he snapped. "You're wasting my time."

"That fair, Mister."

"Put the apples on the boat. Load the potatoes." He grabbed the bearskin eagerly.

"Thank you mister, you save me a heap of sorrow here. A heap." Esther turned to me. "Get them apples on the boat," she snapped. "Watch you don't drop one in the river. You drop one, you jus' as well go in after and drown yourself, 'cause what I do to you be a whole lot worse." Esther pulled twelve bags of potatoes over to the cart. I backed under every one of those baskets of apples and staggered up the bouncing plank to the tittering of the loungers. In those days I had no trouble swinging fifty or seventy-five pounds. It took some practice before I could time my step with the spring of the wood. As soon as I swung a basket down onto the damp logs, one of the white men tucked it into the rest of the stack. With that task complete, I heaved twelve bags of potatoes up into the cart where Esther worked them into position, finding the same balance she had before.

Without looking at the white men, Esther climbed aboard and turned the horse away from the landing. I had to scramble up to avoid being left behind.

"What we do now?" I asked.

"Wait."

I reviewed what I had just witnessed. I had to know more. "How you know he don't have no rocks in with these taters?"

"He don't put in rocks until he get closer to where he goin'. He don't want to haul no dead weight to the river."

"So why he work so hard to hide what he got?"

"Oh, he ain't about to let some colored woman get her way. And he sure don't want those other white men to see. He need

to show who up and who down. And those lazy darkies watchin'
didn't help. No matter."

"I could see him ponder it."

"Good, girl, good. You saw it. He had to think what he gonna
lose if he let me look at them taters myself. He don't lose nothin,'
but he not that smart. I bet he don't know that he get better price
for a load of diff'rent things than for just the taters. You try to sell
too much of one thing, you don't get so good a price."

"He sure like that bear skin."

"You see that too. Good. He probably look for a bear all summer and didn't catch a one. He might get two dollars for that hide,
but some white man smarter than he is make sure he don't. And
you keep your mouth shut. Good."

As we entered the town, so grand to me at the time, but in reality quite shabby, Esther stopped.

"We best be walkin' now."

I listened to her whispered descriptions of the various buildings, the tavern, where True, William's horse waited, the brick
courthouse, where I saw Brownie tied, the blacksmith, the store,
the fur trader, and the homes of white people. Most houses had
gardens and some had slave hovels behind. Even more than at
Morgan's, dried mud coated the lower two feet of every wall. Unlike
market day when the settlement teemed with people, almost nothing moved midweek. Two white men idled on a bench in front
of the tavern, coats off, hats back on their heads. I remembered
to look down as they paused their conversation to watch us. I got
the impression that the only reason that they looked at us at all
was because there was nothing else moving in the town. The only
other Negroes I saw labored quietly at wood piles or in plots of
vegetables.

Esther turned the horse into the shade of an unpainted clapboard wall, causing a dog there to open his eyes. A yellow version
of the ubiquitous mixed breed of the frontier, he examined us
casually without lifting his head. Apparently determining that we
held neither threat nor advantage, he returned to his rest.

"What now?" I asked.

"We wait."

After a few moments, a woman in a faded yellow store-bought dress rounded the corner. Her clothing spoke of her prosperity, or rather the prosperity of her master. Even her blue head wrap, knotted at the side, was of better cloth. A basket hung from each arm.

"I heard you was in," she announced. "You skin those boat men with that fodder?"

"Fodder! I show you fodder, Becky. Just hold those baskets under the back end of this horse and you get better than you grow in that weed patch of yours."

"Least I grow weeds. Twice as good what you rob from the crows up Beaver Creek. Three times."

"We got good crows up Beaver Creek. Best crows in the county. Maybe all of Kentucky."

"Heeee," the woman laughed. "Not sure that be something I brag about. Maybe that all you can brag about. How old that bear skin you give them boat men?"

"Almost as old as you."

"That boat man don't mind?"

"No, he don't mind. He don't mind what he don't know. You out for a walk in the town or you hope to do some tradin'?"

"I might do some tradin'."

"I see your basket empty," Esther prodded. "I ain't interested in what you trade with the men."

"What I hear, you don't trade. You just give it away. I got somethin' else."

"What would that be?"

Becky pushed a hand into a pocket on the dress and produced three silver coins in her wrinkled palm.

"I got some shillin's."

"Where you get shillin's?"

"Mister Clayton bring 'em back from Catlettsburg. Give 'em to Missus. Missus give 'em to me for vittles. Maybe potatoes."

"Why don't you buy potatoes from them boat men?"

"Don't want no part of them boat men. Just squatters down from some holler. Never see 'em again."

"One of them shillin's ought to buy a bag of these taters."

"You may be your master's town nigger," Becky replied, "but you still just a nigger. Steal all you can."

I was getting concerned about the tone of the conversation when Esther and Becky began a serious negotiation. They settled on two bags of potatoes of her choice for one shilling. Esther allowed Becky to pull bags off the cart and to select the ones she wanted. But Esther would not let Becky move potatoes around. The bag was the bag.

"So," Esther said, "Mr. Clayton, he tradin' cows down Catlettsburg?"

"And a horse he don't need. He get her for Missus, but Missus don't ride. He don't want to be feedin' nothing he don't need."

"He got more than three shillin's for all that."

"Oh he get lots more, lots more. I hear him tell Missus he get two hunnit dollars. These just some of it."

"A hunnit dollars! What he do with all that money?"

"He want to buy land, but he find another way to make money easy. He give it to Mr. Osborn."

"Edward Osborn?" Esther asked as if she did not know. "That pretty white man with the tall horse?"

"That him. Mr. Clayton give him money and have to give it back later with percentums."

"Osborn buy that land from old Mrs. Harmon?" Esther knew very well what Osborn did.

"Mr. Osborn give that money to her. That right. Give her Mr. Clayton's money." As simple my understanding of lending was in those days – we had no banks – I saw the implication of Clayton lending money to Osborn. Clayton was not a friend of Morgan. Did Morgan know this? He would know it soon.

Esther and Becky exchanged more talk about her owners and their neighbors. Parker's girl, Hannah, was expecting again. Her master's youngest son was most likely responsible as part of some ugly family custom. White men complained about new squatters from over the mountains as well as wolves and thieves and lazy slaves. Becky competed easily with Sarah in her ability to carry tales about someone else. Never wanting to be compared to Becky and

Sarah, I took to my heart Esther's admonition to keep my mouth shut.

Finally, the talkative slave in her mistress's dress turned to leave.

Esther called after her, "And you be sure to tell your missus just how much those taters cost you. My master be askin' your master." Becky didn't respond. "You have to watch that one," Esther told me. "She give you one and she tell her missus she give you three. Keep the other two for herself."

As I reordered the bags of potatoes that Becky had pillaged, I noticed the slumbering yellow dog had watched the entire transaction, but without moving more than his eyelids. I imagined he understood everything. But my thoughts about this spectator dropped aside for other questions.

"Where Catlettsburg?" I asked Esther.

"Down river. Where it meet the Ohio."

"No river when we come from Virginia."

"We come over the mountains. West. Then back up Beaver Creek. Most white folks go west now on the river.

"What out west?" I wanted to know.

"Kentucky. Tenn'ssee. Cross the river up north, Ohio."

"The river and the land both Ohio?"

Esther nodded at my making that connection. "The river and the land both Ohio. Ohio a state. No slaves in Ohio."

"No slaves? No coloreds?"

"No slaves. But they got coloreds. Free."

"Free?"

"Nobody own you. Nobody sell you. You go where you want. I want to see one more thing."

Bailey

We guided the cart to the tavern, a rough building where white men lingered outside smoking and talking. At the rear, where we stopped, I noticed a Negro seated on the ground in some shade with his elbows on his knees. His bare legs and feet stuck out from canvas trousers that ended just below his knees. I had never seen him before.

"You from the boats?" she asked him.

"Yup."

"Nothin' to drink for you?"

"Nope. Whiskey take money."

"Your master get a drink, but you don't?"

"That about right. You niggers back up here not so dumb as I hear."

"No, we not so dumb. Not so dumb I can't get you a drink."

"Why you do that?"

"Can't stand to see a good man go thirsty. And you got a long way to go on them boats."

"That's a fact. A true fact. But that not why."

"Just want to hear the news." Esther tapped on the back door and conferred with someone out of view. She returned to the cart and retrieved a small pot covered in wax which I knew to contain honey. She also retrieved an empty linen bag closed at the top. The pot disappeared into the tavern and Esther received a plain cup in return. This she tendered to the boatman who looked up puzzled.

"Just want to hear the news. My master always interested in what happenin' on the river."

"Your master?"

"Colonel David Morgan. County commissioner. Richest man in Floyd County."

The boatman licked his lips in thought, then reached up for the cup. He sniffed cautiously before sipping. His eyes closed with the same sense of joy I saw in Saul when we were together.

Esther took a seat next to him in the shade. I stayed with the cart.

"How things on the river?"

"How you mean?"

"Lots of trade?"

The man sipped some more and kept his eyes closed.

"Tradin' good. Anybody with a boat got money."

"Should be a good year for prices."

"That's a fact. I hear Cole say he double, triple what he pay up here."

"Cole?"

"Cap'n."

"Your master?"

"I *free*," the man corrected her. Work for wages. I the pilot."

"That your keel boat at the landin'?"

"Yup."

"Where you live?"

"Cincinnati."

"I Esther. That Phyllis."

"Bailey."

"How far down river you go?"

"Cole run 'tween Cincinnati and Catlettsburg and here."

"Not below Cincinnati?"

"No."

"How 'bout you? Been down to the falls?"

"Been down to the falls, down to Natchez. Once to Nawlins."

"Colonel Morgan want to know about Natchez and Nawlins. Help him with tradin', politics."

"He a colonel. He ought to know."

"You be surprised what white people don't know."

"No, I not surprised."

"He like to know about business. You boatmen get up and down river more'n anybody. Anybody know business it's you boatmen."

"Your colonel can ask his own self."

"He do that. But he smart enough to know that coloreds know a lot too."

"He sound like a smart colonel."

"I hear down below Ohio is Indiana."

Bailey sipped before replying, "That right."

"And then the Ohio come into the Miss'sippi."

"Uh huh."

"Then you come to Injuns."

"Chickasaws."

"Bad Injuns?"

"Naw. They got houses like anybody."

"Slaves?"

"Not many."

Esther looked around and then picked up the bag and loosened the drawstring. She opened the bag completely revealing a design of crooked lines and other marks. This caught Bailey's attention and he studied the writings. He understood.

"Here Prestonsburg," Esther pointed out, "and Cattletsburg, and Cincinnati. And the falls down here."

"Lou'ville," Bailey explained.

"Lou'ville," she acknowledged. "How you get below the falls?"

"Got to be careful," Bailey told her. "But unless low water we get by it. Got to know what you doin'."

"How you get up the river?"

"Not easy." He pointed at the lines on the sack. "You don't have the Tenn'see here. The Cumberland."

"What those?"

"Rivers. Down from the south. Two close together. Cumberland then Tenn'see. So close you walk 'tween 'em before dinner."

Esther pulled some tobacco leaves from her dress and stuffed them in her mouth and began chewing. She offered some leaves to Bailey and he accepted, but put them in a pocket. Instead of spitting, she dipped a sharp stick into her mouth and used the sticky, brown juice as ink to add two more lines.

"Yah," Bailey approved.

"How far?"

"Two, four days."

"Towns there?"

"No, just rivers."

"Where they go?"

"Don't know the Cumberland. Tenn'see go up to, well, Tenn'see. Injuns there."

"More Injuns?"

"Same ones. Chickasaws. Got all the land 'tween Tenn'see and Miss'sippi."

"No white men?"

"Some. They marry Injun women. Build big houses."

"The rest?"

"I dunno, just Injuns."

With Bailey's help Esther used her tobacco juice to record more detail to her map, my first representation of the world around me. By the time Bailey finished his cup of whiskey Esther had a better picture of the land around the bend and beyond the mountains. She left the bag open and laid it on top of the potatoes so as to allow her work to dry in the sun. She bade farewell to the boatman and we boarded the cart.

My mind reeled with all this incomprehensible information and images of towns, more rivers, and white men marrying good Indians. I remembered another reference to Mississippi.

"Mis'sippi where Harmon boys go?"

"Hush! You don't say nothin' about that. You start talkin' about that, you get folks upset. They start to worry. They might try to run away. Coloreds start to run away, it go hard on 'em. Hard on us all."

"Where they run to?"

"North. If they get that far. Now listen close. I tell you this 'cause I know you keep your mouth shut now. Mas' think you might be good to help me when I come to town. But you can't be showin' nobody things like I just show you. People start thinkin' about what over the mountains and 'cross the river and out west, that just make trouble. Keep to your work. Someday you need this. Right now, nobody need it. And you don't say nothin' about Bailey or what he say or do. Not even to that man of yours."

I realized that something very important resided inside Esther's bag. I could not appreciate exactly what, but I knew it had great value. Soon we were on our way back to Beaver Creek, and I noticed we had picked up a companion, the yellow dog from town. For some reason he decided to throw in his lot with the two slaves who bargained for information. By the time we reached Morgan's I gave him a name: Sim.

The Spy

I traveled with Esther once or twice a week, sometimes to town, often to other farms. Ostensibly, we traded. I learned that money consisted of a mixture of American dollars and English pounds and silver shillings. I saw a Spanish coin once. With little cash in the frontier almost all the exchanges involved corn for beans or beans for bread or bread for a chair. A common series of visits involved us taking corn or smoked meat to a farm and trading for some oats or squash. We took those to another place and turned those back into corn again. The more remote farms also offered chickens or ducks or goats. I learned to banter with old Moses and to extract what little information he had. The exercise of my mind in remembering the value of items further strengthened it. And this growing strength made it hungrier for more work, more challenges. Esther taught me to count and to calculate profit and loss. I naturally knew that five chickens was more than three chickens, but she showed me how ten chickens could be more than one goose. Even though our primary mission lay beyond profit, Esther took it as a matter of pride to return to the master richer than when she left. We remained under strict orders not to be too sharp in our dealings, for our other purpose was to loosen tongues and not purses. Someone who had just made a good bargain feels triumphant and less careful about what she says.

Esther could have kept for herself some of the gain. Morgan might never know that one of the hams or some of the cloth went to slave bellies or slave backs. Esther chose instead to be scrupulously honest in her dealings for him. Even in our tiny community, informers could be counted upon to let slip word of some advantage. "Don't never steal from Mas'," she told me. "He catch you stealin', you seen what happen. You be off to Mis'sippi. No need to steal. He do well, you do well. He think he can't trust you, you never know what happen next."

Some would regard Esther as "a good slave." History tells of retainers who selflessly attend their masters' fortunes and even give their lives for those who would beat or sell them. The defenders of slavery often used this characterization of loyalty and natural order to soften their crimes. To them, the slave simply adopted an accepted role in the universe that he assumed dutifully and performed, with careful guidance, competently. They would have us believe that this is the mutually beneficial relationship that The Almighty has imposed on the white man, who dutifully judiciously supervises the munificent system. If abuses occurred, it was the failure of a single individual, not the fault of the institution. Esther, the good slave, of course withheld some information for herself.

My new duties changed my status among the other slaves. As Esther's assistant, I enjoyed the coveted trips to town and other farms and relief from the usual toil. I returned with information for the master and my head full of questions. Mariah treated me as less of a threat, perhaps because she saw that I had my own good job and no longer coveted hers. I still carried white slop and beat white laundry on the rock in the creek, but Mariah no longer shooed me out of the cook house. She remained largely silent though. Knowing that I had the master's ear she was smart enough not to press me for his business.

Upon our return from an errand, Sarah greeted us first with some joke or comment designed to elicit a thread of rumor for her to weave into fact. By watching Esther, I learned how to satisfy Sarah's cravings with observations of no consequence, usually involving other slaves. Sarah found happiness with word of colored birth, colored love, and colored death especially if she was the first to receive it. Esther held information about white people only for the master.

Esther never gave me any of the cast-off clothing that made its way from the master's house to slave quarters. "You just a hand to ever'body, just a slave, a nigger." she told me. "You get a dress from Missus, that change the way folks see you. You need to be just another nigger."

I soon developed an attraction to espionage. A day on the road might be easier than one in the field, but that was not the benefit that I saw. I found pleasure in the acquisition of knowledge, in the use of my brain. My work now involved more than making soap and skimming grease. I went forth into the world and collected something useful and important. I carried this precious cargo back to Esther and Morgan and delivered it intact, like a fresh egg or a live butterfly. To err or omit could prove disastrous for the master and his fortunes, and mine. Spying required awareness and planning so just as the field hand's labor with his arms and back made him stronger, my work with my mind made me smarter. Every visit for gossip also gauged the height of corn or the count of bales and boxes. These tasked my eyes and my ears and my memory. I used small stones and knots on a string to tally the number of full corn cribs at Auxier's or the type of seed being bought at Graham's store. I listened to the idle tittle-tattle of house servants outside kitchens.

To the masters, their slaves were mute, stupid, and invisible. Their chattels existed to serve and were of no further consequence. Morgan knew that slaves were not deaf or blind and not entirely stupid. To that extent, Morgan was ahead of his time. To paint him as a Whig went too far, however. The move for abolition did not really begin until well after his death, and I am certain that he would have opposed us. His fortune and his society chained him to the ownership of human beings, and he would never go against his own interests. He was one of very few white men who regarded slaves as more than just cattle, though. I wish I could have seen that at the time.

Ned

Something much more significant altered my situation in the cabins. God, who was still then a stranger to me, saw fit to bless Saul and me with a child, which surprised apparently only me. All the other consequences of marriage were known to me, but I never extended the miracle of birth and life to myself. God handles such ignorance well and as my baby grew inside of me, I came to understand more of the world and my place in it. Saul, the crops, the mountains, the seasons, the river, all began to make sense. Life and living took on a new meaning. I embraced, if I did not fully comprehend, the propagation of my race. At night, I listened to Saul's slow respiration and felt the connection between him and the life within me. That connection seemed to pass through me and into the earth, flowing back up into the bodies in other cabins nearby, and onward into the trees and the other living things around me. I had stopped being an observer or a passenger and now fully participated in wider marvels.

When Daisy wiped the blood from my little girl and gave her to me, I looked into that tiny, pinched face with the emotion only a mother can know. My body produced a human being, a person, someone who would grow to a woman. My life seemed complete. As I nursed her, Mariah offered kind words, her first ever to me.

"She a fine girl. Be strong. Don't have your eyes, though. What you goin' to call her?"

"We like Pirey," I said.

"Pirey. That sound nice. Pirey. Good."

Saul could not have been happier. To see the love in his eyes as he held our daughter made the world, for a few moments at least, a perfect place. I reveled in the pride of having brought forth life, in the joy in the closeness between Saul, Pirey, and myself, and in the relief that childbirth had not killed one of us. William Morgan's wife, Susannah, took three days to bleed slowly to death after little David was born. And slave women with names forgotten screamed their last pleas for an end to agony in that same way. I was alive. Pirey was alive. Saul was there. Life was good. Pirey filled, for a while, that empty place inside me.

I returned to work with Pirey slung on my back or cradled in the wood box at the kitchen. Slaves were not baptized then, so we had no ceremony to celebrate. I could stop work to nurse her, but if I was carding or weaving, I had to keep at my task.

Word got up to the house that another slave had come along. Morgan's first notice of Pirey came a week later as I carried water up from the well. I lugged the buckets on a yoke and my daughter hung in a shawl slung in front of me. I slogged up the hill toward where Morgan waited. But instead of his usual stance of arms crossed, he adopted a different posture. His riding crop hung from one wrist as usual, but his open hands rested at his sides. He balanced on both feet, set. Gone was the customary confidence and nonchalance. That morning, Morgan the master reflected the tiniest uncertainty. As I trudged closer through the mud, I kept my eyes down, knowing that he would be the one to speak.

"Let me see what you got there girl," he told me. I set down my heavy buckets, and not a little apprehensively, I pulled my shawl away from her face. He brought up the whip and I tensed, but he used the butt to lift the fabric. I stole a glance at his hard hazel eyes as they examined his new property. Pirey had Saul's dark eyes and his beautiful ebony skin. She squirmed at the light and brought tiny hands to tiny face. Morgan's mouth tightened briefly and he took his hand away. "She looks healthy enough. Be needing you again soon."

And that was all. He turned and walked toward the stable, snapping the whip against his boot. The color of a slave baby always interested owners, particularly fair-skinned female slaves. According to the law, a white man forcing himself upon a slave woman was guilty of property damage. But an owner could enjoy some profit from these unions should a child result, so the law was observed in the breach rather than in the main. Never mind the bitterness in the slave community should white men help themselves to black roses. Morgan believed in order, his order. Race mixing was disorderly, and he forbade his overseers and anyone else from molesting his slave women.

Three weeks later, Esther told me to hitch up the cart and load sacks of wheat and corn. I was off to the mill. Esther offered to care for Pirey, but I prevailed upon her to let me take my little girl along. We had not been separated since her birth, and I could not bear to be away from her. Besides, I told Esther, a new baby always attracted attention. Women will want to hold her and men will say kind things. People will open their mouths. The sacks of corn and wheat offered a soft bed, and the motion of the cart and the lazy squeak of the axle quickly put her to sleep.

Although a light spring rain had dampened the dust, the track had yet to surrender to the deep mud that would coat everything for the next six months. I led the old horse down the valley to where another trail led up a stream. Mr. Peter Hamilton's grist mill lay three hours distant, perhaps eight miles. I could make the trip, spend several hours milling the corn and listening, and be home close to dark. A mud colored stray with spots on his face observed me from the safety of the woods then vanished. I looked back for Sim, but he pursued some other adventure that day.

Hamilton built his mill up a deep, narrow valley where a stream fell off the mountain. A log cabin crouched at one side of a clearing. At the foot of the waterfall stood the mill in its house and the great water wheel, the height of invention on that frontier.

I stopped the cart and pulled Pirey down from her cozy bed. Hamilton was engaged in an animated conversation with Mr. Edward Osborn and another man who I did not know. Knowing better than to approach a white man unbidden and certainly never to interrupt three white men speaking to one another, I waited at a distance with my pass at the ready. I took the opportunity to feed Pirey and to listen.

Osborn's voice carried indistinctly. He was finely dressed, as usual. His tan breeches had yet to gather any signs of soil and wear, and his brown frock coat with the high collar spoke of good quality. His long blond hair scrambled across the collar. William Morgan had several coats of that style, but none of that value. Osborn held his low-crowned beaver hat to his side to touch the top of his tall boots. Off to one side he had tethered his beautiful bay gelding who tossed his head, impatient to move again. The best saddle horses are loath to remain still.

I could not hear what Osborn was saying, but from his demeanor and the emphasis in his voice and body, he made a point that Hamilton was unready to accept. The shabby old miller looked to be standing his ground against Osborn, but reluctantly. His old-fashioned tricorn dusted in flour and dirt must have seen him through the Indian wars. His trousers surely dated from before that. Nothing about his appearance or his surroundings suggested that he sat at the hub of economic activity in the county. The mill creaked and the stones ground against each other a few feet away.

The third man stood to one side, watching nothing in particular, but obviously listening with his arms folded. He did not quite fit into the categories of white man that I had known. His full beard was that of a settler or backwoodsman, but his coat and trousers spoke of a townsman. His boots showed a current familiarity with the road. I got the impression of a well-dressed denizen of some tavern, more at home with a flagon in his hand rather than a plow or a tool.

I held Pirey close and took a position behind Osborn and within Hamilton's view. Hamilton would deal with me when he was ready, but I did manage to catch some of the discussion.

"Why would I want more?" was all that I could hear from Hamilton. Hamilton then chose to notice me with a look of irritation. Osborn saw what took Hamilton's attention and with some annoyance, clapped his hat on his head. I doubt that he recognized me as Morgan's. To him I was just another Negro. With no further comment, Osborn went to his horse and mounted, taking up the reins. I saw that the little finger of his left hand was lopped short, evidence of some accident not infrequently visited upon those who work with harnesses. Fingers get caught in fittings just as the animal tests the leather. The cut nips as clean as any with an axe. The gelding fought the bit. Osborn addressed Hamilton without taking his eyes off his horse. "Think about what I said, Patrick." The other man backed away and found his horse, an animal so common in appearance as to first escape my notice. He trotted off down the track after Osborn. I remembered Esther's caution, "Watch what you don't want to watch."

Hamilton turned to me with a face less troubled. "What you got, girl?"

I stepped forward and held out my pass with the instructions for the miller. Without that pass, I could not be out on the road. As long as he held it, I was his. Even though I gazed at the level of his chest, I could see him mouthing the words on the paper. He stuffed the paper in a torn pocket and walked to the mill. Ned, his old Negro, positioned a bag under the chute. White dust paled Ned's skin and hair, giving him a ghost-like quality. Hamilton thrust his hand into the fine stream dribbling out of the mill and tested the quality of his, or rather Ned's, work. He then began to examine the machinery.

The structure was little more than a roof covering the mechanism of wooden gears and bevels and the two millstones and the platform for feeding the hopper. A leaky flume of rough boards on spindly legs ran from the top of the falls a few rods to the wheel. The paddles of the water wheel caught the thin stream splashing from the flume and as much water spilled sideways from the wood channel as down. The hardwood mechanism, shiny with grease, turned with a soft, repeating groan, like some sick animal. Slowly, the great wheel moved, and with it, shafts and gears in an intricate meshing of design and power. One device bent upon another and the force of the waterfall translated underneath into the revolution of one heavy stone upon the other. Hamilton stepped deliberately around the moving parts to watch their work and to guarantee harmony. I imagined what would happen should he make a careless move and be consumed by his own creation.

Ned hauled sacks of grain up the ladder to the hopper which jerked from side to side through some mysterious connection to the rest as it fed the winnowed kernels into the shoe then into eye of the runner stone. Ground meal spilled out the edges into another a box with an opening that fed the bags.

I marveled at the ingenuity of taking water and tricking it into work. Just as when Saul had opened for me the door of knowledge onto a wider world, gazing into that mill made my mind work like those shafts and gears. Crude as I am certain it was, that mill loomed as wondrous to me then as children today find steam locomotives and factories. And this shabby man and his white Negro had mastered it all.

Hamilton the miller got a sixth of corn that was ground and an eighth of wheat, but usually more since he was a scoundrel. He once had a box around his millstones that he told farmers prevented their flour from spilling, but it was just a ruse to collect a larger share of the meal in the corners. One rumor said that Morgan made him remove the box or face the court. This did not improve Hamilton's character, but it eliminated a source of conflict. Morgan despised conflict.

Slaves and pigs got the coarse meal, while white people got flour. My instructions were for one sack of good flour for the house and four of coarser stuff for the rest of the farm. Hamilton ignored me as he and Ned worked the mill. Ned hauled sacks to the hopper and from the spout while Hamilton tended the mechanism with a pot of grease. From time to time, Hamilton stepped out for a pull on a jug. Each time he did that, Ned watched covertly. Ned filled one last sack and pulled it aside with the others. Hamilton waved at Ned who went to the flume that fed water to the wheel. He pushed it, directing the stream of water away from it. The wheel, the shafts, the gears, and the stone stopped with a "chum." The heavy grinding of the mill yielded to the music of falling water, and the shaded mountain valley returned to the sounds of nature. In the wilderness, man and his machines held sway for a short time only.

Hamilton reached out to the cool stream falling out of the flume and grabbed a handful to splash his face and wash his hands. Refreshed and dripping, he found his jug, pulled at it, and recorked it in a single, practiced motion. Then he regarded me and my sleeping infant with curiosity as if somehow I had changed clothing in the past few minutes. Undoubtedly, he had failed to notice that I carried a small child.

Ned saw this, I think. "Drink, sah?" he asked.

Hamilton did not move his eyes from me and muttered something.

Ned quickly stepped to the flume and drank deeply of the falling stream. The water washed away his white cast, revealing a deeply wrinkled face. His hair did not lose color though, being gray all the way through. Relief briefly broke an otherwise inscrutable mask.

Hamilton reached into his pocket and reexamined the pass with the instructions. He ambled over to the cart where the old horse rested, head down and one foreleg crooked. The miller opened one of the bags and let the corn dribble through his fingers. He found the bag with wheat and checked it for chaff and dirt, nodding with what might be construed as approval. He spoke to me without granting me the dignity of eye contact.

"Run the wheat first. Get them bags over to Ned."

"Yassah," I replied. Without disturbing Pirey, I backed the old horse and the cart closer to the mill. I placed Pirey on a pile of straw in the shade and began to unload the bags, stacking them near Ned. Ned looked in each bag and set them nearer the mill. When we were unloaded, Ned stood to one side.

Hamilton waved a hand at the flume. Ned put his shoulder into it until the water splashed down across the wheel. Ned pushed on the wheel and the runner stone resumed its motion. Slowly the machinery came to life, moaning, twisting, scraping, until the runner stone rotated steadily round against the bed. Ned began feeding Morgan's wheat into the hopper. I stood by and hefted bags up the ladder to Ned as needed, but did not dare linger near the hungry gears. Hamilton wandered away. Ned went about his work silently filling the hopper, checking the grind, and watching the speed of the great wheel as the stream splashed across it.

Ned's was not a bad lot. Hauling bags and running the mill was far easier than bending on a hoe or swinging an axe, and he was out of the sun. The small plot where master and slave grew squash required little labor and even my untutored eye could see that the maintenance of house and mill consumed little of Hamilton's or Ned's effort. Ned ate and Hamilton ate and drank. Trades from milling provided them a living.

Occasionally Ned pushed on the flume to change slightly the stream of water that turned the wheel. I was puzzled that he indicated no interest in conversation or in me at all, for that matter. I thought that a solitary slave would hunger for contact with his own kind. But that mystery would have to wait. My task there was not to divine Ned's silence, but to return with ground flour and information. It would not do to stand before Morgan or Esther and say that the miller's slave would not talk to me. I had to find some way to draw him out. I started with something obvious, the mill.

"Ain't seen nothin' like this."

Ned continued feeding Morgan's wheat into the hopper.

"How long it take to run these bags?"

"Mmmmm."

If I could not inspire him to conversation, perhaps he could be enticed into argument. Keeping one eye on the heavy stone dribbling forth flour, I stepped up to the bag under the hopper and shook it and made to examine the product. I stuck my face into the bag, almost earning myself a head full of white.

The back of Ned's hand flashed with the speed of a rattler and caught me across one eye. The blow fell swift rather than forceful, a sting rather than a jar. I would never have suspected that such an old man possessed both such speed and such skill. Quite naturally, I pulled back.

"You dirty up my flour, girl, and that be the best thing happen to you all day."

"I just want to see the flour!" I protested. "I got to use it in Mas's bread."

"Flour from Hamilton's always fine. Don't need no dumb kitchen nigger to help me grind flour. You just keep them bags handy."

At least I got him to acknowledge my presence. I studied the old man. Ned knew his mill. He moved around those terrible gears and that wondrous turning stone as if they were his own bed. Never did he risk being caught in the mechanism. No move lacked purpose. No effort was wasted. Occasionally, he stepped out to the flume and with scarcely a glance, moved it every so slightly. He cocked his head to gauge the effect. If any of those machinations changed the speed of the mill, I could not discern.

One large croker sack of wheat became a smaller linsey bag of flour. Ned shook the last of the grain from the first bag and kernels and chaff fell to the hard-packed earth.

"Pick it up girl," Ned scolded. I got down and gathered what I could. "Watch it! Don't need horse turds in your master's dinner." I held out two hands full of kernels. Ned sniffed in my direction. "Put it in the other bag, girl."

I had a clue to unlocking his tongue. Ned's way was to make the other person look or feel stupid. Perhaps he perceived me as someone whom he could not dominate. The instinctive male needs to establish an order, some precedence among one another, who is on the top and who is on the bottom, some measure of their relative worth. They do this with their wealth, their weapons, and with their laws. The female sex is less inclined to do this. Like those perfidious dogs who yield to the stronger in the pack by lowering their heads and baring their necks, I undertook to let Ned take over.

"How you know just how to move the water to make the stone turn?"

"Just know."

"But why not make it go faster? Be done sooner."

"Show you how stupid you is girl. Go too fast, flour coarse."

"What if it go too slow?"

"Too slow and job take all day. Hamilton take my supper. I have to find a squirrel for my dinner. Ain't no slow squirrels left."

So, Hamilton used food as a weapon to flog his property. One thing I will say about Morgan, he kept us fed. We ate precious little meat and a fat Morgan slave did not exist, but we did not go hungry. Even a slave raw from the lash, ate. Loyalty may not be as strong as fear or hunger, but it is far more reliable.

I remembered the corn cakes that I had tucked into the cart. I looked in on Pirey, who slumbered soundly on the straw. In the distance, I saw the spotted face of my spectator from the trail as he darted back into the forest. I did not see any dogs around Hamilton's, and there was little to attract any. Maybe Hamilton ate his dogs? I have never tasted dog, though some consider it a delicacy. Were I desperate, I would deem it a rare treat. I retrieved the piece of sacking that wrapped my dinner and I returned to the mill.

I opened the cloth and began to break off small pieces of the cake and to eat them. Slowly I worked at the black and brown and yellow disk, hardly the sort of thing we see today, but more than satisfactory at the time. Ned caught my actions immediately but gave only the thinnest of indications. I could tell, though, that my mean repast held great interest for him. I calculated that although Ned was not being starved, his found was meager and monotonous at best. My corn cake represented a significant departure from his regular fare, probably boiled oats twice a day.

"You want some fritter? I tired of fritter."

Ned's response was not to look at me, but to search out his master. He cautiously eyed the shed that served as the miller's home, and he listened.

"Don't have nothin' to trade."

"Don't need to trade. My man kill a turkey. Have it tonight. Roast in a pit all day. Mmm." Slaves had little to boast about, but even the lowest hand enjoyed a brag about food, though my claim was empty.

"Be quick!" Ned whispered as he repositioned himself with his back to Hamilton's shack.

I held out my gift and Ned carefully selected a large piece. In a single move, the cake disappeared into his mouth. Slowly, secretly, he chewed with the same composure I had witnessed when he took a drink of water.

Sensing that Hamilton might disapprove of my charity, I stood with my back to the shack so that Ned needed only to glance and take another bite when he was ready. He did not take a second cake though.

I had been so intent on using food to compromise Ned, I let other considerations fall away. I can only attribute my narrow-mindedness to youth and inexperience, which overcame my other instincts. The first that I noticed that something was amiss was when Ned's head snapped up, not at Hamilton's, where I thought the threat to be, but in another direction.

Ned's body tensed, and he sprang away from the mill with speed I might have expected only of a younger and smaller man. His movements seemed so precise, so efficient, that I still wonder if he had somehow practiced them.

Ned dropped a hand toward a collection of mauls and bits at his feet. He retrieved a tomahawk, one of those Indian hatchets with the long narrow blade. He raised the ugly weapon over his head in a single, fluid move and snapped it into flight in the direction of the horse cart.

I turned to see his target and was presented with a scene that stopped my heart, a horrific picture yet burned into my brain after fifty years or moe. Pirey, my first-born, just three weeks old, hung from the jaws of that flea-ridden, diseased cur with the spotted face. He had her by blanket at her shoulder and he dragged her off her straw bed and into the forest. His firm bite and stealthy moves only just began to wake her. He doubtlessly hoped to pull her quietly a few feet into the brush, and then with a single snap, break her neck before fleeing with her body. I saw the horror of the next few seconds. I pictured her sweet little face in shock as his jaws tore the life from her.

The hatchet vaulted through the air end over end. It struck the ground short of Pirey. My heart fell knowing that Ned had missed and that my baby was doomed to the murderer's teeth. The hatchet bounced over her, though, and the handle struck the dog right behind the ear. Either by skill or by luck – there is no difference – the weapon's blow so disconcerted the thief, that he immediately dropped my baby. Freed of the weight of his prey as he pulled toward the forest, the killer rolled forwards in a somersault.

Ned continued his fluid moves and snatched up a mallet which he hurled almost before the tomahawk had landed. The mallet struck the dog squarely in the side. The animal ran yelping until the forest swallowed him and his cowardly voice.

I ran to my baby and found her crying, but unhurt. The filthy predator had grasped her through her tightly wrapped blanket leaving no marks on her shoulder. An embrace and breast easily calmed her. But that moment of calm caused me to realize just how close run a thing I had just witnessed. The thought of losing my baby and, particularly, to such a horrible fate gave me such a fright that I felt bile rise in my throat. Images of my dear Pirey being ripped apart like some hapless squirrel tortured me and I felt the scorn of my husband and Esther. Instead of sympathy I received contempt. And Morgan would have me whipped. But mostly I realized how close I had come to losing my dear baby. I began to cry, to sob, and I clutched Pirey all the closer.

My wailing drew Hamilton out of his lair.

"What's all this?"

"Nothin', sah," Ned told him. "Old dog just about have the little 'un for supper. All better now."

"Good," was all that Hamilton could offer and he returned to his cabin.

"Don't fret gal," Ned told me and he placed a rough, whitened hand on my back. The baby be fine. We got to be millin'. The baby fine. That old dog won't be back. We keep the baby close. Over here, by the bags."

"I carry her."

He put more grain into the hopper and shifted the bag for the finished flour. As soon as Pirey had her fill of milk, I slung her against my back and took up the bag for the ground flour. Soon the light dust covered me as well. I sneezed several time into Morgan's flour which seemed to rid me of the terrible possibilities had Ned not been so quick with his tomahawk. Feeling measurably better I reengaged him. This shared experience might open his mouth.

"Sure happy you saw that dog," I told Ned. "Old Hamilton not so quick to save her."

"Hah!" Ned caught himself and checked the sack. "Hamilton feed your baby to that dog. He might even have a bite or two hisself. Hah."

"Or that other white man. That Osborn, ain't it?"

"Edward hisself Osborn."

"What so important, he talk to Hamilton?"

"Osborn want to be sheriff."

"I hear that."

"Then why you ask?"

"Why he talk to the miller?" We kept our voices low and continued to grind wheat. Before every utterance, the speaker watched for Hamilton.

"Hamilton see a lot of people, but he ain't in town. Hamilton in a place where he can talk up Osborn and talk down your master. But Hamilton don't take to nobody. So Osborn get Hamilton to hate him less'n he hates Morgan."

"Hamilton hate Morgan?"

"All about flour."

"What about flour?" I pressed, as casually as I could. He continued to feed wheat into the shaking hopper and to watch as I held a sack underneath. More of the dust had collected on his face broken only by the creases in his skin, which seeped sweat. One would think he was ignoring me, but I decided to hold my tongue. Ned acted like one of Saul's upstart colts, cooperative only after the trainer feigned giving up. After the next bag of wheat became flour between the stones, Ned explained.

"Hamilton get a sixth of what we mill. You bring in six bags, he keep one. For the mill. He then trade it. Or use it for mash. Or I get some. Hamilton could just buy corn and mill and then sell it. But he ain't got no money. Nobody got money. Your master got some money. Hamilton borrow some to buy the corn. But he don't make such a good deal, and he end up payin' back your master with some land without makin' nothin. He shoulda just kept the sixth. I can at least eat some of it. But with enough mash, he sleep it off."

I heard other resentment towards Morgan because of his wealth. Esther explained how some of Morgan's land, several horses, and an old slave had come into his possession this way. But for every man who lost something to Morgan, two or three found themselves better for the transaction. Morgan was no banker or money lender. He was an investor.

"So, Hamilton hate my Mas' for that?"

"You master won't give him no more money to buy the grain. Farmers pay the sixth and take their grind down to the river they-selves. Or sell it. Or trade it. Like your master."

"What Osborn got to do with that?"

"Osborn say he fix it so Hamilton get the money he need. Get out from under Morgan. All Hamilton got to do is talk him up come 'lection time. We see people here. Osborn know Hamilton can talk ole' Morgan down."

"So, Hamilton help Osborn?"

"Anybody say they know what Hamilton do be lyin'." I spilled a bit of grind. "Watch it! Hamilton find your meal on the ground, he whup me, not you." I adjusted the bag under the spout and with one hand rubbed the flour into the dirt.

"How long you been here?" I asked.

"Old Hamilton get me from Taylor's mill in Virginia. We come over the mountains. We put up this mill. Set the stone. Run the water down."

"You work in a mill all your life?"

"In the mill, in the field."

"Mill better?"

"Better work. Lonely, though. Let's get in on the corn."

I took a break in the job to clean off little Pirey. I scanned the woods for our spotted friend, but he had moved on. In three hours, Ned and I had milled Morgan's wheat and corn. Ned pulled out what approximated a sixth of what I had brought in. The flour was white with brown flecks mostly and the corn meal was yellow and brown, not what you see in the shops today, but respectable. I had the sacks in the cart, and Ned tentatively approached Hamilton's shack.

"Mist' Hamilton? Mist' Hamilton?" Obviously, the next few moments held some anxiety for the old man. I heard some move-ment followed by violent coughing. After a few moments of this, Hamilton blinked out from behind his door, his remaining gray hair off in all directions. The shadow cast by the door emphasized his age and his stupor.

Hamilton stumbled out and in our general direction before he stopped and began fumbling with his trousers. When he had attended to that piece of his business, he made his way over to the cart and began fingering the contents with his filthy hands. Then he examined the portion that Ned held out as the fee. Either he satisfied himself that the share was correct, or he gave up thinking about it. He waved in my direction and wandered back towards the shack.

"He drink like this a few days, then he stop. Then he drink again."

"You can make yourself some fritters now."

"Nothin' to fry 'em up in. Need a hunka fat."

"Next time I come, I see if I can get you some fat back. Next time I come."

"A egg?"

"And a egg. Couple eggs."

"That be good."

Then I remembered something. "He still got my pass. I need my pass."

"Hold on, girl." Ned walked over to the shack and softly spoke. He opened the door and after a few minutes of patient supplication, he returned with my paper, somewhat the worse for wear. I tucked Pirey in among the bags and lead off with the horse and cart in tow. I was an hour into my return journey when I spied a wagon coming the other way. As soon as I could see that a white man drove, I stopped the cart off the track as far as I could. The wagon pulled by two horses passed me and the bearded man with a broad-brimmed dark hat paid not the slightest attention to me. In back I saw least double the number of sacks that Ned and I had just milled. I quickly calculated that Ned could never finish this milling job in the daylight that was remaining. He would certainly not eat before it was done.

I made home by supper time and I delivered my report to Morgan under the big tree as Esther listened. Morgan asked several questions about Osborn and about the stranger who attended, but I provided little help there.

Morgan listened with his arms folded, one leg at rest as was his habit. His brown eyes examined the distance or the ground, but never me. He nodded slowly as I mentioned my observations of Hamilton's sobriety. I did not share the experience with the spotted dog. When I finished, or rather when Morgan finished, he turned and walked to his house. He offered no comment and no commendation. Esther tapped me as a signal to retreat. As we walked back to the cabins where the smoke of cooking fires filled the air, she spoke.

"We need to watch, to listen. If Osborn go 'round talkin' to the right people, Mas' have trouble come 'lection day. Mas' have trouble, we have trouble. Some day," she continued, "somethin' happen and you need Mas' to trust you. You need him to tell some white man, 'she a good girl'. You need him not to worry about where you is. I can't say when that be or what you need to do, but you get that chance. And you only get that one chance. Just that one."

Later I listened to Saul and Pirey breathe softly in the dark and I reflected on the events of the day. My inattention could easily have led to the bloody death of my baby. Only the quick thinking and uncommon skill of an old mill hand save her and saved me. But somehow all turned out well and I even extracted useful information out of the meal and flour. To what did I owe this good fortune? How did some people end up sold down the river and how did some become spies? And good fortune followed bad fortune. Bad fortune followed good fortune. I had a house with a window. I lost it. I got a new job. I never knew the society of a real family, but now had one. I was like that leaf in the water. Instead of being caught and crushed I was being carried forward. But to where? To what?

Horses

White men set the elections for harvest, the busiest time. The courts convened that time of year. Marriages were formalized and recorded, taxes were paid, estates were probated, fines were levied, and lawsuits were resolved. Every few years the white men held elections.

David Morgan went to town with his entire family and all his slaves. Mrs. Morgan sat next to Peter in the wagon seat. Her three grandchildren rode in the back with the harvest. Esther drove the cart, piled high with more for the market. O'Hara rode his nag at the rear of the procession. William Morgan cantered on ahead out of sight. Morgan brought us along because he wanted the community to see his slaves, a manifestation of his wealth. The big trip to town had become a tradition, and Esther made use of the extra eyes and ears. Sarah hoped to harvest her own bumper crop of tales.

Saul led a colt and a filly for Morgan to sell, and I carried Pirey. The yearlings jumped and pulled at their leads until they accepted the journey and settled down. Hooves and wheels churned the dry track, and we spread out both to avoid the dust that hung in the humid air and just to enjoy a little solitude. Axles squealed, harnesses clinked, and loads groaned. The morning settled into a pleasant communal experience. I may have been a slave, but I could enjoy being a part of something good and something secure, despite any ill feelings.

I shared my knowledge of the now familiar route with my husband while Sim kept pace.

"Just up here is that Peterson place," I told him. "They makin' good this year. Round the bend is a place where we can get a cool drink from a stream. You see the beaver dam there." We walked by ourselves because Saul had the horses. As we neared Prestonsburg, other travelers joined in. A white family took a position between us and the rest of the party. Their wagon lingered near death, and I wondered if it could complete the journey intact. Behind us, O'Hara mumbled one of his incomprehensible Irish ditties. The tune reached the people in front of us, and they looked back and stopped. Saul and I passed them with the horses and as they met up with O'Hara, they struck up a conversation in their own language as they resumed the march. Soon all whined foreign music through their noses.

Just before town, Morgan waited. He turned in his saddle and motioned for Saul to follow him. I went with Saul both to be with my husband and also to listen in the crowd. Sim disappeared preferring the company of his own kind to any crowd of humans. Saul had been working with the yearlings who foaled the same week. They learned to walk and to run together, and they spent their days teasing and racing each other. They looked to be first-rate runners. Saul trained them each on a long line in a circle and had broken them to bit and saddle. The filly was midnight black and the colt was a deep brown. I followed Morgan and Saul to some pasture well back from the river where horses and stock were penned and traded. When men exchange horses, racing followed as naturally as day follows night.

I saw Morgan nod his head and touch his brim to other white men as he was recognized. I hung back as the men moved in to see the rich man's new offerings. Smells of pipe smoke, sweat, and whiskey filled the dry air. More than once, white men thoughtlessly spat tobacco juice that spotted my shift. Saul's horses began to jump and pull on their leads as soon as they saw the crowd. A man stepped up to help Saul and took the filly's lead. A white man quickly pushed the man aside to seize the honor of holding one of Morgan's horses. Draper appeared again, ever alert to curry favor with the powerful man and perhaps to earn a penny for whiskey. The filly fought Draper's artless control. Under Saul's hand the brown colt calmed a bit, but both animals remained anxious in the proximity of so many strangers.

Morgan dismounted and began the process of horse trading. White men ran their hands over the young horses and stood back to admire the fine lines. I could not hear what transpired, but his was not the conversation I sought. Other exchanges attracted my attention.

"That new boy of Morgan's, good with the yearlings," commented one farmer, oblivious to my existence.

"Old Harmon's boy."

"Morgan's pretty good picking his niggers," replied a townsman.

"And his horses."

"He ought to strike a sharp bargain for 'em."

"Can't pick his sons, though."

"No man picks his sons."

"Hmm, Bill Morgan just got to town, that means he should be bare-assed about...now."

"I think you're wrong. I say he was out of his boots five minutes ago."

"Does he take off his boots?"

William's involvement with the octoroon seamstress was common knowledge, but this held less embarrassment to his father than annoyance. Morgan preferred that William attend to politics or business rather than to women. William's transgressions violated Morgan's firm sense of order. But once William's head cleared of lust, he managed to attend to politics and business if less competently than his elder.

"You votin' for Morgan this year?"

"Don't know. Want to hear Osborn."

"Osborn's a fool."

"Promises to keep the niggers and squatters in line." The man remained oblivious of my presence. I doubt that if he had noticed me, he would have tempered his comments.

"Maybe we need Morgan at Frankfort?"

"Maybe. But Morgan been soft on the niggers."

I peeked at the man who made the suggestion about Frankfort, and I recognized him as small planter who visited Morgan occasionally. I moved away, suspecting that he as well as I would be reporting to my master. A wave of laughter washed back from where Morgan was showing his horses. The crowd moved forward to catch the next joke.

"Osborn wants to be sheriff just because he can't make it on his place," the planter said. "He sold his own niggers."

"He has his boys."

"He just bought those pretty clothes and that horse," a third voice came in.

"And that saddle. Has to be the best saddle in the county."

"Morgan has a good saddle."

"Ever looked? Just reg'lar. Just reg'lar."

"Sure knows horses, though."

"He's got a boy who knows horses."

Back and forth the comments bounced, most inane. I began to understand that although Morgan enjoyed wide respect, resentment simmered over his prosperity and his influence. Edward Osborn seemed popular if for no other reason than he had no office. I witnessed there for the first time the habit of the electorate voting with its heart instead of its brains. Change for the sake of change. Throw the rascal out. That has not changed in fifty years, in a thousand years.

A small cheer rose and arms hoisted a boy onto the back of Saul's colt. Saul had replaced the halter with a bridle, but the horse still wore no saddle. The sea of men parted and the boy skillfully guided the animal, a tribute to his own deft hand with animals. He rode the colt at an easy pace out to the field that served as a crude race course.

The coal-black filly, seeing her stable mate leave, reared and pulled at Draper. The dirty vagrant, as unskilled at holding a young horse as at holding work, promptly lost control. She broke away after the colt and the crowd scattered to the cheers of all. Unburdened with a rider she soon caught up and the race was on. The unfortunate rider of the colt stayed mounted only a few more strides before he flew off to the glee of the white men watching.

I heard Saul whistle and whistle again. The horses kept running and paid attention only to each other. As they reached the edge of the wide pasture, they turned and swung back toward Saul. He whistled again and ran out with a rope. Another man followed. The horses ended up close to Saul and he was able to get the rope on the colt and to grab a rein. The man took hold of the filly's halter and soon both horses blew hard and pulled on their leads in the midst of the group.

"I say the filly's better," from the edge of the crowd.

"I say the colt, but can't tell from here. Need a proper race."

Morgan held animated conversation with other prosperous-looking white men. Whether by accident or design, Morgan had shown his horses' good breeding and Saul's fine work. The horseman making a good bargain with Morgan could easily earn his investment back by racing and breeding. Or he could take the animal down river or over the mountains and profit from resale. Saul and the other man led the dancing racers back to be examined more closely.

"Sure wish I had the money to buy a fast horse like that."

"Wish I had the money to buy a slow horse."

"Surprised that Osborn ain't here. He's usually the first to bet on a horse."

"Hear he's tapped out. Owes for that land he bought. Don't need no more debts."

"He get sheriff, he can float."

"Morgan don't need sheriff."

On the talk went. Weather. Prices. Women. Squatters. Horses. Someone from Louisville wanted Negroes to buy, but none of these white men had any Negroes. The British were whipping up the Indians. What if the Indians came back? We'll take 'em, we'll take 'em all. And war was good for prices. Will Osborn take Morgan in the election? I did not know anything about British, but I knew about Indians. I listened and I tried to remember all the strange details.

Several white men clapped as Saul handed off reins of his charges and the young, excitable horses resisted the strangers. Morgan had made his deal, but he did not remain to see them raced or traded further. Morgan mounted Brownie and walked off as the crowd's attention shifted to the new owners.

I joined up with Saul and Morgan on their way back into town. As I walked along next to Morgan's stirrup, I related what I heard. His only reply was to order me and Saul to find Esther at the landing. Our little family, Saul at my side, Pirey on my hip, headed down to the riverbank.

"Did you see her run?" were Saul's first words. He had foaled the both of them and broke them, and he was justifiably proud of his work.

"She fast," I said, knowing I could get an argument, "but I think he faster."

"No, she fastest. You see. She got the drive. She need to be first."

"You sad to lose 'em?"

"Naw. They get to run now. They go to where they can run. And win. Sure would like to see 'em run, though."

"You got one more due in this winter. Do it again."

"Maybe. Too soon to tell if it be any good."

I could keep Saul talking endlessly about his horses. I could not care less for horses. As far as I am concerned, one end bites and the other end kicks. Both ends smell. But I loved to see the animation in my husband's eyes, and to hear his total enthusiasm for his work. He accepted his world and found the good in everything. I doubt that I would ever have been able to lure my own husband into escape from bondage as I ultimately enticed others. In order to survive, Saul embraced his life of bondage and convinced himself things could be no better. He concentrated on his family and the prospect of a sound foal some dark night. Saul said that foals were always born at night so that by dawn they could stand and run from the lions.

Away from the trading ground I spied a group of white people gathered under a tree. This was odd, in my experience, so I began to make note of the circumstance. There were perhaps ten people, all but two of them women. The two men I took for husbands. The other husbands undoubtedly enjoyed free election whiskey in the main square. This new face in town invited my attention, and the intelligence might prove useful to my master. The stranger dressed as a townsman with a black frock coat and a shirt, but he wore no hat. Of medium height, his brown hair hung long, swept back from his ample forehead so that it cascaded over his collar. His trousers and boots showed recent travel over the trail and I guessed him as one more Tidewater or Piedmont transplant. But what was his trade? Newcomers usually brought with them the tools of their vocations such as a mule and plow or a law book or a bag full of potions and lancets.

Then I observed that they were all listening to the man who spoke, not in the oratory of the politicians in town, but in a normal conversational tone. He held open a book, the Bible that later guided my life, but at that moment just paper sheets and unintelligible print. I witnessed the first Methodist preacher to make his way into our country.

"What's this?" I asked Saul, but without signifying to anyone else that the scene had gained my attention.

"Preacher," Saul said. "White folks' religion. Joe tell me about them. White folks like what he say. Pay him. Sing even. Called religion. Church."

"Church?"

"They talk, they sing maybe. But not for us. Somethin' for white folks."

I was certainly accustomed to the multitude of things reserved for white people only or colored people only. Here was just another example of the gulf between our races and our conditions. Still, the newness drew me to inquiry.

"Pirey hungry," I told Saul. "Wait at the landing." He continued on while I found some shade within earshot of this curiosity. I sat on the ground, my back to the tree, and gave Pirey a breast, thereby disappearing from white eyes. Esther taught me how to use my motherhood to best effect, and her instructions proved invaluable many times.

The preacher read from his book, and I could tell that what he had to say held great import for his listeners. I can remember the passage yet since when I heard it a second time, years later, these words from Matthew opened the door to my own salvation and to my life in our struggle. Every Christian has some thought, some passage, some sentiment that embraces their faith and defines their salvation. For me the core of my beliefs came from this Virginian with mud on his boots as he read.

"...for they shall inherit the earth. Blessed are they which do hunger and thirst after righteousness: for they shall be filled. Blessed are the merciful: for they shall obtain mercy. Blessed are the pure in heart: for they shall see God. Blessed are the peace-makers: for they shall be called the children of God. Blessed are they which are persecuted for righteousness' sake: for theirs is the kingdom of heaven."

These words exploded in my head and in my heart. Here were concepts that turned on its head the basis of my world of subjugation and toil – that there was actually a future; that somewhere, somehow, pain and suffering and sacrifice might be rewarded; that there was something else.

I stole a look at the speaker and noticed that his face was one of the most peaceful and composed I had ever seen. Simple Jack had peace in his face, a complete lack of concern for anything untoward. But Jack's eyes revealed the origins of his placidity. His grasp only what appeared before him, and his understanding of past and future came not from experience or learning, but from habit. And almost all the white people I knew had a pinched, pained cast to their faces, angry or disgusted or sad or afraid. Even their laughter lacked the complete release of concern mere slaves enjoyed. All white people seemed, at their core, unhappy to me.

This man, although not expressing happiness, exuded something else, something more subtle, more powerful. As Pirey suckled I looked in her little face and it came to me. She was a baby, only little aware of her world and her life. She knew her mother and her father and just recently began to respond to voices and faces. Nothing threatened her. Nothing worried her. All was good in her world. I saw that this man was not afraid. He did not fear the loss of his farm or his slaves or his power or anyone who had those. He did not even fear death. Not only was he unconcerned about loss, he focused on giving, on broadcasting words and ideas that comforted people and gave their lives meaning.

The ten people he addressed soaked up his message like hungry children. And the message planted a seed in me too, the seed of faith, yet to sprout, but nestled in the loam of my heart. To the slaveocracy, the seed was that of a weed, a pest that would one day overtake the entire garden. I continued to listen.

"Friends, these words are for you. Our Lord didn't just say them to some people in the Holy Land thousands of years ago. He is saying them to you. Today. Right now. The Word of God is eternal. And the Word is here, now, in Kentucky. God does not care if you have one cow or two or two hundred. He only knows that He loves you and that you love Him. These words show that He loves you. These words show that after this life is salvation and justice. This is the miracle of faith. Believe and it is true. Your mercy shall bring you mercy. Your mourning will bring you comfort. Who among us has not cared for a child? Who among us has not experienced the loss of a child? This love and this loss is known by God and you will know God."

The black book he held was the key to his message and within it resided doubtlessly many more truths. I tried to reflect on what I had just learned in order to report back to my master. I knew he would be pleased to have this exciting news. Perhaps he wanted to meet with the preacher? Then I remembered Saul's words about how religion and church were not for us. Why? Here was a message of hope and of peace and of happiness. What could possibly be the harm in that? But there were many things denied me because of my condition of servitude and because of the color of my skin. Perhaps the white man wanted to keep good things only for himself, things like the tenderest meat, good houses, and fine clothes? I understood the base drives of greed and avarice, so perhaps the preacher's words were one more object of value denied the slave? The why of the question seemed to have ample precedent, but I later came to understand that the real reason the slave should not know the Bible is that it would give him a sense of worth and lead him to question the fundamental injustice and inequality of his condition.

The teachings in the Bible ran contrary to the principle of chattel slavery, and to give slaves the Word of God was to risk the destruction of the system. By the time that slaves were allowed to become Christians, God's message of forgiveness and resurrection had been cleansed of any dangerous concepts such as equality and free choice. None of the verses that told the master he could not abuse or lay with his slaves reached colored ears. Rather, preachers gave Negroes the First Book of Peter, Chapter 2 and his "Slaves, submit yourselves to your masters with all respect, not only to those who are good and considerate, but also to those who are harsh." And, of course, there is Ephesians 6 "Bondservants, be obedient to those who are your masters according to the flesh, with fear and trembling, in sincerity of heart."

For the moment, as Pirey slipped off into her sated slumber, I knew only that this faintest of light in the darkness, this tiniest bit of hope tormented my mind with more of the intellectual hunger that I was learning to feed. The preacher closed his book and the two men in the group donned their hats, touched their brims, and headed toward town. The preacher shook hands around with the women, found his own hat, and followed the others.

I got to my feet and walked to the landing pondering how best to handle this intelligence.

Abner

The river landing teemed with people, colored and white, and vehicles and horses and piles and piles of cargo. This was certainly nothing like the river landings at Catlettsburg or Cincinnati or St. Louis, but to me at the time, it was the biggest and busiest scene in my memory. Townsmen and farmers mingled along with their animals and vehicles along the dusty streets and down to the water. At the landing, flatboats, push boats, and keel boats shouldered one another on the muddy shore. They numbered in the dozens, but in the event there could not have been more than ten all tolled. At the top of the bank, sharp traders from down river bargained for the fruit of the land. Wheat, tobacco, corn, rye, fruit, skins, whiskey, and stock were sold, traded, and loaded. The wealth of the Big Sandy country then flowed downstream.

The most enterprising farmers took their crops down to Catlettsburg or Cincinnati on scows or rafts they built themselves. A man could double or triple his profit in this way. Trade along the river had its risks though. Some boatmen left a year's toil and even their lives at the bottom of the Big Sandy River or the Ohio when a badly caulked barge or an ill-balanced load paid the price of poor fortune or ineptitude. Most settlers simply traded what they raised – wheat for cloth, tobacco for iron goods, cattle for gun powder. Evidence of other talents drifted down out of secluded hollows. Leather goods lovingly cut and stitched, wooden utensils intricately carved, and homespun cloth laboriously decorated with threads of color betrayed skill and imagination that rivaled any I have seen since. Some enjoyed the good fortune to exchange what they had for real cash.

A fortunate few might pay off the credit they took over the growing season, assuming the merchant extended credit on hope. For the small frontier farmer life was about hope: hope that the weather or the pests did not steal the crop, hope that the crop would come in, hope that the harvest would bring a decent price, and hope that he could repeat the cycle next year. But I suppose that hope and drive is what propels this country forward. Certainly I hoped for many years to abolish slavery.

Mrs. Anna Morgan negotiated with a boatman over the contents of the wagon and the cart. Relieved of any need to stay busy, I stole some moments to watch her. My mind had sharpened in my experience as a spy, and I found myself examining the mistress with a new eye. My conversation with the mistress held to instructions from her. She always made requests, never the demands that came from her husband and son. Not really courteous to me and Mariah, she was certainly civil.

Like most of the women of the frontier, Anna Morgan sacrificed her youth and beauty to build a new society for her husband and children. Her bonnet hung down her back, revealing long gray hair, still showing some blonde, tied in a single braid. Her new blue calico dress stood a sharp contrast to the homespun of her slaves and lesser neighbors. I took her in at a distance, from behind.

The big boatman pawed through bags and baskets. She stood straight and positioned herself close enough keep the man engaged, but not so near as to threaten him. He shook his head. Her hand swept out gently, but with conviction. He continued to manhandle the harvest. With a final no, he waved her off and left. She stood her ground and watched for the next buyer. Her head tipped toward Peter with an unheard word, and he jumped to rearrange the sacks. Peter rarely moved that fast, even for the master.

William Morgan had three children, little David, who was about five years of age that autumn, and the girls were Polley and Ann. Unlike many plantations, the slaves at Morgan's had little to do with the children of the master, or in this case, his grandchildren. Anna Morgan raised them and did not foist those responsibilities off onto servants. We knew the children only by sight and by name. Mrs. Morgan's remoteness warranted little in the way of discussion around the cabins. Even Sarah failed to bring news of any consequence. If Mrs. Morgan went to town or to another farm, she had Esther or Peter take the reins.

That day by the river, I studied someone almost entirely new to me. I was immediately struck by how people and events seemed to turn around her, a circumstance made even more incongruous by her small size. I put her height at less than five feet, the same as her eldest granddaughter. For several moments, I observed her, or rather I observed those who greeted her. Men touched finger to a brim. Women nodded and smiled and Mrs. Morgan returned the sentiment. All kinds stopped by – planters equal in social and economic stature to the Morgans, and more common folk, the small farmers who clung to remote valleys. It was as if being around her and the bounty of her husband's farm and the brightness of her countenance might somehow acquire for them similar gain. Or they hoped to derive from her proximity some measure of her own quality.

That the wife of David Morgan enjoyed this celebrity should come as no surprise. He was the richest and most powerful man in the county. His wife naturally commanded notice and regard. A kind word or a light moment from a neighbor might find its way back to the master's table or bed. The neighbor that Morgan, being highly intelligent, might remember the information and return the smile with some advantage another day.

My fascination with Mrs. Morgan, so close to me all my life yet so unfamiliar, yielded to something else at the far end of the landing. Another scene, horrific in its simplicity and sad in its finality, demanded examination. Across the bartering and the arguing, the loading and shifting and the laughter was another aspect of the season, unique to that world and only recently and at such a great cost, driven from this land.

A man stood quietly, dressed in the usual brown homespun. Two things distinguished him from the other Negroes at the landing. First, he was naked above the waist, showing a solid chest and well defined arms not unfamiliar with hard work. His skin showed that he suffered neither ill health nor the marks of ill discipline. His black hair contradicted the deep wrinkles of his face. He reminded me of an older Saul. I had seen the man once before, but as I recalled, his hair had more gray then. His name was Abner.

The other thing that set him apart was his isolation from others. He seemed oblivious to the bustle of humanity around him, perhaps because he knew he was no longer a part of it. His gaze fell on the near distance, some object, a wheel, a sack, the mud of the riverbank. But he never looked at another person.

Next to Abner stood an old white man I knew as Taylor, a planter who had fought Indians to claim his land close to the town. He stubbornly built up a farm with substantial, if modest buildings and worked it with his own sweat and that of four or five slaves. He tried the tobacco he grew in Virginia and that sustained him a few seasons. When he tried cotton, the fiber never had a chance in the wasted soil. I noted that Taylor's clothing was well out of fashion – even slaves had a sense of fashion. He apparently possessed neither the inclination nor the means of obtaining anything newer in his twenty years in the Big Sandy country. Despite his slow decline he enjoyed a wide regard in the community. White men nodded at him and stopped and spoke. They regarded Abner briefly or not at all.

From Esther I knew that Taylor intended to sell out and move back to Virginia. Taylor came to the landing to sell his last slave, Abner. Abner helped him fight Indians. The planter did not hawk his property like some farm wife trying to unload her potatoes. Abner's nakedness announced the offer clearly enough.

No chain bound Abner, and his hands hung free. I marveled once again at how a man, like a horse, could submit so easily out of habit and training. Saul cornered a reluctant horse that yielded to him as soon as he put a rope across its neck. So this slave submitted immediately to a brief order to hold still.

Other people at the landing worked the boats and cargo and averted their eyes around the man, as invisible as some deformed beggar. Looking at him acknowledged an awful thing and accepted that the same could happen to any of them. He had a disease that no one wanted to catch or admit existed. For the rest of the slaves, Abner was already dead.

I needed to know more, not for my master, but for myself. My mind had already begun to grasp at knowledge for its own sake, just to know. Why sell a slave if slaves were so necessary? What would become of the slave? What would become of the white man?

Upstream from the landing, where the forest still touched the river, people gathered to shirk their work and to gossip. Most slaves in the valleys toiled alone on isolated farms. A trip to Prestonsburg presented a welcome taste of desperately needed society. Some came to town on regular market days, but for others, the fall was the only visit to a brother or a sister or simply another of his own kind. In the saddest cases a wife saw her husband or a father saw his children.

I found perhaps a dozen people in the shade of some trees overhanging the water. Most looked like field hands. A happy man tapped on a small drum while two children cavorted to his music. The rest talked and laughed while keeping time with his beat. The comfortable joy of the scene marked a sharp contrast to the tragedy across the landing.

My approach to the group with Pirey in my arms drew immediate comments, and the women gathered round me. "Let's see that little baby," asked one called Odessa as she reached for my daughter. "Oh, she so pretty. You Morgan's girl."

"Phyllis," I told her as I handed over my precious bundle.

"You got that Saul. The one with horses. Little girl, your daddy the best horse man in the country. You a pretty child. And you a happy baby. Yes. Yes."

"Not everybody happy," I remarked. Odessa looked at me questioningly. I looked in the direction of the far end of the landing and her eyes fell.

"Taylor's boy. On to Mississippi. Or Arkansas I 'spect." She did not even use his name.

"Sold away?"

"Down the river. See, Taylor make him look younger. Dye his hair."

"Why?"

"Need money. Owe money to your master."

"No," chimed in a servant girl about my age. She was standing ready to take her turn holding Pirey. "Owe his money to Judge Graham. But folks think it your master. People sayin' your master makin' him sell."

Graham was another Indian fighter who once held title to most of the county by virtue of his early surveying efforts. He was a popular man who ran a store and served as judge, but he let others such as David Morgan wield authority in the county. One story held that he gave a wanderer a plot of land on the strength of a fiddle tune.

"But he don't owe to my master, you said. He owe to Graham."

"Yep. Here, let me hold her now." The servant girl took Pirey. "But that what people sayin'."

"Why they say that? Hold her head up, like this. That's it. Why they sayin' these things?"

"Don't know. I just know what they say."

"How you know all this?"

"'Cause I Judge Graham's girl. I hear him talk."

"Who's sayin' that he owes Morgan?"

"That pretty man say it."

"Pretty man?"

"That man from up Louisa. The one with the clothes. The pretty horse."

"Osborn?"

"That his name?"

"He visit Judge Graham?"

"Yup, I hear it myself."

"You heard him say Morgan's making Taylor sell?"

"No, but I hear he say that."

Rumor, but not without foundation. This I would pass along to my master through Esther. But I suspected that he would learn it on his own. What better way to incur bad feeling against Morgan than to blame him for the fall of a leading figure? My thoughts returned to Abner.

"It don't look like Abner goin' down today."

124

"Don't you worry," Odessa said. "That man up from below be around again. He probably take him."

"What man is that?"

"Trader. Nobody you ever want to meet."

"What's his name?"

"Never hear his name. Don't want to know his name. Don't even want to look at him."

"Norton," someone offered.

"He a bad man?" I asked.

"Don't have to be a bad man. He a trader. He buy coloreds and sell 'em down. Might be a good man. But what happen around him is bad. Good men do bad things too."

The talk drifted among all the inane topics known to any group of people anywhere. A field hand appeared with a bundle and furtively took up a position behind the big tree. Smiling men and women, ever watchful, joined him, one or two at a time. I glimpsed a small jug that attracted them all, the byproduct of election time on the frontier. Whiskey loosed votes just as it loosed tongues and the baser instincts, so its ubiquity at election time allowed those denied the vote some of its joy.

Laughter rose as smiling individuals stepped out from behind the tree. Lucy joined the child dancers. She quickly attracted the gyrations of two young men. Lucy stepped and wiggled, and the men threw out their arms as if to catch her, and catch her they sought to do. In only moments, the men began to crowd one another until the inevitable shoving began. Lucy did not seem to notice. Finally one managed to over balance the other, and the stumbled suitor found solace in line at the jar. The one on his feet moved closer to Lucy who had turned her back to him. Their movements began to coincide as he drew nearer. Hands clapped and jeers encouraged them.

I felt Odessa at my ear as she whispered, "There." She pointed her chin across the landing. I saw a man with Taylor, and the two engaged a serious discussion. The people and animals prevented me from obtaining a good view of the two. I retrieved my baby and wrapped her before making my way into the multitude, past conversations and arguments and through the turmoil.

By the time I saw Taylor and the man again, they crouched over a box. Abner watched them, his apathy replaced by intense interest. Some marks on a document unknown to him sealed his future. He doubtlessly understood the import of what he saw if not the details of the process. Taylor pushed a paper at the stranger. The man counted out coins, which Taylor quickly collected. They stood and shook hands. Old Taylor regarded Abner stiffly, and I could tell that their eyes met. Quite uncharacteristically, Abner did not look away. He held Taylor's gaze until the old man turned and walked off. What unspoken words passed between the two who has unquestionably shared so much?

The man who had bought Abner faced his new property, and I saw him clearly, the bearded stranger I had seen at Hamilton's mill.

He spoke in the direction of Abner, but not to him. Norton's driver dressed as a servant and even wearing shoes, stepped up and produced iron manacles, which he proceeded to apply to Abner's legs. The driver gave Abner some order, and Abner reached down for his shirt. The driver spoke again, but Abner did not respond. He just pulled on his shirt over his head deliberately, his face an impassive mask. The driver seemed to take offense with Abner's silence and took a cudgel that hung from his wrist to give Abner a blow to his shoulder. It was nothing painful, but a reminder that he was a prisoner. Abner straightened up for an instant, then slowly dropped his head. Abner turned to look at the landing, taking in his last view of the land and the people that had been his home, a land he helped build. The driver directed Abner up the plank to a spot on a keel boat, behind a stack of bags. Abner limped out of my view dragging leg irons.

His last picture of Prestonsburg was of a collection of his own kind preferring to ignore him and his departure. It was sad enough that a human being was being sold like a sheep or a basket of apples, but to be granted no notice, no recognition of this passage, demeaned him all the more. I wanted to shout to him, "I see you, Abner! I see you bein' sold down the river. You not a sheep. You not a basket o' apples. I think of you. I remember you." Then he was gone, one more piece of baggage on a packet.

The Voice of the People

In spite of having my baby in my arms, I felt empty. I needed to be with people I knew. I searched for a familiar face, Saul or Esther. Even Mariah would be some comfort. No one from Morgan's remained. Mrs. Morgan had apparently sold out and moved on. I walked back to the gathering under the tree where Lucy lustily taunted the men. She moved her young body in time with the drum and her dark skin glistened with sweat. The drummer's hands and fingers gamboled over the taut head of the instrument, all in one with Lucy's hips and feet. I hoped that the dancers and their audience intensified their celebration in reaction to what had just transpired with Abner, as if the effort and the noise would somehow drown out the obscenity. I needed more than a dance to ease my pain.

I walked up toward the courthouse with Pirey. The sleepy town, little more than a village, bustled with white people. I started up the street, but seeing no brown faces, I elected to steal between houses. In the lee of the buildings, the stench of man and animal commingled in the fetor of civilization. I always marveled how a big city like Philadelphia managed to smell as bad as some frontier settlement and always worse than a farm. Animals have their own stink, but add to them the odor of man and his leavings and the effect multiplies. Tiny Prestonsburg was no exception.

I picked up a path that snaked through the gardens in the general direction of the court house. Although the route crossed a number of private properties, we knew to use these back ways rather than the streets. As much as white people depended on their hands and servants, they would just as soon not have to look at them. Negroes stayed out of sight with the hogs and cows and the necessary houses. Dogs challenged me and each other as I crossed through their territories. I even picked up Sim as he continued his own social calls. I had visited these yards before and usually stopped at back doors and barns to exchange pleasantries and blather. But today, the servants had deserted their wash tubs and garden plots.

I found my usual informants behind the tavern along with farm hands. Another whiskey jug proved to be part of the attraction. Esther was there along with Mariah and Daisy and several other Morgan slaves. Men and women sat on whatever was available or they stood. Peter sat on a log with the jug tucked safely between his legs

The group seemed to be of two stripes: those who expressed extreme interest in Peter, or rather in what he possessed, and the rest. Peter continued his role as driver, but instead of assigning work and distributing food, he dispensed corn in liquid form under Esther's watchful superintendency.

"Old Peter," remarked the blacksmith's man, Simon, "let's see how much more you got in Little Suzy there. I say Little Suzy want to kiss all the boys."

"Little Suzy just fine where she is," Peter replied with a smile. Peter had already kissed Little Suzy himself, and he swayed a bit. Morgan had liquor at the farm, but he kept it close in the house. Too many of his hands harbored a taste for the corn, and so did O'Hara. This never prevented the industrious from acquiring spirits somewhere, though never of the quality that the master guarded so well or of a quantity to bring his notice. At election time, whiskey flowed through Prestonsburg like the Louisa Fork. The noise from the crowd inside the tavern and from the courthouse spoke to that. Naturally, some of the drink found its way to the back lots and stables.

Esther's close presence indicated to me that Peter's jug was not just the good fortune of field hands and servants. Esther stood apart from Peter listening to a woman babble about absolutely nothing. Nothing Esther ever did was by chance, and I surmised this was all Morgan's doing with her subtle guidance. Giving the jug to Peter took advantage of both his size and his custom of control. Esther controlled Peter. Morgan controlled Esther. Morgan's plan again.

"Let's have another kiss from Little Suzy," pressed Simon. "Just a little peck."

"You just got a kiss," Peter replied. "You kiss her too much, she won't be anybody special to you. You won't want to kiss her again."

"Don't you worry, Old Peter, Little Suzy somebody I willin' to kiss any time. Any time."

"You can have another taste, but I catch you mouthin' like before and no amount of liquor make you feel better when Suzy's big sister kiss you." He held up his heavy fist.

"Just a tiny kiss," Simon assured Peter, reaching out with both hands. "Suzy won't even feel it."

Peter dropped his hand to the jug and hefted it up to Simon's eager fingers. Shamelessly the blacksmith upended the jug with the massive arms. His eyes squeezed shut in excruciating pain. Morgan's plan for slaves did not include any more than the rawest and crudest of spirits. I never understood how drinkers withstood liquor's horrible taste in exchange for such fleeting effects. Simon was one of those drinkers who cared little how his potable tasted or smelled. He just needed the insidious effect.

Peter's fist into Simon's belly ended the assignation with Little Suzy. I could not tell which hurt worse, the effect of the drink or Peter's blow. Simon lowered the jug, and his tongue chased the drops leaking down his chin. His eyes relaxed not in the slightest.

"Ahhhh," Simon rasped. "Suzy got the fines' kiss in all Kentucky."

"Give!" Peter spat, and he took the jug decisively. He passed it along to a more patient but no less enthusiastic admirer nearby. Little Suzy made her rounds over four or five pairs of lips. None of Little Suzy's other suitors managed to kiss her with Simon's passion, but all seemed to experience the same immediate results, which could only be interpreted as negative. Simon made a half-hearted attempt at seizing the jug, but Peter prevailed and Little Suzy returned to her seat between his knees.

Laughter rose as good feeling washed over the hands and servants. I stopped next to Esther and tugged her sleeve. We stepped away and I related what I had seen and heard at the landing. She took it all in silently until I made the connection between the slave trader and Osborn. She took notice of this. She glanced toward the courthouse just as a brief cheer rose. Someone was speaking to the crowd.

Esther told me to stay there, and she stepped over to Peter who received her whispered message with a nod and a move to pull Suzy closer. Esther then disappeared through a mass of tethered horses and parked wagons. I assumed that Esther wanted me to stand in for her with the gossips, but I wasted my time there. I learned only of the misbehavior of white children and the disgusting details of mistress's toilet.

Esther returned just as the topic, I cannot call it a discussion, turned to the poor quality of potatoes this year. She did not appear unburdened by my information, and I tried to consider what it meant. Osborn hated Morgan. Osborn wanted to be sheriff. Osborn had a connection with a man who bought slaves. All of this only added to my sense of gloom over Abner, and I yearned to be near my husband. I tugged on Esther's sleeve.

"Where Saul?"

"With Mas'. Front of the courthouse."

"I want to see Saul."

"You do that. But soon as you see him you get to camp. Get some fires goin'. We got meat tonight."

Pirey and I worked our way through the horses to where a wagon blocked my way into the square. I stood there to observe the courthouse and the white people scattered about in front of it. I also searched for Saul, but there was not a colored face in sight.

The courthouse was a two story – really just a story-and-a-half – brick structure, the most substantial building in that part of the commonwealth. The first version of wood burned down and Morgan and Judge Graham managed to squeeze enough money and labor out of the electorate to erect a new one. Imposing as it seemed to everyone at the time, it was simply a large room with an office at the back. It served the purposes of meeting place, courtroom, archive, center of town, and symbol of the law. Through it passed all taxes, land transactions, and official justice. In it gathered the men who ran the county, the judge, the sheriff, the commissioners, and the clerk. Who controlled the courthouse, controlled the county. Another small cheer came from the knot of men closest to the building.

I saw more white people than I had ever seen in my life. Many years later, I addressed groups far larger than this, but none of my feelings in front of those events could compare to the awe I felt then. In my world on the farm, Negroes outnumbered white people. White men had the power over us, but I always felt that I was in the majority. This was the case no longer, but it would be just one new realization I would gain that day.

The white people, mostly men, stood, alone, in twos, and in threes. A few spoke, as much with their hands and pipe stems as with their mouths. Most seemed just to listen. I recognized Auxier, Spurlock, Mayo, and Judge Graham. Others I knew only by sight, either from visits to the Morgan place or in my journeys around the county. I caught a glimpse of Morgan through the crowd on the other side of the tiny square.

Edward Osborn walked to the front of the courthouse, and with a nod to the men on the porch, he mounted the frontier hustings, merely a box turned upside down. The audience continued its numerous conversations.

"Friends," Osborn began, but his friends ignored him. He wore fine clothes better than I had ever seen him wear. His dark brown coat seemed made for his tan breeches. His tall black boots gleamed with fresh polish. A bright red cravat supplied an illusion of strength. His voice pitched higher, tentatively. He held a brown, wide-brimmed hat to his side.

Osborn tried again. "Friends, it is good to see you all again." A few heads turned. "It is good to see you again. But it is sad that we only see each other once or twice a year. We have so much in common. The journeys from your farms and your homes are arduous ones made no easier by the uncertainty of your profit. Our labors here on the frontier are heavy and long. We have precious little time to waste attending to problems not of our making. I thank you for coming here to help." The voices dwindled as the crowd gave Osborn its attention. He stood stiffly and failed to engage any one directly in the eye. Instead, he looked over them to the far side of the group.

"We all came to this fine land to build homes and to enjoy the fruits of our own labors. We all seek better lives. We wanted more for our families. We wanted to build a new commonwealth and to be free from the dictates of a few moneyed men. Our constitution and the Declaration of Independence bear out these motives. The founders and the heroes of the Revolution struggled that we all might enjoy the rights of free men and the rights of property. Would that all men followed the spirit of our ancestors embodied in these great documents." A few partisans in the square attempted to raise a cheer but found no recruits.

"Would that all men respected the laws of our commonwealth, laws intended to protect the rights of free men, such as you, the rights of property and God's order in the world." Osborn's arm swept to his left toward David Morgan, who watched impassively from under his hat.

"We have laws that prohibit larceny so that a man might be secure in his home and in his property." Osborn brought his free hand in front of his face as a fist. "How can a man feed his family without the property to produce their food? Property is at the core of our heritage. Property is the basis of citizenship." The hand pointed into the crowd and the voice dropped a note. "Property is recognized by the word of Almighty God. Without property, there is no civilization.

"The law protects the rights of property," he continued, "that a man can hold what he earns and owns. The law also imposes certain responsibilities, certain obligations on free men who live in a free society. One of these obligations is to follow God's will by maintaining the natural order of the universe. Did not God give us this land to transform from a wilderness into a free and prosperous society? Did not God ordain that the heathen Shawnee should yield up this country to its higher use? Did not God place the white man over the African for the betterment of both of them?

"And does not the commonwealth set laws that insure that God's will and God's order are followed on this earth? Friends, I tell you that for all the law's high intention, it is not worth a farthing when public officials themselves," the arm swung again to the left in Morgan's direction, "refuse to listen to it.

"I speak to the fact that the law requires that slaves shall not wander about unless they possess a pass from their master and have a valid purpose. But does this happen? No! Slaves regularly roam about this county to fall into misfortune – or worse, to bring misfortune upon others, upon free men and their families. I do not need to tell you the consequences of ignoring the law, of ignoring God's law.

"I say to you, friends, that what is needed in this county is a new respect for the law. What we need is men willing to work for the good of free men and willing to stand up to those who would flaunt the law. Some of us are troubled by this. I am deeply troubled by this. I am willing to put myself forward to stop this, to bring order back to our society.

"I therefore place myself at your service as Sheriff of Floyd County. I pledge to you that I will stop this blatant disregard for the law. For those who continue to violate the law, there are the courts. Let us end this scourge of shiftless and dangerous Africans upon the roads of this county to threaten our peace and our prosperity. I, Edward Osborn, as your sheriff will bring tranquility and order back to Floyd County. Vote for me and watch as the law is obeyed!"

The Osborn partisans raised their cheer. This time it seemed to catch on with shouts and applause. Osborn remained on the box and the noise seemed to relax him. Several men stepped forward and offered their hands pulling him down from the box. Throughout the crowd, men nodded to one another with stern, determined expressions on their faces.

The crowd of men had shifted. They pushed closer to the courthouse porch without crowding, lining up at a table there.

Judge Graham, sat behind the table. Next to him sat the fat county clerk poised with pen over a paper. The first man stepped up.

"Name?"

"Hammond," the farmer announced himself.

"One dollar." The man held out a coin which the clerk snatched up lest it escape.

"For sheriff?" the judge asked.

"Osborn," the man answered. The clerk made a mark.

"For clerk?"

"Auxier."

And so the free white men of Floyd County exercised democracy. One by one, they paid the poll tax and voiced their choices. As each man uttered a name, I detected a moan of approval from the crowd. Gradually, the men divided so that Osborn partisans watched from one side of the small square, and Morgan supporters clustered to the other. The Osborn forces seemed to have the edge in numbers.

Then I noticed an interesting change in the voting. A man approached the table whom I would not have placed among the propertied class of the county. A farmer with land showed a certain order to his appearance. His trousers might be homespun, but he made an effort at mending rents. He possessed a clear eye and despite his modest means, he stood with an assurance that said, "I may not be rich, but what I have is mine and here I proudly pay the poll tax."

This new man was visibly drunk and obviously poor. He plunked down a coin under the watchful eye of a townsman I had seen among the Osborn deputation. As the strange voter leaned on the table, his escort mumbled to him each candidate's name, including that of Edward Osborn for sheriff. The untidy one repeated what he was told if a bit imperfectly. This pattern repeated itself, with few muttering Morgan's name. When I saw Draper swagger up to cast his vote for Osborn, unassisted, I realized that someone had bought the votes of those who did not have the tax. My master's enemies had purchased Ruth's hangman.

Collecting votes one by one is a tedious process, allowing the spectators to track the progress and to influence the necessary electors. Sponsors ushered forward their charges as room at the table appeared. From the Osborn side of the square one besotted man in homespun and moccasins taunted, "Looks like your man on his way out now. Things gonna be different!" This was met with grim stares from the other side and huddled conversations. I lost sight of Morgan.

"What you doin', girl?" Draper's voice startled me. I turned to find the filthy slave catcher in his tattered hat using the wagon that hid me to steady himself. Tobacco juice stained his beard, and I could smell that Osborn's liquor was no better than Morgan's. "Spyin' for your master? Well, you take a good look girl. You won't be spyin' much longer. Put you back in the field where you belong. You git!"

He started toward me, but Draper never managed walking and drinking with any success. I clutched Pirey close and hurried in the opposite direction bumping several horses in the process. I thought I had seen Brownie on the other side of the square. Brownie and Saul would be together. I had to double back behind the tavern and the houses to circle around the square, all the time alert to the likes of Draper and Osborn.

With some difficulty I found Saul with Brownie and True. Saul was oblivious to the election speeches and was more interested in talking horses with other grooms. Only the arrival of his wife and daughter pulled him away. Juggling the reins, Saul leaned over and kissed Pirey.

"Esther say to go to camp and start the fires. You have to show me where it is."

"Have to wait for Mas'."

"I don't get the fires goin', Esther strop me."

"Esther not goin' to strop you. I'll tell you where it is. Easy to find." He then described a grove of trees along creek that fed into the river. I would find the wagon there and Mrs. Morgan. I just wanted to get away from the crowd that so enthusiastically applauded Osborn, so I followed Saul's directions.

With only the thinnest understanding of politics and economics, I began to fathom these elements. They were nothing I could touch or feel, like the weather or hunger or fear, but they represented forces just as powerful. Like a child who first discovers that the fascination of fire held the possibility of pain and injury, I had just discovered that greed and hate hide dangerous risks as well.

Greed is a thirst of no unusual complexity. Its degrees range from simple ambition to intense avarice. It has a simple goal, and its success is easily measured if not consistently attained. One can count money or cattle or land or buildings. Everyone is greedy in some way, so it is a predictable drive.

Not as quickly grasped is the passion of hate. Hate burns with a flame unlike the coals of a forge or the glow of a stove. These fires are tools, useful and safe if managed well, dangerous if unattended or misapplied. Hate is a flame that flashes unpredictably, a spark in dry grass or a match in gunpowder. One moment it is small, easily held, extinguished with a breath. The next instant it explodes in the face to consume all in its reach. Edward Osborn showed me hate at work. Osborn hated Morgan.

I never firmly established the source of Osborn's enmity. The offenses purportedly committed against Osborn by Morgan numbered as many as the tellers of the tale: Morgan sold Osborn a splayed horse. But I know for a fact that Osborn knew horses. Morgan dishonored Osborn's father in some way during the Revolution. But Morgan was a mere stripling in the ranks against the father's seat on General Washington's staff. A woman. Politics. An insult. A debt. Like any war, once battle is joined, the cause is forgotten and only sorrow and pain are clearly remembered.

The county broke into the camps of Morgan and Osborn. Add to this the usual rift between Whig and Democratic Republican, Virginian and Yankee, Englishman and German, and you have a Tower of Babel spewing conspiracies and falsehoods. As best as I can recall, the factions broke out as follows:

Osborn saw the county full of estates with large houses and gangs of slaves to enrich the aristocracy, of which he saw himself a natural member. Morgan's vision involved small land owners and forges smelting iron with the coal that lay about so plentifully. For this he needed workers, slaves if they were available, but free men if not. Naturally, Morgan saw himself controlling all of this for the common good.

So I suppose it all boiled down to money, who had it, who did not have it, who wanted it, and why. Morgan had it. Osborn did not have it, and he hated Morgan for it.

Mrs. Morgan

I found the Morgan encampment easily, out of town, upstream. The bare, packed ground and fire circles marked visits by other travelers. The cart traces lay where they were dropped and the hobbled mule grazed nearby leaving the scene quiet. The cart with the tent and cooking gear tipped up, tongue to the sky as if resting on its backside. The wagon with the harvest had gone with Peter. The Morgan grandchildren visited their Spurlock cousins in town.

I was somewhat startled when I walked past an immense tree to find someone already in the camp. Mrs. Anna Morgan sat under the tree with her tan bonnet on the ground next to her. Strands of gray hair that had escaped from her long braid hung in front of her eyes. The skin around her mouth clung to some of the brightness of her youth as her face yielded to the wrinkles and jowls of age. She was so engrossed in the book in her hands that only Pirey's cry for a meal caused her to glance up.

"She sounds hungry," the mistress commented, her tone softer and kinder than her custom, suggesting to me that her journey in the book must have been a pleasant one.

"Yes'm. Esther want me to set the fire for supper."

"Feed your baby. We have time." I started to walk away when she told me, "You can stay here."

"Yes'm." Pirey was just fussing and not yet in need of milk so I simply rested just out of Mrs. Morgan's view, my back up against a cart wheel. I had been moving all day and was grateful for the chance to rest. The mistress's eyes dropped back to the book. After a few moments she sighed deeply, stuck a blade of grass between the leaves and closed the small volume.

She turned in my direction. "Did you see the election?"

I was taken aback, not only at the question, but at the source. I did not associate Mrs. Morgan with anything but caring for children and supervising a house. Then I recalled the woman at the landing who deftly manipulated the river man. Mrs. Morgan had talents, even secrets that I had yet to fathom.

"I see it, Missus," I told her.

"What happened?"

"Don't know, Missus. I leave. That Draper run me off. Maybe Mr. Osborn be sheriff?"

"I'm not surprised. He's been working at it. There are plenty of people who would just as soon see Mr. Morgan dropped a peg or two." Another shock. A white woman disclosing her thoughts to a slave. As often as I reported to Morgan, he never commented on the information I supplied or gave me more than I needed for my mission. I drew my own conclusions as to events, if I bothered to draw them at all. I wanted to know more from this woman. This was my real first appraisal of her face. Her eyes perfectly matched her new dress, the color of a summer sky just above the horizon.

"Mister Osborn talk," I said. "He talk hard about coloreds."

"What did he say?"

"Oh, he worried about coloreds off their places, makin' trouble."

"He would, now that he sold his hands away. Servants have to have their passes. You always have your pass, don't you Phyllis?"

"Yes'm. Always."

"Without that pass, you can be whipped. Mister Morgan can be fined."

"Yes'm." Pirey fell in to a deep sleep, so I tucked her in her blanket and set her safely in the wagon before I began a search for fire wood. Ours was a well-used camp, and it took some time to find all that I needed. A season of migration through the Big Sandy country fairly cleaned out the best fuel.

When I got back, the mistress was wrapping Pirey on the ground and talking to her softly. My baby reached for the gray hair that tickled her face. Instead of leaving Pirey to squeal until my return, she had cleaned my baby, a distasteful task for even the most devoted mother, and she added a soft word to an infant who knew neither race nor condition of servitude. I piled the wood where our predecessors had made their hearth, and with the tinder box I set a smoky fire.

"Get some beans going," Mrs. Morgan said. "We have some beef coming. Greens too."

"Fry up the beef?" I asked.

"In the pot. Some to roast maybe."

I pulled a pot off the wagon and went to the stream for water. I got the water on the fire and dumped in beans to soften. Then I began pulling other foodstuffs off the wagon – a bag of flour, meal, and a jar of molasses. I tended the fire and sat down to wait for the return of the rest of our party. As Pirey slept and Mrs. Morgan read, I resolved to risk some conversation.

"Make a good trade at the landing, Missus?"

"We had a good year. Everyone did. There's talk of a war, so prices are up."

"A war?"

"Yes, a terrible thing. It's just talk tough. Up north. Back East. I managed to get a book at the landing. It's been so long since I had a new book. Do you know what a book is, Phyllis?"

"Yes'm."

"What is it?"

"Uh…" Perhaps I had gone too far. "Paper."

"Yes. Do you know what's in a book?"

"Uh, don't know, Missus."

"It's a story. Instead of hearing it spoken, you read it."

That a story could somehow be contained in a stack of papers fit within my understanding. After all, the letters I carried for Morgan bore information. Why could not more elaborate ideas also be conveyed in this same way? That afternoon, the nature of a book or the implications of literature (those contemplations came in another decade) intrigued me less than in what all of this told me about my mistress.

"A story?" I was perhaps treading on dangerous ground by holding a conversation with her in this way, but her soothing voice and her open manner were almost intoxicating. I could easily find myself rebuked, or worse, for such familiarity.

"It's called *Charlotte Temple*, and it's about a young lady."

Much had been revealed to me over the course of the day, and I worked my brain to place Mrs. Anna Morgan into my existing categories for white people. I found that I had no examples to match to her. She was not like any of the tired farm wives or the snarling ladies in town. All the white women seemed to have some annoyance or unhappiness they endured. The first words in any conversation came in the form of a complaint. Complaining formed the principal means of communication among white people. White men greeted one another with comments about weather or commerce or politics and how bad they all are. There was too much rain, or too little. Sunshine threatened drought. Good crop prices signified impending collapse. White women complained about servants, their health, their husbands, and their neighbors. Slaves certainly found no shortage of things to complain about, which they did, with care, but looking at the world positively fit our custom more. The heat of the day flowed into the cool of the evening. Hunger ended with a good meal. Weariness led to rest. This lady did not complain. I had much to explore here.

"Where you learn to read, Missus?"

"My mother taught me, in Virginia."

"It hard?"

"Not with the right teacher. Not with the right books."

"You think I can read?"

"You probably could. But Mr. Morgan might not like that. I know that other folks wouldn't want it. Certainly our new sheriff wouldn't approve."

"Why that?"

"Oh, that's complicated. They might think you wouldn't be happy once you learned to read."

"Reading make me unhappy?"

She looked straight at me, as if measuring me. "I would say with certainty that learning to read would make you unhappy. Sometimes it's best not to know what's on the other side of the mountain. No sense wanting something you cannot ever have. You have your baby. You have your man. You have a good master. That should keep you happy enough. You don't need to have your head filled with ideas."

Another puzzle. Why would such a thing make me unhappy? Naturally, I now know the reason that literacy terrified the slave holders. I am living proof today that their fears were justified. A literate slave is more dangerous than an armed one. The slave who reads can acquire the knowledge to ask the questions about the justice of bondage. The learned slave has access to the arsenal of knowledge, ideas becoming the arms within. And the ideas can be shared, spread, grown, and sharpened. Weapons of iron can only intimidate and kill. The weapons of knowledge threaten only the unjust and kill only ignorance. Given the look of serenity and joy I saw in the mistress's face, she was very happy reading a book. That she could open those sensations by simply turning pages made the small volume magical.

A shout and laughter interrupted my contemplations and my inquiry. The other Morgan slaves approached in a loose and spirited group. Mrs. Morgan took up her bonnet and stood, brushing grass and leaves from her dress. She stepped around the big tree toward the river. She clearly did not want to appear to anyone as having some kind of intimate conversation with a slave. Peter led the parade. He carried Little Suzy in his hand. A string of people followed him, joyous with the boon of the day. The wagon followed led by one of the men.

"Phyllis," Daisy called, "we got a haunch for dinner. Set another fire."

She snapped an order at Peter for the andirons and broach. Only in matters of meals did Peter take orders from women. With one hand he reached into the cart and began to pull out the heavy iron utensils.

"Here, Old Peter," Simon said, "I'll take Little Suzy so's she don't fall and hurt herself."

"You the blacksmith," Peter told the freeloader, "you take these. You set 'em up over there where the girl's makin' th' fire. Little Suzy goin' to rest."

"Oh, happy to do it," Simon sang, "Happy happy happy." Notwithstanding his inebriation Simon palmed the irons as if they were mere twigs. He walked over to where I was blowing on the fire and with a single stab, planted one andiron deep into the hard ground. The other support followed a few feet away. The broach took the haunch which Daisy skinned and trimmed using the wagon bed as a table. The fat and some raw pieces went to the pot.

"And you help with the wood," Peter added realizing that he could make use of Simon's thirst. The blacksmith disappeared, anxious to please Suzy's keeper.

Other people drifted in, most tippled and tittering. But not Saul or Esther. They did not make it for supper, either, and I seemed to be the only one who noticed. Beans flavored with greens and beef, fry bread with molasses, and juicy roasted beef made for as fine a supper as we ever had. Peter's diligence prolonged Little Suzy's demise, no thanks to Simon's close ministrations. Pirey and I retired early to our blankets. The mistress enjoyed her own tent a distance away.

Those late to choose a dry bed awoke to the aftereffects of whiskey and a coating of chilly dew. Hands loaded what was left of the camp without any breakfast and our caravan made its way back to Beaver Creek absent any skipping and laughter. Even the dust kicked by bare feet and shod hooves hung low to the ground, as if held there by the knowledge of another year of toil. I kept looking back, hoping to see Brownie, since Saul would be close behind. Sim caught up with us and also appeared somewhat spent by his visit to town.

My husband did not return until that night. His body sagged onto the bed with the weight of two men and the troubles of Job.

"Mas' have trouble, I think," he sighed.

"Why?"

"It's about the 'lection. After Osborn 'lected sheriff, all Mas' friends seem to go away. Only Mister Lackey stay close. Mas' go to the tavern and men laugh at him. Low, no 'count men, but they all laugh. Even O'Hara laugh, but he drunk."

"Where Esther?"

"She stay in town. Bring the children along tomorrow." Saul's next sound was a soft snore.

Esther showed up the next day, but without the Morgan children. She was accompanied, or rather led, by the new sheriff Edward Osborn and by Draper, who contrasted with Osborn in almost every way. Osborn sported his fine coat and hat where Draper wore the common cloth of his class. Osborn easily controlled his fine steed in its graceful walk, but Draper had to kick his nag to keep up. The erstwhile slave catcher pulled a rope at the end of which Esther staggered, her hands bound in front of her. My teacher's usual confident and alert demeanor was replaced by the blank gaze of the prisoner. The effort at keeping up with two horses obviously wore her down. Osborn stopped near the big tree.

"Tell your master that the sheriff is here," Osborn snapped at Saul, whose duty it was to meet any visitors. "Tell him that I have business with him." Saul hurried off. Draper stopped his horse and gave his rope a tug, causing Esther to stumble, but she did not fall. A dozen pairs of eyes took in the scene from various corners of the farm where people stooped and sawed and sweated. That Esther came home in this way bode well for no one.

Morgan walked down from the house, his head bare. In his hand he clutched his riding whip, the strap looped around his wrist. Morgan stopped short of Osborn, careful to take a spot in the shade.

"David Morgan," Osborn announced, "you are charged with your nigger being off your property without a pass, in violation of the laws of the commonwealth. You are hereby ordered to post a bond of two dollars and to appear before the Justice of the Peace." Osborn's face never changed from its impassive mask. Draper grinned unashamedly.

"She was on my business. She was with my grandchildren."

"She weren't with nobody," Draper blurted out.

"Silence!" Osborn snarled at his minion. Then he turned back to Morgan. "You will be heard in court. Bond to be posted forthwith."

"I don't need to post a bond. I have property. I have more property than any five men in this county."

"The law requires the posting of a bond. Failure to post the bond requires that I take the prisoner into custody."

Morgan's face remained stone, but his color was up. He glared at Osborn a moment before saying, "I have the money. Wait here." The master returned and walked toward the mounted Osborn, holding out the coins. Osborn reached for the offering, and Morgan allowed the coins to fall to the ground.

Osborn spoke first. "Deputy Draper!"

"Yes, Sheriff?" No one within earshot moved.

"Mr. Morgan dropped his bond. Retrieve it on behalf of the court."

"Yes sir." The ruffian fell off his horse more than he dismounted. He scuttled over to the spot in front of Morgan and came up with a coin in each hand.

"David Morgan, you are commanded to appear before the Justice of the Peace at ten o'clock tomorrow morning." Osborn twitched a knee and his horse turned away. "And bring the nigger with you," he added without bothering to look at Morgan.

Draper untied Esther and scrambled onto his horse. The two men trotted off out of sight before anyone moved.

"Come here," Morgan instructed Esther. "O'Hara! I see any-one not working, you'll get stripes of your own." Every hand in sight jumped back to his task or disappeared. I found a pot and went to creek as quickly as I could.

Word spread quickly, in the usual way. "The white men go lookin' for her," Sarah reported. "Esther near Spurlock's and she got no pass. They lock her in jail. Say they goin' to strop her, but they want to strop Mas'."

The next morning, before dawn, Morgan on his horse and Saul and Esther on foot all left for town. Morgan returned by sup-per time and Saul and Esther were with him, but we all saw that something was dreadfully wrong. Esther slouched as if carrying a burden. My usually cheerful Saul stared at the ground, positively grim.

"They whip her," he whispered to me in our cabin. "She don't have no pass. The judge say he won't fine Mas', but he can whip Esther. Draper tie her to a hitch rail, and he pull up her dress. Over her head until she bare naked. He lay into her for ten. She cry and cry. All the white men laugh." No one could muster a question or a comment. Esther was a good slave. In many ways we all aspired to her station of respect and authority. To see everything strong and stable in our world brought down so easily and so quickly was a shock beyond comprehension. We all asked ourselves, what will happen to us now?

And so the new rulers of the county began to assert their power. Pressure on Morgan increased as Osborn and his allies looked to take what Morgan had, first politically, then materially. A cow strayed into a neighbor's corn. Fine of two shillings. Restitution to the neighbor. Osborn hounded squatters off his friends' land, but left them unmolested on Morgan's. White men no longer visited Morgan's to doff their hats, talk horseflesh, and offer deference. The extent of Osborn's corruption came clear when Draper took Walter in for not having a pass. He was driving some sheep to another farm when he was set upon by Osborn's new deputy. But Walter had a pass, duly written out by Morgan himself. Walter told Morgan that Draper tore up the pass and threw it away. Since no Negro could ever testify against a white man, Walter had no defense. This time the Justice of the Peace not only fined Morgan but ordered Morgan himself to lay the ten on Walter. Walter took it without a sound. Walter helped Saul build our first cabin and we felt his pain as our own. The indignities and reverses levied upon our master, and on us, mounted.

I was more fortunate. Whenever I ventured abroad, I kept a clear eye for Osborn's deputy. Morgan countered the corrupt deputy by making a fair copy of the pass to be secreted in my clothing. Should Draper tear up my pass, I could produce another in front of witnesses. But my missions abroad abated to one every two weeks or so. While in town, I did my business quickly and drove straight home without much in the way of intelligence. Servants who used to happily feed me gossip made me feel unwelcome and shared little. My master had lost his station in society and that extended to his property. Good bargains for food or goods became fewer. If I saw Draper, I hid like a hunted rat.

He stopped me one day as I drove the cart. His new duties suited him. He had discarded his filthy clothes and had acquired manufactured trousers and coat. He insisted on keeping his slouch hat though. Men are so funny about their hats.

"Gimme your pass, girl," he demanded. I complied with my heart in my mouth. Although Draper could not read, he could recognize a pass. He held it away from his body between his thumb and forefinger and said again, "Gimme your pass, girl." He then let it flutter to the ground, still soggy from a recent rain.

I jumped down from the cart to retrieve it. I imagined going to jail and being whipped. Would they let me keep Pirey? Who would feed her? I had the copy in my pocket, but Morgan had instructed me not to reveal its existence until I was in front of the judge. If Draper was to destroy the copy, he would have to do it in front of white witnesses. I held the paper up to him.

"Git goin', girl. I got no time to deal with you." He left me there holding the pass up and trying to catch my breath.

Osborn

But my good fortune was limited to avoiding Draper's perfidy. That tiny bit of dubious sunshine eventually darkened as well. Morgan could be counted upon not to endure the insults indefinitely and I am certain that his mind set to work as soon as he saw the election not going his way, perhaps earlier. Saul and I became tools in his plan for survival, resurrection, and retribution. Morgan's ill-starred scheme came in the early spring. Peter found me at the creek washing clothes. Pirey crawled about nearby.

"Back to your crib, girl. Mas' William want you." He hurried out of sight. I first thought that something might have happened to Saul so I felt relieved to find him there. But relief quickly shifted to concern when I noticed him collecting our few belongings, some clothing, a pot, and utensils. William Morgan sat his horse nearby.

"I shouldn't let you take the pot," William commented. "But you'll need it."

A great foreboding came over me which only increased as I saw the worry in Saul's face. He pulled the few items he could call his own into the middle of our blanket. He gathered the corners together and tied them. He hefted the bundle onto his back. The horror of the situation struck me like a mule kick. My husband was being sold! I screamed and ran to him.

"Nooooo!" I cried. "Please, Mas' William, Please. Don't sell my Saul!"

"Shut your mouth, girl," he ordered, almost conversationally, without any malice. William headed off down the road.

"We all goin'," Saul said softly, and he gently pushed me after the young master. I was so relieved that Saul was not leaving me that we had traveled some distance before the complete weight of these events struck me. We were all being sold. The farm that I helped build, that had been my home, and that caused me so much grief and so much happiness retreated behind me. Not a single one of the people who had been my community, for good or for ill, stepped forward to bid farewell. Just as Abner vanished onto the boat at the landing, Saul and Pirey and I vanished beyond the trees, invisible. Others would take our cabin. They would rather forget us than think of how they came to live there. Our names would not be spoken and no mention would be made around the fire of our absence, our past, or our future. Even a chicken killed for the pot was acknowledged for its contribution to the meal. Not so the slave sold away.

As I tramped alongside Saul, clutching his sleeve with one hand and my daughter with the other, I agonized over the future. I wanted to ask Saul what he knew, but the young master was too close. Would they keep us together at the landing? Where would the boat go? All the way to Mississippi? What awaited us there? Would Pirey be able to eat the food? Why us? Why me? I could not stand the mystery.

"Mas' William," I bleated like some stupid sheep, "where we goin'?"

"Being sold," was all he said.

Samuel Johnson said that knowing you are to be hanged in a fortnight concentrates your mind wonderfully. The forest that day bloomed with the new growth of spring. All the smells of the land, unnoticed until now because of their familiarity, came to me like expensive perfume. The high clouds complemented the beauty of the sky. The birds' euphony resonated in stark contradiction to my misery. The hide of William's horse held a certain grace even though it carried the means to my end. Sim trotted alongside us, but could offer little comfort.

150

I resolved to do all that I could to stay with Saul. We might be separated. For some reason I did not worry about Pirey, although I should have done. Traders pulled infants from their mothers' breasts and give them away or worse though I enjoyed ignorance of this horror. Had I suspected this possibility, I do not know what I would have done. Some mothers killed themselves after their babies were robbed from them. Some mothers killed their babies to save them lives as slaves.

Worry gave way to imagination. Perhaps we would go to a landed family who could make use of our talents. Saul was an experienced trainer. I could be a house servant. I pushed out of my mind the thought that we could end up as nameless members of a gang in cane or cotton or rice. Still, the specter of the disease-ridden west followed us. I glanced down and considered if Sim wanted to make the journey out west?

Where the track down Beaver Creek joined Louisa Fork, William reined right upstream instead of left down to Prestonsburg and the landing. The river narrowed here, and I doubted that boats would venture this far upstream. Curiosity overwhelmed dread. For hours, we followed that white man on his brown horse and I clung to all that was dear to me.

William pulled up at a farm only a little larger than one supporting a single family with no slaves. The barn was of bleached, rough-sawn lumber. The outbuildings that could have been slave cabins lay roofless. The house, constructed of better lumber than the barn but also unpainted and worn, had a broad porch and small windows with glass. Unlike the neat appearance of Morgan's, the implements of housekeeping and husbandry littered the ground around the house. A broken wooden rake and a sawhorse on its side lay in the dirt. Morgan insisted that tools find their place when not being used. This man seemed to drop his things at the moment they left his mind. Two scrawny dogs bayed at the visitors.

As we approached the house, I was shocked to see Edward Osborn emerge onto the front porch. He was dressed as one would expect of a farmer, not the dandified politician in town. Instead of tan breeches, he wore work trousers with braces. The candidate's cravat yielded to an open collar shirt.

"Good morning, Sheriff," William said as he touched his hat.

"Morning, Morgan," Osborn answered. "Fine day for some business."

"Yes, and some fine business too."

"I expected to see Mr. Morgan."

"Yes, well, you see actually I'm the seller here. These hands belong to me."

"Don't suppose it makes a difference."

"None at all, none at all." William swung down from the saddle and Osborn stepped down from his porch. They shook hands only cordially.

"Let's see what you have."

"Step up here," Morgan told Saul. Saul dropped the bundle and removed his woven hickory hat. Osborn looked at my husband critically.

"How about the woman?"

"Phyllis. And a fine babe too." William motioned for me, but I froze. He stepped over and grabbed my dress firmly to pull me towards Osborn. "She cooks for us. Good at tradin'."

"So I hear." Osborn regarded me and Pirey as if he had seen us for the first time. "Let's go inside." The men disappeared, leaving us to wonder. Nothing about the farm gave me encouragement.

After a time, William and Osborn reappeared, each with a paper. William folded his and placed it in his coat. Without so much as a glance or a nod at us, he mounted his horse and trotted off.

Osborn hooked his thumbs in his braces and announced, "You belong to me now. You are my property to do with as I please. To work, to feed, to whip, to sell. Don't you forget it."

Behind Osborn, a tired-looking woman appeared. Abigail Osborn was still beautiful, so unlike the other women for whom life on the frontier left them marked by toil and childbirth. A careful examination of her face suggested, not inaccurately, a less than complete understanding on her part of circumstances around her.

Several disheveled children, a boy and two girls, peered around her with no greater exhibition of lucidity.

Saul had the presence of mind to say just the right thing, "Yessah, ever'thing be fine. We get right to work."

"Thomas!" Osborn shouted. "Thomas!" From around the barn appeared a younger, leaner version of our new master carrying a bow saw. "Saul'll help you on that fence. Then he'll tend the stock."

Saul hefted the blanket containing our possessions and followed the youth.

"Girl," Osborn said, "I want some dinner. Let's see if you can cook."

I shifted Pirey and made my way around behind the house to the cook shed. Those who did not cook directly on the hearth inside the house, used a shack outside like at Morgans where an accidental fire would not destroy the house. In the foulest weather cooking moved indoors. At Osborn's the kitchen had an adequate stone hearth with just a rude roof and three walls, leaving the cook to crowd over the fire for any shelter. Thankfully, the hearth stood up off the ground to make cooking a little more convenient. I speculated that the slaves Osborn had sold possessed talent enough to add such touches to ease their labor.

I found a pot swinging from the crane wherein some meat of indeterminate origin and of no particular quality simmered in water. I tucked Pirey into a corner and went about making sense of this situation.

"It's dog," a voice behind me remarked. "We don't have dog much. Thomas shot it." My new mistress stood there not at all disturbed that some strange colored woman took over her kitchen.

"Yes'm." I answered. "You got maybe some 'taters or greens? I can also fry up some cakes." Mrs. Osborn pointed to another shed. I found some sorry-looking turnips and a few potatoes almost beyond use even as fodder. I sliced up the vegetables and put together some dough from meal and grease in the breakfast pan. In an hour, I had a handful of passable corn cakes and a stew that I would have been satisfied to pass up.

I lugged the pot into the house where six hungry people pushed up to the filthy table. Osborne dished out the contents leaving none for me or Saul or Pirey. It would not be the last missed meal at Osborn's. That I received no thanks or compliments for my work came as no revelation. I learned to gauge the success of my efforts by the absence of rebuke or punishment rather than mention of any approval.

The Osborn family consisted of the mother, the father, the eldest son Thomas, and three unattractive children ranging in age from four to twelve. Feeding this tribe kept me busy from dark to dark, and I never understood how they survived before my arrival. I imagine now that their fare was at best, simple, at worst, inedible. Not that there was a great variety of foodstuffs in that country, but with a little creativity by a competent cook, diners could greet mealtimes with some sense of expectation. When I was not engaged in actually preparing food, I foraged across farm and forest for anything that dressed up boiled oats, corn mush, corn cakes, and stews. Some simple snares in the forest provided a squirrel or even a possum to flavor the pot. I learned to prepare enough for my own family without appearing to rob the master's family and to certainly never eat better than they did.

"She not Thomas's mama," Saul told me about Mrs. Osborn. He got the story from Thomas, the oldest boy. "Thomas's mama die and the baby die. Osborn find Missus in Maryland or somewhere. And she have the other three. Thomas don't mind her. He miss his mama though."

To say she was dumb as a post would gibe many fine fences. I learned how to work with my new mistress, which was more like learning to milk a pretty new cow. Too simple for cruelty and too sweet for anger, Abigail Osborn took life as she met it. Little mattered before yesterday and less after tomorrow. A more pleasant, inoffensive member of the white race did not trod the dusty roads of that county. Mrs. Osborn took easily to influence without any sense of losing power, a critical element of intercourse with white people. I took particular care that the new master did not observe me when I invited the mistress to consider an alternative to dog in

the stew. He seemed ever on watch for some threat to his prerogative and to his authority.

Saul and I exchanged our warm cabin for a drafty shelter leaned
against the barn. Osborne's two old slave cabins had become a
chicken coop and a pig sty. Saul worked into the darkness to patch
the gaps and cracks of the lean-to to keep the wind out. Boughs
from the forest formed our bed. We improved the shelter until it
had walls of its own and even a tiny hearth.

"Mr. Osborn want to be a big horse breeder like Morgan."
Saul told me. "That what I do. The other white men bring their
fillies and colts for me to train. Mr. Osborn get money and he
have important men come to him 'cause he now the sheriff. Have
to add on the barn. Me and Thomas can do that. I see Thomas
with the stock. He got the touch. He watch me too. If I not careful, Thomas be the horse trainer. Thomas a good boy. Be a good
man. Say, did you see that Osborn miss a finger?" Saul held up
his index. "Got no finger on that left hand. Hard way to learn a
axe."

That first summer, Osborn's scheme ran its course. He boarded
three young horses, which he turned over to Saul. Saul could have
easily made each into an excellent saddle horse or a racer.

"He got me pulled in three directions," Saul whispered at
night. "He got me training horses, but he got me following him to
town. He want a groom while he be sheriff. And I got work here.
I goin' to tell him if I ride a colt to town with him, help train the
colt. I can't keep walkin' to town. Maybe he want to show the white
men I a good trainer. He like to show off to the white men in town
and aroun' the county. Got to be careful what I say though."

Slowly we accommodated ourselves to this new life. In spite of
the ostracism that we had endured at Morgan's, we both missed
the society of our fellows. Pirey learned to walk, but without the
kinship of children of her own race. No other woman watched
her as I hauled water and cut wood, as I worked the garden, and
as I cooked. Although Osborn used his whip sparingly he never
hesitated to complain and criticize. His children fared no better
in that regard than did we. Only Thomas seemed immune to cor-
poral punishment, largely I suspect, because he was old enough to

resist. The children and the slaves worked so that the master could strut.

One thing distinguished the Osborn family from most other white people I met. That was their shoes. Every one of them, man, woman, child, wore probably the best shoes in the county. Edward Osborn had one area of excellence, one skill which might have held him in good stead had he not aspired to another station. He possessed of a talent with leather, particularly in the crafting of shoes and boots. His father had apprenticed him to a cordwainer, and unlike so many young men so bound, he manifested a touch and an eye that might have found a safe home in an honorable trade. But Osborn saw his destiny elsewhere. Perhaps the only benefit of my bondage at Osborn's was the finest old shoes worn by any slave in Floyd County.

"Mr. Osborn like it when white men see my shoes," Saul told me. "Like his own boots and his saddle and his clothes. He shoulda made shoes instead of tryin' to be a farmer. Be better for us."

Sim stayed on with us, although why was beyond me. He placed import on being respected. If that meant being dominant, so be it, but he never sought to lord it over the other dogs. Naturally Osborn's inferior curs challenged him briefly, but Sim quickly sorted matters out with them. They easily accepted him as the smarter and stronger. If Sim ambled out to the woods his fellow dogs knew to participate at their profit.

From the very first, Sim avoided Osborn, demonstrating further the dog's good sense. I think that Osborn resented Sim because Sim was the only thing on that farm the he could not command or sell or whip. Ultimately Osborn ignored Sim, and Sim remained content to stay out of the man's way. Had they clashed I speculated that Osborn would lose yet another finger at least.

I would have thought that Sim would attach himself to Saul. Dog and man got along well enough, but when Saul went one way and I the other, Sim followed me. Certainly the scraps I threw aside influenced the relationship, but I like to think he saw more than morsels in our companionship. I counted on Sim to be near Pirey if I was not. If the youngest Osborn children tormented their lesser by throwing sticks and rocks, Sim protested. The brats turned their cruelty on swift and agile Sim, turning their insults into a game for him. They eventually bored of the sport which, thanks to the inheritance from their mother, came fairly quickly. Sim forgave too. He pitched in with the Osborn tribe to herd cows and sheep and pigs.

During my husband's absences, Sim became my best companion. Naturally, he could not speak to me, but I could speak to him. Stripped of my adventures around the county and the company of my race, I relied on Sim for what community I could claim. Abigail Osborn could not hold an extensive conversation, assuming she deigned to converse with a slave at all. And I had little to say to the children. So it fell to Sim to be my confidante.

"Did you see how that filly come along?" I asked Sim. "Need to get Saul or Thomas to pull in another log for firewood."

He had that keen canine ability to know when someone, two legged or four legged, approached the farm, and I learned in advance of any other human when Osborn received a visitor or when Osborn and Saul returned. I led myself to believe that Sim heard the animals of the forest whisper to him and he spoke back.

Sim also helped protect the farm from raids by stray dogs, raccoons, or other thieves. He knew enough to never directly challenge a raccoon, but he raised such an alarm to gather allies and make the masked intruder reconsider his foray. One time, Sim's distinctive "I've got a 'coon here" barking summoned Thomas and his gun to a successful kill just a few feet from the front porch. Under Sim's protection, the chickens who slept in the old slave cabin lived long enough to produce eggs and meat for Osborn's table instead of for some predator's litter. In very small ways, we all profited from that stray. Given later events, my family profited in very large ways.

"Mister Osborn learning how it is to be sheriff," Saul told me. "He get fine moneys for bringin' in squatters and stray stock. He got Draper to dep'ty for him now. Draper ride all over looking for fines. You should see Draper now. He got some fac'try clothes. But he only go after squatters on Osborn's friends' land, not on Mas, uh, Morgan's lands. All those rich white men that used to tip their hats to Morgan, tip 'em to Osborn now."

I gave birth to little Ben late in the summer. At Morgan's I had the benefit of a half dozen mothers to help me through the ordeal of childbirth, but that day only Saul comforted me. A baby was not a foal or a calf, so his skill found its limits. Althought having already borne a child gave me both knowledge of what I could expect I knew there was still danger. I told him how I needed one of the women.

Osborn was away at the time, a blessing. Saul approached young Thomas.

"Mister Thomas. Phyllis need help birthin' the baby. Maybe we get a woman from Mister Morgan's?"

"I don't know," he answered. "My Pa not here."

"Mister Thomas, she not get help she could die. Baby could die. A woman can help."

Thomas had to transport himself from being just another child worker to acting as a master and his father had done little to prepare him. But Thomas was a good boy and not without some faculties of his own. He had yet to grow to his father's height although his limbs seemed to want to reach their maximum extension as quickly as possible. His beard recently made its first appearance and his voice croaked. I watched the boy as he looked at me, then to the house, then back at Saul. Mrs. Osborn could not be relied upon to deliver even a slave child and that option never rose to any consideration. The simplest solution would be to send Saul off to Morgan's. We had the plow horse and Saul could return in a matter of hours. But Saul would need a pass and Thomas did not write. Thomas looked toward the stable, then across the gate to where the trail disappeared into the cane where he undoubtedly saw an adventure.

"I'll go," he pronounced. "You stay. Do the best you can."

In a trice, Saul had the horse out of its harness, into a bridle, and Thomas was up. Osborn never bothered to buy a saddle for anyone other than himself so the boy rode bareback. Saul ran to the gate and Thomas trotted through, his long feet hanging to each side. When he returned, he and the horse breathed heavily and he beamed with a sense of the challenge met and the challenge overcome so craved by men. I suspected that this was the first scrap of responsibility the boy had ever known. To him the Osborn farm must have been as much a prison as it was for us.

"Morgan'll send a girl."

"Daisy?" Saul asked.

"Yeah. She'll be along. She'll stay as long as she needs."

"Thank ye Mister Thomas," Saul said, "thank ye."

"Colonel Morgan says I did the smart thing, coming myself. He said I was a good man." Thomas used Morgan's militia honorific, nothing Osborn ever did. Morgan had apparently left an impression on the boy, as had the boy on Morgan. This should have given me a warning of another move in Morgan's plan.

Daisy walked in from the dusk with her bag of teas.

"Got another one comin'?" she asked, more to Saul than to me. In our lean-to she spread her worn hands over my belly and clucked approval. "Tomorrow. No reason you still can't get supper. Be good for you."

Ben was born the next morning and thanks to her potions and her soothing words the birth was uneventful. I was grateful for the attendance of another woman even though she limited her conversation to the matter at hand. She pitched in and served up a breakfast and a dinner to the Osborn family only to head out before nightfall. For supper I stood my post at the fire, my newborn at my breast. In the following months, Saul and I reached an unspoken agreement not to risk other children until our situation improved. Each of us bore this additional deprivation along with our other travails, but I had the advantage of that hard place inside.

A Gift of Apples

Sim informed me that Esther approached Osborn's. She had two bushels of apples, a gift from David Morgan to Osborn, which made a tasty cider. That, of course was not the true purpose of Esther's visit.

"Mornin', Missus," Esther sang to my new mistress.

"What?" As sweet a person as Abigail Osborn was, she adhered to the custom of whites never engaging in courteous conversation with Negroes.

"Mr. Morgan want Mr. Osborn to have some apples. I bring 'em."

Mrs. Osborn walked around the cart and examined some of the yellow and green fruit as if there was a possibility that she would reject the offering.

"Nice," she remarked exhausting her contribution to the transaction.

"Mr. Morgan say I just drop 'em off. We got plenty this year. Plenty." I watched Esther as she took in details of the Osborn farm, which, I might say, was in far better condition than before Saul and I arrived. Mrs. Osborn went back to some task and Esther led the horse around back. "How are you getting along, girl? I see you got more family."

"Alive. We all alive."

"I related to Esther our situation. She smiled at Pirey and Ben and regarded our lean-to sadly. The effusion of my thoughts and frustrations uttered softly and with my head turned so as not to attract any attention, came as a relief.

Esther helped me with the apples and we began cutting them for the press. We sat on the log that I used as a chair and work-bench and whittled the fruit into slices. Ben slept at my side. Just talking to someone while working was as pleasurable as any sensation as I could recall. Oh that I had just one other woman to converse with on that sad farm. Pirey eyed my visitor with some perplexity. At one time Pirey regarded Esther as another mother, but six months to a babe is a lifetime, and she approached the new stranger tentatively. Esther saw her quandary.

"Come, baby, come to mama Esther." Slowly Pirey came close until Esther could softly pull her close. "How's my baby? You get-tin' big now. A big girl. You got a brother." I could see that Esther missed the child who replaced the ones she had lost. Soon, Pirey overcame the strangeness and treated Esther as familiarly as she did me. I think she also found pleasure in another Negro voice. Esther filled me in on gossip from Morgan's. With Saul gone, the stock were not fairing quite as well. All the folks were in good health and exercised caution in wandering too far from the prop-erty. They knew that Draper ranged about the county looking to snatch a slave for the sheriff.

"They got a war," she told me. "Corn is up. Oats. Everything. They need horses too. Mas' been good to Osborn, helpin' him buy land and invest. Except Osborn don't have to pay any money. He sign papers promise he pay. He pay up after they sell and from bein' sheriff. This fall, when the crops come down to the river with the prices up, he do fine. Everybody do fine. Mas' just have to stay on the right side of Osborn. 'Til the next election.

"That how you come to be here," she explained. "Mas' sell you to Osborn, only it look like William sell you. Osborn and William, they don't have such bad blood. But Osborn don't have to pay. Not yet. He in Mas's debt. William's debt. That the way Mas' want it. When Osborn make his money, then he pay. But Mas' work it so that Osborn can't pay and you come back. Make Osborn look bad for next election. Maybe make him lose the land he got. Mas' got a plan."

"How long Saul and I got to stay here?"

"No tellin', no tellin'. I think Mas' want you all back. The Missus unhappy that he sell you off like he do. Real unhappy. White people so funny when it comes to ownin' other people. Buy, sell, whip, but sad when we leave."

"Missus don't whip," I corrected Esther.

"No, she don't," but white people still funny.

"I even miss Sarah and her guff."

"Osborn use his whip?"

"Not so bad. 'Bout the same as O'Hara, a swipe every now and then. Osborn mostly leave us here to work. The children work too. Thomas, he strong and fair. Osborn just treat us all the same."

"Thomas did a good thing when he come for Daisy. Mas' tell him so. It like nobody ever tell him like that before."

Esther made me happy. A familiar face in a forest of strangers, a refreshing voice in a desert of silence. I found myself relaxing for the first time in half a year. Even though I had my children and a husband to cradle my head in the smelly darkness of our drafty shelter, this connection with the outside world, with the idea of community fed a hunger so familiar, that I had stopped noticing it. Esther was poppy, easing my pain with the music of her words. No soldier, limbs shattered on the field of battle, ever experienced a greater relief from whiskey or laudanum. On the one hand I unburdened myself of what troubled me. On the other hand, my loneliness and isolation seemed to magnify. Had I grown up on the Osborn farm, far away from any society with my own kind, I would have been far happier. But having been exposed to the benefits (and the drawbacks) of society, my situation felt so much the worse.

"You keep your eyes open here."

"I don't see nothin'," I told her. "I don't talk to nobody. Here all day. Sometimes Saul go with Osborn to town, but he stay with the horse. You the first person I talk to since I got here. Except Daisy. I talk to Saul. And the babies. Not the same."

"You see who come. How they are. You see how the farm is. You might hear some things they say. How those yearlin's coming?"

"Saul been with Osborn in town and too busy with other chores to do right by the horses. He get them out maybe once a day. Not enough to bring 'em along good. He been showin' Thomas how he work. Thomas got a touch for it. Not like Saul, course. Someday I think."

"Sound like Thomas holdin' things up around here."

"Oh, maybe. Without him, our lives be hard. Hard. He keep the other children from picking on the baby. He keep them at work. Or away from work. He be a good master."

"Well, you watch. You listen. You never can tell what goin' to happen."

When apple slices filled two large pots, Esther climbed aboard the cart and started out. I walked alongside with my hand on the side just to have some last connection with the outside world. Then the vehicle lurched to one side and my fingers slipped away. As I watched Esther cross the stream and disappear into the cane, my isolation returned with a vengeance. The opium of her voice wore off leaving the pain from before and a sickness.

That was Morgan's plan.

Soldier

Fall gave way to winter and 1811 became 1812, although I knew nothing of calendars in those days. With our work and Thomas's willing help the farm managed to improve. We did not lose any stock and our fortunes improved. One market day, Osborn took his whole family to town along with Saul. This left the farm even lonelier than before, but I had less work to do and could actually rest. Or I could rest as much as a mother with two babies can rest. I spent the time tending to our own meager habitation, filling chinks in the wood with mud and finding shakes for the roof. Saul and I had talked about building a proper cabin before winter, but he felt he had to be politic with the new master in a matter such as this. We elected to wait until after harvest when the work slackened, to justify such a project to him. The coldest nights Saul prevailed upon Osborn to allow us to sleep on the floor near the hearth in the house.

Saul had already spotted some trees he could fell and buck, and he marshaled the other tools and wood that he would need. He had the skill and the knowledge, but with just the two of us a new cabin would rise slowly. We gave thought to building a chicken coop to allow us to move into the old slave cabin the chickens used. Maybe Thomas would help.

I expected the family before dusk and as the day waned, I set a pot for stew. At almost dark Sim told me that the family returned. Osborn rode his horse out of the cane followed by the wagon filled with Osborns, driven by Saul. I noticed that Thomas was not in the seat as was his custom but I paid it no more mind. I returned to my work in the cook shed, putting the pan with the corn cakes nearer the fire to warm them.

The Osborn children disembarked from the wagon, but without the usual bickering, a peace I ascribed to exhaustion. They visited town but once or twice a year and such stimulation tired them. Osborn wore his customary dark countenance. In a few minutes I deposited the stew and the cakes on the Osborn table and retreated as they fed, so many two-legged hogs. Thomas had yet to join them from helping Saul stable the horses. Saul joined me at the hearth outside to share that portion of the stew I held out for us.

"Thomas gone," Saul told me after his first bite of dinner. "Gone to the soldiers."

"The soldiers?"

"Up north. They have soldiers in town with nice uniforms. Blue. With pretty gold. Never seen such clothes. And a drum. Beatin' on the drum. And a flag. They want men for the war. Some other boys, they come to Thomas, get him to go with them. Some white men talk to him too. Mister Osborn not happy. Thomas and Mister Osborn argue, but Thomas go anyway. Marked in a book. The other boys got guns. Thomas don't have a gun, but the boys find him a gun. They won't let him join up without a gun. The soldier in blue, he showed how them to march with the drum."

I had little understanding of wars and soldiers and fathers and sons and how the events of the world could reach down and touch me. That horrible knowledge came years later to my great suffering.

"Mister Osborn, he argue with the soldier, but the soldier say Thomas can go if he want to. The other boys, they tease Thomas. They say he not a man. They off to get the glory. Kill Injuns. Kill redcoats. They talk about lots of glory. What this glory? They don't tease nobody else. Mr. Osborn, he say he put the soldiers in jail, but he can't do that. People watch them fight. Well they don't really fight. They just argue. Mr. Osborn, he have to back down and he don't like that. His son go off to the soldiers and he shamed in front of the town. Not sure what hurt him more."

166

"Who goin' to help us here?" I wanted to know.

"Nobody, I guess. Just us."

Saul was right. Without Thomas's hands and back, his work doubled. The other Osborn children could herd and pick, but the hard labor fell onto Saul and me. More importantly, Thomas had kept his brothers and sisters to their tasks. Children need as much attention as slaves when it comes to labor. Mrs. Osborn could never comprehend the role of child overseer, and slaves do not give orders to the master's children. I missed Thomas already.

It fell to Osborn to return to the direction of his farm. But he had tasted the sweet wine of celebrity and then the vinegar of public disgrace. He would much rather have spent his time riding about the county, frightening poor squatters and solitary Negroes, collecting fees, and being recognized. The attraction of his office and his desire to recover his image proved too strong for him to replace Thomas's efforts entirely. He rode off at least once a week to leave me all the work to Saul and me. Slowly, the small prosperity and weak efficiency that had evolved over two summers atrophied. Chickens ran wild until they could not be lured back into their hutch. Despite Sim's protection many fell prey to the denizens of the forest. Sim knew not to feast on the chickens otherwise Osborn would just have shot him. Cattle and pigs wandered until the sheriff himself became subject of a complaint from a neighbor before the Justice of the Peace.

"The horses almost go wild again," Saul moaned. "I got no time to work them. I got no time to work just one."

One owner rode to Osborn's to claim his property, looking forward to profiting from Saul's tutelage. The horse might as well as been entirely unbroken. When Saul finally got her saddled, she became impatient and almost threw the boy brought in to race her.

"Edward," a white man told Osborn, "this cannot stand. I agreed to pay you twenty dollars to make this filly a champion. All I have here is a wild horse. This is worse than a wild horse. I will not pay."

"Isaac," Osborn answered, "she's just nervous. My boy works this horse every day. He did. Thomas helped him. My boy here's the best trainer in this country. He's been sleeping when he should have been working. I'll take it out of his hide, I promise you."

"Your boy's stripes ain't worth twenty dollars to me. They ain't worth a farthing. I don't care what you do with him. But this horse is nowhere near a trained racer. I want my horse, and I'm not paying you."

"Isaac, the filly just needs to calm down. I've seen her run. She's a winner. That's just spirit."

"Not from where I stand, Edward. We made a bargain. Twenty dollars for a runner. Do we have to take this to town? I know you're the sheriff, Edward, but twenty dollars is twenty dollars."

And so the men contended. The boy with the owner managed to bring the filly into line somewhat, but even I, no particular student of any horse, could tell that the animal remained unruly and undependable. When Saul got her by the bridle and spoke in her ear, she behaved, but the jockey did not express any trust. What deal the white men struck, I could not tell, but the owner departed unhappy leaving Osborn unhappy.

Saul and I both knew what was coming. The gloom gathered over the Osborn farm like the darkness in the sky just before the wind of a thunderstorm. I tried to work, but Saul's screams reached across from behind the barn. Each cry recorded one stripe across my husband's back. Each cry cut a piece from my soul. After three, I could not count. It could have gone ten, or twenty, I do not know. His screams hammered me, one upon the other, as if I too were being beaten. When I saw Osborn return to the house, I felt relief knowing that Saul's pain was over. I waited until Osborn was inside before I ran behind the barn. I found Saul, his arms tied wide to a fence rail, his back raw. He still stood on his own, but his head rested on his punishment bar. My fingers fumbled at his bonds until his arms fell free. For the first and only time in my life, I saw my husband cry. His deep sobs spoke of pain and shame and despair.

Osborn apparently stopped his assault as soon as he drew blood, so the wounds healed without leaving scars. This did not lessen the insult to Saul, having been punished for his master's own poor judgment. Nothing could address the despondency that weighed down both of us.

Had Saul been kicked by one of his horses or mauled by a bear, either would have been injury enough. But such wounds were the results of natural things, animals doing as Nature and God had designed, nothing more than misfortune. Saul's pain and our situation were not the work of God or of Nature. Here the hand of Man swung the whip, as guided by the infernal one himself. For the kick of a horse, Saul needed only to be careful the next time. For the bite of a bear, we stayed clear of the monster's domain. There was no fleeing the master, though, not ever. This was our life. We worked, we shivered, we starved, all so that we could be punished and starved again. This was how we would spend the rest of our lives and how our children would spend their lives, joy being the absence of pain.

Thornton's Lick

Esther arrived at Osborn's in the cart bundled against the weather, her familiar face the warmth of the sun after a cold night. When she did not come immediately and greet me, I felt offended. Was she not going to speak to me? Was there more bad news? Her duty required her to seek out Osborn with the letter from Morgan. Osborn called me to him to reveal the contents.

"Mister Morgan is sending hands up to Thornton's Lick for salt," he told me. "Go along. I want you back in three days. Longer than three days and... Just don't be longer. I need you here." He went to the house to write a pass on Morgan's note. I experienced an odd sense of gratitude to Osborn my tormenter for allowing me out of his thrall for the company of a dear friend. I stole a few moments to tell Saul as he repaired a fence. He nodded with approval that his wife and children might flee the bitterness for a few days.

Osborn had no desire to care for slave babies, so I took them with me. Esther helped with dinner and loaded empty kegs for the salt coming back to Osborn. The sooner I got the family fed, the sooner I made away from that place. The Osborns slurped and grunted over their midday meal as we headed out, the children tucked in blankets between the salt kegs. Esther and I walked alongside the cart. Sim followed occasionally casting off into the forest after some hapless rodent.

A holiday feeling caused me to giggle drunkenly, a sense of wonderful release having washed over me as if I walked through a waterfall. I was back with my old friend and my teacher, away from my dreary life. I could not stop chattering like an angry squirrel. Esther just listened and answered my questions about the people I knew. Sarah lost a baby. Peter got kicked by a mule, but was recovering. Mrs. Morgan came down with the ague for two weeks. The Morgan children had it too, but not so badly. None of our people caught it. The war up north improved crop prices. Word of a terrible battle up north told of many Kentucky men dead. The slave trader, Norton, was back in town. When Norton was around, Draper became particularly active looking for Negroes away from home.

"Thomas go off with the soldiers," I told Esther in a desire to offer some news of my own.

"He march off up north," Esther told me. Leave it to Esther to know more about my master's family than I did. "To Ohio. To Canada. That battle might've been him. You know Mas' get those boys to join up. He give those boys whiskey. He told them they get more if they get Thomas to join up too. He even get the gun for him. Mas' spot the boy when he ride up to our place when Ben come."

Another Morgan scheme, this one to slyly undermine Osborn by robbing him of his most valuable personal and economic asset. The plan was simple and it was brilliant. But it threw more work onto Saul and onto me and further impoverished our lives. Even though Morgan no longer owned me, he managed to find a way to hurt me and those I loved.

"Thomas the only good white boy there," I told her. "Now we do his work too. Osborn have to work and watch us and watch his children. I like it better when he off bein' sheriff."

"And when he watchin' you and his children, he not watchin' Draper." Esther almost spat the name of the vagrant deputy who terrorized the poor. "Draper doin' his own sheriff business now. Collectin' his own fine money. Not bringin' it to Osborn. Draper just a stealer."

"Mister Osborn find out, he whip Draper."

"Osborn prob'ly won't find out. People think it Osborn got Draper doin' it. Least, that's what people think. Hate Osborn for it."

"Why they think that?"

"Mas," was Esther's only reply.

After two years at Osborn's, the stirrings of intellect along with my fascination with politics began to take form again, like a summer rain shower on grass gone brown.

"Mas' want to be sheriff?" I asked.

"Don't know. Don't think so. But Mas' workin' to make sure Osborn not sheriff. Make sure Osborn not nothin'."

"Then we come home?" The glimmer of hope for an end to our ordeal was almost painful.

"Don't know. But I think you be comin' home sometime. Sometime. Don't know when. Just don't know." I suspected that Esther did know, but since all I cared about was getting us clear of the Osborn farm, I would have believed anything. I just wanted my cabin back and to be warm and safe. Then Esther changed topics. "Saul ever talk about that old Injun?"

I had to struggle to recall. "Rabbit? He had a Injun name. I forget. But it mean rabbit."

"Where he live?"

"Saul never know. Somewhere back in the mountains. Maybe the lick."

"Why he think that?"

"Well, Rabbit always have salt to trade. One time, one of the Harmon boys see Rabbit's tracks up there, goin' back up the hollow. I guess he know Rabbit's tracks. Saul figure he have a cave up there. Why, Morgan want him too?"

"No. What else Saul say?"

"Just that Rabbit's people gone. He know where they gone to, but he can't go there. Some problem with his people, he think. Thrown out maybe."

We went first back to Morgan's to pick up Sarah and her husband, Amos. He loaded several axes and pots and more kegs for the salt, plus victuals and some sailcloth. In less than an hour, all of us were on our way into the wilderness above Morgan's. The salt lick was tucked back up a narrow hollow along a game trail little widened by human use. A sterile pool bereft of reeds or cane greeted us. White crystals collected around the muddy edge pocked by thousands of animal tracks. We collected what salt we could without including rocks and dirt. The best salt bringing the best price came from reducing clean water. Dirty salt went to the slave cabins, so we exercised great care in our work. We strained this salt through the sail cloth.

By dusk, each pot boiled brine over a long fire. Tending the fire and pouring in more brine required little effort, allowing us time to relax and to talk. Amos's artful axemanship produced a day's worth of wood in little more than an hour. Lucky for him that the lick had not been used since the fall so he had good, dry wood near at hand. For dinner we had a possum stew flavored with fresh wild greens and roots. Esther prepared much more than I thought we needed, and we could not finish it. That night, we took turns keeping the fire up and dumping in more water to boil away.

Sarah's incessant babble, once such an irritant, sang to me as familiar, sweet music. I even engaged Sarah in some good-natured banter, but being isolated for so long, I was no match for her wit, honed by daily use. Like any muscle left long unused, my tongue had withered and I felt as stupid as simple Jack. Ben seemed to grow a little in the hands of the other women. He looked up at Sarah when she held him and laughed at her inane blather. The new surroundings and the new voices fed his little mind with tasty nourishment. Amos doted on Pirey. The glow of good society wrapped me in a soft, warm blanket.

Esther seemed distracted. She answered any questions with curt responses or none at all allowing Sarah to expand on topics about which she knew little. Esther watched the woods as if she expected to be pounced upon by a panther. Late into the night, Sarah talked herself to sleep leaving just the crackle of the fire. Esther and I remained awake, I because I did not want to miss a moment of this pleasant time and she for her own reasons. In the magic of the fire and in the silence, my reverie subsided as I drank in the totality of my life and the events of the past year.

As I clutched my blanket and stared into the coals of the dying fire, Sim stirred with a particularly sinister growl. His hackles went up like I had never seen before. My first reaction took me to where Ben and Pirey slept and I made ready a firebrand. Should the animal come too close, I would snatch up the burning wood and make him sorry he did not just have a lick of some salt.

Esther stood but did not go for fire or a weapon. She stared into the darkness alert with her hands open. I saw a bear appear, just his outline, standing on his hind legs, as tall as a man. I took hold of the wood in the fire. I knew not to swing it until the enemy was upon us lest the fire on the brand go out. I resolved to plunge the fire into his mouth, thinking not at all of my own safety and his powerful claws. I hoped that Sim would join my attack.

But the bear turned into a man, a man whose appearance shocked me no less than a bear's. Although no bear, he was still a stranger, so I kept my fingers on the burning stick. Sim's growling abated, but he kept his head low and stayed next to me, his eyes on the visitor. The rest of our party slumbered on.

"Pata-lani," Esther stated calmly, soothingly, using the name I could not remember. "Friend."

The shabby figure stepped closer into the light, and I saw my first Indian. The apparition wore rags and bits of skins, nothing could I characterize as a specific item of clothing. His homespun leggings, a different color for each leg, stretched up his thighs and disappeared under an apron. His shirt was a sort of shawl, but sewn under the arms, giving his arms the appearance of wings. Shabby as the shawl was, it bore interesting patterns embroidered with no mean skill, nothing I had ever seen any white man or slave display. His features were very different than Esther's, thinner, just not as thin as a white man's.

"Food," Esther said, pointing to the pot on the ground near the fire. She hefted it by the bail, for by this time it had cooled, and set it out toward where he stood. Then she held out a wood spoon. He stepped forward and took the spoon, then the pot. We watched as Pata-lani, also called Rabbit, cautiously slurped up the remains of our dinner. Finally, he tipped the pot to get the last stew, set down the pot and stepped back into the night.

"That the Injun Saul tell me about?" I asked Esther.

"Yeah, that him. We see if he come back."

"Tonight?"

"Maybe. But tomorrow for sure. We make sure he has somethin' to eat. Phyllis, I'm going to sleep. You watch the fire and you keep them pots full. If you want to sleep, you tell Sarah."

I tended the fire all night and my children slept off the exhaustion of their excitement. I stared into the flames and let the joy of the moment shove aside any past or any future. For a slave the past is a few good memories amid so many bad times. As for the future, the slave has little prospect. I looked forward only to another day of companionship and relief from the sharp tongues and dull wits of my owners. If nothing else, I had more salt-making trips to look ahead to – a few days a season when I might enjoy moments of solitude, comfort, and fellowship such as this. Closer toward dawn I woke Sarah who complained weakly, but did not resist. I slept through to full light.

Rabbit reappeared later in the morning with four fat grouse. In the daylight, he looked no less horrific in his costume, but I could see from his expression that he represented no threat to us. The scars on his cheeks, some sort of Shawnee decoration, intrigued me. Some Africans bore similar marks, but home-grown Negroes did not continue the practice. Without a word, Rabbit squatted and began plucking the birds as expertly as any cook. Feathers drifted in the air and Pirey, at first terrified by the apparition from the forest, ran after them with glee. As he finished each bird, he tossed it at Esther's feet and she cleaned it with her knife. Sim made short work of the innards. Rabbit rigged a spit and soon the grouse dripped fat onto the coals giving our camp the aroma of roasting meat. Amos and Sarah kept their distance, not quite sure what to make of this strange being.

Rabbit knew some English, there being no one left in the district who spoke his own language. Esther introduced all of us by name, and he seemed to understand that we came from Morgan's. She pointed to me and Pirey and said, "Saul, horse man."

Rabbit beamed and asked, "Saul here?"

"No, Osborn's," she replied. "Saul woman," she explained as she pointed to me.

"Good horse man."

Esther took up a stick and stepped over to some mud. She then began to draw the streams and rivers of Floyd County that I recognized from earlier demonstrations. "Morgan," She stuck the stick at the mouth of Beaver Creek. "Prestonsburg," took another point. She waved the stick over the marks. "Kain-tuck-ee," She extended the lines north until she drew two lines to represent a much larger river. "Ohio."

"Ohio. Shawnee. Home," Rabbit nodded. Soon the two of them jabbered away in a mix of English, sign language, and marks in the dirt. They only stopped talking for Rabbit to eat roasted grouse or for Esther to keep the rest of us at the salt.

Rabbit left for a time and returned with a squirrel and a rabbit for our supper. Sim easily took to the stranger. Both of them were cut from the same wood, smart, independent, and resourceful. I felt a flash of jealousy when my companion Sim paid so much attention to the hunter, but I reined in my sense of possession. Sim was not my dog. He was not anyone's dog. He made his own decisions. By dusk, little more than scattered feathers, bones, and bits of fur remained of the animals.

Rabbit and Esther resumed their strange discourse. I tried to follow it and paid particular attention when Esther retrieved the cloth bag which she opened to reveal her accumulated notes on cartography. She laid it out next to the marks in the dirt and used tobacco juice to copy what she and Rabbit had drawn. This version included more details farther away – the Great Falls of the Ohio and more rivers, some flowing from the north, some from the south.

"Shawnee?" Esther asked again.

"Shawnee," Rabbit said, pointing north of the Ohio. He moved his stick below the Ohio. "Chickasaw. Shawnee." Esther marked her scrap of cloth. On went the exchange and Esther added more animal blood to the design until she had, I later realized, a simple but not inaccurate version of the rivers that drained the Valley of the Ohio and the trails that intersected them. I drew closer to gather more of the exchange, and Esther reminded me that I had salt to make.

"Mississippi?" she asked. Rabbit dug a deep furrow far to the left of the rest. Obviously, Esther's understanding of the lands to the west held great importance to her, but I could not comprehend why. The only place of interest to slaves, aside from their own neighborhood, lie vaguely north, and that was as remote as Africa or heaven.

After the second night we had filled three iron pots and four kegs with good, clean salt. We filled the cook pot last. Everything loaded into the cart and we headed back down to Morgan's.

"Why you want to go to Mis'sippi?" I asked Esther as we walked along.

"Hush."

"Why go to Mis'sippi?"

"Maybe Mis'sippi where I *don't* want to go to."

What a puzzle. We unloaded the cart at Morgan's and the two of us took the cart back to Osborn's with his salt. The weight of reality once again found my shoulders. The brief interlude had ended, and I returned to the life of a slave.

William Morgan came loping up the road from the direction of Prestonsburg. His unbuttoned coat flapped open and his mother's blonde hair bounced with the motion of the horse on his uncovered head. Esther clucked to the horse to pull the cart to one side, and he gave us no more of a glance as he rode past than he gave to one of the trees in the forest.

"Mister William still leavin' his hat everywhere?" I asked.

"Mister William leave hats all over this county." It won't be long before you start seein' another baby wearin' one."

"Boy baby anyway," I laughed. "Maybe the girl babies wear 'em too so the brothers don't marry the sisters."

"Way he's goin', won't be any but brothers and sisters here 'bouts."

In my scouting missions for Morgan, it never occurred to me to report back on the sightings of William, generally in the vicinity of women, some with husbands away. The county never truly suffered any real danger of population by William's issue, but he did have a

178

way with isolated wives for whom a well-dressed and charming visitor proved irresistible. I do not know what suspicions a husband might have about an extra blonde child, but in Floyd County such families enjoyed a certain sufferance in repayment to Morgan for loans or land purchased. William's reputation with his fists and a knife precluded any of the traditional redresses available for tarnished honor. At the affected farms a switch to the offending spouse supplanted a duel. On the frontier survival meant more than honor and a healthy child outweighed bloodlines.

We arrived back at Osborn's in time for me to reassemble the kitchen from three days of misuse by the mistress, and I got a supper going. Saul stole away from his work to hug me and his children. Edward Osborn was off being sheriff, so I was greeted only with the complaints and insults of his hungry children. Mrs. Osborn expressed no interest in the two kegs of salt. Once I fed the family, I retreated to our hovel. In the dark, our lives settled back to dreary normality. The possibility of more salt trips softened the drudgery of my future.

A Pot Upended

That winter of 1813, we stayed alive. Cold and work met us at every turn. Like a pack of wolves which has trapped hapless sheep, the winter weather circled us waiting for an instant of inattention to move in and kill. I was never warm. I could be less cold, but I was never warm except while hovering over the hearth. The hardest time was with Saul at night, our children huddled between us. As anyone who has ever slept with children knows, such rest is fitful at best. Little ones fuss and cry and wet. I could roll one way, away from Saul and Pirey and Ben, and my back froze. The other way, and it was my face that suffered. I rested, but I did not sleep. I do not think I slept at all for months. Our small hearth did little to warm us. Without any way to draw off the smoke, we almost suffocated.

When the late storms hit us full on, cooking moved indoors around the hearth. This was good and bad. I was out of the wind and the rain and the snow as were my babies, but so was everyone else. I had to work around the Osborn children who sought the same precious warmth that I did. They became quite skilled at sliding in to the open space I needed to tend to a pot. Should the fire wane it was I who went outside to buck and split more wood. In Thomas's absence the children abandoned his cautions against tormenting the slaves. And Osborn could be counted upon to add his own irritation to any interaction.

181

Large soggy snowflakes melted on the ground as soon as they landed. Saul and I rose before dawn. He shuffled down to the stable while I got a pot of hominy going and fried up eight pieces of salt pork. Ben wheezed in his bundle at my side. But my constant movements only unsettled him and exposed him to more cold. I tried to wrap him together with Pirey, but she pushed him away, and she was too young to be scolded by me effectively. The human-legged hogs gathered at the table and carped at me to serve them breakfast.

When the pot of thick hominy was ready for humans, I hefted it off the crane using a rag against the hot bail and balanced it with Ben's weight. The route between the hearth and the Osborn table was just a few steps. But the effects of cold, Ben's weight, and the hot pot effectuated a confluence of factors that caused me to overlook a mallet left on the floor.

The result was a graceless tumble, losing both my baby and the family's breakfast. I cried out the instant that I lost my footing. Ben slipped away and the pot started its mindless descent. Ben landed safely, due to his heavy blankets, but I delivered the pot to the laws of gravity and misfortune. I howled not at any possible injury to my child or because of any concern for the family's meal, but with the knowledge of a white man's malice that was certain to follow.

The master's breakfast spilled across the floor, some of it draining through the ample cracks in the flooring. Osborn jumped to his feet and set upon me before I could rise and salvage anything.

"You stupid cow! That's my breakfast! Can't you even walk?" He then laid into me with a switch that he kept in the house for his children. I clutched Ben close to me and all the master's blows struck my sides and back, well padded against the weather. Had he used his riding crop I surely would have taken on some scars, but the lighter stick did not leave marks. It was my good fortune to earn a beating proximate to the less lethal weapon. The thrashing served more to vent his rage than to have any real effect on me. Nonetheless, I felt every stripe.

Osborn must have realized that time spent flogging me was minutes lost in recovering what could be saved of the meal.

"Quick, girl! Get up! Pick this up! At least some of my children shall eat. You shall not."

I scrambled to my knees, even laying Ben aside in order to use both hands. I scooped and shoveled into the pot what of the hot, sticky mess I could, managing to save about half. Flecks of dirt made their way into the food. Since I made no practice of having clean hands to prepare my master's meals, who can tell what else was imparted to the Osborn breakfast? I presented the salvaged meal to a cacophony of complaints and insults from three Osborn children, members of an enraged mob, each reinforced by the insults of the others. Even the youngest, not more than six, joined in, although I question whether she understood what she was doing. Mrs. Osborn spooned up equal, but reduced portions, the master served first.

"I sorry, Mister Osborn. I trip on that hammer," I told him.

"You wouldn't have tripped if you put down that bastard brat," he snapped just before shoving a spoon into his mouth.

"Baby sick, Mister Osborn." At that point, Ben let out a deep, wet cough one would credit to a child three times his size.

"Get that...thing away from my family," Osborn commanded. I took a corner of the filthy blanket into which I had wrapped Ben and tried to wipe the snot from his nose, only to leave bits of cooked corn in its place.

Osborn let out a sigh and slowly shook his head, his eyes closed. Although I never, ever will bring myself to sympathize with a man like Osborn, I saw that his world had closed in on him. On a bleak March morning, his meager breakfast arrived tainted in dirt in a house only a little better than some squatter's. The master horse trainer whose skilled hand was going to guide him into the local gentry failed, through Osborn's own missteps, to deliver. The gang of slaves he envisioned tending to his every need turned out to be a clumsy woman and a convulsive child. The lofty position of sheriff had its honors and benefits, but earned him at least as many enemies as it did friends. Instead of a talented posterity, he found himself surrounded by whining, sniveling, needy underlings. His one son who could have helped him push his ambitions beyond his front gate marched around in snow up in Ohio. The hominy that dripped through the boards of his floor surely represented his plans for power and wealth and respect. Whether his failures were the result of his own ineptitude or the machinations of others, his despondency ran just as deep. I had no intimation how his deep melancholy would injure me.

The Osborn children fed with their customary gulosity. I often remarked to myself the similarity between them and animals at a trough. Mrs. Osborn, her head covered with a shawl against the cold, stared at the table and ate slowly.

"I make some more, Mister," I told Osborn. "I make some more right now."

"Your breakfast is under the house," he told me. "And your dinner too."

"Yessah. I make more right now." I retrieved the now clean pot from the midst of Osborn's ravenous tribe and huddled over the fire. The pieces of salt pork, my own piece included, helped to calm the rancor. I ran to draw more water and puffed hard to get the fire up again. It was almost an hour before I had a suitable meal, this one without the fat. The diners were no less noisy and insulting, but they got fed.

Gone

Ben was better, I was better, and the rain and snow had stopped. Saul left with Osborn the day before. Despite Osborn's sharp tongue a trip to town meant Saul had only to keep up and to care for the horse. I ached for my husband's warm arms and soothing voice the night before. I consoled myself with the thought that Saul would have a night in town where he could talk with other men while Osborn went about his business. I pictured him outside the tavern joking and bragging with other men. Saul did not gossip, but he brought back some entertaining stories. I saw in my mind his bed in the straw of a horse stall, warmed only by Osborn's horse.

We needed soap. One thing I will say for sweet, simple Mrs. Osborn, she was clean and she tried to keep her children clean. For myself, I found that cleanliness, washing my hands and face in particular, gave me a certain sense of value, not to mention comfort. I applied this practice to Pirey and to Ben too. It was no mystery to me why those who did use soap helped to avoid the spots and sores that poor people seemed to attract. Soap making was a regular chore.

We had a hopper of wood with sloping sides used to make the lye. I filled it full of ashes, then water. Corn shucks and straw kept it from leaking. The water soaked slowly through the ashes and drained liquid out the bottom into a pot. That was the lye. If it stayed on my hands too long, I got a burn. I boiled the lye and added fat, pounds of it, whatever I had collected. The fat melted into the hot lye. I stirred this into a syrup.

Seeing the rancid yellow waste transform into something useful gave me a minor sense of accomplishment. I even lost myself slightly in it, watching the bits of grease crumble in the thick soup, bits of waste magically becoming something useful.

I planned dinner and supper in my head. With my work over the past year, the garden produced a wider variety of food – snap beans, pumpkin, sweet potatoes, and peas. I managed to put up much of these. The pumpkins I cut through the middle and hung the circles to dry. The sweet potatoes I boiled and skinned and dried. With Mrs. Osborn's help and some of the children, we strung green beans on thread and hung them out of the sun to dry. Peas we dried in the sun. I transformed the Osborn root cellar into a cornucopia of tastes and smells. This coming year, I wanted to try my hand at pickling, but that required salt. That meant another trip to Thornton's, something to look forward to. The only way to get sulphur was to trade for it, and I considered how I could suggest that to Osborn. Thomas would have been a good avenue, but Thomas was gone.

I settled on beans flavored with molasses and pork for supper. I started soaking the beans after dinner. Sim ran into the yard from down the road as if he was being chased. It was too early in the season for bears so I assumed he fled some other hazard. If he had seen some cougar he would have told me, but he said nothing. It had to be Osborn and Saul. Sim was just getting out of Osborn's way. Osborn was particularly testy when he returned from business and Sim found peace beyond Osborn's reach or better yet, out of his view. That Sim should flee the man with such alacrity struck me as a bit strange. I should have known to watch Sim more closely.

Osborn came fully into view out of the cane on his tall horse. The animal had the slow steady walk of any fine saddle horse and Osborn's body easily met the steed's gait. Without commanding it, my face stretched into an unaccustomed smile in anticipation of Saul's beaming grin, that same grin that had captivated me long ago at Morgan's. Leave it to Saul to transform an arduous journey into a joyous homecoming. The trip to Prestonsburg took several hours and Saul might lag behind the master on his saddle horse. Indeed, Saul preferred as much distance from Osborn as he could hazard without earning a blow.

Osborn approached the gate. He kept his head down as he was wont to do recently so I could not see his face. Whether withdrawn into some deep thought or he just wanting to block out the ugliness of his world, I did not know. Osborn's thoughts did not concern me. I concentrated on where the track came out of the trees and cane, straining for the slightest movement and my husband. Slowly, imperceptibly, the anticipation turned to puzzlement. Puzzlement became discomfort. Discomfort then became pain. Pain became horror.

Osborn customarily stopped and waited for Saul to unhook the latchet. Saul pushed open the spindly contraption that swung on its leather hinges and waited for the master to enter his domain. Once Osborn made his entrance, Saul secured the gate and followed. That day, Osborn sidled his horse up to the fence, leaned down, and worked the worn rope off the post before pushing the gate open. Between the time he leaned down and straightened up again, no more than a moment, mere seconds, the whole meaning became clear. My head throbbed and I swam in a dream. I hoped I was in a dream. I begged to wake up in the chilly shed next to a stable. But there was never a waking from the nightmare of slavery.

As Osborn rode toward the house I stumbled toward him. Upon my approach the gelding naturally stopped, expecting me to take his bridle. I met Osborn's angry eyes.

"Mister Osborn, where Saul?" I pleaded.

"Sold," he stated flatly.

"Sold!" I cried. "Sold where?" Maybe my husband was as close as a neighboring farm? I might see him only on Sundays, but I would see him and he would see his children.

"Down river."

Osborn made to get off the horse, but I prevented that by mindlessly striking out at him only to have my fists fall on the innocent dumb animal. Its reaction was to jump, forcing Osborn to fight to keep his seat. He recovered quickly from my surprise move and from the sheer shock at being attacked by a black slave.

187

He struck at me twice with the short whip strung on his wrist. Then he jumped from the horse and began flailing at me with the braided leather. I felt none of it. Not at the time.

Doctors will tell you that pain cannot be remembered. They offer platitude to help you endure their butchery and to ease their own consciences. This is true. I have now borne six children and no longer feel the hurt, but childbirth was a joyful occurrence and for me and the agony quickly passed. I have fallen and hurt myself. Like any woman who has spent her life over a fire, I have been burned. I felt an assassin's knife tear my flesh. The memory of all those unhappy hours and days is unpleasant, which is as it should be lest we linger again too close to the fire or forget that every one of us has enemies. But there is no revisiting of the pain itself, though. And some events are so traumatic that nature shields us from the torment. Some divine mechanism frees us from the immediate sensation and scars over the memories.

When Edward Osborn thrashed me for striking him, or rather, for striking his horse, I was in tremendous pain, a hurt that caused me to do the unthinkable and lash out at my master. Something protected my mind from the physical damage from Osborn's whip and boots. Osborn's blows did not compare to the agony that overcame me.

My life had been torn from my body. I was robbed of the only joy I knew in that meager existence, the only other soul in the world truly matched to mine. Had I lost a leg or an eye, I could not have been injured more. At least an ugly stump or an empty socket would be an outward indication to an observer of what I had suffered. Any human being would sympathize with me. But who would know that my dear husband had been sold away, without even the opportunity to tender a goodbye kiss to his wife or the briefest of embraces to his children? Gone, as if he were dead. Who could tell that I wanted to die?

I cannot account the number of lashes that Osborn struck. My face swelled and welted as did my back and legs. I must have taken the first blows to my head and then fallen to protect myself. I have some recollection of Sim barking and snarling, so he may have managed to intercede. That would have been very risky for him, since Osborn would have been happy to pound my yellow friend into the dust or gut him with that big knife he always carried. I do remember being injured and walking and working with difficulty. I cannot tell you how I did it.

Like an amputation wound that scabs over then grows to an ugly scar, the loss of my husband became a great mark on my character, a new face for the slave known as Phyllis. I knew no waking moment without that invisible knowledge. I can mark perhaps several turnings in my life, such as my freedom and finding the Lord, when my entire journey through this world changed. Losing Saul was one of these.

I do not know what I told my children. Ben was yet an infant. For a time Pirey asked, "Papa?" But babes have knowledge of little beyond their own reach.

A few months later I learned of Saul's transport, whispered by Lucy in town. She did not witness the event, but such an account found wide distribution.

"Mr. Osborn come to town with Saul, just like he do. That trader Norton was in town too. The one from the boats. The one been buyin' up folks. He offer Mr. Osborn cash money for Saul. Right there. No yesterday, no today, no tomorrow. Folks say that Saul don't want to go. He beg Mr. Osborn not to sell him. He have a family. But that nigger that work for the trader he grab him. Before Saul know it, there was this rope round his neck. That nigger figure he just lead Saul away like one o' his colts. But nossir. Saul took one pull on that rope and make that nigger fly like a bird.

"Draper there and it take him and the nigger both to get Saul down and tied. Draper help 'em." Lucy closed her eyes for the next part. "Draper pretty hard on him, folks say. All happen when I back here. That trader get mad and he yell at Draper not to leave no marks. I don't know, maybe not so bad. They take him to the boat, and they off before sundown."

"The money Osborn get enough for what he owe the Morgans for now. Go right from the trader to Osborn to the Morgans. But the Morgans not too happy. No, not what they wanted, I hear. Talk says Osborn outsmart the Morgans, but I don't know. You think they be happy to get their money."

That was the last I heard of my dear husband, a second-hand rendering of one more innocent disappearing into the darkness.

Alone

With Saul gone, I took on some of his work with the stock, the one task I was least suited to perform. Saul talked to his animals, and he understood what they had to say. I could barely look at a horse or a cow without some animosity arising between us. Milking, feeding, harnessing, and grooming became a struggle for all parties. The third day that Osborn's dinner arrived late and undercooked, he ordered his wife to prepare dinner and supper, but I still had to be involved or we would have undercooked oatmeal forever.

On the good side, my children found some refuge from their tormenters. Osborn ordered the two oldest children into the fields and pastures to attempt the tasks that Saul and Thomas had once easily, and even cheerily, completed. Osborn worked too, when he was not off being the sheriff.

I sunk to a new low in my life. Had I been less gifted with an intellect, I might have struggled on in blissful fatuity. I would not have been bothered with questions of why or who or with concepts of retribution and justice. I would have taken on the wounds of loss and assault and pushed them aside in favor of concerns about chickens and pigs and manure. But Almighty God chose to bless (or curse) me with this mind that thirsted for answers. Why was Saul sold? How did we come to this place? Where would we go from here? Who will pay for all this? What is my justice?

Amid my dolor of widowhood – I was for all practical purposes a widow – I pondered and I pondered. Naturally, my feelings toward the man who took my husband clawed as hateful as can possibly be imagined. All I had in the world were my children and my husband and he took my husband. My hate ran so deeply that it turned back in on itself like a wild fire leaving only blackened ruin. I was, in a way, purged of all emotion leaving only my intellect to observe and calculate.

I could have killed Osborn as easily as I sliced the throat of some stunned hog. I thought of knifing him in the barn or slipping poison into his food. I heard poisons being whispered about at Morgan's, but only among the most trusted of conspirators. If I waited patiently and inquired cautiously, I could learn what leaves and roots to gather, how to grind them, how to conceal the taste. I could have killed the entire family and been miles away before the crime was discovered.

I planned on going to town with Osborn and stealing away to find the cook at the tavern. She possessed the secrets for miscarriage and passion and spells – beyond even Daisy's ken. The whispers spoke of poisons too. I only needed a few moments with the woman. One scheme involved getting a pass from Osborn for the morning that I poisoned breakfast. That way I avoided capture if Draper or his like encountered us on the road. Days and perhaps weeks might elapse before my crime were discovered by which time we could have crossed many mountains.

Where would I go then? The reality only frustrated me all the more. I knew enough to know what I did not know, the route and the means to freedom, had there been one. People believe today that if an escaped slave could somehow just follow the North Star to the Ohio River, he found freedom. Ohio was still not freedom. Only Canada, far, far to the north, represented real freedom, but I was ignorant of Canada.

Death offered escape, a cool, perpetual void. Were I then a Christian, I would not have feared death. I would have known that my Maker awaited me on the other side with his arms open wide to take me to his bosom. But I was an unlettered heathen, kept from The Word that would have enlightened me and freed me from the fear of death. I feared death more than anything. I could not abandon my children, and I could not take them with me. I just could not harm them. I had to live for my children. I had to live.

I found my only solace in work to exhaustion so that I might collapse for a few hours free of the burdens of my life. In our shabby shelter, I clutched my babies both for warmth and for the desperate touch of something human. Even then, dreams tormented me, dreams of happier times, dreams of the horrors of yesterday, dreams of the dread of tomorrow.

Still, I thought. As I carried fodder through the icy morning, I asked, what has happened to me? As I washed Osborn's clothing in soap that left my hands cracked and raw, I inquired, how has this come to be? As I ate another bowl of mush I wondered, who did this?

One day, still sore from his beating, I saw Osborn with his next eldest boy, a lad of seven or eight. I have completely forgotten his name. Unlike Thomas, he was small for his age and profoundly unencumbered with an understanding of anything other than his mouth and his stomach, some cruel inheritance from his mother. Osborn tried to teach him how to hitch the horse to the wagon, but the boy's hands were too small for the heavy tack. The child struggled to fasten the yoke strap to the belly band. His fingers just could not negotiate the pieces. Thomas or Saul accomplished this task in moments. Saul could probably have had the horse hitch himself. In Saul's absence, it fell to Osborn those days to harness the horse so he tried to teach his son.

"Pull, damn you," Osborn growled. "You weakling! Your brother was harnessing horses when he was six, five. I was doing the same. One of your sisters can do this."

"I can't," he cried, "my fingers are cold." It was indeed cold that day. I could also tell that the boy was afraid of the horse and with good reason. Fender was sneaky and nasty, watching for any opening to kick or bite.

"Put the strap in the buckle and pull it back!" Osborn taunted. "Perhaps one of the girls would like to try?"

At that point Fender, good for little more than pulling a plow, stepped forward, pushing the boy off his balance. He fell back into the icy mud with a yelp. He sat up and hugged his knees and cried and cried and cried with shame and frustration.

I fully expected Osborn to start whipping the boy as he would me, but he did not. Instead, I saw that same look from the morning I spilled his breakfast, a blank, despairing gloom, the aspect of a man at the end, pinioned and staring at the noose. He did not even shake his head. He turned his attention to his surroundings, and I could see him consider his domain – broken down plow horse, weak, despondent child, dilapidated home, surly slave, debt-ridden farm. I knew what he saw. For what paltry pleasure it offered me, I knew he felt punished.

As much as I disliked the Osborn child (why cannot I remember his name?) and the entire Osborn family, I could not let him lay in the mud. He was a child. If that wagon did not get hitched the farm would eventually suffer. My children would be the first to go hungry from the food not produced. I planted the axe in a log and made my way down to the harnessing lesson. It's what Saul would have done, just pitch in and help. I felt an obligation to perpetuate Saul's good nature.

"Help with that, Mister Osborn?" I asked. I am certain that the expression of initiative on my part caught Osborn unaware and left him suspicious.

"Buckle it up," the master said as if it were my job all along. "God knows this one can't."

I stepped in front of Fender (how can I remember the name of and unworthy horse, yet forget the name of a human child?) and gave him a slap on the nose just to let him know I was there. "Ho, Fender," I told him, "no sense puttin' it off. Got to work now." Fender offered a moment of hesitation when he undoubtedly considered taking a piece of me. Then he realized that I had him by the bit. Horses will always test the new rider before cooperating, and you have to watch for that moment. Saul taught me that. Fender shifted his weight in submission and waited for my move. I hooked and buckled the stiff belly band to the yoke strap and took care of other fixtures – yoke strap, hame strap, side straps, and quarter strap. In the meantime, the boy crawled out of the mud and took the reins into the box in an effort to resurrect himself in his own eyes if not in his father's. I received not the slightest acknowledgment for my effort and returned to the wood pile.

That bleak winter lingered for weeks before yielding to spring. A heavy snow rendered our hovel untenable, and Ben got sick again. I used up Daisy's potions on him. I prevailed upon Osborn to allow us to sleep on the floor near the hearth. Ben managed to recover. Then Pirey caught cold. My children sniffled and wheezed every winter. It seemed everyone in the Osborn household coughed their way through those months. I bundled my feet and head and hands and cooked and cared for stock. Since Osborn's position as sheriff brought him an income, cash money or kind, we stretched the year's corn and squash and beans into the planting season. His children grew a year and produced a bit more labor for the farm.

I watched the farm's fortunes carefully. Farming is a delicate business in the best of times. You plant and hope there is enough rain to sprout the seeds, but not too much. In the summer, you want sun and a little more rain, but not too much. Pests plotted to take what little you had. I imagined that the crows and deer and pigeons conduced to take turns ravaging young plants. And in fall, when the stalks and vines hung heavy with their fruit, a wind or hail storm could wreak havoc in just ten minutes. In those brief moments, a bumper crop became empty desolation, plenty devolves to starvation. All that summer, I felt one hailstorm away from a long walk to the landing and a trader's chains.

Once a month, a tough old chicken fell under my axe to soften for a day over a slow fire. My snares yielded up a victim or two. By adding enough turnips and dried peas, I stretched the stew to feed all of us, the master's family first. Osborn usually returned from sheriff business with a sack across his saddle. My heart soared knowing that the family, and by extension my children and I, found some additional nourishment for a few more days. I kept track of his movements and discerned that every Saturday and most Tuesdays he rode off to Prestonsburg in his fine clothing and wide hat to perform his official duties. If he did not return that night he cozened some lodging in town or on the way.

Getting the crops in the ground took longer that spring because we had fewer hands. Then the rains came late. Osborn plowed, not out of any equanimity on his part, but because he needed me to cook and plant. He pushed his children into the fields and told them to watch me as I patted the corn into hills. Two or three of them seldom performed as efficiently as I was alone. Osborn and I handled the stock, with some help from the boy. Other tasks, once carried by men, fell to children with predictable results. The children fell sullenly into their new routines as aware of their lack of success as they were of the weight of their labors. My loneliness still dripped an open wound, and the malaise that sought to bury Osborn's farm kept it from healing in any way.

I began to see Osborn as the man he was, competent at leather work and self importance, but hopeless at higher pursuits including farming, politics, and business. Had he become a shoemaker or a saddler his skill would have carried him into a respectable place in society, more secure than elected office. He fell instead victim to his own dreams of importance and wealth oblivious to the fact that other men manipulated him with temptations just beyond his complete understanding. He could not even choose a wife well. To him a pretty face bested aptitude.

His almost unlimited power of arrest and fine earned him respect if not fear. He enjoyed gifts and loans and bargains. For a strong man, these perquisites can be easily balanced against considerations such as duty and citizenship lest he become too prejudiced in favor of the few. For every partisan benefit, there hung a countering and potentially damaging opposing force. A strong man like Abraham Lincoln could steady, even juggle the competing influences of a dozen men and their cabals as deftly as any circus clown. Edward Osborn possessed only the strength of a child and the balance of a common drunk.

As I labored through that spring and summer of 1813, my long dormant skills of reason shook off the dust of disuse. I weighed Esther's comments against my forgotten impressions of David Morgan. My mind stretched its muscles as if awakening from a long night's rest. I pulled together facts and intelligence from beyond the Osborn farm to understand how the wider world controlled my life. Edward Osborn emerged into a new light. I began with the fact that Morgan and Osborn shared enmity. Such things change little, even with offerings of apples, salt, and slaves. From what I knew of Morgan he could never countenance an enemy of Osborn's stature without seeking to defeat him in some way. Osborn's ascension to the office of Sheriff not only represented a victory against Morgan in the election, but it changed the scales of forces which Morgan always sought to control. Osborn was happy enough to enjoy the profit and honor of his position, but he did not hunger for it like Morgan did. Hunger burns a stronger motive than happiness. Morgan's hunger set him to niggle away at Osborn's prosperity and influence with debts and obligations beyond his skill to overcome. He schemed to enlist young Thomas into the army and march him away.

I considered Morgan's role in my own life beyond as the one who sold me. Esther revealed that David Morgan still controlled me though, and still drove events in my life. Saul and I were just means to Morgan's end, that being the reduction and destruction of Osborn. Osborn presented to Morgan a problem to solve, like a sick animal or a debt. Morgan pushed me and Saul in front of Osborn to make him stumble. Osborn stepped and faltered, but he trampled my family in the process.

David Morgan determined that we should live in isolation from our community. I began to see the world no longer simply as random occurrences that blessed some and bloodied others, but also as events with causes. I later understood that some things were truly acts of God such as a flood or a cyclone that destroyed a home. But many things, most things, like where and how the home was built or what fools won election to office, came at the hand of man. For every act of man, there was a reason. And for every act of man there was someone responsible. Men made events. What evolved in me was the realization that to best control events, one controlled men.

I saw Osborn up close and watched a proud man – but not really a bad man – decline in front of his community and in front of his family. Osborn was the runner facing downhill. At first his strides come easily on the slope and he attains great speed. Then his desire to win exceeds his skill and he hurls forward out of control. A stone, a twig, or a spiteful shove and he crashes to the ground with destructive force. The race is lost and the runner is mortified.

Was I, the prisoner, beginning to make concert with my jailor? Did we have the same enemy?

Visitors

I labored throughout the summer. We brought in the harvest, beginning with the squash planted in the corn hills. Then we took on the stunted corn. We, that is I, with some help from Osborn and his wife, cut ears from the stalks and carried them, a bushel at a time to the crib. The stalks ran shorter than usual and the ears smaller. The dearth of corn became truly evident to me in the process of shelling kernels from cobs. I started with a pile of ears from the crib and, one by one, I stripped off the husks. Then I took each stunted ear and scraped off the kernels against a sharp board already shiny and worn smooth from other, more successful autumns. As any laboring person knows, there is a difference between the kind of work that simply maintains, like grooming stock or hauling water, where there is never an end, and work which produces a useable result such as spinning or building. So it is with husking and shelling the corn. I started with a pile of harvested ears and ended up with bushels of shelled corn for humans and for stock. I expended effort and watched my work grow to realize at the end some result.

To vary the tedium, I selected a fixed number of ears and husked them, stacking the result in a neat pyramid, six rows across at the bottom, then five, then four, until there was just one at the top. After moving the husks out of the way, I sat with the shelling board between my knees over a wide trough. With all ready, I plucked the ear off the top and ran it over the sharp edge of the board, shaving off the kernels. The naked cob landed in another pile, and I took the next ear. Slowly, the trough filled with kernels until it held enough to empty into a sack or a basket. I kept my mind alive by changing the design of the next pyramid or the way I ran the ears over the board.

But my mind was not satisfied by simply playing games with stacks and piles. I thought again and again as to my situation. Always there was why? Why was my husband taken from me? Would it happen yet? Would my children and I soon disappear into the unknown?

Harvest is violence. Men chop living plants at their peak of life and bind the dying stalks in bundles. After the crop withers in the sun, the ears are ripped from their homes and then imprisoned in cribs. Hands husk bushels of corn by stripping the coverings in quick, assaultive moves, but the violence has not ended. Hard blows on the shell board force kernels from the cobs which gave them life. Pummeled by the injustices of my servitude, I easily transformed innocent ears of corn into surrogates for my enemies – Osborn, Morgan, and the trader. An ear became a man as I tore away his arms and dismembered the rest of his body. My victims never cried out, never complained, and never exhibited the slightest fear. They always submitted, as if they knew this fate punished them for their crimes.

In spite of my daydreams, I always ended at the same place, the same cause – not just "the peculiar institution" that was truly the root of it all, but my former owner, David Morgan. He was the cause. He was to blame.

The morning limped along under a cloudless sky. The heat rose from parched fields littered with dead stalks. Marauding crows glared insolently from fence posts and outbuildings evaluating their next act of thievery. Two of the braver bandits patrolled the ground on foot just out of my reach. Sim slumbered at my side after a night of guarding the fields and cribs from plunderers. I shifted my work from shelling to crushing boiled corn for dinner.

Although I worked alone in my thoughts Mrs. Osborn and her children continued to husk knowing that their next meal came from my efforts. The youngest kept the debris out of our way. I sat on a log off to the side in my own bit of shade. Mr. Osborn worked in the house repairing his fine boots, since his means had fallen below the ability to purchase new ones. The bitter exchanges of the master's children and the incessant hum of flies broke the stillness; a mellow farm moment on the Kentucky frontier.

I once saw a painting by a famous artist in a fine house in New England. The work bore the title "Bounty." The farmer and his family, all white, happily hauled and gleaned grain. They wore simple, but clean, colorful clothing, and they all worked in cheerful harmony. They might have even been singing a song together. I doubted very much then that the painter could have sold his painting had he portrayed anything but a bumper crop. No painter could ever hope to sell a painting of the Osborn farm that day.

The next moment lives in my memory. Mrs. Osborn and the Osborn boy and his sister husk as best they can. The youngest stacks husks and makes a game of it. Pirey plays in the dirt with the empty cobs tossed to the side. Ben sleeps next to me, protected from the flies by my shawl. I lean to take the next ear off the row with four across and Sim comes briefly into my view. Everything is still so clear. The bowl of soup. The bugle.

Sim's eyes open, not slowly as when he wakes naturally, and not quickly as if he is suddenly roused. His lids part purposefully, revealing dark, focused eyes. His ears – pointed like a wolf's, but turned down at the ends in some compromise among his ancestors – tip forward a little. I know the move that always presaged news, a traveler in the forest. We often receive men with business with Osborn, but deer probe out of the trees too in search of a meal. Bears and wolves can lurk in the shade so we watch for them. The animals of the forest speak to one another of friends and enemies and Sim hears them.

Some of the possibilities hold the promise of a meal, even several meals. With luck the wandering deer ends up over my fire. Naturally, the work of butchering Osborn's kill falls to me, but even this bloody task breaks my tedium. Butchering requires some art and skill, slicing the throat to bleed the carcass just so, skinning, opening the cavity carefully so as not corrupt the meat with bile or urine. The odd occasions when we eat meat often suffer from Mrs. Osborn's inept use of a sharp knife when she punctures an organ to taint our meal.

So, Sim's messages from the forest affected no small interest in me. He heard cardinal tell squirrel to run higher in the tree. The squirrel warned the rabbit to find his burrow. Esther and Saul taught me to watch not so much for the big changes in the forest but for the little ones. A pigeon flying to you could be flying from something. Turkeys are shy, and if you see one, something has caused him to come out of hiding.

Sim raised his head and cocked an ear to catch more sound. Whoever, whatever approached did so at a steady pace. That obviated the deer which always paused to listen and watch before moving on again. One Osborn child threw an ear of corn at another causing a complaint and a bawl. Mrs. Osborn rebuked them both. Sim ignored this all. His throat twitched once and rested. It twitched again and remained taut. The muscles of his shoulders tightened too.

Sim gave off the customary cry announcing a visitor, a long woo-oo-oo-oo that began sharply as he raised his nose. His hackles lifted and he jumped to his feet. He ran toward the cane and slipped under the fence as smoothly as if there had been no fence at all.

The broad black hat of William Morgan emerged out of the cane. His head grew to a rider on a horse. The horse walked easily as he stepped into the stream, splashing up silver water in the sun. Behind William rode his shorter father, David, wearing a new white hat with the low crown of the style becoming fashionable for planters. The two men watched the Osborn house intently. William reached the gate first. He leaned down and unlatched the rope and pushed the gate open. He rode through, and the elder Morgan followed, but did not bother to close the gate. It swung indecisively. Sim circled the riders alertly and followed them into the yard as if it were he who had granted their entry and allowed them through.

The Osborn boy ran to the house and Osborn appeared in his doorway, at the top of the steps. He hoisted his galluses over his shoulders and kept his thumbs hooked behind them. Both

Morgans stopped and dismounted slowly. William approached the steps and placed a foot on the bottom step. He produced a piece of paper and handed it up to Osborn. Osborn opened it and read. He read for the longest time before William spoke, his words lost to me.

"I am the sheriff!" Osborn shouted. "You cannot serve a writ upon the sheriff!"

I missed William's measured reply which included a soft gesture toward the paper, then a motion back to his silent father.

"This is an outrage! You have no right!"

More calm words from William.

"They are *my* property! No!"

David Morgan took two slow steps to the side and avoided Osborn's eyes. William's voice rose enough so that I could catch his words.

"Edward, the judge and the commissioners have all signed the writ. It is valid. Colonel Morgan here is a witness. If you refuse to comply, I shall return with a warrant. You know what that means. Even sheriffs can be arrested. Unless you post a bond, you will sleep in your own jail. I have come for my property."

Until the mention of property, I viewed the exchange with a sense of detachment, as another mysterious interaction between white men. But when William mentioned property, I knew my children and I were the cause of this visit. Any time white men talked about Negroes, particularly their Negroes, little good came of it. I was an object and my children were objects. My sense of gloom only increased when all three men turned and looked at me, squatting on a log about to shell some more corn.

"Phyllis!" William called to me. "Come here."

"I'm the master here!" Osborn screamed. "You cannot give orders on my land! This will not stand! I will have *you* in *my* jail!" He screamed with a rage that even I had never heard before, a bellow from the bottom of his belly, as if the cry would somehow save his life.

I put down my work and got to my feet, slowly. David Morgan took off his hat and stepped towards Osborn. With Osborn at the top of the steps and Morgan on the ground, Osborn towered even more over the small man. Morgan's head came to Osborn's knees. Morgan spoke and as I drew closer, I could hear.

"...for the niggers to hear. And your family. We can resolve all this in town. But the writ allows us to take them. Right now this is all among gentlemen. Let's keep it that way. Among gentlemen. Please, Edward. Let's be gentlemen."

Osborn stepped back into the house for an instant, then leaned out and called to me.

"Phyllis! Come here!" he yelled. "Get your brats."

I turned and gathered up Ben and tugged on Pirey's arm. Pirey buried her face in my side as I approached the white men. You cannot imagine the terror I felt as three white men stared at me, but a life of submission allowed me no other course of action.

"Go with these... gentlemen until I get this business straightened out. You won't need anything. You'll be right back."

I could not move.

"Hurry!" Osborn snapped. Then he calmly addressed his visitors. "Get off my land."

"Thank you, Edward," David Morgan softly replied. "You are always a gentleman." He put his white hat on his head, gave the brim a tug, and reached for a stirrup. Two bounces and he hauled himself up into Brownie's saddle. William, the taller man, mounted more skillfully. They turned their horses to leave. William looked back at me, clutching my children, and when he saw us rooted in place, he only said, "Come on, girl. Get the gate."

I followed, struggling with both my babies who were not as small as they once were. Pirey toddled along hanging onto my hand. I closed the gate behind us, and we scampered across the cool creek and into the cane and forest. Pirey had to run to keep up with me and the horses. Even before we entered the forest, I saw that we could not last.

"Mas' William," I begged, "little Pirey can't run. Please."

William stopped and turned. He looked back towards Osborn's then regarded me a moment. "Get her up here. Tell her to hang on. I'm not going to worry about her. If she falls, she's yours."

I hoisted Pirey up to the cantle and placed her hands on the straps there. Her eyes widened with terror. "Hold on baby," I told her. "Hold on." As the horse stepped off, I hurried along beside to give her some comfort. Soon she obviously enjoyed the pleasant sensation of riding. Little Pirey, in her crude sack shift and with her hair sprinkled with bits of corn husk, contrasted sharply to the tall, neatly dressed host. I doubted that William thought any more of his passenger.

The track allowed two horses to ride abreast but not with me walking alongside, so I soon dropped back. Pirey clutched the straps and watched back at me. With her little legs, she really just crouched atop that big horse rather than rode it. As long as William walked, she had a secure seat.

Sim joined us walking alongside me. Once on the track, I briefly considered running, but how far would I get with a baby? Where would I go? What would become of Pirey? Perhaps I could find Rabbit? He could hide me. No one had found him yet. But no one had found him because perhaps no one looked. He might not entertain a fugitive who would compromise his own invisibility.

Gradually, I ginned up the numbness to cope with the dark journey. I tried to keep a good face for Pirey, but I cannot but think that much of her fear came from me. Sim sensed my troubles and stuck close as if to add encouragement.

The Morgans did not speak. I found this somewhat unusual. They always had something to talk about, particularly on the trail. Their silence was the least of my concerns, but I could not help but notice the omen. I strode on through the warm morning, the great trees largely blotted out the hot sun, one small relief.

Sim stopped in the trail and turned. He growled once, then growled more fiercely. I heard it too. A horse at full gallop. I stepped to the side to let the rider pass as I was expected to do and saw Edward Osborn in shirt sleeves atop his fine gelding, riding at full speed down on me through the gloom of the forest. As he rode through patches of sunshine, something flashed brightly. He passed me in an instant.

William and David Morgan heard the approach as well. William turned to his left and reached back with his left arm to steady Pirey, a gesture that I found touching. With one hand full of reins and the other on Pirey, he could not protect himself. Osborn fell on

William in an instant and lunged at him with his huge knife, the one that his father received from General Washington. Osborn planted the blade right in William's chest with a sound like a keg of water being hit by a log, a terrible, resonant drumbeat. Blood erupted from the wound. William fell back onto Pirey and his horse sat back on its haunches. Both William and Pirey fell to the ground in bloody heap. I shrieked for my baby.

David Morgan saw the attack over his shoulder just as the knife struck William. The older man kicked his horse. Osborn, still with the knife in his hand, swiftly and deftly as I am sure any veteran cavalryman could, rode on, down onto Morgan kicking Brownie to run. Brownie had just begun to leap out when Osborn planted the knife in Morgan's back. Morgan threw his arms wide and rolled away. Osborn lost the weapon in Morgan's back as Morgan fell to the ground.

I ran to Pirey and found her stunned under the inert body of William Morgan. The knife had taken him squarely in the heart and blood covered both of them. I wrested Pirey free. She bawled through the blood, but exhibited no other injury. With her and Ben in my arms, I scuttled off the trail, certain that Osborn would attack us next. From the protection of a tree, I looked down the trail and saw him on his heaving horse surveying the carnage strewn before him. William lie on his back as his blood seeped into the dust. A few rods away, David Morgan sprawled on his chest, the knife handle protruding upward. Osborn looked completely composed. He walked the horse to David Morgan's body and stopped. Blood smeared his hand and forearm hanging casually at his side. Dust floated through the shafts of sunlight that broke through the trees.

"Richest man in the county," he said to the body. "County commissioner. Colonel of troops. State legislature. Not much good to you now. Now we are both nothing." Osborn regarded his work for a moment, then walked his horse toward me. He sat straight in the saddle, as if he were parading up the main street of Prestonsburg. I froze, but not without considering the best way to retreat from him into the forest. I could never outrun a man with two children in my arms. I might prolong the inevitable by fleeing, but he would overtake me soon enough. The foreknowledge of my death left me with a small sense of relief and freedom from all my pain. The end was at hand at last. The two men before me died quickly. I hoped that we would die quickly too. Sim stood close by me to share this last battle.

For once, I looked straight at Osborn. If I were to die, I could at least look into the eyes of my tormenter and murderer. His blond hair hung in some disarray from his hard ride. His white shirt showed flecks of his victims' blood. Osborn reached William's body, but he did not stop. He walked his horse past me and my sobbing Pirey staring straight ahead. Soon I found myself in the silence of the forest with two dead white men in the dust.

I set Pirey and Ben down and walked over to look at William on his back. His brown eyes looked stupidly into the trees above us. His chest glistened with bright red. The knife had pierced through to his heart, and he had died in an instant. A white bit of bone stuck out of the wound. With his head thrown back I hardly recognized him. He recently had his hair trimmed and he carried a small pistol in his belt. Had he predicted Osborn's reaction to losing property? He probably expected more of a warning. Had he not protected Pirey with his free hand he might have reached his weapon.

David Morgan's body rested face down some distance up the track. Osborn's knife protruded straight up. I walked up and examined the body of the man who crafted my own personal disaster, the man who such a short time before had demanded fear and respect. The man who brought me my husband. The man who released my mind, then locked it in a dark room. The man whose ambitions resulted in the destruction of my family, whose inept manipulations caused his own demise.

It was such a strange sensation being in the presence of two men who had been part of my life for as long as I could remember. But in all those years, I had never been able to really look closely at either of them. I never noticed the wen on the side of Morgan's head.

I stood transfixed at the reversals in fortunes. A moment ago, I faced death. Now I was alive and out of danger. My bitterest enemies lie dead. Even slaves know that if a man kills a white man, he will be hanged for it. Osborn had just killed two white men. White men will ask questions. Will they think I murdered these men? I had to think clearly. What should I do next? I could not go to my master. Who was my master? Whose property was I?

Suddenly, bloody bubbles erupted from the knife wound in Morgan's back and his back gave off a sucking sound. His arm moved to push himself up and the dead body came alive. He struggled and rolled, revealing the dirty face of a stranger contorted in pain. Frothy blood covered his lips and dripped into the dust. He opened his eyes then slumped forward. He pushed himself over again and noticed me.

"That bastard," he muttered. "That worthless bastard. Couldn't tell when he was done? I had him." Then he saw me and closed his eyes. "Phyllis. Good girl. Get help. Get O'Hara. Get Peter. Get Esther. Good girl."

"Why you sell me, Mas? Why you sell me and Saul? Why you do this to me?"

"No, get help. Do as I say. You're a good girl. Where's my son?"

"He dead," I told him. "Why?" I repeated, "Why you do it to us?"

Morgan took a breath, half of which came in through the hole in his back, and he coughed out more frothy blood which mingled with the dirt on his face. "Get me some help, damn it," he spoke into the dust.

"Why you do it?" Having in my control the man who controlled me all my life hypnotized me.

"I...can't...talk," he managed. "Help."

Accused

Where to go? Where to run? How far could I get with my babies? As much as I wanted to flee my life and this new horror I knew well enough that there was no escape. Safety became my first concern. Here in the forest Osborn lurked like some deranged animal. Would he return for me? But we had really only gone a short distance from the Osborn farm and it offered the closest choice distasteful as it was. But Osborn would be there and he would kill me. He would kill my children.

Esther would know what to do. Mrs. Morgan would know what to do. Brownie browsed nearby and I easily got her reins. I put Pirey in the saddle and led Brownie in the direction of the Morgan farm. My fright took over my body and I am certain I shaved an hour off the journey.

As Brownie and I arrived at the slave quarters I was encountered questioning looks and suspicious whispers.

"What you done, girl?" Sarah asked with great suspicion. "What you doin' here? Where the Mas'? Where Mister William? What's all that blood?"

"Esther," I pleaded, "where Esther?" The journey allowed me to gather my thoughts and to formulate a plan. "Need to see Esther."

Esther appeared and despite the confusion of people gathered around she quickly grasped the implications of what she saw. "What happen, girl? What happen?"

"Mas' and Mister William come to Mister Osborn's," I started, having practiced my words on the way. "They take me away. Me and my babies. Some paper. Mister Osborn, he mad. He ride after and he kill Mas'. He kill Mister William."

Gasps from those watching.

"I come here."

Even Esther needed a few seconds to order out this news. "You sure they dead?"

"They dead. Mister Osborn killed them with his knife. They dead. Near Osborn's."

Esther ordered Daisy to take Ben from my arms and dragged me up toward the house, past the big tree. At the house Mariah gaped at our approach.

"Missus Morgan, please, Missus Morgan," Esther called out. Anna Morgan appeared at the door. The Morgan children peered out from behind her. "Missus Morgan, Phyllis say Mister Morgan and Mister William, they killed by Mister Osborn."

A look of shock overtook my former mistress, but she was not one to be easily struck dumb. "Are you certain, Phyllis?" she asked. "Tell me what happened. Tell me everything."

I repeated myself with little difference than a few moments before. Mrs. Morgan's eyes stayed wide, but shifted from me to some point in the distance. Her hands clutched her apron then released the fabric.

"Esther, find O'Hara. Have him come here." Searching out the overseer took some time. He was superintending the felling of trees with Peter's help at a distant corner of the property. In the meantime, Daisy and Sarah cleaned William Morgan's blood off of Pirey and gave her something to eat. Someone cleaned blood off Brownie and Esther passed along the instruction that Morgan's mare be readied for the overseer's use. When he finally reported to the house we watched him nod obediently as Mrs. Morgan instructed him, then instructed him again. Finally the mistress retreated into the house while O'Hara waited, hat in hand. She returned and tendered a paper which he pocketed. He then rushed down to the stable where a man waited with Brownie.

But O'Hara never rode out. Osborn's deputy, the no account Draper loped in with fire in his eyes. People usually withdrew to cabins or fields upon his approach. But I had nowhere to run and Esther would not run. He fixed his gaze on me and pounded over forcing us to step away to avoid being trampled. He swung down and in a single move struck me with his crop knocking me to the ground.

"Thought you'd hide here?" He screamed. "You can't run from me. You can't kill white men and run from me." He cut at me again with the crop.

"Please Mister," I begged. "I don't kill 'em, Mister Osborn kill 'em." But he kept hitting me. As much of a deputy and a slave catcher as Draper might have been, he really had no skill in beating someone. Most of his blow fell on my arms which protected me.

"Draper!" cried Mrs. Morgan as she ran down. "Draper! Stop it! Stop it!"

"This nigger killed your husband Missus," he sneered past missing teeth. "And your son. I found 'em. I found 'em in the road. She killed 'em with a knife. We're gonna swing her for it."

"Phyllis says Sheriff Osborn killed them."

"Well I say she done it. I'm taking her to town. When Sheriff Osborn finds out, we're gonna swing her."

"You fool. Why would she kill Colonel Morgan? Why would she kill my... Mr. Morgan? They had a writ to seize her, to bring her here. If you are looking for who killed them you look for Sheriff Osborn."

"Oh I'll look for Sheriff Osborn. But first I'm taking her to the jail. She can wait in the jail for me to swing her."

Mrs. Morgan continued to think quickly despite having just learned of the deaths of her son and husband. "Then you won't mind Mr. O'Hara's help. Such a dangerous killer will need two strong men to guard her."

Draper could not hide his puzzlement.

"Mr. O'Hara, you ride to town with Dep... Mr. Draper here and if he mistreats Phyllis in any way, I will have the damage taken out of his pocket. And if he doesn't have any money, he will learn the life of a bondsman for he will spend years working it off here. Alongside our other hands. Under your whip." I will always admire that small, graying white woman's ability to cow a dirty rogue, but my admiration came later. My first concern was being accused of murder and being surrendered to Draper.

Only because the knot on Draper's thick rope hung in front of my throat did I not strangle to death. The gap where the two sides of the noose came together allowed me just enough room to breathe. The rough hemp burned my neck as I stumbled along behind the deputy, like a pack mule or an errant cow, which is what he thought of me, I am certain. With O'Hara in tow he did not risk any additional violence.

We reached Prestonsburg at dark and Draper pushed me into the jail, a tiny, windowless dungeon of logs that smelled like a privy. Draper added leg irons to the shackles on my wrists. My exhaustion allowed me to collapse into a deep sleep and to avoid the reality of what awaited me. Whatever dreams transported me out of that fetid place ended with the clatter of Draper's key in a lock and an explosion of light as he opened the door.

"Out!" my jailer commanded. I crawled out, consumed by thirst. Without a word, I stumbled in my chains to a horse trough, earning me several blows from Draper's whip. The green water tasted heavenly. After a few short drinks, Draper hauled me up by my hair and pushed me toward three white men standing nearby.

I recognized Alexander Lackey, Morgan's son-in-law and a prosperous planter in his own right, and Judge Graham in their town clothes, breeches and frock coats. Lackey's boots and trousers bore the dirt of recent hard traveling. The third man also carried dust fresh from the road. Judge Graham was clean. Lackey spoke first.

"Your name is Phyllis?"

"Yassir," I managed. Having that many white men stare at me so intently, I believed that Draper would soon be pulling on the rope that would choke the life out of me.

"You are the property of William Morgan?"

"Y–" That did not sound right to me. "Nawsir. I belong to Mr. Edward Osborn, the sheriff. I his prop'ty."

"She doesn't know about the writ," black breeches and brown boots stated.

"Hmmm," Lackey said. "Tell us what happened yesterday?"

"Yesterday?"

"Yesterday, girl. Speak up."

I suddenly could not remember what happened. I looked down and all I could see was the heavy boots of the white men who were going to kill me. Lackey had the nicest boots. Graham's were the cleanest. The third man needed to visit a cobbler soon and I thought of Osborn.

I had been robbed of all that was familiar and dear and never felt so completely abandoned. That isolation resulted in a sense of release from my family and society. It was just me. I could help no one and no one could help me. Any decision I made for survival I made for myself. My children were gone. My husband was gone. Nothing mattered any more but life. Slowly, I gathered my senses.

"Do you hear me, girl?" Lackey wanted to know.

"Yassuh."

"What happened to Colonel Morgan? And to Mr. William Morgan?"

"Mr. Osborn."

"Mr. Osborn what?"

"Mr. Osborn. He stab them."

"Did you see Mr. Osborn do this?"

"Yassuh."

"Tell me what you were doing?"

"Suh?"

"Were you going someplace?"

"Yassuh. Mr. Morgan – Colonel Morgan – and Mr. William. They come to Mr. Osborn with a paper." The words tumbled out of me in no particular order as I replied to the questions.

Finally, Lackey became more direct. "Did you kill the Morgans?"

"Oh nawsuh, nawsuh. I was just walkin' behind Mr. William. With Ben. Pirey, she riding with Mr. William. He pull her up 'cause we slowin' him down." As lucidity returned to me I could see the

213

white men were trying to understand what I knew before they hanged me. I had to overcome my fear and tell them. "He ride up, and he stab Mr. William. Then he chase Colonel Morgan and catch him and stab him."

"Do you recognize this?" Black breeches held out an object with dried blood.

"Yassuh. That Mr. Osborn's knife. His father's knife. He stab Mr. Morgan with it. And Mr. William."

"Where did Mr. Osborn go?"

"I don't know, sah. He ride off."

Then the white men stepped back and conversed. I did not hear all that was said, but black breeches raised his voice with "… nigger can't…" and I lost the rest. I strained to get more, but the men pulled away from me. When it was obvious I would learn nothing more there, I turned to Draper.

"Mr. Draper, sah, can I get some water?

"In time. In time. For now, just shut up."

"Mr. Draper, suh, where my babies?"

"Morgan's. Now shut up, ya know what's good for ya."

"Water, sah?"

Draper gave a disgusted wave with the handle of his whip and I gloried again in the slimy wetness of the trough. I suffered later for the bad water, but I could not live without it. Draper tapped me with the whip.

"Back inside, girl." More clatter locked me into broken darkness again. I felt the rancid water begin its infernal work in my gut. Before payment for my desperate thirst came due, the door opened and Lucy, the judge's girl, gave me a bowl of food and bucket for my needs. I made short work of the cold fritter, and as I paid the bill for my thirst, that bucket became my dearest friend.

Years later, I read of the agony of Edmond Dantes. I knew well what that fictional character endured, because I suffered as he did, locked away with no hope of redemption. But where Dantes plotted his elaborate revenge, I hoped. I hoped I would see light again, that I would see my children, and that I could return to my life, even my life at Osborn's. I wished I could undo the events of that day. If I doubted those dreams, I hoped that Draper would pull quickly on the rope and my end would come with a quick snap and a minimum of suffering. I remembered Ruth and wondered what I could do to hasten death. Should I kick or should I resist the urge to struggle? Ruth went quiet after a few moments. Perhaps death at the end of a rope was surprisingly merciful?

After a period of intense disorientation, a prisoner begins to focus his mind on the tiniest of matters until things of no real consequence adopt monumental proportions. My mind would not tolerate simply sitting in the dim light and waiting for the door to open. I began to explore my world. As I found a new feature, I would mark it in my mind so that when I received my meals and a jug of water and emptied my bucket two times a day, I could use the light from the open door to see more of the inside of my cell. Gradually, I recorded the details of my home. The cataloguing became an important means of passing the time.

The cell was perhaps eight feet wide and six feet deep, big enough for half a dozen slaves awaiting transport or two or three white men finding sobriety. The roof sloped so that I could just stand at the tallest end next the door but had to stoop at the back wall. The only entry came through the heavy plank door, which opened outward. Logs made up the walls, like any rude cabin but without mud and straw caulking. The gaps allowed thin light and some air that warm autumn and I recognized that should my imprisonment extend into winter, I should suffer grievously. Of course, there was no window and no chimney. The roof was logs too. The lowest logs of the walls were buried to prevent the inhabitants from digging their way out, I supposed. I was probably the worst criminal ever housed in the Prestonsburg jail, the county having just experienced its first murders – the first since the Indians left. My greatest discomfort came from my chains. You have seen the scars on my wrists and ankles chewed by the rough iron.

As my own odors replaced those of my predecessors, the smell offended me less. The bucket allowed one means of keeping the room clean, and fresh straw brought in by Lucy contributed to my lodgings. I worked to hear and catch glimpses of the movements of the town. I was well familiar with Prestonsburg, and I worked to match what I knew with the sounds that came to me under the door. I could hear Simon's forge and a chicken coop. Children threw rocks at the jail to torment me, the first prisoner who might hang. Their taunts of "Dance, nigger, dance" at first troubled me, but I gradually inured myself to them and attempted to differentiate the speakers.

After three days, someone besides Draper unlocked the door, and my strict regime relaxed somewhat. Lucy told the guard, a local man named Oscar hired for a few cents a day to keep the keys and look in on me, that she could not leave the plate. She had to wait until I finished eating the beans. This required me to dine outside while Lucy and the guard watched. The meal in the fresh air truly made my food something to look forward to. I sat outside and chewed slowly to make sure the moment lasted. The guard was loath to watch some slave eat and stepped away so the meals provided an opportunity for me to learn from Lucy of current events.

"They lookin' for Osborn," she told me. "That his knife they find near Colonel Morgan and he run away."

"My babies?"

"Your babies at Morgan's. Esther has 'em. They fine. They safe." I could not hope for any more for them.

"What they do when they find Osborn?"

"Put him in here, I guess. They have a trial. At the courthouse. Make him guilty. Talk of hangin' him. They keepin' you here 'cause they don't know what else to do with you. I get you some meat tonight. Some greens."

"They know where he at?"

"Maybe so. Draper leadin' the men. He think he gonna be sheriff, so he ridin' hard. Out all the time."

"What if they don't find him?"

"Don't know."

I languished in that cell maybe three weeks, a time brightened only by fresh straw, a cold fritter, and an empty bucket. One day a new sound came to me. It came from the throats of many people, but different than the crowd in front of the courthouse on election day. Election voices shouted husky and sharp and mirthful, fueled by liquor. Arguments abounded. These new voices gave off a higher pitch, urgent with no levity. I strained for more detail, and I quickly discerned that these to be Negro voices. Peering between the logs revealed nothing. I tried to get the direction, but my vantage through the cracks denied me any information. Lucy appeared at the door with Oscar, her face a mask of horror.

I shuffled out of the cell and rather than grab the bucket as was my routine, I craned my neck in the direction of the new sound, down towards the landing where joyous dancing and clapping once drifted up from the water. Today I heard a moan of misery like cattle being slaughtered. I turned to Lucy, and I did not have to ask the question.

"Sold," she uttered.

"Who?"

"Morgan's people. Your people."

At Lucy's words, I dropped my plate of food and bolted. The chains about my wrists and ankles clattered and banged and the heavy iron shackles cut into my skin. Still I ran. Oscar stammered and babbled before I heard him shout, "Uh, stop, dammit, stop. Got a runner! Got a runner! Help!" Someone had loaned him an old, unreliable musket. If he shot at me, I never heard it. I ran between the houses to the main street and down towards the landing. The iron dug further into my flesh, but I did not feel any pain.

I caught the scene as I crested the riverbank, perhaps two or three seconds of movement. The river was very low that time of year, so the big push boats reached almost completely across the stream from where they were beached. Fifteen people who had been my family and my neighbors clustered in one group as the trader Norton and his Negro drivers took them one by one out to a boat. Sarah had been loaded in one boat and was sitting on the bottom. She babbled drowning as she gripped the sides in terror. I do not think that any of the people had been in or on a boat before, so stepping into those canoe-like contraptions was quite disconcerting. The boats rocked easily and seemed ready to sink. The trader's Negroes pushed and struck people with cudgels, aggravating the situation and almost upsetting the boats. Norton stood off to the side with Alexander Lackey and two other white men. Actually, Lackey and the white men stood somewhat apart from Norton, who superintended the loading. Simple Jack sat in another boat, dazed and silent. Daisy stepped in Sarah's boat next, but with Sarah over-balancing each time the boat tipped, the process proved slow and cumbersome.

The rest of the people huddled together, bedrolls and sacks of meager possessions lay on the muddy ground. Mariah sobbed and Ike held her close. Peter carried Pirey, who understood that something frightful was happening. Peter stood there, his brave and dispassionate self, but I knew he was not unmoved. Esther carried Ben and her sack and watched the trader and his minions closely.

I made for Esther who turned toward the commotion of my flight and pursuit. She stepped away from the group and held little Ben out towards me. At that point Oscar's musket butt took me in the back. With a gun in his hands, he could not struggle with me, but he could keep me from rising. Several white hands pulled me up, and I was back in custody.

I screamed. I cried. I begged. I kicked. It was simple for the white men to just grab the chains between my shackles and drag me back to my cell, but I still fought. I craned my neck to catch a glimpse of my children. My escape and recapture further upset the people being transported, and Norton's Negroes attacked them. The last view I had of my son and daughter on this earth was there on that landing, in the arms of others. Pirey reached her little arm out to me, and she was crying. Of little Ben, I saw only that he had grown in the few weeks since my arrest. He was beginning to look like his father, and he reached out for me too. Pirey spoke my name, "Mama." My imagination grasped and magnified every detail because in a few short moments, they were no more to me.

The white men, layabouts from in front of the store and the tavern too lazy even to ride with Draper on his hunt for Osborn, and Oscar handled me roughly as they dragged me by the shackles back to my cell. By the time they kicked me inside I bled from new gashes in my wrists and ankles, but I still did not feel any pain. I attacked the door even before Oscar had it closed. As he turned the key in the lock, I let up a long wail that I hoped was heard at the landing. The lock rattled again and the door opened. My bucket hit me in the shoulder before I fell back into striped darkness.

The Law

The next morning, Oscar opened the door again, this time ready with an ugly club. Lucy spoke under her breath as I ate her beans.

"When the Morgans die, they was this, this will. That's how white people give away prop'ty when they die, they have a will. That's what Missus told me. Well, there was so much land and stock and slaves that the Morgans had, men started fightin' over it. See, all the property, the land, the money, the stock, the people, really belong to William. It go to the children. William's children. But they children and they can't own property. But they can't take it away neither. So white men stand up and say, *I* be the guardian. And someone else say, no, *I* be the guardian. Because the guardian is the same as the owner, you see, 'til the children get old enough. They already talk about marryin' off the girls. And they only twelve, fourteen. A man who marry one a them girls get rich right away. The boy, he only eight."

"Anyway, Mr. Lackey, he get to be guardian 'cause he married to the Colonel's daughter, William's sister. And that's like he owns it all. And he decide it time to sell the people. He say he can't be runnin' a place with people, and it a good time to sell, he say, with the war and all. And some white people mad at him. Sellin' off folks is bad for the other owners. It upset their people. But some think he doin' the right thing. Get rid of the niggers, they say. Get rid of 'em all. And Mrs. Morgan, she very upset. She want to go to court. You got to eat, Phyllis. I make that special for you. Took it out of the judge's supper. Eat it. Please. Can't give it back to the white folks. Just give it to the dogs."

I could tell that Lucy had gone to some trouble to pilfer meat and prepare the beans with molasses. It was hardly a feast, but better than most slave food. Still I was not hungry.

"That trader come to town," Lucy went on. "Norton. He had gold, real gold. Mr. Lackey, he say slaves no good up here. Time to sell. And he sell. It so sad. After you run, those drivers have to drag Peter to the boat. He don't say nothin'. He just hold still with your little girl. Those traders push and pull. And they hit him and hit him. Still he don't move. With Pirey in his arms. They finally got him in a boat and they gone. They even took that yellow dog. Eat. Please."

"Why not me?" I wanted to know. I was property too, no different than the others.

"That trader ask that. He remember you. He hear about you. He figure you fetch a fair price. The judge, he say no. He want you here 'til they find Osborn. They still lookin' for him. They got Osborn's knife next the Colonel. They know a girl can't kill two white men with another white man's knife. They know Osborn run away. And you see it all." Then her voice dropped. "Some of the white men want to hang you anyway. Eat."

I ate Lucy's food, not because I was hungry, but to show gratitude for her efforts on my behalf. At that moment, I did not care if I hanged or not. Hanging would get me out of that stinking prison. Hanging would end my pain. I did not fear dying now. I had no reason to live. I grasped for solutions, for possibilities. If they hanged me, my pain would end. But if they did not hang me, what then? Would I be sold to the trader on his next visit? At least I might follow my children. It stood to reason that the trader would follow his same route down river and that I would end up on a plantation with Pirey and Ben and Esther and Peter. That possibility made me hope that I would not be hanged.

I could go back to Osborns. But how would it be after I saw what Osborn had done? Would he even be there? Who did I belong to? Osborn? He ran away. Mrs. Osborn? Morgans? They were dead.

The guardian? The children? Did the trader buy me? Would he take me to my babies? The heart always yearns for the best, and I imagined being taken to some farm where I would find everyone I knew. My babies would be there, and I would gather them up in joy. Then I would look up to see Saul's smiling face, and the world would be right again. Back and forth, the visions swung between death and life, despair and joy, darkness and light.

Perhaps a week after the sale of the Morgan slaves, the door clattered open at midday. "Out!" shouted Oscar. Lucy stood there wide-eyed, not with a plate of food, but with a broom. She hurried past me into the cell and began cleaning. A tick full of fresh straw waited on the ground. Oscar reached out and grabbed the chain to my wrists and pulled me toward the courthouse.

Dirty, sweaty horses and with dirty, sweaty men jammed the square in casual groups passing around a water dipper. They noticed Oscar and me but gave us no further attention, giving me some comfort. If I was bound for a noose, they would watch me closely for signs of fear. There was some other purpose to this gathering. Oscar stopped on the low porch of the courthouse and dropped the chain. He pointed to the dirt of the street, indicating I should wait there. The presence of so many other white men insured that I would comply. He opened the door and stepped inside briefly before coming back out and pulling me after him.

The Prestonsburg courthouse stood as the seat of government for that part of the Commonwealth, but its form was remarkably simple. The building of sawn wood and brick was no more than a meeting room with rough benches. White men, some dirty and some clean, filled the room. Oscar led me through the crowd to a desk and Judge Graham. On a bench to one side, Edward Osborn sat, now bearded, dirty, his once-fine clothes torn and muddy, his long blonde hair a tangled, greasy mess. Osborn did not look at me and instead regarded his soiled hands. Manacles like mine hung from his wrists. Behind Osborn, Draper regarded me smugly over folded arms. Over the past weeks, Draper had assumed a minor prominence in the town as the leader of the hunt for Osborn, and this unaccustomed office caused his already intolerable arrogance to grow.

"Come here, girl," the judge ordered. I stepped to the desk. The noise of my chains pierced the silence. I had exchanged a few words with Judge Graham in the past, nothing beyond those necessary to deliver or receive a message from Morgan. I dropped my eyes to the heavy ledger open on the table in front of him. His right hand held a quill ready to write.

"Is this the man you saw kill Colonel Morgan?"

I could not answer. My presence in front of so many white men struck me dumb.

"Speak up girl," Graham ordered.

"Yassuh," I croaked softly.

"What?"

"Yassah," I utter a little louder.

"Yes, what?"

"He kill Mas' Morgan."

The judge dipped the tip of his pen into a bottle of ink and proceeded to write very deliberately. Before he finished, Alexander Lackey stepped over and whispered to Graham who looked up startled.

"Yes, of course," he said. "Girl, raise your right hand." I froze. "Your right hand!" Oscar grabbed my right arm and shoved it into the air. The manacles dragged my left hand up too. "Do you swear to tell the truth?"

I did not understand and I could not answer.

"I said, girl, do you swear to tell the truth?"

I had nothing to say. The judge sighed in exasperation.

"Girl, Phyllis, you know me. You know I'm not going to hurt you. You know that, don't you?"

"Yassuh."

"Do you know what the truth is?"

"I think so, sah."

"Are you telling the truth when I ask you if Sh...Mr. Osborn here killed Colonel Morgan?"

"Yassuh."

"He stabbed Mr. William Morgan?"

"Yassuh."

"And he stabbed Mr. David Morgan?"

"Yassuh."

"And cut his throat?"

My own throat seized up. I forced a reply. "Yassuh."

Osborn lifted his head and looked directly at me. I did not meet his gaze. I did not have to. He knew.

"That will have to do." Graham went back to his labored writing. He ended a sentence with a period and looked up at me again. "Is this the man you saw kill William Morgan?"

"Yassuh." Osborn did not take his eyes off me.

Another dip in the well, and the judge wrote in the big book.

"Do any members of the grand jury have any questions for this witness?"

I heard some grumbling behind me, but I dared not turn.

"Take her outside." Osborn watched my every step.

Oscar led me out like some sheep through a pack of hungry wolves. He found some shade for himself next to the building while I stood in the sun. Having been locked in darkness over the past weeks, I elected sunshine over any discomfort from the heat to just enjoy the light. And free of my cell for the first time in weeks, my eyes feasted on every sight. The simple buildings stood taller, and the muted colors shone brighter. Even the dried mud on walls and fence posts seemed rich and vibrant.

My reverie dissolved as I noticed the white men loitering outside the tavern. Malingerers collected there often, and their numbers waxed and waned with the season. Many men had crowded into the courthouse and they craned their necks for some scrap of the proceeding, but the tavern crowd did not appear interested in court. I slowly became aware that they did not seem to be discussing the scene in court, rather the sheep outside – me.

What did they care about me now that Osborn had been captured? The killer was in custody, and the law would take its course. I was exonerated of any culpability. Without my help, this tragedy would have gone unresolved, or more sadly, resolved against my favor. What was their interest in me? The distance that separated us made it easier for me to examine these individuals without appearing to be staring at them. Gradually, I identified a few white men whom I managed to place as partisans of Osborn's in the past election and definitely not members of the Morgan camp. Few had names for me, but I recognized a poor farmer called Calhoun and one called Harper. Bishop tanned leather badly. They were of the lower sort in the county, men who never seemed to prosper despite the opportunities around them, just the men who resented Morgan and were quick to blame their misfortune on slave owners and their slaves.

I soon provided my own answer. Osborn was their leader, and he now he wore chains, deposed. Their champion resided in the hands of Morgan's friends, men who would hang Osborn for his crimes. But they did not place the blame for Osborn's misfortune and their own on the head of the person most responsible, Osborn. And they did not consider that the court and the law might have some role in the drama. No, they focused on something and someone whom they already despised and who they thought might control the outcome – me. I was the one who caused the dispute between the Morgans and Osborn. I was the one who saw Osborn kill two men. I was the one who testified. All this was my fault. I now had to consider not the possibility of being hanged as a murderer, but of being hanged as a witness, just for being there.

Not that I really cared one way or the other. With my husband and children gone, my life was over. A rope would be a quick way to end all my pain and no more agony than I now experienced. What difference would it make why I was dead, as long as my pain ended? That mob could save me the trouble of hanging myself, and I could be assured of success. The freedom of oblivion, to suffer no more, still tempted me.

Draper and another man pushed aside these macabre thoughts as they led Osborn out of the courthouse and through the crowd. They marched their prisoner off in the direction of the jail. The tavern men stepped back sullenly, but none offered any comment or troubled to impede Draper's progress. How proud that dirty slave catcher must have felt with his prize, a white man, a white man who was the sheriff. No Roman general in a triumph paraded himself better than Draper that day.

The courthouse observers, mostly townsmen and prosperous planters, crows loitering around a harvest, spilled out of the building, oblivious to Oscar and me. The arrest of the sheriff for two murders was the biggest event in that county's history and the moment would not pass without much consideration and discussion. I caught snatches of conversation, most of which meant nothing to me.

"...indicted..."

"...trial..."

"...a nigger can't..."

"...who's going to pay?"

"...lawyer...Lexington."

"...no, Cincinnati."

"...Kentucky."

The voices seemed as entertained as perplexed.

Alexander Lackey stepped off the courthouse porch and motioned for Oscar. My guard listened intently to a message murmured in his ear. Oscar then stepped off, dragging me after him. Instead of heading toward the jail, though, we walked in the opposite direction to a stable in back of the town. I followed him inside into a stall still foul from its last occupant. There he unscrewed one of the manacles and looped the chain through an iron ring affixed to a sturdy post.

"Mr. Lackey says you stay here for now" was all that Oscar told me before leaving me alone. A horse in the next stall peered through a gap in the boards to examine this new event before going back to his own business. Using my feet, I moved enough clean straw around to make a comfortable seat of sorts, but in order to sit, I had to hold my hands over my head. I wondered how I was going to sleep or how I would attend to personal matters. Although the stall was dirty, it was not a smell I was unaccustomed to. After so many weeks in my own stink in that dim cell where Osborn now languished, the stable was positively homelike.

"Phyllis?" The voice beckoned out of the gloom. I opened my eyes to see Wilson, the old stableman who belonged to Alexander Lackey. "You want somethin' to drink? I can get you somethin' to eat."

"No, they goin' to hang me. I just want it over."

"You want me to fix your chain? Look like it hurt."

"What?"

"Your chain. Don't look too good with your hands up like that. Here." Wilson stepped out of sight a moment, and I heard iron on iron before the loop holding my hands up fell on my head. Wilson stepped into view with an iron pin in his hand. "We move that ring around. I just need to take it out'n the post. It just holds in there with this here pin. Can't leave it out, though. Wouldn't do if they find you loose." Wilson refastened the loop through a hole in the wall lower down allowing me to sit comfortably and even recline. "Get you some more straw. And some water." Within half an hour, I enjoyed a prison measures more comfortable than the hole I had slept in before. Wilson went about his chores in and around the stable, and he looked in on me. Lucy came by with food.

"They got Osborn in there now," Lucy explained. "Only he got a real bed. Those tavern boys get him some whiskey. They going to keep him there til his trial. A month, they say. Keep you here too. It funny, bein' a horse better than bein' in jail. Show you what white men know."

Despite the shackles and with Wilson's help, I made a credible bed for myself. I got fresh straw and fresh air, such as it was in a stable. By laying back and crossing my arms I found a few moments of sleep before my hands began to hurt. Wilson gave me a horse blanket that reeked of a dozen different owners, but it smelled no worse than I did. As the light faded, I felt my tiny bedfellows stir for their nightly insect sojourns for food and society. A dubious brown cat peered into the stall to examine the interloper on her hunting grounds. As soon as our eyes met, she jumped out of view only to return silently a few moments later. She seemed unconvinced that my presence did not affect her supper, so I pushed my empty bowl toward her. She tentatively approached the treat and her gaze twitched between the potential meal and the obvious threat. While keeping me in her scrutiny, she licked the bowl clean. I reached to her, but when the shackles clattered, she disappeared.

The abandonment by a brown barn cat just amplified my melancholy. I lay back and closed my eyes. What sleep I had was tortured by images of my loved ones lost. Their faces and their voices spun about in all sorts of improbable ways. Pirie stirring a pot. Little Ben driving a wagon. Saul standing in water. Even Sim appeared, observant, cautious, calculating. Sim actually spoke to me, saying in a strong and clear voice that he would watch the children and help Esther with them. In the background were the rest of my friends, even those who tormented me. They laughed and they cried. I called out to them. "Wait for me. Wait for me." The pain left when I pushed these thoughts of them out of my head. Freedom from pain meant denying my family.

"Just cut her throat," the voice said. "No need to work at this any more than we have to."

"No," another man slurred, "I want t' see her swing."

"String up your own nigger. I say we bleed this one right here and be done with it. Besides, she's chained. You got a key?"

"Don't need a key. Hang her in chains."

I opened my eyes to dark shapes standing over me. Enough moonlight crept through the sides of the stable to tell me there were three and the voices told me that they were white men – white men smelling of whiskey and murder. The end had come. I would no longer be haunted by ghosts. Oblivion and the end of pain was only moments away. I knew from bleeding so many hogs that once they opened the vein on my neck, sleep followed. I even turned my head away from the intruders to expose my neck to the knife. I gladly surrendered my life to end this agony.

"Maybe you're right. Would have been nice to see a little show."

"Grab her. Get the chains. Let's get it done."

As desperate as I was for death, something in me fought off the murderous hands. This only earned me kicks and punches. Anyone who has butchered knows that you either kill your meat at once or make certain that the animal is tightly bound. These erstwhile butchers either forgot this lesson or misjudged the fight in a lowly slave girl. I wanted to die, but I did not want to die. In the darkness confusion reigned. Three drunken men and one chained animal struggled in a crude horse stall. They kicked and punched and cursed. I flailed about, and I felt the chains and shackles bite into soft flesh not my own. Perhaps I resisted so that my end was not my own decision but that of others? It is one thing to jump off a cliff willingly and another to be pushed off. I know now that there was another hand in this all, another power.

That power found its way into the pistol butt of one Noah Draper, slave catcher, deputy sheriff, and cock of the walk in Prestonsburg. Draper dispatched one of my killers with skill I would never had credited him with. He must have felt pleasure in attaining a certain talent at felling human beings with a single blow. The drunken white man fell on top of me with a weight that robbed me of breath.

"No one kills niggers in this town less it's me," he announced. "No one kills niggers in this county less it's me. I'm the law. The judge wants this one alive. I do all the nigger killin' here." I heard the pistol butt meet muscle and bone and a second body crashed to the straw screaming. The man on top of me stirred, and I felt warm fluid on my face. Some dripped into my mouth with the acid taste of puke.

I coughed and pushed at the body on top of me until it moved. More chaos in the stall with curses and threats and stumbling, but no blows and no knife thrusts toward me. A lantern carried by voices appeared overhead. Draper loomed over a stricken man with his pistol, butt forward. Other white faces gathered behind him, some grim, some shocked. I had seen Draper lord it over Negroes, but now he wielded his power and authority over white men. As much of a monster as he might have been and as malevolent as he might have become, Draper saved my life. I do not doubt that he would have been happy to watch me twitch and twist as I bled a river into the straw. Somehow God commanded him to be my savior.

"Pull him out of here," Draper ordered. "And him." Hands wrestled my protesting murderers away. Horses in the stable stomped and jumped at the disturbance. Draper took the candle lantern from his helper. He stood there in the dim light and regarded me without the contempt I had come to expect from him. Now I was a problem, a puzzle. His mandate was to keep me alive, and he had to draft a plan with limited tools. He stepped back, walked around the small stable, then stood over me again. He stuffed the pistol in his belt and retrieved a key which he used to unscrew one of my manacles.

"Get up," he told me and he dropped the open manacle on my chest. I pulled the chain through the iron ring and stumbled to my feet. "Out," he said.

I followed this new master out of the stable into the clear night, carrying the means of my own imprisonment, but only half confined now that one arm was free. A small crowd of white men had gathered to gawk.

"Whatcha goin' to do with her, Draper," one voice taunted, "put her in with Osborn?" This produced drunken laughter from the onlookers and some lurid comments, but no response from Draper. I followed his dark form carrying the candle lantern to the blacksmith's home next door where he pounded on the door.

"Mallory! Open in the name of the law!" After some moments and cursing from within, the door opened to a powerful and angry blacksmith in a nightshirt.

"Draper, you dog," Mallory growled, "this deputy sheriff business has addled your brain. I'm going to have you locked away with your master. You can sleep off your whiskey there."

"We'll see who sleeps it off. I want your help."

"You need more chains? Have you arrested the rest of the county? What's she doin' here?"

"Osborn's boys tried to gut her. Judge Graham and Mr. Lackey say I got to keep her alive til they decide what to do. I can't keep her in the stable, and I can't lock her in the jail. I can lock her with your boy. We'll tell him to watch her and to shrub anyone tries to hurt her."

Mallory eyed me and considered the request. "How long?"

"Can't say. Take it up with Judge Graham."

"How much?"

"Take it up with Judge Graham. I don't suppose your boy'd mind the chore."

Mallory smiled. "No, don't suppose he would. This way." Mallory stepped past me and we followed him to the forge in the back. "Simon! Simon!"

Simon, Suzie's erstwhile beau peered out of a corner. "Yassuh?"

"Simon, do what Dra...the sh..., the deputy sheriff says."

"Boy," Draper said, "I want you to keep watch over the girl here. Some folks don't want her around, and I don't want to pay a white man to watch her. You keep her safe. Anyone tries to take her or hurt her, you stop 'em. You got a hammer here?"

"Yassuh, fine hammers."

"Use a hammer if you have to. Just keep her safe. White or black, I don't care. Keep her safe. Anything happens to her, Simon, you pay for it, and you know what I mean. You understand?"

"Yassuh."

"You keep her safe. You take that hammer and you knock anyone who comes near her. Anything happens to her happens to you. If she's dead, you better be dead too. You understand?"

"Yassuh."

"Give me your hand." Draper set the lantern on the ground. Simon tentatively reached out with his left hand, and Draper grabbed it by the wrist. He turned to me and snatched the open shackle from my hand and clamped it around Simon's wrist. But Simon's huge forearm was more than the manacle could easily accommodate, and Simon jerked back as Draper tried to close the iron and pinched him. Draper cursed and started to push again on the closure, then stopped. Simon's huge arms defied any shackled designed for the wrist of an average human. Draper pushed Simon away and grabbed my chained arm. Using the tool he unfastened the remaining manacle freeing my hands. I immediately began to feel the wounds left by the iron.

Draper then knelt down and undid one leg iron moving it to Simon's ankle. In a few seconds, Simon and I stood bound as one. "You stay with Simon, girl. I'll be back at daylight." Draper pushed us into the darkness of Simon's room and pushed the door closed. As insufferable as Draper had become, he adapted well to his position of authority. He could have as easily let those drunks bleed me and be done with it, but he elected to do some duty. Deep under that layer of dirt lay the seed of a man which just needed a sound purpose to sprout. How many men of no account before The War grew in that horror to become great leaders? General Grant himself had been bankrupt. General Sherman was regarded as crazy.

I heard Mallory ask Draper as they left, "Who's going to feed her? How's he goin' to work with those irons on him?" I could not hear Draper's answer.

Simon's room allowed the two of us to stand together next to his pallet in the dark. I felt him look at me with the same look of shock that had greeted Draper's orders. My mind still reeled from the episode in the stall that found me locked at the ankle with this big man. Finally, Simon spoke.

"You been sleepin' with pigs?"

"Horses. And myself," I replied.

"Look like it. Smell like it. Those white men try to kill you?"

"Guess so. No matter."

Simon's pallet was the first real bed that I had seen in weeks and my lack of sleep and my exertions in the stable had left me spent. Without asking any leave from my host, I dropped onto Simon's bed and faced the wall, but my leg curled back in Simon's direction. Simon quite willingly followed me. I curled away from him so he was left to find his place facing my back. As I sought sleep, I felt his hand explore my person under my shift. He pushed at me with the urgency that the male animal so uniquely expresses, but lacking any response from me, his advances relented. I do not know if Simon slept, but I did.

Dawn found Simon and me shamelessly answering nature's call together in the colored privy. As he built up the fire in the forge for the day's work, the chain hindered his progress. Lucy brought me and Simon a breakfast of grits, a rare feast for me. Draper arrived after several hours and unburdened Simon of his guest. From the deference Simon showed me, I sensed he would have been willing to continue his obligation for at least another night on the gamble that I found the experience less loathsome.

Carrying the empty shackle I limped with Draper back to the courthouse and inside. The tavern men watched silently. One sported an angry red gash in his head. In the courtroom this time, there was just Judge Graham, Alexander Lackey, and the diminutive Mrs. Anna Morgan. The judge sat behind his table with his great ledger open. Draper stopped me in front of the judge.

"Release the prisoner," the judge ordered. Draper unlocked the remaining manacle without hesitation. He gathered the chain entirely proud of his important role in the business of the county. "Phyllis," the judge continued, "you are given over to the custody of Mrs. David Morgan, on her bond, until such time as your ownership and the will of this court can be determined. Mrs. Morgan will return you to the court at the time of trial. Court's adjourned."

Mrs. Morgan regarded me with a slight smile, but her blue eyes bore a great sadness and more wrinkles than I had noticed before. She had lost much in the past weeks, her husband, her son, and almost all her property. She did not even have a man to help her run her farm. Being returned to Morgan's was not a fate I had anticipated. I imagined being hanged, butchered, being sold off to Mississippi, fleeing into the forest, even being dragged back to Osborn's by my murderous owner. But Morgan's never seemed a possibility at all.

"Let's go home, Phyllis," she told me. I followed her to the once familiar wagon pulled by the same old horse. "You drive."

I fumbled for several minutes with the harness and the reins as I moved from condemned prisoner back to slave. The movements of my body like walking free of irons, once done without thought, produced sensations fresh and sweet. I felt I could fly. The past weeks faded away. I got into the seat next to my old mistress, or my new mistress, and I managed to turn the team back towards Beaver Creek. I was free, but not free – safe, but not safe – alive, but not alive.

We drove in silence, passing fields being harvested, some by black hands, most by white hands. Scythes flashed in the sun in a slow steady march as fields transformed into God's bounty bound for the landing and the river. As I saw the stalks fall I imagined the people I knew who were harvested from this land and sent down to the landing like so much wheat or corn, just to be shipped away and to be consumed somewhere far down the river.

The Farm of Silence

For the first hour I drove in silence, stunned by this change in fortune and overwhelmed by the transformation in my situation. One moment I languished in chains, robbed of humanity, smelling of my own foulness, and confronting my end. The next moment, a murderous mob sought to bleed me. An instant after that, I slumbered next to an amorous blacksmith. Now I drove a once-familiar wagon staring at the rhythmically laboring haunches of an old horse. Had the last three years and the last several weeks really happened? Was it a dream? Would I wake up in the barn? Or in my cell?

As my mind cleared and cognition returned, I began to grasp the new reality. All the disparate events connected into a snake-like chain, and I accepted that I was driving a wagon back to Morgan's farm on Beaver Creek. My motherly instincts quickly surfaced. That undying tie between my children and myself tugged at me, painfully. I was moving away from where I needed to go, away from my children, but away from the pain. This path was wrong, but it was right. My family left in the opposite direction, on boats, down around the next bend in the river. That was where I should have been going. My husband was already lost from view and I felt my children pulling further away. Where once the track from town to Beaver Creek led to home and safety, it now seemed both another jail and an escape.

I glanced back to see Mrs. Morgan sitting in the wagon bed apparently deep in her own thoughts, so I saw no occasion for conversation. She could have fit on the wagon seat next to me as one would expect from a mistress, but being the independent soul she was, she availed herself of some empty sacks.

Onward we rode for hours and those haunches never wavered from their even gait. I slowly recovered from the role of prisoner back to that of free slave, if such a state is possible. The Morgan farm emerged from the forest just as it did every time I returned home behind this same old horse. The first thing the traveler saw was the split rail fence between the track and the pasture. A single rail leaned to the ground begging for repair. The small barn then appeared. This rude structure was one of the first buildings we erected on arriving from Virginia, and it housed slaves and stock until the cabins were built. Soon, the main barn, the slave cabins, the big oak tree, and finally Morgan's house each hove into view as if emerging in some elaborate theatrical tableau – the impresario slowly pulling back a curtain of forest to reveal a once-thriving community.

But where delicate plumes once marked small chimneys, the air shone clear and still. Gone was the sound of axe against wood as were the soft songs and easy conversations of women about their chores and the calls and laughter of men at work. Morgan's farm reposed in the autumn afternoon no longer a living being, but a fresh corpse. Pens and stalls lay empty. Gates stood open where the executors had left them in their haste to seize up the Morgan wealth. Whoever took the stock must have considered the goats to be of no value, for they seemed to have survived the legalized pillaging of a dead man's estate. A few loose chickens pecked at the ground or roosted on fence posts. A scrawny hog scuttled out of a slave cabin to stop at the door of another to sniff before entering to forage. Roof lines sagged in sadness, robbed of the lives that lately dwelled so blissfully under them. Even the main house gave off the air of mourning.

All around Morgan's signs of neglect foreshadowed decline. A farm requires continual attention or it gradually sinks into the ground. The farmer fights a constant struggle with the land as he wrests profit from it. It seems that the earth stolidly yields up only what it is forced to. The farmer thinks he dominates the land with his plow and hoe. He believes that the crop he harvests is his and not the result of sun and water and seed and soil. But crops are temporary, and one season's inattention allows the forest to creep back into the fields with the saplings and vines that once grew there. Cabins and barns pretend permanence. Any lack of vigilance and soil and sky conspire to leverage the structures down and reduce them to dust. Boards work loose from walls and the walls lean. Fences sag until they topple. In enough time without man's efforts, the farm returns to the earth without leaving a trace. In only a few weeks, the earth's progress against Morgan's was already apparent.

"They let the fire go out," Mrs. Morgan commented. "At least they aren't burning wood that has to be cut."

"I get the fire goin', Missus," I told her without thinking. How quickly I resumed the role of obedient servant.

"No, I can start a fire," she answered softly. "You tend to the horse and milk those goats. We don't want them to dry up. I need your help here. Everyone's gone now."

"Mr. O'Hara?"

"He rode off with Draper. I haven't seen him in weeks. I'll get out here. Take care of the horse. I'll send David down to help. The girls can herd the goats. Maybe you can teach them milking."

I stopped the wagon and began unhitching the old horse, once the poorest in the Morgan stable. The stable and the smell of the tack room brought back sweet memories of the happier time when Saul made Morgan the envy of every horse breeder in the county and me the happiest and proudest woman in the world. Empty pegs awaited the collar and harness, but more pegs bespoke tack snatched away by the looters. I pulled the horse into his stall and got him some of fodder from the wagon. The mundane work of brushing and currying was actually quite refreshing after my imprisonment, and I tried mightily to concentrate. Young David arrived and stared at me first with awe, then with curiosity.

"Missus say you help," I said. "Can you curry? I unload the wagon."

"Sure." He stepped up, and even at the age of eight, his head came just below mine. I handed him the brush, and he started with a crude stroke against the old horse's hide. The horse jerked away from the inept movement.

"Here," I told him, "try this." I showed him how to place one hand on the animal to tell it where I was going to brush, then brush. "Easier on you, and easier on the horse." He grasped the idea immediately and the horse quickly accepted his ministrations. "Go with the hair on the hide. Good. Now back here. Good. Get all his sweat out. Go easy down here. Good." Young David seemed to have some touch with the animal without the uncertain manner of so many learning to handle stock. David's father William knew horses too, but his grandfather, as far as I know, never groomed his own horse.

The leather bucket for the goat's milk was upside down on a fence post and from the flies disturbed within I realized that the novice who had been doing the milking had neglected to wash it. Polley, the eldest girl, soon joined me.

"Nana says I'm to learn from you milkin'. I already know how." Polley got the family blonde hair, and she wore a fair-quality dress of manufactured cloth, but made at home. The girl perched on the brink of womanhood, and I remembered Lucy's comment about the powerful men of the county plotting to marry her into some influential family. Women and girls, even white ones, fared no better than Africans when it came to white men and their greed.

"It easy, but you got to have a clean bucket." I was used to respectfully addressing Osborn's children, but unaccustomed to instructing them, and I had no memory of ever speaking to the Morgan children. "Come on." I led her to the creek below the slave cabins. "The old milk rot and sour the new milk. I wash it here. Not by the well. Don't want the bad water in with the good up there." I set her to work scrubbing the leather bucket with lichen snatched from a log. I went over to the slave cabins to find another bucket.

The chickens had fled their pen through a broken door, which was probably just as well since there was no feed there. The slave cabins looked as if they had been ransacked by thieves. Benches lay over on their sides. Bowls, broken utensils, and bits of clothing lay about. Esther's cabin, my cabin, the one with the window, was worse, probably because she and her driver husband, Peter, had the most possessions. A small bed lay at the foot of Esther's pallet and silently spoke of her last guests. Here my babies had slept the night before they were taken to the landing. I stepped over to the little bed and placed my hand there, hoping to make some connection with my missing children. The cedar chips just felt cold and dead like the rest of the cabin.

Over the dead fireplace the empty crane spoke of a pot taken in the looting. The other cabins were similarly strewn with the debris of simple, but once-secure lives. Some fugitive chickens had taken up residence in the men's cabin as evidenced by manure and eggs. In the cabin I once shared with Mariah and Ike, I found the small wood pail that she used for the slave children's share of milk.

After some instruction on cleaning, I took Polley and the buckets to the goats. I showed her how to corner a nannie with swollen teats and tie her to the fence. Polley's hands were not used to the work and she tired easily, but she showed willingness and demonstrated not a little pride of what she had accomplished. Mrs. Morgan had apparently been trying to keep the goats milked, but two had gone dry and would not give again until bred. It was just as well since we had fewer people to feed. Polley and I delivered the milk to the house and the mistress set me to work laying in firewood. The fuel for the kitchen usually supplied by slaves had been depleted to nothing. Mrs. Morgan apparently cut only as much as she needed for each meal. I quickly calculated that were I to have a hot supper, I needed to get to work right away. Fortunately, I had dry wood available, and I set to work bucking and splitting. Young David, done at the stable, silently stacked the cut wood for me. By the time supper was ready, I had enough fuel for a meal or two ahead.

Mrs. Morgan had a pumpkin soup on the hearth in the main house. No need to use Mariah's outdoor kitchen with so few people to feed. The mistress proved a far more competent cook than Abigail Osborn, having been raised without slaves to do her cooking. Anna Morgan, widow of the richest and most powerful man in the county, still knew her way around a kitchen, unlike her grand-daughters. She now endeavored to impart to them the lore of hearth and home since they would soon be wives and would need some abilities in their new homes. Once they became the chattel of their husbands, they would be out of the grandmother's reach and care.

Mrs. Morgan hoisted the pot onto the family table and the children took their seats greedily. I stood back waiting for my turn after they had their fill and as usual, I worried that there would be enough for me. The mistress surprised me by saying, "Get that bowl. Sit."

Polley, William's eldest, seemed to have her grandmother's quiet confidence as well as her blond hair. She asked many questions, often to her brother or sister or to me knowing full well that none of us had the means to answer her. Her manner was that of professor grilling students just so they would remember who was student and who was teacher.

David was the youngest and took after his father with a long body, wavy blond hair, and arrogant brown eyes. He was big for his age, and I predicted not a few broken noses and broken hearts in his future. The two of them eclipsed Anne in the middle, whether by lack of skill on her part or clever discretion I will never know. Their mother died when David was born, so the grandmother became the mother, a role she managed easily.

Mrs. Morgan dished out the soup into five equal portions, upturning the pot over her bowl last. When the children did not immediately devour their meal, I worried that their grandmother was a poor cook and that they were avoiding an unpleasant task. Having never eaten with white people before, I watched for a cue for my next move. Instead of spontaneous gorging or an order to eat however, Mrs. Morgan bowed her head. With her hands in her lap she recited, "Almighty Father, we thank you for this fruit of your bounty, and we pray for your help in this season where others hold our lives in their hands. Amen."

"Amen," answered the children who then seized their pewter spoons and dove into their bowls. Such was my second real taste of faith and another step in my path as a Christian. Naturally, I did not know at that time that the journey had begun, but I sensed again the possibility of other forces in the world beyond white men and the weather. I understood that outside my reach and beyond my view someone or something manipulated seasons and events. This was the first time white people had expressed that in front of me. The preacher spoke in terms of salvation and justice. Here I saw recognition of power and gratitude for gifts received. It was like walking through a dark forest and suddenly finding a tuft of strange fur at head height on a tree. Some immense animal had passed by and without seeing or hearing the creature, I was aware that it was real and large, much larger than I.

That imponderable yielded to my hunger, and I took up my spoon for one of the finest meals of my life. Young Polley pushed the plate with fritters at me, and David snatched one for himself.

"Leave that one for Phyllis, David," Mrs. Morgan softly chided, "she hasn't eaten this well in weeks and weeks. She's a good cook. She'll make you more. Better than I can. We're going to need her help this winter."

David looked at his grandmother suspiciously and dropped the morsel back onto the plate without even regarding me. He returned to his meal, and I caught the slightest smirk on Polley's face. That simple piece of fried meal tasted wonderfully.

"Mama," Polley asked Mrs. Morgan, "why did Phyllis come back? Why didn't she go with the rest of the hands?"

The mistress chewed slowly and before she was entirely finished replied, "It's complicated." I suspected she hesitated to discuss business in my presence, but I was wrong. She was just trying to translate arcane legal events into something the children would understand.

"Phyllis was there when your father and your grandfather... died."

"The sheriff killed 'em, killed 'em with a knife," David offered proudly.

"I know that," Polley assured him. "We thought *she* did it. At first."

"Gonna hang her," David added.

"Yes," Mrs. Morgan continued, "that's all straightened out now." She chewed some more. I found the meat in the soup particularly stringy, like slave food, and we all chewed. "Under the law, the guardian takes over. Your Uncle Alexander became the guardian. He decided to sell off the people and the stock. But Phyllis was…in jail and couldn't be sold." More chewing. "I got the judge to give her to me, to us. She can help us here until we…they decide what to do with the farm. We have to get the apples in and down to the landing." There was more that she was not telling, but I assumed those were legal mysteries that might make no sense to the children or to me. I surmised that there were other secrets behind all these events.

I milked goats and picked apples, cut wood, cooked, fed the horse, but not entirely alone. The girls stumbled through kitchen tasks and learned washing. David yearned to prove himself a man and undertook to care for the stock. His affinity for the one remaining horse and even the goats called up in me painful feelings over Saul and even young Thomas.

As the warm days waned, I experienced a growing gulf between me and my babies. Every day, they floated further down the river, deeper into cotton country, farther from me. Gradually, I lost touch with their faces and their voices. Ben's laughter became just a smile. The words of Pirey's childish questions lost their distinctness. Those words I could remember her speaking became just words and not spoken in her voice. The kindness being shown by Mrs. Morgan, mirrored by the children, recalled a happier time, making me all the sadder.

I ate with the family three times a day, but never joined in the conversations except to answer questions. Every meal they prayed and every meal I became more aware of the emptiness that existed without the Word of God. Mrs. Morgan asked for God's help and His forgiveness, things I did not yet understand. I yearned for the comfort and strength that the prayers seemed to give to her. The words seemed to be of inestimable value and great power. To suspect there was more to the world than what I could see and touch and to suspect that the powers over me were other than those of owners and overseers only teased my mind further.

A week after I returned to the farm, Draper rode up to the house. In his metamorphosis from slave catcher to interim sheriff, he acquired better clothing to go with his new boots. He even had a good horse, one that Saul had trained for Alexander Lackey. Pride and arrogance replaced his obsequious slouch. He walked up to the house and removed his hat for Mrs. Morgan. A certain swagger replaced his old furtive, often drunken gait. After a few words, Mrs. Morgan brought her hand to her chest. They conversed for some time until Draper stepped back and donned his hat before taking to horse again. He rode off and Mrs. Morgan disappeared.

At supper, the mistress announced to us all, "Phyllis and I are going on a trip for several days. Perhaps several weeks. Something has happened with the hands down river, and we need to see what we can do."

"What happened?" Polley asked.

"Something. It seems that many of the people are down at Owensborough. There has been some trouble." My heart jumped.

"My babies?" I blurted out still very much out of place. "My babies there? What trouble?"

"Mister Draper didn't know about your children. He told me of the trouble. You children will stay with your Uncle Alexander. Maybe he will send some of his hands to tend to the farm. Phyllis and I are going to Owensborough."

"There is other news," she continued. "Mr. Edward Osborn has broken out of jail. He's gone."

The River

Two days later, at the same landing where I had seen my children disappear, I stepped aboard a push boat. I carried some food tied in a blanket. Mrs. Morgan directed me to take a seat in the bottom of the narrow hull. The boat sat low in the water with the beneficence of the country, sacks of grain and baskets of apples carefully balanced. The two boatmen pushed the boat away from the shore and used long poles to guide it into the middle of the river.

I watched the country pass by knowing that this was the last that Saul and my children and my friends had seen of their homes. The Big Sandy drains the land between Kentucky and Virginia in wide, slow meanders nudged back and forth by the mountains. The bends loop around dense forest, slowly yielding to axe and plow. The farther downstream we traveled the farms grew in number but not in size or prosperity. The fields stretched out bare, having just been shorn of their bounty. The country took an easy breath between the hard labor of autumn and the first winds of winter. Streams and branches added their flows, and the river grew larger. The boatmen used their poles to fend away from snags and to stay in the middle of the languid stream where the current carried us downward.

"Some say Osborn was strung up," the lead boatman told Mrs. Morgan. "They made to look like he lit out. Some say he got help and got out of this country. He's gone, and it don't look like they interested in findin' him."

Our boat took us as far as Catlettsburg on the Ohio. Catlettsburg and its broad landing actually had painted houses, and long boats, schooners, scows, keel boats, rafts, flatboats, and other craft crowded the shore. The town gathered all the river traffic from that part of Kentucky and Virginia and took a sip of the growing flow of people and goods from east to west.

Mrs. Morgan found a keel boat, and within hours we set off down the great Ohio River. In those days, before steam, keelboats did the real work of the Ohio using sails or poles or long oars to get up the river. The voyage downstream was accomplished by rowing to mid stream and riding the current west. Four men manned the sweeps as the captain steered with an oar at the stern. Our boat was about forty feet long and reflected years of hard use and little care. It had never known paint, and from the frequent bailing of water from the hold, it promised to sink if neglected more than a few hours. The captain tried to get Mrs. Morgan to have me do the bailing, but she refused unless he remitted some of passage money. The house on top on which passengers rode threatened to resign from the enterprise out of sheer exhaustion. But somehow the vessel held together.

Captain Jenkins, if that title can be applied to the white man in charge of such a mean conveyance, looked like one of the barrels in his hold. What he lacked in stature, God compensated with powerful arms. The river man pushed the tiller with ease. All of the crew save one was white. The lone Negro was Henry, who I assumed belonged to Jenkins or was hired out by his owner. All of the river men affected broad-brimmed hats against sun and rain, trousers that ended just below the knee, and bare feet, the better to negotiate the shallows through which they so often found themselves struggling upstream. Each, including Henry, also possessed an ugly knife at the small of his back.

My world widened with the Ohio. I could easily ford the Big Sandy and Beaver Creek at low water, but the Ohio threatened to swallow me up. From the middle of the river the land shrunk to just two dark green lines in the distance. I clutched my bundle, afraid the random collection of old boards would finally surrender to the hungry waters. A lack of cooperating wind meant the crew rowed to keep to the middle of the river and add their effort to our progress. We saw other keel boats under limp sails being polled upstream. Downstream traffic included rafts piled with the belongings and even stock and vehicles of settlers bound for the open lands of the West.

I did not relax until Jenkins steered us to the Kentucky side. The green line in the distance grew into a forest again then trees and the river bank. Mrs. Morgan traded my cooking services for a share of what the boatmen had and what they pilfered from the cargo. I built a fire on the shore and soon had a pot going. Big Sandy potatoes and vegetables allowed me to make up a tasty meal. As they conversed, I worked in the middle of things, present but invisible. Besides the two of us, there were five boatmen. That's when we learned the details of the trouble that Draper had reported. Word on the river traveled quickly if not accurately.

"Cut their throats," the captain told Mrs. Morgan. I could feel the eyes of the others on me as I tended the fire. "Threw 'em overboard. Got to the Indiana side an' ran. Took a week to round 'em up. Not sure how many got away."

I had to summon every ounce of my own slave discipline not to blurt out a question about my babies. Here was word of them so close, but I dared not speak out. Mrs. Morgan must have sensed my anguish and tendered some questions.

"Did you hear anything about any children?" she asked. "There were at least five children that left Prestonsburg."

"Didn't hear nothin' about no brats. They gonna hang six of 'em next week. Men not brats. Biggest thing to ever hit that town. People coming from up and down to river to watch. Too bad. Six prime hands. Bring a nice price in Memphis."

"What of the others? The ones... the ones that won't hang?"

"Sent on I 'spect."

"None of the white men survived?"

"Nope."

"One lived, I hear," a boatman volunteered. "I hear they found the trader's niggers. One didn't have no head."

"What they ought to do," another interrupted, "is take and hang 'em in different places. So's all the other niggers can see what happens when you kill a white man and run off. Hangin' 'em all in one place just makes for a big show. Need to let all the niggers see."

"But nothing about any children?" Mrs. Morgan pressed.

"Anybody hear about any little 'uns?" Heads shook no.

"Still," the one in favor of separate hangings said, "I ain't shippin' on no boat full o' niggers. Give me a hold full o' nice, quiet corn. No corn never cut no white man's throat. Fine with me if we didn't have no niggers 'tall."

I bit off my anguish as I spooned up a rough stew to men who neither thanked nor acknowledged my work. With seven plates and a pot to clean in the sand of the river, I had plenty of work in which to bury my fears. Mrs. Morgan sweet-talked Jenkins out of space inside the keel boat for the night, incurring protests from his crew who had to settle for the deck or the shore. Jenkins set the men to take turns on a watch, pirates still presenting a threat along the river. "They watch for migrants on rafts and don't tussle with a full crew," Jenkins explained to his passenger," but you can't be too careful. Fella I knew disappeared down from here a year ago. Don't know if it was pirates or just the river. The river can be hard enough. You get high water at night, and you might not wake up."

The soft rocking and pictures of my children made my rest fitful. When I finally drifted off to sleep the river men's shouts shook me awake as they got underway in the dawn.

Back in midstream, the boatmen worked the sweeps deftly as they rode the current. This left them with little to do except speculate endlessly about everything, mostly about the virtues of women and girls, seen and unseen. As much as they estimated the carnal qualities of imaginary strangers, I got the impression that their own knowledge was limited to the basest of encounters behind taverns amid stink and garbage. At no time did I hear a conversation worthy of the term. Mrs. Morgan, met all veiled overtures with a tight-lipped gaze that could freeze a forge. I drew a few inquisitive stares, which I returned with a glance away and, if possible, retreat.

I made certain to remain close to my mistress and never to offer anything in the way of invitation or acceptance.

During one stop at a riverside settlement on the Ohio side, Jenkins went ashore to seek more cargo and Mrs. Morgan trailed along for news. I warmed a pot of beans on the shore this being a frequent stopping place. I could hear the white men on the boat.

"You know," said the river man who always made the most lurid comments, "I think I'll go down and borrow the widow's bitch."

"Not this trip you don't," replied another voice. "Not so long as she's cookin' *my* dinner. You tumble her, we'll picking turds out o' our stew. My stew too. Seen it. Young buck thought he'd get some juice and she pissed in our soup. She went for a swim, but that didn't help my soup. Leave her be. I find somethin' in my stew I don't like, you'll both eat it in the river." After a moment during which the first man undoubtedly considered this new information, I heard him change the subject to the weather.

An hour or so later, I handed up the beans with an insincere, "You gent'min eat up now, eat up," which was met with a careful examination of the fare. Notwithstanding the warnings, Henry, the Negro ventured off to where I ate my beans for some conversation. He took a place on the same log.

"You got people on that slave boat? The one that killed the white men?"

"My babies. Boy and girl. All the people from our place."

"How'd you not go?"

How to explain that? How to express the twisted series of events? How much to trust him? At one time I would have been pressing him for information, but that part of me hid deep in its burrow like a hedgehog somewhere between the lean-to at Osborn's barn and the jail in Prestonsburg. Sensing that Henry did not really care about my answer, I just gave him, "Don't know. Missus just keep me."

"Those prob'ly her blue eyes. That why she keep you. Who's your daddy, her brother? She got a son?"

I did not answer.

"Don't say you don't know. Where you think you get them eyes? That's what they do. They sell off ever'body but their own. That how my Nana get free. Her daddy own her. He set her free. My mama born free. I born free."

"They don't sell me 'cause they got me in jail."

"Ah. Bad you in jail, but good you not sold. Why they got you in jail?"

"They think I kill some white men. Colonel Morgan and Mister William. Then they catch Mister Osborn. Missus take me home."

"Lucky for you. Like them eyes and that honey skin. I say you belong to your Missus and you more'n just a slave."

"No, nobody never said."

"No, they never say it. They never own up that the massa be down in the quarters takin' his pick. Well it true. You got a white daddy and I say you kin to the missus."

There it was, out there in front of me, the question I never answered because I did not want it answered. I had accepted my fair skin and my eyes, but chose never to push it further. I never asked about my father because I did not want to know. I could not deny it any longer now. William Morgan began his roaming ways as a youngster in my mother's cabin. That was why his father left her in Virginia. He needed to remove any further distraction for his son on whom he needed to build a new life in Kentucky.

So much else became clear – never being really accepted by Mariah or the others and Esther's special attention to me. And Morgan's actions. He brought me from Virginia. He picked me to help in his house. He brought me a husband. He made me his spy. Then I saw something that filled me with profound regret. He sought to retrieve me before Osborn sold me away too.

Suddenly I did not know who I was. One moment I was another slave, the property of white people, working without rest, pining for her lost love ones. The next moment I was the daughter and granddaughter of powerful white men, having both benefited from scraps of privilege tossed my way and suffered from their miscalculations. Now I was being pulled along by my mistress – my grandmother? – in an effort to find my babies. Her babies?

Henry interrupted the anarchy in my mind.

"You ever thought of bein' free?"

"What?"

"Free.Work for wages. Like me. Not same wages as the white men, but wages."

"I don't know."

"Don't need your mistress to free you. Just get up and walk. I walk where I want. Work where I want. I want work on the river, so here I am. Jenkins he fair. If he beat me he know I leave. Then he have to get some no 'count white man. And it cost him more. Coloreds hear he beat me, they don't go. I just don't go Kentucky."

"Why you don't go Kentucky?"

"No free coloreds in Kentucky. You see how I never leave the boat? 'Cept to haul. We get to Cincinnati maybe we go for a walk. I help you find a place. I help you find work. Your mistress never find you there. Big city. Lots of people there watch out for you."

Before I could consider this incomprehensible offer, Henry changed the subject, or rather, he changed direction. His subject never changed.

"You got a man?"

"Sold Saul away. Last year."

"That so sad."

Only one other man looked into my eyes like that. Henry tried to use his words and his mind on me instead of his hands and feet, and I was vulnerable to that approach. In those moments as he ignited the new understandings about myself and where I came from, he tickled awake my baser instincts beneath my belly long ignored. I could not help myself.

"You got a woman?" I asked.

"No one special." He skillfully turned the subject back to me. "You cook good. Your mistress lucky. And you got them pretty eyes. You do well in Cincinnati." Maybe out in the country. Lots of people hide there."

"Tell me 'bout Cincinnati."

"No town like Cincinnati," Henry beamed. "No place like Cincinnati. People live there free. Even runaways. Nobody sold away. White folks don't want us around, but they want us around. Somebody got to work for 'em. Some free folks even got their own farms. I no farmer. I love the river. Maybe someday have my own boat. I think about buyin' ole Jenkins's boat but I do better. Got some money with Mama. Save it. I get a boat some day. Take care of it."

"Where you go on your boat?"

"Anywhere I want where there water. Pittsburgh. Lou'ville. Anywhere." His eyes sparkled with enthusiasm like when Saul planned our cabin. "I hire my own crew. Maybe hire a cook. Maybe hire you for a cook. You could make money. Buy your freedom even. Not have to be a runaway no more." He shifted ever so slightly closer to me as he sought a bit of comfort. I did not recoil in disgust or terror.

"I got to find my babies," I told him. Henry was not unattractive, and he spoke better than any Negro I had ever met, even Saul. Saul was tender, patient, peaceable, and my love. And this man was tender too, even respectful, and he demonstrated an intelligence that only a foolish slave would reveal. Henry was not a slave. He was a freeman. He did not have to hide his brain or his dreams. What sort of a creature was this? An appealing one with ideas, dreams.

"I think your babies safe. You find them sure. They down below waitin' for you." He reached out to touch my hand. "You see 'em soon."

Jenkins interrupted us as he stepped forward and silently spooned up beans. He made no effort to accommodate Mrs. Morgan who followed him. She got what was left.

"No news, Phyllis," Mrs. Morgan told me. "We've got to get down to Owensborough. "Everyone has a story. Rumors."

"My babies?"

"Nothing at all about any of the children."

Henry never came back. I do not know if he would have resumed his kindly overtures or what my response would have been. My confusion over finally admitting my true origins so disconcerted me that the more animal desires abated. Other emotions shifted too. Instead of feeling some society with our people sent down river I experienced a distance, a pull in another direction, but not toward my white blood either. All my life I regarded white men as something unpleasant, something wrong. White men worked me and punished me and subjected me and those like me to injustice.

The white man was cold weather and illness and bad food. Was I supposed to be part of them? Did it make me like them? Who was I like?

As the great current of the Ohio carried us along I remembered the leaf in the stream. It floated by on its own and never let itself be sucked into the soggy clutter at the edge. I was that leaf, separate, destined for some other place. My people and my babies and my husband were trapped at the edge to be ground into unrecognizable soup. I should have felt sadness or anger or something. The information and thoughts crashed instead against that hard place inside me, that place that grew out of being different and alone. Henry did not transform me, but he opened the tiny flow that broke a mighty dam.

I might have abandoned Mrs. Morgan on the Ohio side and turned away from my quest for my children. I considered it. She was not the type to call the slave catchers, and I could have disappeared among free men and free women, perhaps cooking for Henry on his boat. My mind grappled with the possibilities and flirted with the glimmer of what might be called a dream. I actually imagined a life beyond bondage. Still the dimming images of Ben and Pirey and Saul pulled me, with flagging strength, in another direction. Henry had only to hold out his hand, and I might have followed my loins and my head and abandoned my family.

Henry smiled and nodded but gave no further acknowledgement to me. Halfway through the third day, Cincinnati, starting with smoke on the horizon, emerged on the right into view. And if little Catlettsburg was a city for me, then Cincinnati grew into a veritable metropolis, a sea of humans and buildings that seethed and roared with an energy I found mystifying and intoxicating.

Added to all this were the many soldiers mustering to confront the British and the Indians up north. War raged and the river became the main highway of supply and attack. Some soldiers wore blue, but the volunteers still wore their frontier homespun, leather breeches, and fur caps. All carried shiny muskets and new blankets. Straps and ropes for other equipment crossed their chests. They shouted and milled about until they managed ragged, raucous files behind officers on nervous horses. Any number of goats, horses, cattle, and sheep added to the chaos. Piles and piles of goods in sacks and boxes promised to form another city. A few hard women waited in carts behind the lines of troops. I had never witnessed such a fury of commerce.

Henry had just jumped ashore with his rope when an officer in a cocked hat called out, "We'll pay gold if you will take supplies up to Fort Meiggs." Captain Jenkins quickly leaped into the mud to learn more. After an animated conversation, he swung back up on board.

"Sorry, Missus," he reported to Mrs. Morgan, "but the Army needs me. You're gettin' off here."

"But I paid you as far as Owensborough!" she argued. "You took my money! I need to get to Owensborough, and you're going to take me."

"No, Missus, I'm going with the Army, up north. You can find a boat goin' down below."

"You took my money!" The captain spent the fare money on more cargo to fill out his hold. "I'll go into town and get a writ and attach your boat," she threatened. "I'll swear a warrant with the sheriff."

"By the time you do that, we'll be half way up the Miami. You paid me a fair price for a trip this far. I'll sell this and give you half your money back. Things are different. There's a war. The Army here needs my boat."

By this time, the four river men paused in their tasks and listened, enjoying the scene of someone standing up to their captain, something they dared never do.

"Do these men know about the Shawnee and what they've been doing to boats up there?" Mrs. Morgan asked. "Did you tell them about the men who were found with their hands nailed to their boats and then scalped while they were still living? Those are the ones they found. The lucky ones. Two men they didn't find. That's because the Indians took them back to their women. And I don't think they became husbands. Didn't you hear about the River Raisin? Butchered three hundred Kentucky boys. Some of them in bed, sick, wounded. That's where you're going."

Jenkins had an answer. "The Army'll protect us."

252

"That Army?" Mrs. Morgan pointed to a mob of frontier recruits ignoring the shrieks of sergeants. A disgusted colonel on horseback could only look on. One of the volunteers, unfamiliar with military discipline, punched back at an officer and a noisy fist-fight ensued. "I'd rather *walk* down to Owensborough than to trust my hair to them. The Shawnee will nut you with your own knives. You will choke to death on your own balls."

"I've made up my mind," Jenkins announced. "I'm goin' north with the Army. And these men're comin' with me." He stepped past my mistress and addressed the boatman. "Frank, bring up the lady's traps and put 'em ashore. I'll sell this load to the quarter-master, and we won't have to handle it. Just take it on up."

"Bring up our things, Frank," Mrs. Morgan ordered, "we're going to keep our hair. You go with Captain Jenkins. The Army'll protect you. Just as soon as they're done brawling. Good luck to you men. The best I can hope for you is that you die quickly. Best thing is for you to shoot yourselves first. You have guns don't you? But we're not leaving your boat until I get my money back."

Jenkins swallowed hard as he considered his next step. By removing our possessions, the way opened for their trip north to fight Indians. Venable, the noisy one with the plan to hang Negroes all up and down the river spoke next.

"As long as you're givin' the lady's money back, Jenkins, you can pay me off too. I heard what's happenin' up north. I'll let them soldier boys take care of you. I think I'll take my chances down here."

"Me too...captain," came another voice from the back. Henry wisely remained silent, but nodded in agreement.

Venable sat down on the wooden deck and folded his arms. "You come on back from the Army with our wages, and we'll be quit of you. I'm just goin' to take it easy and wait. If you won't keep your word to take the lady down to Owensborough, you might not keep your word to us about our wages. We'll just wait." The others joined Venable, leaving Jenkins to go finalize a deal for his cargo and to find a new crew.

In an hour, Jenkins returned with a buyer, but not from the Army. The officer with the gold disappeared. Mrs. Morgan got some of her fare back. I found a place far up on the landing to wait for Mrs. Morgan and new arrangements for our journey. I took in the sights and sounds of that wondrous place.

The landing stretched for what seemed miles. Instead of a single track leading from the river to the town, a dozen wide roads left the shore through clefts in the bank. Feet and hooves and wheels churned the bank into thick mud. Higher up the bank the mud became dirt and then dust. Beyond the landing, I saw a city of houses and buildings beyond number pulsing with the life and the profit of the valley. I fully expected Henry to touch my shoulder and invite me into the city, but he never appeared. He probably went home to his mother, or maybe his wife.

I noticed the Negroes at work. A few men hefted sacks and boxes and two or three seemed employed with tools on boats and rafts, but I did not see any gangs of people under the direction of an overseer as I knew in Kentucky. Almost everyone was white, and they seemed to work with equal effort as the Negroes. It was a curious sight. In Kentucky, slaves did all the work and whites watched. This was Ohio, a free state, where humans did not own humans, a state where families were not sold away like furniture or cattle. I would come to learn later that Ohio had its own distaste for people of my color, but I could see that this place was different. Indeed, the rest of the world was different than Kentucky and the South.

The Army volunteers adjourned their differences and marched, after a fashion, to some camp inland. Their supplies continued to pile up as more boats and rafts arrived to discharge the fruit of the interior. I could not help but notice that as sacks and baskets and bales grew into heaps intended for the Army, dissolute characters took advantage of the chaos and helped themselves to what they could carry. Military planning had yet to evolve to the point where the Army guarded the supplies that it needed for battle. In the time that it took Mrs. Morgan to find us a new vessel, fully the contents of one keelboat made its way out of Army hands.

Mrs. Morgan found us a flatboat on its way to New Orleans. The farmers counted on a better price a thousand miles away than at Cincinnati or Louisville, and they had built the boat with their own hands and loaded it with grain. They also brought along some pigs. Their plan was to float all winter to the great city on the Mississippi and then walk home with their profit. This was their second voyage and they spoke confidently of the river and its hazards. Only the falls at Louisville concerned them. The time of year was low water and they had no guarantee of their ability to traverse the rapids.

Micah Peterson headed his clan of three sons ranging in age from fifteen to twenty. Mrs. Morgan easily found her way into their good graces by means of my cooking. Micah appreciated being relieved of that thankless task. They had vegetables and potatoes with which I was able to make some excellent stews. The boys caught fish which were unknown to me, but with a little instruction, I managed to cook these too.

The flatboat offered much more room than the keel boat, and Mrs. Morgan and I enjoyed a measure of privacy in the A-frame cabin amidst the cargo. The men used a long sweep at each end of the boat to guide it to the middle of the stream and over to the shore at dusk. When possible, they moored a distance away from shore and always kept a guard. No throats were cut and the falls did not kill us.

Naturally I began to regard my mistress differently and I watched her closely. She still gave me quiet, patient instructions, often with a "please." When I gave her a plate of food she said, "thank you." But she always did that. In our little cabin she kept to herself. If I was related to her by blood she gave me no indication.

Within a week, we found ourselves easily past the falls and at Owensborough where the interlude ended.

River City

I smelled the jail before I saw it. Having recent personal experience with such institutions, I knew well the stench of human habitation in close confines mixed with the reek of sadness and the rot of despair. The jail in Owensborough held six men whose doom was not only certain, but whose deaths were to be celebrated amid a revel of hatred, like animals slaughtered in some heathen rite, which it was. My old friends lay chained in a squalid darkness, waiting to be dragged out and strung up before a crowd of villainous enemies whose glee would be fueled by the victim's twisting death throes, men whose crime was to seek freedom against the living perdition of plantation life in Mississippi or Louisiana. Walking through the dusty streets of the river town, I followed close behind my white mistress for fear of violence from the vile populace.

Small, proud Mrs. Morgan strode up to the thin, dirty white man who stood guard over the brick jail. His weaponry consisted of a grimy musket and a rusty sword. A dirty red sash circled his lean waist as some badge of office. He reminded me of a hungry Draper before the rise to sheriff, another layabout whose principle business was the apprehension, detention, and torture of Negroes.

"Deputy, I am Mrs. David Morgan, wife of Colonel David Morgan of Floyd County," she announced. "I have permission to speak to your prisoners."

He leaned over to spit a stream of brown juice before speaking. "I heard. You can talk to one at a time."

"I shall speak to Esther."

He spat again. "No Esther. No women."

"What happened to the women?"

"On to Mississippi, I s'pose."

"The children?"

"Mississippi… I s'pose."

"Peter then?"

"No Peter."

"Ike?"

The white man rolled his tobacco into a different cheek and then turned to two men seated against the building. "The one with the head," he ordered. The men in the shade struggled to their feet and stood by as the guard worked an iron key into an immense lock. He stepped back and the men pulled open the iron door onto a flood of fetidness and the moans and cries of the wretched prisoners within. The light from the door revealed a mass of bodies writhing like worms under an old corpse. Mrs. Morgan stepped back at the sight and the smell, and I felt compelled to do the same. Accustomed to the horror, the men entered. Amid the clatter of iron manacles and cries of agony and protest, they retrieved a human being I barely recognized.

Ike was thinner, filthier, and far more ragged than the last time I had seen him at the landing. I had shared a cabin with Ike and Mariah throughout my youth and I could barely mark him as the same man. An untreated wound on his head oozed yellow and red out of brown dried blood. His wrists and ankles bore red wounds from the heavy irons. Straw and dirt clung to his hair and clothing. He blinked at the bright light and seemed disoriented. One of the jail slaves looped a noose over his head and cinched it so that he could not run.

"You goin' to hang me now?" he asked the men, but they just pointed to Mrs. Morgan. He squinted at her in bewilderment, trying to match the image with his memory. His face relaxed as he realized that he was confronted with the face of a distant, happier time. He licked his dry lips and said, "Missus? That you? Oh, Missus, I so sorry. I just so sorry."

"Are you thirsty, Ike?" she asked. "Do you want a drink?"

"Yes'm, that be nice, real nice. Real thirsty."

"Phyllis."

An empty bucket and gourd sat next to the jail, obviously intended, but not recently used, to provide for the prisoners. Without asking, I snatched it up and found a pump at a trough with reasonably clean water. Within moments, Ike drank eagerly, water spilling down his chin and into the dust.

"How about some water for the others?" Mrs. Morgan asked the white deputy, but he only shrugged. I refilled the bucket and placed it at the iron door, which stood ajar. One guard pushed it inside, tipping it over. Water flooded onto the dirt. A cacophony of cries protested the waste. The bucket came back to me, and I filled it again, this time stepping into that rancid atmosphere amid growls and shouts. I retraced my steps three times with the bucket and returned it to that reeking darkness. I heard a familiar voice call my name several times, but I could not discern who was speaking.

"Ike," my mistress asked, "tell me what happened?"

"When?"

"Start with when you left Prestonsburg, home."

He did not speak for a few moments, collecting his thoughts, reaching back to before the present horrible reality. He brought his hand up and touched the wound, then rubbed his face as if to clear the fog.

"They come to the place and tol' us we got to go. We take some clothes. Mariah take some food. Had to leave ever' thing. You weren't there Missus. They walk us to town and put us on them boats. The little boats. Took us down river. Said we was sold off. Goin' to a new home."

"Did you stay on the little boats?" Mrs. Morgan prodded.

"Yes'm, til we got to a big town."

"What side of the river?"

He held up his left hand.

"Was that before the big river?"

"Yes'm. Put us on a big boat."

"The same men?"

259

"That Mister, ah, Norton. And his driver. And two other white men. And their driver."

"White men?"

"Yes'm. They had other folks there. We all got on the bigger boat, a raf' they call it, you know, and headed down. That when they put chains on us." He held up a wrist with nasty gashes.

I could not wait any longer and interrupted. "My babies? Where my babies? Pirey? Ben?" Ike looked at me as if he just realized I was there, but without recognizing me.

Mrs. Morgan held up a hand and motioned me back. "Go on, Ike," she continued, "what happened on the boat?"

"Got on that raf'. Had a little house. Only we don't stay in the house. We stay outside. The white men get the house. One of the other men, of the new men, already have chains, he talk about Mis'sippi. He say we goin' die there. The white men, they whip him, whip him bad. Name Arthur. He here."

"How did you run away?"

"Esther."

"What about Esther?"

"She start talkin' to Peter and to me. She say, 'we get to that side of the river, other side, we be free. No slaves there.' I don't know what she talk about. Free. But Peter, he know. And the other men, they know. And they talk. But real quiet."

"What did they say?"

"They talk about gettin' over to the other side and runnin' away. We goin' to Mis'sippi, and it bad. We got to run. They have us on the top of the raf', the flat boat. The white men, they live on the inside. They got us chained, and they don't feed us much. Some beans. Ate the fritters."

"Did they chain everyone?"

"Yah. No. They don't chain the children. Or that dog. That damn dog. He won't leave. Them drivers, they try to throw him over, but he too mean. He stick close to the children. And Esther. They keep with Esther." Ike offered a slight smile, probably the last smile of his life. "That dog. He got so those drivers won't have nothin' to do with him."

"What did Esther do?"

260

"Esther talk. Talk to Peter and me and the men. She say, get to the other side. She want to find a rabbit. Don't know why. Run away. When they ask what about the white men, Esther just look at them and say, 'You goin' to Mis'sippi. You goin' to Lou's'ana. You goin' die. They whip you 'til you die.' She watch all the time. She see the keys for the chains. Norton got 'em. Even them drivers don't have no keys. Need the keys. So, at night, we stop and tie up. Always on the same side. The slave side, Esther say." Ike held up his left hand causing him some pain.

"She watch Norton. He get up in the night and go to the side to make water. The other white men, they sleep. So, she and Peter, they wait up with the other men. When Norton get up to make water, they get close to the drivers and hold them quiet, hands over they mouths. Real quiet. When Norton done, Peter say real low, 'Marse, come look at this,' just like one o' them drivers. That Norton, he sleepy, so he not thinkin', he come over and Peter grab him.

"Peter, he pull Norton up and he choke him. Norton, he fight, he kick, he hit Peter with his own chains. But he don't make no noise 'cause Peter choke him and hold him up. You know he so strong. His feet in the air, Peter so big. Then Peter make one big move on Norton. Norton he jump once and then he still. Kill him like a chicken.

"That make a noise and the other white men, they come out with a gun. One, he shoot the gun, boom! Fire. Smoke. Peter hit 'em with chains. The gun, it have only the one shot so we grab the white men. I just do what the other men do. Esther, she get the keys from Norton, and she unlock us. Get the chains off. The other men, the ones that get on later, they jump on the white men and beat 'em with the chains. Then they in the water. With the drivers."

"The white men went into the water?"

"Yes'm. But it dark, we can't see where they go. One white man get away. I see him later here. That how they find us."

"What did you do when you got the chains off?"

"Well, me 'n the other men, we watch how the drivers work the boat. We get them long poles goin'. Before light, we on the other

261

side, and we lit out. Don't know what way. One of the new men, he say, 'follow the stars. He show us where in the sky. He say, follow that. We go through the woods. Stay away from white people. Don't see no colored people. The children, they hungry. Nothin' to eat. Everybody hungry. Children can't go very far."

I closed my eyes at the thought that my babies suffered in their flight. Surely Esther would find a way to provide for them.

"Then the catchers, they catch us. Got dogs." With that, Ike dropped his head in despair. "They catch us. Hit me. Hit me bad. Tie us up. Drag us back here. Took the women away. Mariah. The children."

"My babies," I blurted, "what 'bout my babies?"

"Yes, Ike, what about Phyllis's children. What about Esther?"

Ike cast a furtive look at the man who held the rope but stood just out of earshot. He dropped his voice nonetheless. "It dark that night. I don't see 'em. Esther, she say, 'You men get on them paddles. I untie us from the bank. Just start on them paddles. Get to other side fast as you can'. So I get on one of them long paddles, and I use it like I saw them do. Never done that. Peter he help Esther."

Mrs. Morgan lowered her tone as well. "Did they get caught by the catchers? Esther and Peter?"

Ike continued talking to the dust. "We get to the other side, and it's dark. We start runnin' and I follow the others. We just run. We lose some people in the woods. I don't see him with us. They catch Peter? They kill him?"

Mrs. Morgan ignored his question and maintained her interrogation. "Did Esther talk about where she was going?"

Ike seemed to consider this before asking, "Water?" I brought over a gourd and he drank from it. "She just talk about catchin' a rabbit."

"Ike, you're hurt."

"Yes'm. Catchers get me. One of them swords."

"Who else is here with you?"

"Just Walter."

"Is he hurt?"

"No'm, don't think so."

"And the other women? The men? The children?"

"Catchers catch 'em. Ain't seen 'em since we got catched."

"Have another drink. We'll get you some food. I want to talk to Walter," she told the deputy. Ike returned to the jail, and Walter the carpenter came out, his great arms and deft hands bound in iron. He squinted in the strange sunlight as Mrs. Morgan questioned him.

"No'm," he told her, "don't see Esther and Peter after we get off. The other men fight with the traders and the drivers. I don't do nothin'. That trader say I killed a white man. I don't kill nobody. I don't hit nobody. Those other boys hit the white men. Peter." I knew Walter as a peaceable man, more interested in building than in destruction. "They goin' really hang us all Missus?"

"I don't know Walter, I don't know." Then, "I'm done here," Mrs. Morgan announced. "I'm going to arrange for some food. Is that all right with you, Deputy?"

"Have to ask the sheriff. Hangin's in four days. No sense wastin' good food."

"I'll talk to the sheriff. Phyllis, you stay here and help these men with the water. Just like you used to do for Colonel Morgan." She turned and left.

"Yes'm," I told her. "I be right here." It was a moment or two before I understood that I was to do more than just carry water.

The deputy's two assistants were Nate and Timothy, slaves rented to the sheriff to help detain the condemned. I asked them why they could not get water for the prisoners.

"All we supposed to do is guard," Timothy replied. "Sheriff say he goin' to hang six niggers, and he don't care if it us or them. If any them get away, he hang us in their place. If any of them get's shot gettin' away, he hang us in their place. None of these niggers is gettin' away."

"You right," Nate added seriously. "And if more'n two get away, he hang us twice he say." I doubted that Timothy believed that he would be hung twice, but Nate certainly did. I had to resurrect my dissipated skills as a spy to learn more about the slave revolt. I had nothing to trade, not even gossip, so I had to start the conversation somewhere.

"Lots of soldiers on the river. Many come through here?"

Timothy had the quicker mind. "Soldiers through here a month ago. More in today. They want coloreds to haul for 'em, drive stock, but my master say if we go up in Ohio, he never see us again. He say the Injuns love the taste of nigger meat."

"Who your master?"

"Mr. Elliston Marquardt of Castle Rock. That your mistress?"

I had to speak the next words carefully because there was so much more. "My mistress Mrs. Anna Morgan of Floyd County. Colonel Morgan's widow."

"Never heard Floyd County. This Breck'ridge County."

"Floyd County upriver. In the mountains."

"These men from there. These your people?"

"We all Colonel Morgan's people. Then he get killed. And his son." I was amazed at how easily those words flowed. That hard place inside me. "Then they sell folks away."

Why'nt they sell you away?"

"Mistress keep me."

"Why you down here?"

"Mrs. Morgan hear what happen and want to see after her people." I decided to leave out my own interest in events. "Don't even know what happened until we talked to Ike and Walter. They really kill those white men?"

Timothy watched to see if the deputy was paying attention, which he was not. "Boat come down with a white man on it. He say his slaves run away. They kill two white men on his boat and his drivers. Then run to the other side. Indiana. Sheriff, he get dogs and men and go over and help catch 'em. I go too."

"How many they catch?"

"Hmmm. These six. Some other men. Women. Children."

"What children?"

"Hmm. Three. Boys and a girl."

"How old?"

"Hmm. 'Bout ten, I s'pose."

"You sure? Any babies? A boy, couldn't yet walk. A little girl?"

"Hmm. No, no babies that young. That white man who come in, he send 'em down on another boat. These six they goin' to hang. For killin' the white men. He try to get 'em back, but the sheriff say they got to hang."

"No baby boy, no little girl?" I pressed.

"Didn't see any. Maybe someone else catch 'em."

Then I remembered something. "How about a dog? Was there a dog that come back with the slaves? Did you catch a dog? With the children?"

"No dog don't think."

"Anyone see a dog maybe fightin' with the sheriff, the deputies?"

"Nope. He have his own dogs. Any dog get in their way be meat. Meanest dogs around." Sim would not let my babies go without a fight, even if it was his last.

That spark of hope still lived in my heart. Perhaps Esther and my babies had escaped. I had some idea now what escape was, and I knew that in spite of the threat of hanging, cold and hunger in the wilderness was better than bondage and Mississippi. As I turned the facts over in my head I wondered how the sheriff could catch able-bodied slaves and still fail to catch a man and a woman with two small children. Esther was crafty, but I questioned even her ability to stay out of the hands of bloodthirsty hunters and their hounds. The killing of white men stirred the entire country-side to a terrible vengeance, and but few forces on this earth could stop them.

I brought water until the thirst of the six men seemed quenched. I also disposed of the slop pail that had not been emptied in days. Every time the door opened to admit the full bucket and retrieve the empty one I tried to identify those within. Aside from Ike and Walter, I recognized no one. The other condemned men must have been those taken aboard in Catlettsburg. They all sat around the walls of the little cell, legs toward the center, their legs chained together. Ike was not the only one with untreated wounds. I found some hay that helped provide some comfort and soak up the wet.

Mrs. Morgan returned after a time, and I followed her to a house where I picked up some beans and bread. These I took back to the cell. The beans made their way to the prisoners, but the deputy and his minions purloined the bread. Future deliveries included enough food for this tax.

Mrs. Morgan found lodging in a house, and I was permitted a tick on the kitchen floor, not at all private, but warm and dry. I ate with the servants, a man and a woman owned by Mr. Herndon, a white widower lawyer who acted on behalf of the six condemned slaves. The man, Forney, cared for the lawyer's stable and home and drove the carriage. He was also hired out for day work. His wife, Alabama, cooked and did laundry for boarders. Forney called her "Bama." When they learned my connection with the runaway slaves, they seemed at first awestruck at someone who actually knew the people who killed for their freedom. Then they became solicitous because of the looming executions of my friends.

Mr. Herndon had a prosperous law practice, allowing him a spacious home, the largest building I had ever entered, larger even than the courthouse in Prestonsburg. He even had rooms for paying guests. The servants prepared meals on a real iron stove – a marvel beyond imagining. Alabama could set a fire and control its heat with various louvers and handles. She could also keep a pot and a pan going at the same time and even bake without burning herself. Real baking took place in a brick oven in the back. Forney and Alabama lived over the stable, and although they put in long hours, they seemed content and loyal.

"Got people coming from everywhere to see these hangin's," Forney told me. "Biggest thing ever here. Ever. Hung a white man about five years ago for murder, but that's all. Town fillin' up. More'n court sessions or 'lections."

"My children on that boat," I told them. "We tryin' to find them. If we can't get 'em back, I want to go with them."

Both people stared at me incredulously. Why would anyone willingly go to Mississippi, even to be with their children? But Forney and Alabama had no children and had little understanding of the love of a mother.

"They catch your children?" Alabama asked.

"Don't know. No one see 'em. Or Esther. Or Peter. Peter Esther's husband. She takin' care of my babies. She lose her own babies to the fever."

Owensborough prospered along the river from the cotton grown inland. One of the new cotton gins operated there, making the town a magnet for the white gold destined to be "king." Gangs of slaves unloaded wagons full of bolls into the gins under the sharp rebukes of drivers and overseers. Bales of ginned product waited on the landing bound for mills in the east. But Owensborough lacked the same sense of industry I noticed in Cincinnati. Indeed, all along the left bank of the river, the slavery side, little indicated much in the way of ambition. Thistle overtook the fields and fences and barns showed more neglect than attention. Even the animals demonstrated a slovenly attitude toward life. I got a greater sense of poverty there than in the river settlements of Ohio and Indiana populated by free persons, even free Negroes.

The market for Owensborough occupied an open area back from the river where farmers could park their wagons and offer for sale the last of their harvest or some home-manufactured wares. In most cases, white women negotiated sales while servants waited and engaged in gossip. Alabama was well known at the market and her master's prominence and prosperity made her a target for every offer and pitch. But Alabama was a seasoned buyer and would not be deflected in her mission to spend her master's money wisely. Her fortunes were her master's fortunes. If he prospered, so did she.

"Mr. Herndon a good master. He don't beat us like some, and he don't 'prove of masters who break up families. Some of the masters, they owe money and go sell folks. Sell the children. That's how we come to be owned. Mr. Herndon get us for a debt. We s'posed to be sold to a trader. Do anything for that man. He try to keep 'em from hangin' those folks. In court. Lot of white folks don't care for that. That sheriff, he bent on hangin' somebody." I told her what Nate said about what would happen if someone escaped. "That the sheriff. I sure hope hangin' these six don't give him a taste for it. I hope it keep him happy. Be glad when this all over."

My venture to the market was not without benefit, however. I noticed a man with a hat, a round, brimless affair, with certain designs on it. The curious lines turned back in on each other to create a not unattractive pattern against his drab slave clothing. Having no brim to protect the wearer from the sun and rain, I suspected that the owner found more pleasure with its appearance than with its ability to shield him from the elements. I knew these designs from Rabbit's shawl at the salt lick. I followed my instincts, and he was visibly pleased when I asked him where he got his hat.

"Get it from a Injun. He trade it to me. A real Chickasaw."

"Where he come from?"

"He say he goin' north."

"Where he from?"

"Injun lands. West."

"He goin' to the war?"

"Maybe. He trade me this for some food. They live west, 'cross the Cumb'land, 'cross the Tenn'ssee."

"It a fine hat. Many Injuns west?"

"West and south. Injun land. Theirs. White men take the rest." The mention of Tennessee brought to mind the map that Esther carefully recorded inside her bag.

"Tenn'ssee south? Cumb'land south?" I asked.

He smiled. "Tenn'ssee a state and a river. Cumb'land a river."

"The Chickasaw in Tenn'ssee?"

"No, Chickasaw land Kentucky, 'cross the Tenn'ssee, 'cross the Cumb'land."

More became clear. Esther, my teacher, had her eye not on free states to the north, but Indian lands to the west where the white man's laws did not apply. Then the cold, brutal, brilliant genius of her actions on the river also became clear.

"Our people were purchased by Norton and his partner," Mrs. Morgan told me. "Our people were their property. Now that Norton is dead, they all belong to his partner, the one who escaped. They are all gone down to Natchez and I certainly can't buy them back now. No one saw your children. I don't know how we will find your children, Phyllis." She sat there in Herndon's parlor, her hands tightly clasped and her eyes down, loathe to look in my face as I received the news. Any other white person would have told me in the kitchen or the yard or perhaps not at all. But my mistress extended thoughtfulness, even respect. Was she mindful that through my babies' veins flowed her blood? "The best we can do here is make it comfortable for Ike and Walter. They are going to hang, and I can't stop it."

"Yes'm," was my only reply, and I returned to cleaning ashes from the stove and fireplaces.

I imagined leaving Mrs. Morgan and striking out on my own toward the Tennessee River and Chickasaw country, but which way? Esther had cunning beyond words and even though she carried two babies, she had Sim's eyes and ears and Peter's strong arms to keep them safe. Peter was no fool. If I had to strike out through the wilderness I would want to have him along. She knew that north of the river was the first place the catchers would look for the rebels. She insured this by telling the others to make for the Indiana shore. In the confusion and darkness she slipped off the boat with Peter to flee to the south and west. While the sheriff and his dogs swept the Indiana country for the runaways, she had two weeks or more to work their way out of the country. My babies were in good hands, probably better than mine.

I became known in the town as the only survivor of a plantation full of slaves. Strangers nodded to me as I tended to the prisoners and helped Alabama with the marketing. If anyone heard any word of escaped slaves on the Kentucky side of the river, they never approached me. I knew not to ask questions about fugitives headed south or west lest some faithless wag set importance upon some missing food, strange tracks, or shadows in the night. In our struggle for abolition, our worst enemies often came not from the masters or the slave catchers or even the politicians, but those of our own race. Some believed that their only recourse for continuation in positions of benefit lie in the unending repression of their own race. Some were so ignorant they simply knew no better. So many tragic ends on a rope or in a bonfire began with a Negro informer.

Sacrifice

As the day of white retribution approached, every Negro felt the suspicious eyes of every white man and white woman. Those people with tasks at the market or in town quickly concluded their business and disappeared. Every spare bed in Owensborough filled with travelers, two to a bed, and public houses became riots of whiskey-fueled blood lust, carnality, and gluttony.

Were it not for Mrs. Morgan and me, I fear that the condemned men would have starved before they hanged. I hoped they saw death as a release from their suffering. Since the deputy and his assistants ate due to the beneficence of Mrs. Morgan, they became more disposed to my visits. Twice a day I brought food for nine – six prisoners and three guards – and fresh water. Mrs. Morgan and Mr. Herndon hired a doctor to properly bandage Ike's head wound. The sheriff and doctor resisted but could not turn down the fees she paid. The morning of the executions, the deputy turned me away, after taking his own portion of the meal. The brave rebels were to die on empty stomachs. I learned no more about the rebellion or the missing fugitives.

For the hanging, the governor directed that a regiment of volunteers, on its way north to the war, be diverted to keep order. Several hundred newly enlisted frontiersmen marched into town and made their camp. Their colonel was Leander K. Wallace, who became the guest of none other than Mr. Ebenezer Herndon, my mistress's host.

Colonel Wallace was also a lawyer so he and Mr. Herndon shared their respective opinions on politics, war, society, and literature. I got the sense that Herndon found in Wallace a kindred spirit, a rare intellectual in a land of those fleeing the rule of competence. The lawyer-turned-soldier was a natural leader – intelligent, educated, strong, and ready with an easy wit. He established his headquarters in Herndon's parlor, so I had a chance to observe him. Every day, his officers trooped in with their reports and conferences, and I served refreshments under the eye of Alabama. With his officers, the colonel exuded authority but remained patient and respectful, which earned him their loyalty and their energy. This ran down to the volunteers, whom the officers drilled all day. My travels to the market took me past their encampment, which drew a steady bevy of spectators wasting time before the hangings. In spite of the soldiers' lack of uniforms I noticed their files grow straighter and their movements more precise.

"Soldiers cannot cause trouble if they are kept busy, gentlemen," I overheard Colonel Wallace say to his lieutenants. "There is nothing more dangerous than a soldier with time on his hands. Once we start north, we won't have this chance to prepare. You can be assured that the British can keep to their lines under fire. Napoleon has taught them well. The hard way. Best we train now. Let them become accustomed to your command. Let them know your voices in their sleep. Let each know the man next to him. Congress has promised land to this rabble, but we cannot rely upon greed for their obedience."

Several of the volunteers succumbed to drink nonetheless, earning them floggings or other public admonishments like being tied to wagon wheels. Negroes knew to stay away from these spectacles of white men being punished.

Colonel Wallace noticed the diminutive, blue-eyed widow boarded with him. His long hair ran to dark blond, which he tied in the old-fashioned way with a blue ribbon, adding to his charismata. In his blue uniform with the buff facings, Colonel Wallace cut a figure not unlike the images of General George Washington.

I could tell that Mrs. Morgan found Wallace intriguing, probably because of her late husband's smaller stature and short hair. She was also alone in the world save for grandchildren who might not be hers upon her return home. When the soldier was not being a colonel or arguing the fine points of law and politics with Mr. Herndon, he engaged my mistress in educated conversation about literature and philosophy and even the weather. I never heard such animated discourse. The colonel's words rekindled the fire in her brain and ideas became flames. I knew well the loneliness of life on the frontier and denial of intellectual stimulation. Her laugh and her emphatic voice, entirely strange to me, rang throughout the house in the evening. When not attending to the prisoners or fighting the fate of her former slaves, she could as often as not be found at the parade ground watching Wallace drill his regiment.

From the upper floor, the Herndon house had a clear view of the gallows in the square. Unlike his neighbors, Herndon did not rent space at the windows or allow an audience on his roof, so his was the only house where people did not crowd into every vantage point. That left the windows to Mrs. Morgan and to me and the servants. The regiment, under the command of Colonel Wallace, formed an irregular cordon around the ghoulish spectacle and men with muskets kept the drunks back.

The gallows was a simple affair, just a beam set across some triangle supports at the center of the soldiers. Surely this mean device must have disappointed those who came miles to see this celebration of cruelty and who expected an elaborate stage and display. The sheriff intended to expend no more funds than necessary in dispatching the condemned. Had there been a single tree large enough, I suspect the sheriff would have used it rather than build anything at all.

Having only seen Ruth hanged, I did not know that there were several ways to kill a human being with a rope. The conventional method we hear of today is, of course, to drop the victim through a trap door allowing the noose to break his neck. Death comes instantly or, at least, with minimal suffering. The hangman carefully calculates the prisoner's weight to match the drop, and as with any craftsman, he prides himself in the swift and painless dispatch of the miscreant. In those days the trap door was a relatively new development in this infernal art, and it required sophistication in preparation and application. These abilities, knowledge, and inclination far exceeded those of the sheriff of Breckenridge County.

A cruder option saw the hangman push the victim off a platform, again providing a drop that might break the neck. Platforms, whether constructed or driven, also lent a theatrical aspect to public execution. The sheriff and his guards paraded the principal actor onto a stage over the heads of the audience to drop or swing or dance as fortune and science provided. In the frontier variation, the sheriff mounted the prisoner onto a horse or into a wagon and then whipped the horse. The sudden jerk supplied the leap into eternity. This latter method was less certain to avoid agony but was simple to arrange, and in the heat of mob violence, speed had the advantage over ceremony.

For the rebel slaves of Breckenridge, whose greatest sins were to be born African, the sheriff saved for their deaths the cheapest and cruelest method. Whether this choice was to provide the maximum in entertainment or the maximum in deterrence, I do not know, although my guess is with the former. Had his intention been to persuade other slaves from resisting the lash of their masters, then slaves should have been witnesses. As far as I know, Alabama, Forney, and I were the only Negroes watching, and we hid within the Herndon house. I hope that others spied secretly from attics and lofts, fascinated and horrified only wanting to share some last communion with their unfortunate brothers.

The sheriff set the hangings for eleven o'clock. A deputation of court officers, including Mr. Herndon, arranged themselves to one side of the gallows, in top hats and frock coats. A gray sky obscured the sun and clouds spat snow indifferently. Six nooses dangled from the cross beam, the ends of the ropes lay coiled on the ground. In the direction of the jail, a stir in the crowd rose to jeers as a phalanx of soldiers with muskets broke through the crowd followed by the first of the condemned, arms pinioned with rope, in between two white deputies. He was one of the men I did not know, but his name was Samuel. Upon his first sight of the gallows, he collapsed. The crowd jeered with glee as the deputies dragged him under a rope and proceeded to secure it around his neck.

The sheriff, a tall man in a beaver hat, stepped forward and read from a paper. I could not discern all the official legalistic words, but I caught the last one. "Proceed!"

Two white men, took up the loose rope, walked backward four or five steps and lifted the man off the ground. A roar from the crowd rose along with his twisting, kicking body. His mouth gaped open in a silent cry and his eyes bulged. Ruth's ordeal came into my mind. The men on the rope, enthusiastic in their dark duty, pulled too far and Samuel's head struck the cross beam, there to swing as his life was throttled away. The crowd surged with excitement but the volunteers held them in check under the watchful eye of officers with swords drawn. Colonel Wallace barked at men who deigned to glance at the spectacle rather than attend to their duties in keeping back the multitude. Only occasionally did Wallace turn to look at the gallows. The body quickly stopped struggling, and I am informed that death typically ensued within a quarter of an hour.

The deputies retreated to appear again with another man. I recognized Walter the builder, but felt no other reaction. He had a wife and two girls, now on their way to Mississippi. His eye and skill built my cabin, the one with the window, and he had a hand in nearly every sound structure in Floyd County. The deputies pulled him forward, but he denied the drunks the pleasure of seeing him cringe. He walked straight and stood tall. I wonder if his last views in the world were of buildings he could duplicate or improve upon. The noose, the sheriff's warrant, and Walter swung next to the first man. The men on the rope knew their work this time, and Walter's head did not strike the cross beam.

Ike with his bandaged head came next. He and Mariah and I shared a cabin for almost ten years. I hoped that his end would be as painless as possible. He kept to his feet and just hung his head in resignation until he jerked upwards. He kicked twice next to Walter and hung still. After twenty minutes, three bodies draped from the cross beam. Dark stains in the dust beneath their feet documented their bodies' last spasms. The crowd seemed to have calmed a little, death having lost some of its novelty. Alabama sobbed next to me. Mrs. Morgan shook her head and muttered words like, "Disgusting" or "Tragic."

I found myself oddly unaffected by this horror, however. My mind clearly grasped and recorded the happenings, but my heart could not find cause to react. I had just watched two neighbors, nay, brothers, strangled unto death, but I felt little emotion over their suffering. Reason dictated that I should be biting off cries into a rag or sharing comfort with Alabama. I watched Alabama, who did not know these men or their history, and Mrs. Morgan, who worked so hard to save and comfort them show their humanity, but I stood there shamelessly cold. What monster could view this spectacle and feel nothing? Had that hard place inside me pushed out all feeling?

I thought back to the last man I had seen die, David Morgan, his frothy blood leaking into the dusty track, no crowd to watch him, just one witness to cheer his demise. My feelings for Morgan ran so high that his death should have elicited from me the same macabre glee that consumed the square below. But then, as now, I just watched human life slip away, unmoved.

The fourth man was marched forth. The hangmen hoisted him up, but the load proved too much for the cheap cross beam, and it broke in a crash. Four bodies collapsed in a heap, one of them struggling against the noose. The crowd let out a mournful "Awwww" at being denied another killing. Laugher rolled over the mob as deputies pulled the still-living victim to his feet. As the sheriff and the officials decided how to proceed the man stood there stunned.

This mishap required that another, heavier beam be procured, erected, and reequipped with ropes. This took an hour or more. Once the new beam was erected, I saw some discussion among the sheriff and his deputies. The sheriff had promised the mob six bodies swinging. Even Colonel Wallace was drawn into the debate. Finally, rather than risk another catastrophe, the sheriff ordered the dead left where they lay and three ropes reset. The deputies pulled the fourth man under the beam, his knees now very weak with the clear knowledge of being hanged. How many are hanged twice? Soon he alone swung from the beam. The last two prisoners followed in practiced succession until three black corpses twisted in the air. Once the sheriff felt satisfied that he had done his duty, he ordered the hangmen to hoist the other three bodies until the mob had their six.

In due course, all were cut down, but the crowd was slow to disperse. Nate and Timothy, now free of their obligation to supply six victims to the gallows, drove a wagon into the square. They loaded the bodies, but some drunks rushed forward and seized up one of the ropes to drag a body off the wagon. Nate and Timothy could not intervene, but an order from Colonel Wallace resulted in the rioters being clubbed away without their grisly souvenir. Nate and Timothy restored their tragic cargo and disappeared between two lines of volunteers. When Colonel Wallace marched his regiment away, more drunks descended on the gallows and tore it apart as keepsakes of the travesty.

Forney and Alabama and I returned to our duties to prepare dinner for Mr. Herndon and his guests. Forney and Alabama were silent in the shock of what they had witnessed. I remained silent simply because I had nothing to say. I might as well have observed a horse being saddled as having witnessed a mass execution. Had I become so pummeled by my experiences of the past few weeks to be robbed of my compassion, or did these events just exploit a fundamental flaw in my character?

The hangings transformed me in a baptism of sorts, a cleansing, a new beginning. At the beginning of the day, I was a victim myself, punished by the slaveocracy and by fortune, beaten, and spent. By early afternoon I had nothing left. My neighbors were gone. My husband was gone. My children were gone. And I was a part of two worlds – white and black – but a real member of neither. Another might be left a docile shell, bereft of any spirit, a perfect slave to work and breed and suffer and die. Not for me. Like some piece of iron thrust into Simon's forge, I received the coals' heat until red hot. Taken from the fire, I laid the hard place inside me upon the anvil and had the impurities hammered out to form a tempered blade to be wielded in a sacred cause. Like any weapon, I still needed an edge applied. The edge would come later, but fundamentally, I stood as hard and as cold as any fine axe. Or Osborn's knife.

The blade came with a sheath or a scabbard. My rashness in the past had set in motion a sequence of events that might have easily ended badly for me, at the end of a rope like the six martyrs. I would never trust emotion again. I had to trust my mind and to a lesser extent my heart. Sentiment must have no place in my future.

Freedom

The drunks from the square drifted back into the country-
side, and the town returned to some semblance of its past
character, feeding cotton through the gins and across the
landing, onto the river. Slaves reappeared and went about their
business with no mention of the murders. Boats landed with gangs
of slaves to be sold to planters nearby or bound for Memphis and
Vicksburg and New Orleans. Ginned cotton, the fruit of slave
labor, shipped on to markets in Europe and New England and the
planters got rich.

Mrs. Morgan and I remained at Herndon's. Alabama and
Forney patiently softened my crude country ways until I became
a passable house slave, cleaning, cooking, and even serving at the
table. Alabama taught me the mysteries of her iron stove, and we
shared lore of kettle and hearth. With her brick oven in the yard
and the last of the season's fresh produce, we laid Herndon and
his guests some memorable feasts.

I expected any day to be told by Mrs. Morgan to be ready to
leave in the morning for home. She still had to resolve the matter of
the Morgan estate, and nothing further kept us in Owensborough.
As I looked out at the river and contemplated the slow journey
back upstream I knew I had to make a decision. I considered one
more time following Esther and Peter. I calculated the possibilities of finding them and concluded that I never could. I imagined
walking through the woods until I met someone wearing Indian

clothing. A while further and I found Esther and my children safe from the slave catchers.

The blade of my reasoning sliced through each of those visions. A simpler woman would have followed these impulses and be a lone Negro wandering the roads and tracks of a strange country. She would wear chains again before the week was out. I lacked Esther's cunning, Peter's strength, and Sim's keen senses. They were all bent on staying free and would not leave a trail nor would they advertise their presence. If the catchers could not find them how could I? Quite simply I had nowhere to go. I took my only comfort from the not unlikely prospect that they all were safe and free.

I learned one reason for Mrs. Morgan's apparent inaction when, one morning, I discovered a blue ribbon on the floor of her bedroom. That same day, Mrs. Morgan called me into the parlor where Mr. Herndon and Colonel Wallace also attended. All were seated while I stood. I once might have trembled with fear, but that day found me calm.

"Phyllis," she said, "my business here is done. I have made a decision about you and you need to understand some things. It was Colonel Morgan's wish that upon his death, you be given your freedom. I'm sure that was my son's wish. It is my wish. Your children too were to go free. But we cannot find them. I do not think we will ever find them. If we could find them they are the property of someone else now. I do not know where they are and if I did, I don't have the money to buy them. Mr. Herndon has helped me execute your manumission. You are being set free."

With that, Herndon held up a legal document and read, "'I Anna Poteat Morgan of Floyd County, Commonwealth of Kentucky, hereby certify that I discharge and manumit from my service my negro woman named Phyllis, nineteen years of age, of fair skin and blue eyes, and this writing is to be a perpetual bar from my heirs or representatives holding said Phyllis as a slave. Owensborough, County of Breckenridge, this 12th day of December, Eighteen Hundred and Thirteen.' Phyllis, you are from this day forward free. You are no longer a bondsman. You are free to hire yourself out and to keep what money you earn.

"But, Phyllis," he continued, "and this is very, very important, so listen carefully to me – you must leave the Commonwealth of Kentucky within thirty days and you must never return. You must leave. It is best if you just go north to Ohio or Indiana. Do you understand?"

People often mention doors opening in their lives, when opportunities presented themselves and the course of the journey changes. For me a door closed, the last one of a series of doors going back to the hangings, my discovery of my real father, the loss of my children, and the loss of Saul. A door closed on my life as a slave and I stood there stripped of family, friends, home, society, and even history. I had no idea what lay before me, but everything lay behind me.

"I free?" was all I could muster.

"Yes." Mrs. Morgan answered. "And you must leave. You will not be able to stay and search for your children. You must not look for them. You will have to let them go and trust in God that Esther will care for them. No one seems to know where they are, but when they are captured, they will be returned here and sold. You cannot stay here, or anywhere in Kentucky. Let your children go. They are gone." She need not have said this. I had already made my decision.

"Where I go? What I do?"

Colonel Wallace spoke. "Phyllis, I can use a servant, someone to cook for me and my officers on the campaign. Mrs. Morgan tells me you have cooked for hunters. Campaigning is like hunting. You are free to accompany me and the regiment. But if you join us, you must agree to stay for the entire campaign. You will earn money from me and from my officers. When we are mustered out, you will be free to go about your business and to keep your wages. You have your freedom, and I am offering you work."

A door opened.

"I go with you, Mas'?" I asked.

"I'm not your master. I'm colonel. Yes, you cook for me. I will pay you. This paper," he reached for the document in Herndon's hands, "says you are no longer a slave. You are free. I need a cook and you need a position. We will strike a bargain."

I looked at the three white people in that parlor and I saw, not the imposition of judgment on some prisoner, but expressions of sincere concern for another human being, something I had seen before in blue eyes of Mrs. Morgan. With everything happening so quickly, my instincts took over. Not the emotion of a mother robbed of her children, or the impulse of a woman who lost her man, rather some darker traits that had served me before when I weighed circumstances and instantly arrived at a solution and a decision rather than a reaction. I was free. I had to leave Kentucky. I was being offered passage by a man whose character I had seen and heard spoken well of. The hardness within pushed me toward the colonel and his regiment, not after Esther and the children. My interests and my future lay across the Ohio and up the Wabash not down the Mississippi.

Herndon handed me the document that I have shown you many times. By taking that piece of paper willingly, I turned my back on my babies and left them to their fate. I hoped that they were safe. I knew they were safer than under my care. The cold blade of reason cut them away.

****

Wallace had a servant in the regiment, but that man wearied of patriotism and discharged himself from the regiment. This left Wallace without a cook, so in the field the colonel ate beans and hardtack with his men. Not to mention the colonel's distaste for soldier food, this risked loss of the remoteness required for his station, and he had far to go with his regiment before they stacked arms for the last time. The colonel needed a servant to maintain appearances, particularly among other commanders. Just as slaves enjoyed status from the stations of their owners, so the owners felt esteem for the quality of their slaves. Some white men acquired slaves and servants as much for the appearance of prosperity as for any real economic benefit and Wallace was one of these.

I left Herndon's that same day to join the camp where a lieutenant, his badge of office a white cockade pinned up at the side of a broad-brimmed hat, took me to the colonel's headquarters wagon. The wagon fell within the province of an aging teamster by the name of Smith. He was a typical hairy woodsman with leather breeches and homespun shirt and coat. "What she do?" Smith asked the lieutenant.

"Cook for the colonel."

"She drivin' for the colonel too?" Here was Mariah, defending her precious job.

"You handle a team, girl?" the lieutenant asked.

"Nawsuh," I quickly lied. Lying to white people still came easily despite my change in civil status.

"Guess she ain't drivin' for the colonel. Just cookin'."

"Well, she ain't ridin' with me."

"Guess she can walk then." With that the lieutenant returned to other duties.

Smith spat and I could see I would get no further assistance from him. I foraged in the wagon and found the colonel's fry pan, pot, andirons, and some hard tack, not much with which to start my life as a freedwoman. I discovered a folded tent, poles, ropes, and camp furniture. The colonel's personal baggage and field desk were still at Herndon's where they would reside as long as Mrs. Morgan resided there. The next two days allowed me to lay in some basic needs like molasses and salt pork and other fixings with the help of the colonel's purse.

The regiment included some commissary wagons and about a dozen white camp followers listed on the rolls as laundresses. No one enlisted in this late levy had property of any kind let alone slaves so I was the only Negro there. Each of recruits, like Smith, was lured to Kentucky and the Army by the promise of land warrants. I surmised that the colonel detailed Smith to the wagons because of his age and he handled the mules well enough.

On the morning of the third day the camp stirred before dawn and the regiment marched to the landing to board ferries and boats the officers procured from along the river. After the haste and delay attendant with any military movement, Smith whipped his mules onto a flatboat with soldiers and Negroes manning oars.

I looked back at Owensborough where I saw Ike and Walker murdered. One of the white laundresses rode across with me. She ignored me entirely, but I had occasion to regard her. She joined the regiment with her soldier husband and recalled any of the hard-used farm wives from upriver. The couple hoped to earn a few dollars and a land warrant to start a new life as something other than vagrants or squatters. Like me she used her blanket as a shawl and wore moccasins. The river town slowly disappeared. Thus my life as a slave dissolved into a muddy smudge on the far shore. Of Pirey, Ben, Esther, or Anna Morgan I saw or heard nothing ever again.

Ohio

As with most tales of military service, this one involved mud, cold, and mindless boredom. What does one remember of boredom? I cooked and tended the colonel's camp. I tried to stay clean and warm and dry. Despite being the only Negro in camp, I worked without notice and fell back on my custom of solitude. The soldiers found the laundresses and frontier women more to their liking.

One experience did mark that year for me. A lay preacher, one William Abercrombie, served in the regiment and filled idle hours with readings from his care-worn Bible. This expanded upon those words I heard from the preacher in Kentucky and the prayers Anna Morgan and her children recited before meals. For the first time, I was able to consider some of the messages that ascribed power and glory to The Almighty and the teachings of his Son, Our Savior, Jesus Christ. Although lacking in any theological sophistication, Abercrombie's lessons did make me believe that above all the evil that I had witnessed, and after a life of suffering, something better, something good awaited me and awaited us all. Abercrombie was not so much a Christian that he would consider baptizing a Negro, but he willingly shared his faith and teachings with me. In Kentucky he could be fined or worse for preaching to me, but Ohio held no such prohibition.

Free of the need to survive my mind drifted to these mysteries and I embraced them. God's Word showed me that my life held a purpose beyond doing the bidding of the white man. God commanded that I love Him and that I love others, even the white man. Our Savior offered the forgiveness of sins as a path to resurrection and salvation. I saw in the stories from the Bible, indeed from Jesus's own life some connection with my own. Sin, even the sins of others, cast us into suffering in the wilderness after which we would receive forgiveness and rebirth. At the end of it all came judgment and eternal life. My true spiritual education came at the hand of your father in his church in Philadelphia, but I started down the path around a fire in a muddy army camp.

Central to Abercrombie's words was forgiveness. This did not excuse the necessity of fighting and killing our Indian and British enemies (whom we never met), but we could still forgive them after we killed them. And in forgiving them we laid the basis for our own forgiveness and salvation. Later in my life I engaged in another fight, the one against slavery and those enemies I did meet. Nothing could excuse the utter and total destruction of the slaveocracy, but in the end I knew that they deserved forgiveness, just as I deserved forgiveness.

Abercrombie taught me that one day I would meet my husband and children again in the Hereafter and we would enjoy the freedom and happiness denied us in this world. To see them again I needed to love God and love others.

An entire year of duty passed and our only casualties came from disease and accidents. We heard that other volunteers faced the British at New Orleans in a carnage which proved to be a waste of life though at small cost to the United States. Thus passed the Kentuckians' chance for glory. In March 1815, Colonel Wallace mustered out what was left of his regiment, giving to each man his discharge paper, which he could exchange for a land warrant, something as good as cash. I was not a soldier so I received no such warrant, but I had saved a few dollars from the colonel and his officers.

"Phyllis," Colonel Wallace told me, "the Army is done with us. I hear need of lawyers up in the Western Reserve. Cleveland they call it now. I'm done with Kentuckians. You are free to follow me. I may need a cook. Or you can make your own way."

I of course had no way of my own, so I followed him, driving the headquarters wagon which he took as part of his payment for loyal service. We headed east with a few of his men also curious about the growing city on Lake Erie.

Cleveland, opposite her younger sister Ohio City, proved to be another muddy, smelly collection of houses on the brink of becoming a town hard by the lake. Lake Erie was the first ocean of any type I had ever seen stretching out over the edge of the world. The whole time I knew Prestonsburg, maybe one new building went up in a year. In Cleveland hammers and saws banged and sang from dawn to dusk. The settlement grew busier each day, as newcomers arrived to stake out lots and throw up buildings and houses or brought in food and fodder and lumber and goods. Every day was market day.

Wallace made our first home in a rooming house, then with another lawyer. I slept in the kitchen with the other servants, white and colored. I met Negroes who were born free and who had never known the sting of the lash. What I found different from the household of Mr. Herndon in Owensborough was that free servants – white and colored –worked for a time, then collected their wages and moved on, sometimes to other employers, and sometimes to open hostelries of their own or to buy land. In the three seasons before we moved to Mr. Wallace's new home, I worked alongside a half-dozen different men and women. The employers were not cruel in any way, and they paid the prevailing wage, but these people always sought something better.

"Goin' to rent a place out near Doan's," James Bolton told me. "Cook good food, have a few beds, make it nice. Maybe buy it someday. It don't work out, we move on." Bolton and his wife came from Philadelphia. I had never seen even white people in the mountains express that much ambition. Although I was free to find other work, I was horrified at the prospect of no owner or no employer. Such is the seduction of slavery, but at what price? This was the reality of my new land: freedom, choices, dreams, risks.

Leander Wallace practiced law in Cleveland, and as a war hero (no one seemed to notice that we never saw action), he enjoyed success and notoriety. People called him "Colonel," but he never introduced himself that way. He fit in with the other newcomers with dreams fueled by the opportunities in the lake port where the largess of the interior shipped north, east, and west. Businessmen, adventurers, and speculators sought him out for his not inconsiderable skills as a litigator and adviser, and they rewarded him handsomely for his work. He received fees in cash and also investment opportunities. I continued to enjoy the status as the servant of an important man. In not more than four years, prominent men offered his name for judge and he assumed an office he occupied with honor and distinction for the rest of his life.

Mr. Wallace's popularity took him away from the house almost every evening as he called upon colleagues, allies, and even adversaries. This social whirl brought to him the acquaintance of Mrs. Luella Matteson Miller, a widow with auburn hair and the blue eyes and quick mind of Mrs. Anna Morgan. After that, he spent his evenings in her company until she joined him in his home as his wife.

The new Mrs. Wallace brought along her own cook, a spare, graying Frenchwoman by the name of Estelle, whose family had perished in the Terror. Estelle's sorrow as a fugitive and exile left her with a perpetually pinched mouth. I do not think I ever heard her laugh or cry, or saw her smile. She was not by any means uncordial, just marked. I too had lost a family to a terror, but I pushed on, with God's help, without forgetting them, and I eventually found other ways to remind the world of the crimes committed against me and my family. I only learned of her history from Mr. Wallace, since Estelle revealed none of herself that did not involve household duties.

Perhaps because the two of us shared loss and escape, and now service to the same family, she endeavored to teach me the French way of cooking – on a modern iron stove using delicate pans and baking in an oven. "Pheelus," she would say to me, "keep zee zauce stir zo it no burn." The fancy iron box of the stove's oven could not compare with a real oven, so Estelle arranged to build a proper one of brick – much nicer than Alabama's – where I built a fire within. After the requisite burning, she, later I, swept the coals out. "Hold hand here, count one, two, sree, and zee offen ees hot for zee bread." The steady heat produced loaves and cakes of legendary quality.

I did not find Estelle's sauces and marinades entirely to my taste, but Mr. and Mrs. Wallace and their guests craved them. Estelle's cooking and Mr. Wallace's growing prominence made a seat at their table much desired by many with influence and by those seeking to gain it. I learned from Estelle and from Mrs. Wallace the proper way to set a table and how to serve dishes. These skills further enhanced my stature among other colored servants in the community.

Sundays, as the Wallaces attended their church and Estelle attended hers with the Canadians, I found my way to a warehouse near the river where a white man named Reynolds preached to Negroes. We gave Reynolds our pennies in his support and afterwards we shared with him the borrowed bounty of our employers' larders. Those Sundays, I continued my education as well. For a few more pennies Reynolds taught some of us to read. I returned to the Wallace home and over the week make my way through Mr. Wallace's discarded newspapers. Reynolds knew that he could cadge something to eat at the back door for a translation of the last month's events. In a few years, I could read from a newspaper and the Bible, and write a letter. Education was part of my journey, like climbing a wall or swimming a river.

I learned that although Negroes in Ohio were legally free, we were not in any way welcome. In the South, whites accepted black slaves, albeit as chattel, but seldom expressed the silent scorn I witnessed in the free North. There were just a handful of us in Cleveland, perhaps no more than a few dozen to start, and we clustered together like survivors after a shipwreck clinging to some overturned boat.

Summers followed winters and springs, and any thought of rescuing or seeing my family again became so much melted snow. Their faces blurred and their voices faded. A word caught my eye in an old newspaper. Reynolds helped me understand. The Chickasaws sold the entire western portion of Kentucky and Tennessee beyond the Tennessee River to the United States in exchange for money and land beyond the Mississippi. I read closely for details of the transaction, which was described in only the most positive terms for both parties as if two men happily traded land for money and each left the table the better for it all. I knew, however, that any bargain with white people and the government wielding the color of law rarely happened as represented. The white man and his government always took the better of the deal. As history unfolded, I was correct.

But the transfer of land titles did not occupy my thoughts. Esther and Peter headed south from the Ohio River and then west to make for Indian land. They carried my babies to the Chickasaws who were now moving further into the wilderness. I imagined Pirey and Ben growing straight and strong, free of the lash. Sim watched the woods for enemies. The story of the Chickasaws closed the door on my children forever.

The Shoemaker

My experience scouting for Morgan left me with a good eye for the sharp dealings in the market and shops. Estelle had enough of the language to get by among the stalls, but I had the better of her in dealing with the farmers and traders who sought to press upon us their meanest products in exchange for the highest price. I found the market in Cleveland to be far livelier than any I had seen in Kentucky. Farmers in the slave state showed little enthusiasm for their work. In the North, work produced profit and more work meant more profit. People talked faster and, I think, they thought faster. Even though a potato seller might view me with suspicion and disdain, she knew I carried the purse of a wealthy man, and she worked hard to get it from me. I enjoyed the stimulation of negotiating and shopping sharpened my mind.

One spring day, Estelle and I shouldered our baskets and ventured out to shop for one of Judge and Mrs. Wallace's dinner parties. The berries were coming in, and Estelle wanted to create a tasty concluding course for roasted beef, potatoes, snap peas, and, of course, one of our breads. But she never knew what she would serve until she surveyed the market through her scowl, the hawk in a treetop eying the field for the hint of a careless mouse. Once she spotted her prey, she swooped in to the blanket or the cart with me in trail and proceeded to carefully pick over the offering, well aware that the best sat on top and that lesser fare hid beneath to be foisted upon the buyer in a sleight of hand.

Estelle then angrily denounced the farmer, entirely in French, of which I knew nothing but "petite" and "merde." I knew however, Estelle and her tones and gestures. We established a custom where she shopped and I concluded the transaction. If she felt the item just not acceptable, she shrugged and moved on. If it was acceptable, she shrugged, started to move on, then returned to insult the seller and the merchandise. That was my signal to attend more closely.

Sweeping her hand back and forth over the vegetables meant that they suited the Wallace table, but that I should bargain dearly. Estelle stood next to me, frowning to make it clear that my transaction was hers. If Estelle pointed with her finger while she poured contempt onto the farmer's wife and her hard work, I could buy near the asking price, but never, never the asking price. Not infrequently she encountered some French-speaking Canadians, and she transacted matters herself. Still it was my job to count out fewer coins than requested until our corrivals surrendered. I think Estelle enjoyed seeing a white seller concede on her asking price to a Negro.

In those days farmers either walked the mud streets with bags or carts, or they held forth from vacant lots or street corners. Since building lots did not remain vacant long in Cleveland, the market, such as it was, kept moving. Women with baskets knew where to start looking for the farmers who, like birds, flocked together briefly only to then scatter. We found our sellers that day sprinkled about the square, an open expanse of mud set aside for a park some day.

It being still early for berries, Estelle found the offerings beneath contempt, and Cleveland heard it all in staccato French. But she managed to find some for pennies that might suffice. Estelle tasted snap peas from perhaps three carts until she pointed to the ones on a blanket behind which sat a white woman in an apron and a straw hat. She endured impassively Estelle's torrent of French until Esther signaled me to enter the transaction with "How much?" The woman wanted ten and we settled on seven.

Estelle then began picking out four dozen of the best while the woman tried to slip in her choices from underneath. I refrained from handling the food with my hands since the touch of a Negro reviled many white people. I could pick up what Estelle chose to buy, but I could not handle a potato or a carrot or an onion unless I paid for them first.

Next to the snap peas woman a peddler had spread his dirty sheet and displayed several pairs of newly crafted shoes, some belts, and two pocket-books. The white man's hands darted over the shoes as he showed them off to a German woman who wore shoes of wood in the foreign style. The shoemaker himself sported good boots as befitted one who knew his trade. But the rest of his clothing betrayed but a distant experience with prosperity: worn trousers, soiled shirt, and braces of tentative integrity. He tied his dark blond hair in the back with a piece of leather. A heavy beard concealed his face. A piece of straw suggested the stable that sheltered him the night before. Something about his movements struck familiar. Then I saw the finger of the left hand that stopped short in an ugly stump. I knew that hand. I knew that man. His beard hid a face much older than the one I remembered.

"Look there," he told the German woman, "them stitches tight, solid. Them shoes last you years, years."

"How much?"

"Three dollars and cheap at that," the man replied in a sound that pulled me back to the mountains and the years I forgot. "They cost you five dollars in a shop." The last time I had heard that voice it spoke to David Morgan's bloody body more than five years before. Here was my old master, Edward Osborn, broken out of jail, not strung up, run from Kentucky, hiding in Ohio, and far beneath the exalted circumstances of his life before.

The shoemaker managed to get two dollars from the German woman, and from the way he licked his lips I knew that his next stop was not at another farmer's table for breakfast. That transaction concluded he glanced around to pull in his next customer. His eyes passed right over me as if I did not exist.

"Hullo, Missus," he called out to a white woman strolling by, "nice pair o' shoes for your mister? New, made 'em myself. Take a look. Might fit you too." She regarded his wares briefly and him not at all. Two other strollers similarly ignored his pitch of, "Shoes Missus? Shoes?" Only because I stood immobile almost in front of his sheet he finally took notice of me. "You buyin'?" He inquired with irritation. "Shoes're three dollars."

At one time, this man's word and tone evoked from me a cowering withdrawal and fear of his hand or riding crop. At the very least I expected more insults and orders. His words took me back to that sad farm, and I stood there speechless.

"I know you," he said, unsure of what he saw.

"I know you too, Mr. Osborn," the freedwoman told him, the only surviving witness to his crimes.

His eyes widened at the realization that before him stood his old property and the reason for his plunge from honored official and planter to vagrant squatting in the dust. I wondered if he ever even thought about our last meeting – not the one by the side of the road, but the one in front of the judge – just before Draper took him off to the jail. I wondered if he thought about the husband and father he sold away.

"You run away?" he wanted to know. This was so typical of a white man. He sees a Negro and assumes that she is a fugitive, abroad without her pass, illegal.

My wits found their balance again in my head along with darker feelings from my guts. Ideas and images swam in front of me like the fish in barrels at the lakefront. Here sat a prospect I had never imagined and I needed an answer to the question, what do I do?

"I free. Mrs. Morgan free me. I got a paper."

Osborn got to his feet bringing his eyes just above my own. "And you're here in Ohio," he said.

"Work for Judge Wallace." I held my head high.

The mention of a judge seemed to give Osborn pause.

"But *you* run away," I continued. His eyes swept to each side to see if anyone witnessed our conversation. Estelle traded gossip with one of her Canadian acquaintances and forgot about me. Like Sim smelling fear in a man or another dog, I caught Osborn's trepidation.

"I had help," he said. "No good reason to stay."

"Your friends help you?" I asked.

"Some were my friends and some not. It seemed that not many wanted to see me hung." Osborn then began to gather his thoughts as well. "I hear they wanted to hang you. Maybe it was good for you I did run away. Maybe it was good they didn't put me on trial. You can't testify against me, but I could testify against you. I still could. Maybe they'll hang us together."

Despite Edward Osborn's fall from planter, slaveholder, husband, and sheriff, and his indictment for murder, he still held some advantage on me – the advantage of knowledge and truth, probably greater than the lash. For that I had to grant him a measure of respect as well as some apprehension. The intervening years as a fugitive seemed to sharpen his wits as such an experience is wont to do. Did he gain any wisdom on his journey? This itinerant shoemaker knew my secret. He now represented the only real threat to me and my freedom. I had to assume that he had acquired some of the aptitude that so eluded him in the past. If Osborn had undergone any transformation in the preceding seven years, so had I. Where flight and fear had undoubtedly honed his sense of survival, freedom and education had sharpened my understandings of the world and the universe. I realized that our meeting in the market was as if two strangers had finally met having only heard rumors about the other. We were now confronted with the truth and everything we had heard was in question.

This left Osborn and me in something of a stalemate, an *impasse* as Estelle would say. I had power over him and he had power over me. Who had the more power? Who would act upon the power? Then the answer came to me as I am sure it had already come to him, why act at all? What were our interests here? I did not need him exposed and he did not need me exposed. Each of us needed to be apart from the other and away from Kentucky.

As we stood there another shopper stooped over his sheet to look at the shoes and belts, but Osborn' eyes silently asked me, what do you want to do? Part of his freedom for seven years depended on not showing fear and he showed me no fear. Where once he demonstrated arrogance and impatience, he waited now for my next move, calmly and ready to act. Edward Osborn had changed, perhaps for the better, the better for him. Was it the better for me?

As I was a problem for him to resolve, he was a problem for me. He knew the truth of that day on the road leading away from his sorry farm. But to act on it was to expose himself to prison and a rope. That did not prevent me from acting, however.

My knife had served me before, perhaps it could again. Osborn would not go far today, probably no further than the next whiskey seller. Osborn needed only to step out into the Ohio night for a moment to relieve himself, and his trouble and mine would end. I kept several blades sharp for the Wallace kitchen, and no freedwoman ventured abroad without some means of defense. More than one nameless stranger turned up lifeless in the mud of the Cuyahoga leaving behind two lines in the newspaper. No one would decry Osborn's loss. I could do all this alone. A Negro woman in that town learned to move in the shadows at night, even if only on an errand for her employer. I would linger around the market and see where the shoemaker bought his whiskey. That would save time and allow me to plan further.

I felt Saul watching me. He held softly the halter on one of his master's horses. He did not speak and his face offered no clue as to his advice.

As I stood there other visions passed before me. Hands seized me out of the dark to drag me out of another dungeon, this one of stone. I stood in front of Judge Wallace as he coldly pronounced sentence. A jeering crowd filled the square to see me hauled up to the crossbeam. My knife was not the answer.

Now that I could write, I could notify Judge Graham in Floyd County that I had found Osborn. Would he believe me? Would he want the information? Was Graham even alive? Would anyone remember? Then I saw the wisdom in Osborn's escape. With Osborn gone, the whole problem of Osborn and the Morgans' murders went away. The men of the county divided up the Morgan children and their bequests so who wanted to punish a white man that helped make them rich? They might even help themselves to Osborn's land and his widow. But if they believed Osborn, what might happen to me?

Saul closed his eyes and slowly shook his head. I saw Esther. She reached out to my children. Her lips moved, but no sound emerged. Ben, walking now, glanced back at me without any recognition. Then he and Pirey responded to Esther's gestures and moved away from me.

In those few moments, seconds really, I felt my old faculties return, powers not of the heart, but of the head, skills that stripped away the purely sentimental and emotional. I was now a Christian and believed in resurrection and forgiveness. Could I forgive Edward Osborn? Could he forgive me? But Osborn had nothing to forgive. Osborn might even owe me a debt. Had David Morgan lived, he would certainly have seen Osborn hanged for William's murder. Osborn and I both had seen enough mistakes of the heart and of the mind.

I broke the silence by turning to the man who stopped to look at Osborn's wares.

"He want four dollars for them shoes," I said. "I say they only worth three. Them good shoes, but only worth three dollars."

I stepped back and turned to find Estelle. We had an important dinner to prepare.

I remain,
Your loving mother,

Phyllis Wallace Lewis

Acknowledgements

The germ of this work begins with the scholarship of Martha Heineman whose query in an old genealogy newsletter led me to explore the story of the Morgan murders. Marshall Davidson of Floyd County, Kentucky continued the work of his uncle Andrew Jackson Davidson who documented the incident and erected a headstone to the victims. Don Osborne researched and published an account of the murders of my ancestors by his ancestor. Karen Salisbury of Gloucester Point, Virginia discovered her Aunt Winnie Fitzpatrick John's trunk containing the long lost order books for Floyd County, Kentucky and returned the books to their rightful place. The order books provided additional details about the lives and deaths of the characters portrayed herein.

The staff at Colonial Williamsburg happily shared their knowledge of life and technology of early 19th Century Virginia and Kentucky. There is nothing like conversing with a real human being about the intricacies of an ox cart, cabin construction, or food preparation while they are right in front of you. The Library of Congress in Washington, DC preserved the old histories of Floyd County which carry the earliest written accounts of what happened in 1813.

The students and staff at Portland State University Vinnie Kinsella, Parisa Zolfaghari, Matthew Warren, Kay Tracy, Brian D. Smith, Levi Rogers, Tom McCluskey, Sam Lansky, Pat McDonald, Jennifer Knutsen, Brian Kirk, Maureen Inouye, Mary Darcy, and

Rose Gebken who incorporated an early version of this story into their book development class and provided me with invaluable feedback.

Virginia Story and Vicki McCown helped transform a draft into a final document and provided important affirmation that my efforts were well spent.

And finally I would like to express my deepest gratitude to Janet Sittig, Kathy Kaye, Bob Fogerty, Brad White, Rick Paul, and Maurice Robkin who patiently critiqued my chapters as they dribbled out over the years.

About the Author

David Wilma is a freelance writer and historian with five books, a video documentary, and numerous articles to his credit.

Made in the USA
Lexington, KY
21 April 2011